"If you like a fun tale set in a well-developed world, pick up the Destroyermen series and kick back and enjoy."
—SFRevu.com

Praise for Taylor Anderson's Destroyermen novels

Distant Thunders

"The fun of watching eager aviators take to the air in carved wooden aircraft leavens the nostalgic sense of worlds being left behind and cultures forced by war to undergo unpleasant changes. Anderson raises questions about the morality of chemical warfare, genocide, and summary execution in wartime while holding out the possibility of diplomacy with relentless killers."

—*Publishers Weekly*

"Action sci-fi doesn't get significantly better than this.... Anderson launches a new Destroyermen trilogy ... with this complex but fine and fast-paced tale." —*Booklist*

"An action-packed entry with strong relevant moral questions about the rules of combat engagement running throughout the adrenaline-pumping storyline. Taylor Anderson is one of the best at military science fiction as his plots combine cerebral thought-provoking issues within a great adventure tale; the alternate realm of the Destroyermen saga is worth the journey." —Alternative Worlds

"Simply put, this is great stuff. Anyone that has flipped back and forth between the various channels on cable/satellite TV devoted to documentaries about World War II and the ones about the science fiction genre will enjoy this immensely. Anderson does a spectacular job in keeping the history, flair, and can-do attitude of the aptly named 'greatest generation' integrated with an alien world full of unknown pitfalls and dangers. The characters are well developed and easy to identify with and care about, and the story stays fresh and exciting.... Read it—you won't be disappointed." —Fresh Fiction

continued...

Maelstrom

"Anderson's trilogy of cross-time naval action, Destroyermen, maintains its high quality to the end of this thundering concluding volume. . . . The climactic battle is long, bloody, and suspenseful almost to the last. The ending here doesn't quash hopes that we may see Anderson's displaced World War II Destroyermen again." —*Booklist*

"The pace was fast and kept me wanting to read just a couple more pages. . . . The ensemble cast has a little something for everyone. From a heroic leader and a tortured enemy to power-crazed enemies and wisecracking crew. If you like a fun tale set in a well-developed world, pick up the Destroyermen series and kick back and enjoy." —SFRevu

"With its blending of historical fact, thrilling battle scenes, and science fiction, *Maelstrom* is a novel that anyone who loves reading both military and alternative history SF books will want to add to their libraries."
—BookSpot Central

"Experienced military SF readers will enjoy the attention to technical and historical detail." —*Publishers Weekly*

Crusade

"Even better than the excellent *Into the Storm* . . . intelligent action, more skillful handling of a very large cast, and an obstinately maintained refusal to slow the pace."
—*Booklist* (starred review)

"Anderson throws in tense land battles against overwhelming odds, a massive typhoon and a phenomenal aerial duel, but despite the pyrotechnics, at heart this novel is about how honor and ideals can bend or break under the stressful, life-and-death conditions of total war."
—*Publishers Weekly*

"*Crusade* continues an entertaining story arc and exploration of war, honor, and evolution on a world similar to our own. Taylor Anderson is emerging, with two novels in quick succession only months apart, as a solid and imaginative storyteller." —SFFWorld

Into the Storm

"Taylor Anderson has brought a fresh new perspective to the tale of crosstime shipwreck. The action is gripping and riveting. . . . The characters are sharply drawn and very human—or inhuman, for two interesting species of nonhuman sapiens are included—and the description vivid. I dipped my toe into *Destroyermen: Into the Storm* and when I looked up, it was two in the morning and a working day had vanished! Anderson is a new talent to watch, and I look forward to the unfolding of this series, and his subsequent work."

—S. M. Stirling, author of *A Taint in the Blood*

"Taylor Anderson and his patched-up four-stackers have steamed to the forefront of alternative history. All aboard for a cracking great read!" —E. E. Knight

"Anderson's outstanding first novel combines alternate history and seafaring in a way that recalls S. M. Stirling's splendid *Island in the Sea of Time* trilogy . . . nonstop action . . . works out in the context of extremely high-level achievement at both world building and characterization."

—*Booklist*

"Anderson's alternate history debut combines a love for military history with a keen eye for natural science. Reddy is a likable protagonist, epitomizing the best of the wartime American military." —*Library Journal*

"Paying homage to such tales as *A Connecticut Yankee in King Arthur's Court*, *Robinson Crusoe*, and William R. Forstchen and Greg Morrison's *Crystal Warriors*, Anderson expands on familiar concepts with high-tension nautical battles and skillful descriptions of period attitudes and dialogue." —*Publishers Weekly*

The Destroyermen Series

Into the Storm
Crusade
Maelstrom
Distant Thunders

DESTROYERMEN
RISING TIDES

TAYLOR ANDERSON

A ROC BOOK

ROC
Published by New American Library, a division of
Penguin Group (USA) Inc., 375 Hudson Street,
New York, New York 10014, USA
Penguin Group (Canada), 90 Eglinton Avenue East, Suite 700, Toronto,
Ontario M4P 2Y3, Canada (a division of Pearson Penguin Canada Inc.)
Penguin Books Ltd., 80 Strand, London WC2R 0RL, England
Penguin Ireland, 25 St. Stephen's Green, Dublin 2,
Ireland (a division of Penguin Books Ltd.)
Penguin Group (Australia), 250 Camberwell Road, Camberwell, Victoria 3124,
Australia (a division of Pearson Australia Group Pty. Ltd.)
Penguin Books India Pvt. Ltd., 11 Community Centre, Panchsheel Park,
New Delhi - 110 017, India
Penguin Group (NZ), 67 Apollo Drive, Rosedale, Auckland 0632,
New Zealand (a division of Pearson New Zealand Ltd.)
Penguin Books (South Africa) (Pty.) Ltd., 24 Sturdee Avenue,
Rosebank, Johannesburg 2196, South Africa

Penguin Books Ltd., Registered Offices:
80 Strand, London WC2R 0RL, England

Published by Roc, an imprint of New American Library, a division of Penguin Group (USA) Inc. Previously published in a Roc hardcover edition.

First Roc Mass Market Printing, October 2011
10 9 8 7 6 5 4 3 2 1

Printed in the United States of America

To: All my "Best Gals"—
Rebecca, Christine, Jennifer, and Nancy

For: The Purple Hearts. God bless you.

ACKNOWLEDGMENTS

As always, I'd like to thank my friend and agent, Russell Galen, as well as Ginjer Buchanan and all the great folks at Roc. I can't stress that enough. Unlike a lot of authors, I suppose, I live "out in the country" and don't have a long list of literary clubs, writers' roundtables, and constructive critics to thank. I do have a lot of good friends who are generally highly educated—both academically and in the less-forgiving "University of Hard Knocks," attended during the course of real, adventurous lives. These friends are not always *completely* objective, I fear, so Ginjer and the copy editors at Roc are my last line of defense.

My parents, Don and Jeanette Anderson, remain my first, primary editors, since they're the ones who have to thrash through the initial rough drafts and try to make sense out of gibberish. As members of the generation that I write about in this series, they also prevent me from saying some stupid stuff that people "back then" wouldn't have said. In that same affectionate vein, I want to thank Tom and Jody Thigpen for their lifelong friendship and support. Tom's knowledge of petroleum engineering will also become increasingly valuable as this series progresses. (I like to joke that my dad invented the first means of "out of sight" communications, and Tom pounded the first hole in the ground looking for "black stuff"—around the time Methuselah was born.) Being childhood pals, they probably managed both feats together, with the assistance of gallons of yucky Scotch, and were likely trying to do something completely different at the time.

Otherwise, all the people listed in previous volumes remain high on the list of "usual suspects" and all have contributed in various ways, from technical expertise to character inspiration. Many of my characters are "real," though none are specific people. They are composites. Virtually every goofy stunt described in the series is based on some real event, and I'm somewhat dubiously honored to have witnessed quite a few of them firsthand. One of the great advantages of knowing a lot of people from all walks of life is that you never run out of characters!

For various reasons, I must add a few names to the "usual suspects" list. Long overdue is an appreciative mention of my many friends—and occasional colleagues—at Tarleton State University. They probably think I've lost my mind, but I think some of them have secretly read my books. Also overdue is an appreciative hug for my aunt Terry, whose grit, stoicism, and friendly cheer always remind me of what "stern stuff" Brits are made of. Kate Baker is a swell gal, and she's been doing great work to update my Web site and blog. A facsimile of "Tikki's" "Killer Kudzu"—submitted to the "Order of Darwinian Delight" contest on my Web site—will make an appearance. Additionally, Tom Potter, Michael Walsh, Bruce Kent, R. P. Scott, John Schmuke, Aaron Wehr, and a guy named "Ed" all made valuable suggestions. Colonel Dave Leedom, Mark Wheeler, and my barnstorming dad continue to do their best to keep the "Allies" airborne, and (Bad) Dennis Petty never lets me forget that throughout human history, something, somewhere, has always needed killing. Of course, Jim Goodrich never fails to provide constant examples that no matter how weird or ridiculous a situation seems, it can always get weirder.

The tides of the sea rise and fall, with great energy and exuberance. At certain times, they rise higher than others. The moon is the chief engine behind this, I am told, but it moves them with a singularly predictable, faithful regularity. The flood of war similarly flows and ebbs, but with a wild, ungovernable capriciousness that cannot be anticipated with any degree of confidence. It is more like a storm, a tempest, often unforeseen and almost never adequately prepared for. It can ebb with a breathless suddenness that leaves one wondering what all the fuss was about, or it can rise against the highest, most invulnerable peak in a mad rush of relentless violence. Also unlike the dependable tides, war need not necessarily ebb. Like nothing in nature, it appears, war seems able to flow and flow, and build endlessly upon itself like an ever-mounting gale, flailing vengefully about, long after its contingent parts have been exhausted. When all is said and done, one must contemplate the possibility that such dubious intangibles as "luck" might actually exist, because they, and God, remain the only things worthy of faith.

—Courtney Bradford, *The Worlds I've Wondered*
University of New Glasgow Press
1956

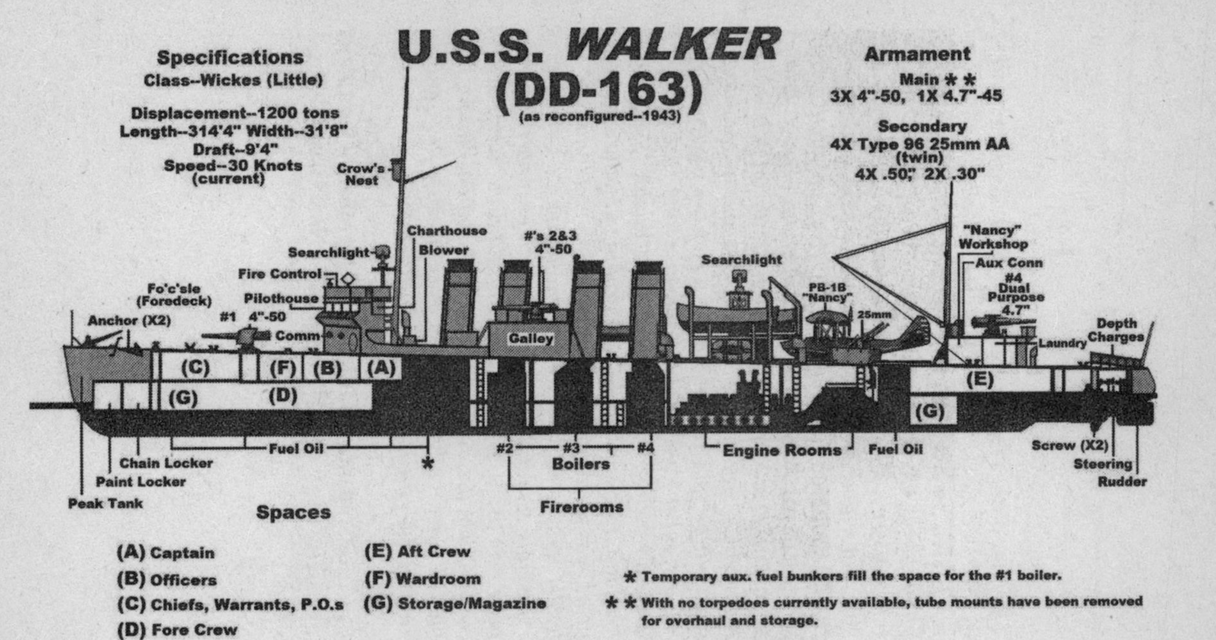
U.S.S. WALKER
(DD-163)
(as reconfigured--1943)
Specifications
Class--Wickes (Little)
Displacement--1200 tons
Length--314'4" Width--31'8"
Draft--9'4"
Speed--30 Knots
(current)
Armament
Main * *
3X 4"-50, 1X 4.7"-45
Secondary
4X Type 96 25mm AA
(twin)
4X .50," 2X .30"
Crow's Nest
Charthouse
Blower
Searchlight
Fire Control
Pilothouse
Fo'c'sle
(Foredeck)
Anchor (X2)
#1 4"-50
Comm
#'s 2&3
4"-50
Galley
Searchlight
PB-1B
"Nancy"
25mm
"Nancy"
Workshop
Aux Conn
#4
Dual
Purpose
4.7"
Laundry
Depth
Charges
(C)
(F)
(B)
(A)
(G)
(D)
(E)
(G)
Fuel Oil
*
#2
#3
#4
Boilers
Firerooms
Engine Rooms
Fuel Oil
Screw (X2)
Steering
Rudder
Chain Locker
Paint Locker
Peak Tank
Spaces
(A) Captain
(B) Officers
(C) Chiefs, Warrants, P.O.s
(D) Fore Crew
(E) Aft Crew
(F) Wardroom
(G) Storage/Magazine
* Temporary aux. fuel bunkers fill the space for the #1 boiler.
* * With no torpedoes currently available, tube mounts have been removed
for overhaul and storage.

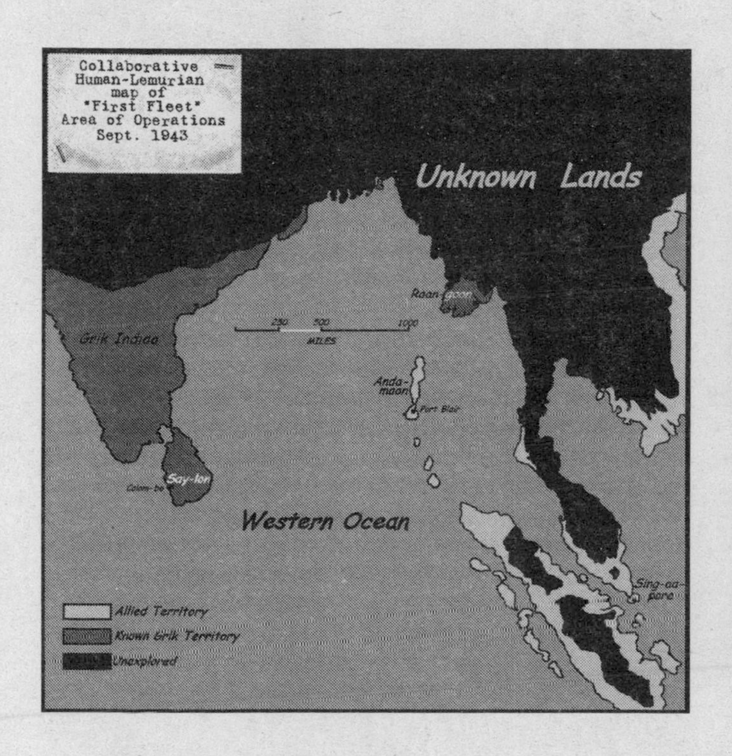
Collaborative
Human-Lemurian
map of
"First Fleet"
Area of Operations
Sept. 1943
Unknown Lands
Raan-goon
250
500
1000
MILES
Grik Indiaa
Anda-
maan
Port Blair
Say-lon
Colom-bo
Western Ocean
Sing-aa-
pore
Allied Territory
Known Grik Territory
Unexplored

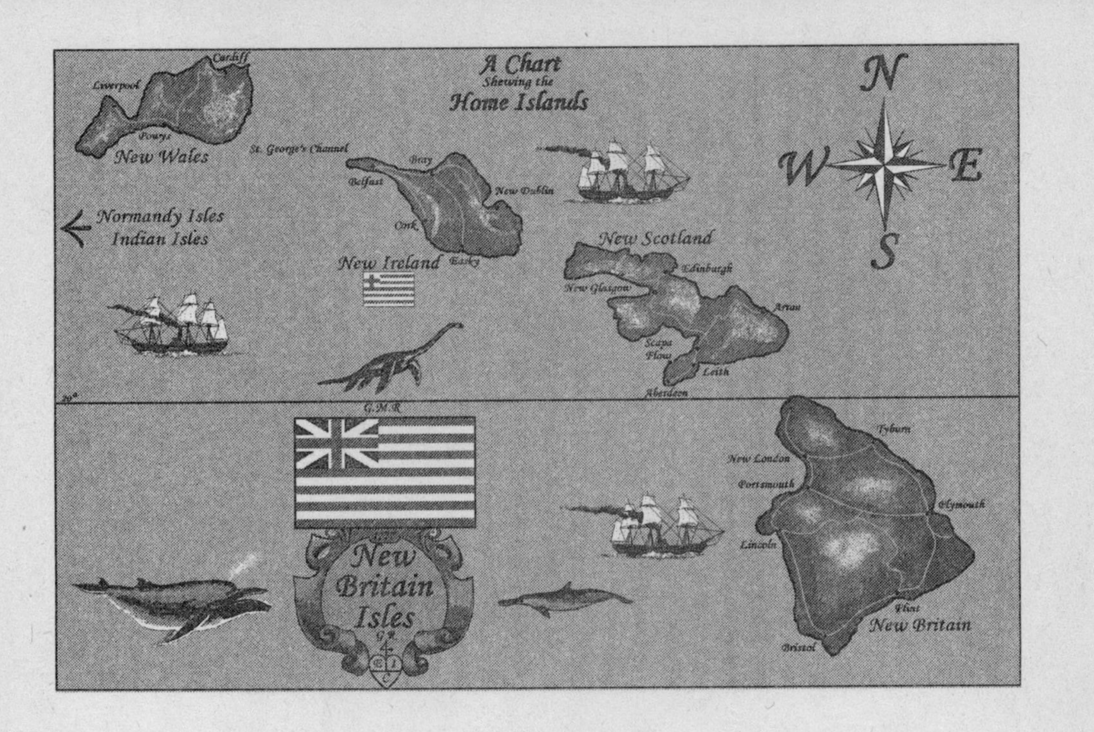
A Chart
Shewing the
Home Islands
N
W
E
S
Liverpool
Cardiff
Powys
New Wales
St. George's Channel
Bray
Belfast
New Dublin
Cork
Easky
New Ireland
Normandy Isles
Indian Isles
New Scotland
Edinburgh
New Glasgow
Arran
Scapa
Flow
Leith
Aberdeen
20°
G.M.R.
New
Britain
Isles
Tyburn
New London
Portsmouth
Plymouth
Lincoln
Flint
New Britain
Bristol

H.I.M.S. ACHILLES
(His Imperial Majesty's Ship)

CHAPTER 1

The atmosphere in the wardroom of the old Asiatic Fleet "four-stacker" destroyer USS *Walker* (DD-163) was no longer animated; it was more . . . subdued and sickened than anything else. The sultry, rotting breeze off the unknown atoll to windward entered the portholes and swirled in the cramped compartment, resuscitating an all-pervading aroma of mildew and sweat. Three beings sat stiffly, tiredly, uncomfortably behind the green linoleum–topped wardroom table, facing aft, waiting for the final prisoner to be brought before them. It had been a long day, in many ways, and the fiery, righteous passions that had inflamed the earlier proceedings had finally dwindled to mere disgusted embers of their former selves. The aversion, horror, and anger the "court" felt toward the prisoners they'd judged was still very real and palpable, but it had become an exhausted, mechanical thing by now, and everyone—the judges, prosecutors, and even the defense—just wanted the whole thing over at last.

Captain Matthew Reddy, High Chief of the American Clan, and Commander in Chief (by acclamation) of all Allied Forces united under the Banner of the Trees, stared through the porthole at battered *Achilles*, anchored alongside. They'd nearly lost the Imperial steam frigate to damage sustained in the battle against the "Company" ships. She'd suffered even more sorely in a vicious little storm that brewed up shortly after, before they made this unexpected landfall that afforded some protection while she and the rest of the little fleet performed emergency repairs. Now the two "prizes" that *Achilles* and *Walker* had taken intact—the HNBC (Honorable New Britain Company) flagship *Ulysses* and the pressed Imperial frigate *Icarus*—were already practically ready for sea. *Ulysses* had fled the action and been only lightly damaged, and *Icarus* had been wrested from her Company commanders by loyal sailors and hadn't participated in the fight. *Achilles* was mauled by HNBC *Caesar*, but ultimately sent her to the bottom. Even *Walker*, with her comparatively long-range guns, had taken a beating, and throughout the court sessions her old iron hull had reverberated with the sound of clanging blows from inside and out, as punctured plates were replaced (they could do that now, at least) or heated, bent back in place, and reriveted.

Walker wasn't new anymore by any possible definition, but after her resurrection and rebuilding, she'd at least *looked* almost new for a while in her fresh, darker shade of gray that the Bosun finally approved. Her appearance had certainly been a far cry from the shattered, half-sunken wreck she'd been after the Battle of Baalkpan. Herculean work had been accomplished to return her to duty and, ultimately, to ready her for this particular mission. It was really a miracle that she'd ever floated again, much less steamed so far, fought yet another battle, and arrived safely at this place. Sometimes, when Matt gazed at her, he had difficulty believing she had.

Neither Matt nor the Bosun had participated in her refloating and rebuilding; they'd both been off aboard *Donaghey*, leading the Singapore Campaign. They hadn't witnessed the unending hours of wrenching labor, ingenuity, and tireless dedication that resulted in her gradual but almost complete restoration. They'd returned home from the war in the west prepared to embark on literally *anything* available to chase the Company criminal Walter Billingsley, who'd abducted Princess Rebecca, Sandra Tucker, Sister Audry,

Dennis Silva, and Abel Cook. Kidnapping the princess was bad enough. She and her "lizard" friend Lawrence—who'd also been taken—were heroes of the Alliance and the Lemurians held them to their hearts. But Sandra's abduction was even worse, if that was possible. Not only was she a much-beloved heroine who'd saved literally thousands of lives with her own hands and her medical and organizational skill, she was the woman Matthew Reddy loved. They weren't married or even officially engaged, but that made no difference to the Lemurian " 'Cats." To them, she was their Supreme Commander's "mate." Nothing, not even the all-important war, could or should interfere with his pursuit of her captors.

There was genuine concern for the other hostages too. Sister Audry had few detractors, despite her heretical teachings. Quite a number had even converted to her church. She was considered by all to be an honest, pious female, if just a bit odd. Abel Cook wasn't well-known, but he was "one of theirs." Dennis Silva was a genuine hero, and though unqualifiedly deranged, he'd almost come to symbolize the human Americans in some indefinable way as far as the Lemurians were concerned. He was big, noisy, and irreverent, but in an almost childlike, inoffensive manner. He was brave to the point of recklessness, but tender with younglings. He'd sacrificed much for a people and cause he barely knew, simply because it was *right*—and he was capable of unparalleled violence toward anything that posed a threat to his new friends. His ongoing affairs with human nurse Pam Cross, as well as the equally rambunctious Lemurian Risa-Sab-At, were also a source of much gossip and amusement among the Allied 'Cats, even though—and perhaps because—the affair seemed to cause such consternation among his "own" people.

For whatever reason, the Lemurians wanted all "their people" back, and therefore, somehow, they and a smattering of Matt's own destroyermen, who'd been left in charge of salvaging his ship, not only did so but had her ready for him when he needed her most. Matt rubbed his eyes. It had been a miracle, sure enough. But he'd almost begun to expect miracles where the Lemurians and his destroyermen—all his People—were concerned.

He shook his head. Time to get back to business. Despite his misgivings, he'd agreed to serve as President of the Court at Commodore Jenks's request. His ship had been attacked without warning and he knew he couldn't be entirely objective, but Jenks had argued that his was the only ship without either a Company or an Imperial Navy presence aboard. Since all the Company and Imperial Navy crews and officers were potential defendants, prosecutors, or witnesses to the primary charge of "Knowingly and Deliberately Attempting the Foul Murder of Princess Rebecca Anne McDonald," heir to the Governor-Emperor's throne, in the false certainty that she was aboard Matt's ship, the trial would conclude if the accused were guilty of high treason, not a deliberate act of war against a sovereign state—or USS *Walker*. Attacking *Walker* was merely the means by which they'd demonstrated their treason. Matt's crew was aggrieved that the guilty wouldn't hang for murdering the shipmates that had been lost, but as long as they hung for something, the crew was partially mollified.

Again, because they'd agreed that no Imperial personnel should sit on the court, Matt had been forced to choose the other two judges himself. On the surface, Bosun's Mate 2nd (and Captain of Marines) Chack-Sab-At was an easy choice. The young Lemurian's honor and integrity were beyond question, as were his physical courage and sense of justice. Of all the 'Cats Matt had come to know, Chack was, in many ways, the most remarkable. He'd literally been a pacifist before the war against the Grik, but he'd since become a consummate, skilled, and resourceful . . . Marine. He always reverted to his "old" status of bosun's mate aboard *Walker*, the ship he now fully considered his Home, but he'd become much, much more.

That was part of the problem. The young Lemurian, once able to take such innocent and childlike joy from the grand adventure of life, had become a virtual killing machine. Fighting the Grik was one thing, however. He'd been able to keep that separate, apart. He'd built a wall between his soul and the things he'd done to save his people. The battle they'd been forced to fight against other *humans* had apparently loosened a few of the stones in that wall. He clearly didn't understand it, and he was confused. Lemurians simply didn't fight other Lemurians—with a few notable exceptions. He'd known and accepted from the start that humans *did* fight other humans, and he'd even helped fight the Japanese humans who aided the Grik. But *these* humans, these "Imperials," were the very descendants of the ancient "tail-less ones" who once came among his people and gave them so much in terms of technology, culture, and even knowledge of the Heavens. Essentially, Matt supposed Chack felt as if he'd met the ancient saints of his people and discovered they weren't saints after all.

Matt knew Chack's feelings weren't unique. The very voyage they were embarked on had done much to undermine some fundamental tenets of Lemurian dogma. Even the fact that they'd traveled this far without falling off the world had been sufficient to do that to a degree. Lemurians knew the world was round, but apparently only those now aboard USS *Walker* really understood the simple truth that gravity pulled down, no matter where you went. This didn't come as a basic physics lesson to *Walker*'s now predominantly Lemurian crew; it challenged many fundamental "laws of things" as far as they were concerned, including such mundane things as where the water came from that fell as rain from the Heavens.

Chack—and all his people, ultimately—had a lot of stuff to sort out, and as essential as it had become for them to enter the "modern world," Matt felt a profound sadness as he watched Chack's and the Lemurian people's . . . innocence . . . drain away.

The third member of the tribunal had been a slightly controversial selection. Courtney Bradford had been a civilian employee of Royal Dutch Shell before the strange Squall brought them to this world. An Australian, he'd been a petroleum engineer and self-styled naturalist. Quirky and brilliant, the man was also a moderately reliable pain in the ass in an unintentional, exuberantly oblivious sort of way. Despite his personality, Matt considered him an obvious choice for the assignment because not only was he Minister of Science of the Allied powers; he also enjoyed the dubious and well-deserved, if slightly nerve-racking, title of Plenipotentiary at Large.

Matt had been genuinely surprised when Commodore Jenks himself raised an objection to Courtney's appointment on the grounds that this was to be a military trial and no civilian could sit in judgment of a military man. Matt countered with a simple question: "How many navies does the Empire have?" Jenks had been flustered, as if the question had never occurred to him before. Perhaps it hadn't. He finally, thoughtfully, admitted there was only one Imperial Navy, and "Company" ships weren't part of it. That being established, he readily, almost eagerly, agreed that it was perfectly appropriate for a civilian to sit in judgment over what were, ultimately, civilian pirates. As prosecutors, Jenks and his exec, Lieutenant Grimsley, had pursued and stressed the treasonous pirate theme throughout the trial, and Matt suspected they were practicing an argument that Jenks intended to lay before the Lord High Admiral of the Imperial Navy in regard to the actions of the "Honorable" New Britain Company as a whole.

Matt's own exec, Francis "Frankie" Steele, reluctantly but competently presided over the defense, with Lieutenant Blair of the Imperial Marines to assist him. Despite their reservations, both men took their duties seriously and were scrupulously, almost torturously fair, but the preponderance of the evidence and the vast numbers of witnesses for the prosecution left them relying almost entirely on "reasonable doubt," which was recognized by the Empire. Unfortunately for most of their "clients," there wasn't any doubt at all.

The trials were finally over, and this day had been dedicated to summoning the prisoners to hear their fate. A total of fifty-one HNBC officers and Company officials had been charged and tried. Of those, thirty-one had been found guilty of the capital crime they were accused of. According to the Imperial trial procedures and Articles of War that Matt had agreed were appropriate under the circumstances, there was only one possible sentence for them: death by hanging. Even now, the condemned men were being ferried across and hoisted, one at a time, to the tip of the main yard of *Ulysses*. Thirteen were guilty of arguably lesser crimes, for which they would be imprisoned at the first Imperial settlement they reached. Six were actually found not guilty of anything, as far as even Jenks could tell, other than being Company toadies who'd mistreated the naval personnel placed under their authority. They hadn't had any idea what the true nature of their mission was.

Still staring at *Achilles* through the porthole, Matt was glad *Ulysses* was out of sight. He had no concern that they might be hanging innocent men, but he'd seen so much death in all its forms over the last couple of years, the cold-blooded, methodical hanging of men was not a mental image he needed to add to the album of his troubled dreams. Not while he was attempting to remain as objective as possible and trying very hard not to hate the Empire as a whole for what some of its people had done. Not while he thought he might enjoy the hangings a little too much . . . He glanced at the other "judges" beside him and sighed.

"Let's get this over with," he murmured quietly.

"Forgive me, Captain Reddy . . . Captain Chack. You as well, Mr. Bradford," Jenks said apologetically. "I knew I was asking a lot of you. Of you all. But this . . . process . . . was utterly necessary, I'm afraid. We still have a long voyage ahead, and an unknown situation awaiting us when we arrive. We haven't caught up with *Ajax* and Commander Billingsley, nor had any of the ships we fought sighted or spoken them. With this delay to make repairs and the delay we must endure a little farther along while we await your replenishment squadron, I fear we may not catch Billingsley at all. We must assume he will reach New Britain, or one of the other main islands before us, and we must be prepared to counter his version of events. That assumes, of course, that he makes his presence known when he arrives. We have no conception of his agenda or how the Company means to use its possession of the princess—not to mention the other hostages. Taking the princess will have been bad enough, once known, but taking the other hostages, your people—" He stopped, knowing full well one of those "people" was the woman Matt loved. "That has made this an international incident," he ended at last.

"It was an act of war!" Matt reminded him. "Besides the hostages he took, he destroyed Allied property and killed people when he did it!"

"Rest assured, Captain Reddy, I shan't forget. It will be our business, yours and mine, to convince the proper people—hopefully the Governor-Emperor himself—just how significant an act that was, not only from the perspective of avoiding conflict between our peoples, but how that might affect our future cooperation against the Grik." He frowned. "Trust me in this—having seen and fought those vicious buggers, I'm quite a fervent convert to your assertion that they pose a monstrous threat not only to our way of life but to all life on this world." He gestured around at the compartment and, by implication, the proceedings underway. "This unpleasant business will have been *expected* of us, and not to put too fine a point upon it, many of these traitorous scum will actually escape the hangman if the Company is allowed to take a hand. In that case, not only will justice never be served, but we might find *ourselves* in the dock facing a—I believe you call it a 'stacked deck.' If we hope to accomplish anything when we reach New Britain, ours must be the official, legal, indisputable account of the events that have transpired."

There came a knock on the passageway bulkhead beyond the beautifully embroidered curtain that had replaced the vile, stained pea green curtain that had hung there when Matt first took command of USS *Walker* a lifetime ago. The new curtain was still green so as not to clash with the cracked and bulging green linoleum tiles on the deck, but some Lemurian artist had lovingly embroidered the U.S. Navy seal and "USS *Walker*, DD-163" in gold and colored thread. The thing was beautiful, and in stark contrast to the spartan interior of the wardroom.

"Enter," said Matt after a slight hesitation.

Juan Marcos, the bold, inscrutable little Filipino steward who had, by force of will alone, established himself as Matt's personal steward/butler/secretary, moved the curtain aside with a grim expression. The final prisoner to come before them was none other than the captain of *Ulysses*, the flagship of the Company squadron that had attacked them and then fled so ignominiously in the face of *Walker*'s vengeful salvos. As flagship, *Ulysses* carried the greatest weight of metal and the most powerful guns. She had most likely been the ship that fired those first unexpected broadsides that damaged Matt's ship and killed several of her crew. The Company captain's later protestations of innocence and remorse only added to the contempt in which *Walker*'s crew held him. He was a murderer and a coward. Currently, only his cowardice was on display. When the 'Cat Marines practically carried him into the compartment and he saw his own sword laid upon the table, its point arranged in his direction, he already knew the verdict and began to blubber. Any sympathy Matt might have felt toward the man evaporated, and his voice was harsh when he spoke.

"Captain Moline, it is the judgment of this court that you are not a naval officer and are therefore not subject to punishment for certain infractions of the Imperial Articles of War of which you have been accused—even though it's my understanding you did swear, upon receiving your HNBC commission, that you'd abide by those articles. That being the case, this court has no choice but to find you not guilty of the crimes specified under articles two, three, four, twelve, thirteen, fifteen, seventeen, eighteen, nineteen, and twenty-seven of which you've been charged."

Matt had never considered himself a cruel man, but he

couldn't stop himself from pausing, ever so slightly. Just long enough to see the first rays of hope begin to bloom in Captain Moline's eyes. He abruptly continued, in the same harsh tone.

"However, even as a civilian, you're still subject to certain specifications within those military articles, and of course you're entirely subject to numerous civil charges as they exist for the protection and punishment of non-military subjects of Imperial law. No provincial Assize court or Home Circuit being in the vicinity, it's my understanding that, according to Imperial law, this court must assume the duties normally prescribed for them. If you were being tried by a civil court, you'd certainly face at least the charges of high treason against your sovereign and nation, piracy, and attempted murder of a member of the Imperial family. I could add other charges, but there'd be no point. Any of these are capital crimes, and this court finds you guilty of all specifications."

"But . . ." Moline floundered desperately. "I was following orders! The orders of a representative of the Prime Proprietor's personal factor!"

Matt paused and took an exasperated breath. He glanced at his notes. "Yes. You testified that a 'Mr. Brown' presented you with sealed orders that were to be opened in the event you sighted this ship—a 'dedicated steamer with four funnels,' you said. You also said these orders directed you to lure the described steamer as close as possible and destroy it without warning."

"Despicable orders, but orders nevertheless!" pleaded Moline.

Matt continued relentlessly. "Orders you did not question? Commodore Jenks assures me that even masters of Company vessels are free . . . are *required* to question orders they consider criminal or immoral—it's in your charter!"

"Much of what is in the charter has no meaning now," Moline moaned. "Questioning orders is no longer encouraged or even allowed!"

"The charter reflects Imperial law. It does not supersede

it!" Jenks accused. "Neither do the orders of rogue Company officials! Regardless of what the Company might or might not encourage or allow, you are still subject to Imperial law!"

Moline looked at Jenks and his eyes grew dull. "You have been gone a long time, Commodore. Who are you to say what supersedes what?"

Jenks jumped to his feet. "Honor supersedes treachery!" he practically shouted. "Duty to the Governor-Emperor supersedes any conceivable 'duty' to a Company . . . creature . . . in the office of the Prime Proprietor!" With a visible force of will, he composed himself. When he continued, his voice was dry and emotionless.

"If your 'Mr. Brown' had not been so conveniently killed in the exchange of shot with this ship, perhaps some of what you say might be verified and your own guilt mitigated to a slight degree, but not enough to save you from a rope." He glanced at his own notes. "You testified that these 'sealed orders' were destroyed as soon as you were acquainted with them, so clearly even 'Mr. Brown' recognized their criminal nature. It has been established by numerous witnesses that Ensign Parr, whom I dispatched aboard *Agamemnon*, duly reported to the first authorities he met—Company officials!—the survival and rescue of the princess, as well as her intention to take passage on this ship. Numerous witnesses—virtually *Agamemnon*'s entire original crew!—also report that they were transferred and sequestered aboard *Icarus*, a less powerful and capable ship, before they could report to any naval or Imperial authorities. Finally, both *Icarus* and *Agamemnon* were pressed into Company service! Imperial Navy ships and crews were illegally seized by, and placed into the service of, Company pirates bent on committing high treason! Regardless of any 'sealed orders,' these acts were no secret to you. That you continued in command of *Ulysses* is abundant proof that you made no objection to these other crimes at least, and obviously made no attempt to thwart them! Even if you are as utterly stupid as you would have us believe, you are at the very least guilty of being an accessory to a blatant act of piracy!"

Jenks paused, catching himself. His voice had begun to rise again and his fury toward not only Captain Moline but the HNBC itself threatened to overwhelm him. Matt suspected Jenks's emotions were stirred by terror as well: not physical terror—he knew Jenks was no coward—but a growing terror of what they might discover his precious Empire had become in his absence. Matt could identify with that kind of terror: he felt it at the edge of his consciousness every moment of every day. He somehow managed to function and perform his duties—he had no choice—but he was genuinely terrified for the safety of one Nurse Lieutenant Sandra Tucker, who even now was still in the maniacal hands of the Company minion, Walter Billingsley . . . as far as they knew.

Matt cleared his throat. "Further demonstrations, protestations, or even admonitions are pointless at this stage. As previously stated, Captain Moline, you've been found guilty of the crimes described by Commodore Jenks. It is therefore the order of this court that you be taken from this place to the deck of the pirate prize *Ulysses*, where, according to the customs of your service, you will be bound hand and foot and hanged by the neck until you're dead." Matt glanced from the frozen form of the prisoner to the two Marines. "Get this bastard out of my sight."

Brad "Spanky" McFarlane scrutinized the toil underway in the crew's forward berthing space with a critical but generally satisfied eye. Standing in the steamy compartment where hardly anyone ever actually slept, he struck his trademark pose—hands on his skinny hips, his absolute authority over everything in his domain radiating from his diminutive but powerfully wiry frame. Before him, a party of 'Cats adjusted shoring timbers while two men held torches against a warped steel plate, heating it to a dull reddish orange. Radiant heat from the torches and the steel they played against only added to the stifling temperature of the berthing space, even with the portholes open. Absently, Spanky wondered again what kind of idiot designed this ship and so many like her with the portholes in the forward berthing space so close to the waterline that they could almost never be opened—at least not in any kind of sea, or while the ship was underway. If it hadn't been for the meager light they provided in daytime, he probably would've plated over them during the reconstruction.

Periodically, the smoking timbers were pounded against the plate, pushing it a little closer to where it had been before the large roundshot bent it inward. It was the last one; all the others that had been displaced nearby had already been re-formed. The racket of the sledges against the timbers in the confined space was terrific.

"Almost there, Lieuten-aant McFaar-lane," cried a 'Cat between blows. Spanky nodded. He was far more than a mere lieutenant now, he was "Minister of Naval Engineering," or something like that, but he didn't care. Usually he couldn't even remember whether his "official" Navy rank was lieutenant commander or commander, but it couldn't have mattered less to him. Nobody would try to tell him what to do when it came to his area of expertise, and right now, aboard USS *Walker*, doing what he was doing, he was the ship's engineering lieutenant, and that was it. As far as he could recollect, he and the Skipper were the only officers currently on the ship still performing their "old jobs."

Spanky and Chief Bosun's Mate Carl Bashear were inspecting the final touches on the repairs to *Walker*'s hull. They'd already fixed several similar perforations acquired during the sharp action with the Company traitors. The hole that opened up the forward engine room had been the worst, not only puncturing the hull—right at a frame—but also knocking a double hole through one of the saddle bunkers. They'd salvaged most of the fuel, pumping it into bunkers they'd already run dry. They even saved most of what leaked into the bilge, just in case, but fixing that damage had been their most critical and difficult repair. They had found the roundshot that made the holes—and nearly took

Brian Aubrey's head off—rolling around in the bilge. Jenks identified it as a thirty-pounder. This struck everyone odd, since the Grand Alliance had sort of based its shot sizes on the old British system, and its closest equivalent was a thirty-two-pounder. The Brits themselves seemed to have abandoned the very system they brought with them—or adopted another. Oh, well, that wasn't Spanky's concern beyond the proof it provided concerning who'd shot it into them. *Ulysses* carried thirty-pounders. Even now, unless he missed his guess, her skipper was swinging for it.

"Nice to be able to fix something right for a change," Bashear rumbled. It was a positive statement, but still came out with a tone of complaint.

"Yeah. Havin' enough guys for a job makes a difference—not to mention havin' somethin' to do it with."

Their labor pool and equipment list were far better than they'd ever been when they'd attempted similar repairs in the past; they had spare plate steel, rivets, and plenty of acetylene—even if it popped and sputtered—and *Walker*'s crew was actually somewhat over complement for a change too. Almost two-thirds of that crew was Lemurian now, but they took up less space and more would fit. Many were Chack's Marines, who had shipboard duties as well. Spanky was generally satisfied with the growing professionalism and competency of all their "new" 'Cats, and he'd long been pleased with the "old hands," who'd signed on as cadets when *Walker* first dropped anchor in Baalkpan Bay, but there was just no way he'd ever get used to certain aspects of this new navy they'd created.

He sneezed. Lemurians sweated more like horses than men, kind of "lathering up." They also panted. Bradford said they'd developed this somewhat unique method of heat exchange due to their environment. They also shed like crazy, and Spanky was allergic to the downy filaments that floated everywhere belowdecks when they were hard at work.

"C'mon, Carl," he said. "These apes and snipes are working together so well it turns my stomach." There were grins at that. "I don't think we need to keep starin' at them to keep them away from each other's throats."

"I just don't understand it," Bashear commiserated. "Whatever happened to tradition? Where's the pride? You'd almost think they *like* each other, to look at 'em get on so. Ain't natural."

Spanky chuckled. The old rivalry between the deck (apes) and engineering (snipes) divisions still existed, but it had been "tamed down" a little without the caustic presence of Dean Laney aboard. He'd been of the "old school," in which duties were strictly defined in an almost labor union–like fashion. The Bosun wasn't much different, but he'd adjusted to the new imperatives. Laney hadn't. It hadn't been so bad when Chief Donaghey had ridden herd on the man, but after Donaghey's death, Laney became a tyrant. There just wasn't room for that on something as small as *Walker* anymore. On this mission, Laney had remained behind to supervise the production of heavy industry—something his obnoxious personality was well suited for. And besides, the running—mostly—joke was that if somebody "accidentally" dropped something big and heavy on him, the world would be a better place.

In the meantime, the Lemurian apes and snipes on *Walker* got along much better. None of the 'Cats liked the Imperial term "Ape Folk," even if, as far as anyone knew, they'd never seen an ape; they understood it was derogatory and condescending. In contrast, the "deck apes" didn't mind that term at all. It was occupational . . . and almost fraternal. They embraced it just as the engineering divisions accepted the title of "snipes" in much the same way. There were still pranks and jokes, and a competitive spirit existed between them, but they'd all been through far too much together to lose sight of the fact that they were all on the same side, part of the same clan, living on the same Home. Spanky, who'd had a little college before joining the Navy as a mere recruit and rising as a "mustang," was reminded of guys from different college fraternities who played on the same football team. In spite of his remarks to Carl Bashear—remarks expected of him—he liked it this way.

"Where're we goin'?" Bashear asked as they left the repair detail to their work and moved aft.

"Something I gotta do, then I'll go topside with you and have a look at that winch. You say it ain't blowin' steam?"

Carl shook his head. "Nope. Nothin' blows steam around here 'cept the fellas now and then." He shook his head. "That ain't natural either. That gasket stuff Letts came up with works almost too good. No, there's something else, and I gotta get it fixed. The Skipper wants Mr. Reynolds to fly tomorrow, or the next day, when we get underway." He pointed in the general direction of land. "According to our charts, that thing's not even supposed to be there. The Brit charts don't show it either, for that matter, but they do show a lot of stuff a little farther along that ain't right." Bashear scratched his head. "So far, west of here, everything seems about the same. Nothing too out of the ordinary that different sea levels wouldn't account for, other than the occasional volcanic island that ain't where it's supposed to be. What's the deal with these atolls and stuff?"

Spanky shrugged. "Ask Mr. Bradford. He knows all that stuff. From what I gather though, these pissant desert islands and atolls pile up on old coral reefs or something. Kind of random. No reason they had to show up the same place they were 'back home,' since there was no real reason them other ones formed where they did. Just luck that the first coral pod—or whatever they are—took root where it did. The islands are in the same basic area, but no reason they should be *exactly* the same either."

Bashear looked at him skeptically. "Well, either way, the Skipper wants Reynolds to fly." He chuckled. "Now that he's fixed all the holes in his plane. You heard one of the holes was 'self-inflicted'?"

"I heard," said Spanky, "and you ought to cut the kid some slack. Most of the holes *weren't* self-inflicted and there were a lot of 'em. All he had to shoot back with was a pistol, for Crissakes. So he got a little fixated on his target.

Happens all the time. Just think how many observers prob'ly shot their own planes to pieces back in the Great War." He grinned. "Think how many times those battle-wagon boys blew their own observation planes over the side just in exercises, before the war! You get 'em in a real fight, they'd probably blast their own damn ship!"

"Well, anyway," Bashear continued as they worked their way aft, "Skipper wants him to chart shoals and such from the air so we'll know if we can ever get something big through here, like a 'Cat flattop. I can't lift the plane without the winch."

"Right," Spanky replied, and left it at that. Reynolds had taken a lot of ribbing for shooting his own plane, but the kid had guts. Once he'd finally decided what to do with himself, he'd become a good pilot for one of the tiny, rickety-looking "Nancys," or prototype seaplanes Ben Mallory had designed. Spanky wouldn't have gone up in one of the things, and he respected anyone willing to do something he wouldn't.

Together, he and Bashear cycled through the air lock into the forward fireroom. 'Cats looked up as they passed, nodding respectfully but remaining at their posts. The number two boiler was lit. Cycling through to the aft fireroom was almost like passing through another Squall to a different world all over again. In contrast to the peaceful routine they'd just left, the aft fireroom was a scene of chittering excitement, shouted commands, and almost frantic activity. Black soot floated in the air along with the downy filaments of Lemurian undercoats. Spanky sneezed again and blew his nose into his fingers. He no longer slung the snot at the deck plates as he once had, but wiped his fingers on a rag hanging from his pocket. Somehow, slinging snot at *Walker* just didn't seem right anymore.

"Tabby!" He had to shout to be heard over the commotion in the fireroom.

Tab-At, or "Tabby" as the original "Mice" (a pair of extraordinarily insular and unusual firemen who actually looked quite a bit like small rodents) had christened her before she became one of the Mice herself, looked up from where she stood, striking a pose similar to the one Spanky himself often used. Her hands rested on admittedly shapelier, disconcertingly feminine hips, even though she belonged to an entirely different species. The tail that twitched beneath her abbreviated kilt at Spanky's shout undermined the image to some degree, but oddly, not too much. As usual, whenever Spanky encountered her, she wasn't wearing a shirt either. This time at least, she probably hadn't been doing it just to get his goat, since her silky gray fur was lathered with sweat and covered with soot. Even so, Spanky had to take a deep breath and force himself not to bellow at her for being out of "uniform" once again. Her beguilingly . . . human . . . well-rounded breasts were the very reason he'd dictated that every fireman must wear at least a T-shirt on duty. None of the firemen in the aft fireroom had T-shirts on now, because for this task he'd given special dispensation. That didn't mean Tabby or the several other female "firemen" they now had were included in that dispensation. Spanky had thought that was understood. Apparently it wasn't. 'Cats could be very literal-minded—especially when they wanted to be.

"Tabby," he repeated, "get over here!"

Bashear looked at Spanky curiously, wondering what this was about. That he hadn't thrown an instant fit over the lack of T-shirts was strange enough. His opinion on that was common knowledge and a source of some amusement. None of the female deck apes (and there were a lot more of them) had to wear shirts for special duties that anyone else might remove theirs to perform. But Spanky McFarlane had bent as far as he intended to just by letting females of any sort into his engineering spaces. If they were going to be down there, they were going to wear clothes! Tabby tormented him constantly, but he was torn by his own personal axiom: if somebody does something that bothers you, either pretend it doesn't or make them stop. In Tabby's case, he couldn't figure out how to do the second, so he tried unsuccessfully to do the first. He wasn't fooling anybody.

Oddly, instead of undermining his authority, his . . . predicament probably strengthened it. Early on, he was viewed by many 'Cats as some sort of omniscient, unapproachable wizard. They now knew he wasn't, but although they weren't terrified of him anymore, they were amazed that a mere mortal such as they (albeit without a tail) could be so knowledgeable about machines. Wizards and magicians didn't have to know things, or so the tales of younglings said. They just cast spells and things occurred. Spanky couldn't cast spells; he actually knew things, and he'd come by all that knowledge the hard way: he'd learned it the same way everyone else had to, and they respected him immensely for that.

Tabby hopped over the 'Cats on the deck plates that were hauling debris from within the number three boiler with a hoe-shaped tool on their hands and knees. Others gathered the stuff up and put it in heavy canvas bags to be taken topside. Amazingly, Tabby snatched a T-shirt from a valve wheel as she approached and pulled it over her head.

"You wanna see me, sir?" she asked.

"Uh, yeah." Spanky gestured back at the work. "That bad, eh?"

She shrugged. "Whoever overhauled that boiler did a piss-poor job on the firebrick. Waadn't me. I guess with the hurry we were in, somebody got sloppy."

"Probably so. You were supposed to tell me if you wound up having to tear it down and rebrick it, though."

"We be done by tomorrow," she assured him. "I didn't think it was worth buggin' you about."

Spanky took a breath. "Now you listen to me," he said in a low, intense tone. "Anything that affects this ship's readiness to steam at a moment's notice—anything the Skipper needs to know before he can make a decision based on that readiness—is always worth buggin' me about, no matter how trivial it seems. Last I heard, you were planning on replacing a few firebricks, and I specifically told you to let me know if you had to do more. I didn't hear from you, so I came in here thinking we still had three boilers, in a pinch.

Right now, the Skipper thinks he has three boilers, but he doesn't, does he? All he's got is two—with a lot of crap in the way of one of 'em. What if a squadron of them Brit, Imperial, Company—whatever—frigates suddenly shows up on the horizon? The Skipper'll be deciding what to do based on his *certain knowledge* he's got three boilers! Don't *ever* just jump up and crack this deep into something without telling me first! Is that understood?"

Tears welled in Tabby's large amber eyes.

Spanky was stunned. "Goddamn!" he managed. "Are you fixin' to *cry*?" His voice was incredulous. His own eyes went wide when Tabby's tears gushed out and coursed down her furry cheeks.

"I . . . I so sorry!" Tabby practically moaned. As usual when she was upset or excited, she lost her careful drawl. "You got so much . . . so much other stuff; I just want to not bother you with more! I sorry, Spaanky! Please no be maad! I never, ever do nothing you no tell me! I wear shirt all the time! Just please no be maad at me!"

For a moment Spanky and Bashear were both speechless. Tabby sniffled loudly a few more times, then tried to collect herself. She began wiping the tears on her clean shirt, smudging it with wet soot and firebrick dust.

"I'll swan," Bashear said softly.

"Shut up, you!" Spanky growled. He turned back to Tabby. "Ah, lookie here," he said clumsily. "No sweat. Just don't do it anymore, see?" Tabby nodded almost spastically. "All right, then." He looked around, staring at anything but her for a few moments. If the work detail had heard or even paused in their labor, he couldn't tell. They were still drawing the broken firebricks and passing them along to others, who dropped them into sacks. Finally Spanky looked back at Tabby. He was glad she'd apparently composed herself. He hadn't come here to jump all over her; he actually had something else on his mind. Still, what he'd said was true and needed saying. Especially now.

"Look, Tabby, just get the job done, now you've started it. I'll report the boiler's down to the Skipper." He gestured at the detail. "Things look well enough in hand." He paused. "You're doing a good job here in the firerooms. Those squirrelly Mice taught you all right, God knows how. I expect you know the old gal's boilers as well as they do by now." He paused again and took a breath. "Here's the deal. I made Aubrey chief down here because he was a torpedoman. He knew turbines and steam plants, but he never was really all that good with the big stuff. Never should've used him like that. Should've left him working with Bernie Sandison back in Baalkpan." He shook his head. "Well, Aubrey's dead, and I'm going to split Engineering back into two divisions: steam plant and propulsion. Every fireman on this tub is a 'Cat now, and it would be stupid to take some guy off something else and put him in charge in here when you'd know more than he would, so as of right now, you're chief of the boiler division, got that?"

Tabby's surprised eyes began to fill again.

"But only if you don't start cryin' over it, for God's sake!" Spanky added hastily. "There will be *no* cryin' in the firerooms, clear? Not ever!"

Instead of answering, Tabby lunged forward and touched him on the cheek with her muzzle, tongue slightly extended. Spanky knew the gesture was a Lemurian version of a modest, chaste kiss. Passionate kissing involved much more licking. Even so, he was thunderstruck and didn't have a chance to say anything before Tabby bolted back to the detail she was overseeing.

Bashear, uncertain how Spanky would respond, guided him back toward the air lock and they cycled through. "C'mon," he said. "I still need you to look at that winch."

"What the hell was that all about?" Spanky asked quietly, still torn between shock, fury, and . . . God knew what. "What the hell's got into her? I *had* to chew her out about letting me know, but I figgered she'd make some crack and get back to work! Then she starts bawling! And that . . . whatever she did to me . . . Do you think she's crackin' up?"

"You really want to know what I think?" Bashear asked as they went through the forward air lock and headed for the companionway.

"Well . . . sure."

"I think she's sweet on you," Bashear said seriously.

"Horsefeathers!"

"Sweeter than honey on a comb. I wonder how many engineers ever had sweethearts in the fireroom. Not many, I hope."

Spanky turned on him. "Shut the hell up, you goddamn perverted, filthy-minded ape!" he said hotly.

"There!" Bashear said. "Now that's more like it. Thought I'd never get a rise out of you!" His voice became serious. "She *is* sweet on you though, and it shows. A lot. What're you gonna do? Turn Silva?" That was the increasingly accepted term for men suspected of having "taken up" with a Lemurian gal.

"She ain't 'sweet' on me," Spanky protested. "Sometimes she's downright insubordinate!"

Bashear nodded sagely. "That's always the first sign. 'Cats ain't really all that different from us, you know. Once you get past the fur and ears—and, well, the tail." They'd reached the weather deck and were passing under the amidships gun platform that served as a roof for the galley. Chief Gunner's Mate Paul Stites was supervising a maintenance detail on the number three, four-inch-fifty. They were installing new oily leather bushings in the recoil cylinder. Below, Earl Lanier, the bloated cook, had left a heap of sandwiches on the stainless steel counter. Bashear snatched one. "Wimmen is all the same," he continued. "Even 'Cat wimmen, I bet. They take to thinkin' you belong to 'em and they start treatin' you like dirt. Take advantage. I been married twice, so trust me, I know." He looked at Spanky. "You want my advice?"

"No."

"You can't just ignore it," Bashear advised anyway. "You treat her like a dog, pretend she ain't there, it'll just get worse. I don't know what it is about 'em, but every time I try to get rid of a dame, they just try harder. You can't chase 'em off."

"Well . . . supposin' you're right—which you ain't—how would you make Tabby get over her fit?"

"Easy," Bashear said around a mouthful of sandwich. "Be nice to her. I never could keep a dame I really wanted. Nobody can. It's the rules."

CHAPTER 2

East Africa

"General of the Sea" Hisashi Kurokawa strode slowly beside the immense, deep basin, lightly slapping his left boot at every step with a short, tightly woven whip. A wisp of dust drifted away from his striped pants leg with each strike. The handle of the whip was garishly ornate and the gruesome golden sculpture capping it appealed to his sense of mockery. It looked strikingly like a flattened Grik face. Beyond the basin, a hot wind blew swirling dust devils amid a sea of Uul workers swarming over the flat, denuded landscape that bordered the wide river, and the hazy orange sun blazed fiercely down from above. The wind reeked of rot, feces, and an untold number of partially cannibalized, festering corpses. Those scents were renewed each day as the defecating, dying thousands toiled, and the stench was almost unbearable. Yet bear it he did. To show weakness of any sort under the circumstances was tantamount to suicide in the great game he played.

Skeletal frameworks arose amid this teeming mass, erected by muscle power alone. Once again Kurokawa marveled at the discipline that could accomplish so much with such apparently mindless labor. Groups of Grik Uul performed many of the same functions as various machines in a factory. Some shaped massive timbers with a tool resembling an elongated adze—and that was all they did, while other groups were dedicated solely to moving the timbers to areas where still others set them in place. A little farther along, other "teams" did the same thing with an only subtly different timber. It was the most wondrous example of non-mechanized mass production he'd ever seen, and the scope and specialization of the endeavor surely put the construction of the Great Pyramids to shame.

There were overseers, to be sure, that served much the same purpose here as sergeants and officers might in battle. They orchestrated the timing and direction of every task. Some led bearers to the next mighty "skeleton" where their particular timber was required. Others lashed a continuous stream of bearers, burdened with massive tree trunks felled in the ever more distant forest, toward the timber shapers' tools. Uul dropped from illness or exhaustion everywhere he looked, only to be trampled to death by those behind them. Some took quick, passing gobbets of flesh from the often still-moving dead.

Kurokawa was sickened, but enthralled. Such discipline! Such symmetry! Such simple, mechanical grace! Grik industry was driven by a living Grik machine. When a part broke down or wore out, it quickly and automatically replaced itself with another! He felt himself on the very cusp of some profound revelation concerning the most fundamental nature of things. He was a naval officer but also an engineer, and the complexity of machinery had fascinated him even as a child. Here, however, was a machine that appealed to him in an almost spiritual way, not because it was complex but because of its almost perfect simplicity. He still considered himself piously devoted to his emperor and had utter faith in Hirohito's divinity, but he felt close to some sort of personal . . . reformation.

He paused a moment, peering into the immense basin.

The labor underway down there was of another sort entirely, utilizing completely different materials and techniques. It was also, of necessity, using a lot of his own men. They were the overseers in this case, each with a team of translators and runners, but as miserable as the working conditions were on the expanding plain above, it was pure hell down in "the Hole." Some of his precious men had actually died just from the heat! He didn't consider them "precious" for their own sakes. As far as he was concerned, most were traitors. If that were not the case, he would still have the mighty battle cruiser *Amagi* at his disposal. They had failed in their duty to him and the emperor by allowing her destruction at the pathetic hands of—

He forcibly calmed himself, taking deep, flared-nostril breaths. He'd begun to realize that his tantrums accomplished little. They terrified and intimidated his men but had no effect on the Grik. Besides, he always felt drained after they ultimately ran their course. Better to hold the hatred in, let it help fuel him. In any event, what made the treachery of those who died of something as ridiculous as *heat* even more egregious was that *Amagi*'s survivors were "precious" only as an irreplaceable resource. Their value was reckoned in respect to what they knew, by what they could do for *him* to elevate *his* prestige and secure *his* position. There were too few of them left as it was, and after the last "culling" following their defeat at Baalkpan, he had fewer than four hundred. He needed to use them sparingly, but he *did* need some for this . . . and other ambitious programs. He grimaced and resumed his leg-slapping stroll.

Another man carefully paced Kurokawa, trying to stay just slightly behind but close enough to hear any possible word that might pass his true commander's lips. He was taller, slimmer, and unlike Kurokawa, who always wore the dark blue, increasingly elaborate uniform made by the finest Grik tailors, his was white, and still genuine Imperial Navy issue. The man's name was Orochi Niwa, and he'd recently rocketed from the rank of a lieutenant of *Amagi*'s small SNLF (Special Naval Landing Force) contingent to

"General of Hunters" in the army of the Grik. Regardless of his new rank and the . . . army . . . he served, he was fully aware who—literally—owned his life. He had no illusions that Kurokawa liked him or even really trusted him; Kurokawa would sacrifice him without remorse if he perceived the slightest reason or advantage. The only purpose for his exalted status was that Kurokawa knew he himself couldn't actually be everywhere at once, and he'd instituted far too many "projects" to personally oversee. Besides that, he also wanted—needed—a Japanese presence at the war councils of the Grik where tactics were discussed. Kurokawa attended those councils dedicated to grand strategy, and his input was now much appreciated, but he readily admitted he had no real knowledge of, or interest in, land warfare. Niwa did. Niwa had also made it abundantly clear that he was wholly aware of his "place." Regardless of his Grik position, he still served Kurokawa, and through him, the Emperor.

"I suppose we should hurry." Kurokawa seethed, picking up the pace. "Our 'masters,'" he snorted, "will be waiting." Niwa didn't point out that the Grik High Command had probably been waiting for the better part of an hour. He didn't say anything at all. Together, the two men strode more briskly among the yard workers, occasionally dodging groups fixated—almost like ants—upon their tasks. Finally, after they'd left the basin and the majority of the dust and stench behind, they joined a group relaxing under the shade of a crude wooden structure, taking their ease and enjoying elaborate bowls brimming with cool liquid. Niwa politely refused an offered bowl. He had no idea what was in it, but assumed it would be something vile and repulsive.

"You are late—as always," growled General Esshk, standing to loom above them. Esshk was the most imposing Grik Niwa had ever seen; the mere sight of him always made Niwa cringe a little, at least inwardly. Esshk was First among Generals in the Army of the Grik, and he usually dressed the part. Bronze breastplate, greaves, and cuffs, along with a scarlet cape and kilt gave the vague impression of a Roman tribune. The tufted bronze helmet he held under his massive arm completed the ensemble. A smoky black crest rose slightly atop his head as he spoke.

"I have been inspecting the work," Kurokawa said by means of explanation, not apology.

"How does it proceed?"

"Well enough on the . . . traditional vessels," he replied. "Slower than I would like on the other."

"What is lacking?"

Kurokawa shrugged. "Heavy equipment, cranes, pneumatic riveters, a steady supply of good iron instead of the useless cast plating you continue to force upon me. Qualified yard workers most of all."

"The cast plating is what we can do. The same iron served well enough for cannons!"

"And it will shatter the first time a shot is fired against it!" Kurokawa stated, voice rising. "I have told you what is needed and how to make it, yet still you send me the same thing. Have you learned nothing?"

Esshk seethed. He knew Kurokawa was right. He was always right about such things. He'd even seen the plating shatter when a gun was tested against it. "The Celestial Mother grows impatient," he temporized. "We stand on the brink of losing Regent Tsalka's domain. We have withdrawn from contested lands as you suggested, despite the . . . difficulty . . . but Ceylon is important!"

"And I told you we would lose it before we could take it back," Kurokawa replied, repeating an old argument.

"But that is precisely where much of your 'steel' is made!" Tsalka interjected, speaking up.

Kurokawa bowed to the Regent. "Indeed. So we must hold it long enough to produce and remove as much as possible before it falls. Complete the new foundries here, and it will be a lesser loss."

"My own realm!" Tsalka almost wailed.

"This has been decided already," Kurokawa flatly stated. "You will get it back. In the meantime, I must have true steel, not only for this project"—he waved at the basin—

"but for others. There can be no 'flying machines' at all, for example, without steel."

Esshk glanced at the newly appointed General Halik. Halik had been a mere "entertainment fighter," basically a gladiator, for many seasons and had grown quite too old for that. That was precisely the reason he'd been "elevated" and tapped as a general. He seemed to have naturally developed an instinct for defensive fighting. It would still be a year or more before the first "defensive" forces were ready to deploy, and they'd be little more than hatchlings even then, but in this new kind of hunt, this "war," much was being accomplished on the fly. Esshk was certain their enemies had many of the same issues to contend with, but most likely some were direct opposites. As prey, they needed to learn offensive tactics, while a whole new class of Grik that was capable of defense had to be grown.

In the meantime, Halik had sponsored the elevation of other warriors in whom he recognized certain traits, and hoped they would serve as a nucleus for his new cadre of junior officers. Esshk had a sinking feeling that war as his people knew it was changing forever. Perhaps their entire society would ultimately be unrecognizable, but he would accept that if it meant his very species might ultimately survive. Some didn't yet recognize the threat and were not particularly supportive, but he'd gained the tentative support of the Celestial Mother, and that was all that mattered. He looked at Halik. "Is there nothing you can do?"

"In Ceylon?"

"Indeed."

"I would have to go there and see for myself," Halik said. His speech had improved amazingly over the last months. "A true 'defense' may not be possible, but spoiling attacks might slow the enemy advance. Grasp time."

Tsalka was nodding, but Esshk was thoughtful. Halik represented much more to him than just another general. He might be their only hope.

"Very well. You will go there by the safest route. Do not allow yourself to be slain! That is a command! You still have much to do." Esshk's eyes turned to Niwa. "You have worked closely with General Halik. Perhaps you should accompany him. Together you will learn not only the . . . 'tactics' of the prey—" He caught himself. "I mean, the 'enemy,' but you may better learn how we might counter them during this . . . transitional period. General Niwa, you will learn about the Grik alongside the Grik. General Halik, you will learn more about the enemy from one who knows them better."

"But General Esshk!" Kurokawa and Niwa protested at once. Niwa realized what he'd done and clamped his mouth shut. Kurokawa, on the other hand, continued. "You would deprive me of my own best counselor?"

Esshk peered at him. "I deprive myself of Halik, but then, I still have you. I have been given to understand you *need* no counsel."

"Not at sea!" Kurokawa sputtered. "But I am no land general! I have never claimed to be. I do understand land *strategy*, and how it must be combined with that of the sea, but to fully appreciate that combination, I need my best land *tactician*." Kurokawa paused and blinked, realizing Esshk had goaded him into admitting, for the first time, that he *didn't* know everything. Damn him! Esshk might only now be learning the subtleties of modern war, but he had long been a chess master of debate and intrigue. Kurokawa had almost forgotten that. He had also forgotten, or finally learned, how important it was to have someone near him he could trust—somewhat—and even speak candidly with on occasion. Niwa, subservient and cowed as he was, was the closest thing to a "friend" Kurokawa had on this world. Now Esshk would deprive him of even that.

"Exactly," said Esshk, and he drove the final nail. "General Niwa will be more valuable to us both after this experience. He will be General Halik's Vice Commander, and the two of them will learn from each other and the enemy at the same time. At least one should survive to return with the tactical observations we desire."

"Thank you, Noble First," Halik said humbly, and it suddenly became clear to Kurokawa that Halik had *requested* this! Why? He looked at Niwa and saw his nervous expression. *How can I use this?* he thought. *I stood up for Niwa and he will remember that. Niwa has an opportunity to gain Halik's and even Esshk's trust more fully than I ever could. I will . . . miss . . . Niwa, but perhaps this might work to my advantage.*

Kurokawa gave Niwa a small but significant nod. "Oh, very well," he said. "It does make sense, I suppose. You may have him so long as I have your word he will not be required to 'destroy himself' or any such nonsense if he and General Halik cannot save Ceylon."

Esshk seemed surprised. "General of the Sea Kurokawa," he exclaimed, "have I just seen you display concern for a member of your pack? How uncharacteristic!"

Kurokawa inwardly smoldered. He knew Esshk would take it that way and it exposed a vulnerability, but it was worth it to gain Niwa's ultimate trust.

"I am concerned for both General Niwa and General Halik, as well as our cause. We cannot spare either of them."

"There we are agreed," Esshk said. "Fear not, the destruction of Uul warriors and their leaders is at an end. You were right regarding how wasteful it is. Even in defeat, not all are 'made prey,' and even those who are . . . provide a valuable service."

Kurokawa wondered about that last comment, but shuddered slightly at what he thought it probably meant.

Esshk appeared satisfied with the proceedings thus far. He lapped at a bowl of . . . something, then looked expectantly at Kurokawa.

"Mmm," Kurokawa said, looking at Niwa. "General Niwa, I believe you know General Halik?"

Niwa controlled an impulse to gulp. "Yes, Cap— General of the Sea."

"Good. I will therefore accept your enthusiastic offer to participate in this important and glorious mission!" Kurokawa affected a false, grotesque smile.

"Uh . . . thank you, sir." Niwa looked at Halik, who was staring back at him now.

"That's the spirit!" Kurokawa beamed genuinely. "General Esshk?"

Esshk looked at Halik, then Niwa. "You will leave almost immediately with a significant escort of ships," he said. "It is a dangerous sea. The escort will be loaded with supplies, but they well might be the last we send. Try to defend Ceylon as long as you can, and fill every homebound ship as full of 'steel' as possible. Those ships will likely not return to you."

"Yes, First General," Halik said.

"The two of you must defer to Vice Regent N'galsh, of course, but in reality you will command Ceylon and all of India. Every Hij and Uul there will obey you. Use them, but try not to waste them. Send me more like yourselves if you discover any." Esshk stood. "Now, we all have much more to do than lounge about, enjoying the view." Niwa almost coughed. "I suggest," Esshk continued, "that Generals Halik and Niwa remain here a short while." He looked at them. "Get to know one another better. Decide if you have any special requirements."

The meeting broke up then. Even Kurokawa disappeared into the swirling dust that seemed to be growing worse, leaving Niwa and Halik alone under the increasingly dubious shelter.

"Why?" Niwa asked without preamble.

"You interest me, General Niwa," Halik said. "I think I might learn much from you."

"Like what?"

"Like how to survive when you are surrounded by enemies. I have learned to do that in the arena, but to do so every day . . . that is different."

"What do you mean?"

Halik rasped a chuckle. "I think you know." He paused, catching occasional glimpses of the horror in the dust. "We are warriors, you and I, accustomed to holding the sword in our hands. Our masters have never done that; they are not allowed, so they fight with their minds and words and barely know the feel of a sword. We are important to them because they think we can fight with our swords *and* minds." Halik looked at Niwa, and Niwa would have sworn the Grik was excited! "We will leave this place! That cannot disappoint you. Then we will see if they are right!"

CHAPTER 3

Yap Island (Shikarrak)

Chief Gunner's Mate Dennis Silva savagely hacked at the indifferent army of spiny, bamboo-like shoots standing before him like a shield wall of personal foes. The swath of "bamboo" couldn't be more than a mile wide at most—judging by the crummy "chart" Silva had, the whole island wasn't much wider than that across this point—but it seemed endless, and the party's progress through it had been excruciatingly slow. Even the mighty Dennis Silva was beginning to tire. Sweat glistened on his skin, collecting grime and fragments of the shredded flora, and the patch covering his ruined left eye was soggy and blotched with salt. He stopped for a moment to catch his breath and untwisted the canteen from the rope belt around his waist. Sloshing it experimentally, he unscrewed the cap and took a shallow swig.

"Now I know what a ant feels like," he pronounced a little breathlessly. " 'Cept I don't guess ants have to gnaw their way through everything to get anywhere."

The rest of the small party accompanying him was at least as tired as he was after swinging their decidedly inferior cutlasses to widen the path behind him. Silva was doing the lion's share of the work, but the steel in his pattern of 1917 Navy cutlass was of infinitely better quality. In response to his statement, his companions could manage only a few gasping grunts. The heat was hellish and the humidity oppressive, but the sun didn't bother Silva anymore. He was tanned so dark, his various smudged tattoos had become merely darker, unrecognizable discolorations on his skin. In contrast, his now longish hair, matted beard, and the light, curly hair that generally covered him from neck to feet had turned almost pure white. For clothing, he wore only his battered "chief's" hat the Bosun had given him, a pair of cut-off Lemurian-made dungarees, and "go-forwards" he'd fashioned for himself.

He was otherwise equipped with a large shooting pouch, slung over his shoulder, made from the almost indestructible hide of a rhino pig. It contained all the implements, components, and accessories necessary to keep the "Doom Whomper," the 100-caliber rifled musket he'd made from a Japanese anti-aircraft gun, fed, maintained, and happy. He'd given his pistol belt to Sandra Tucker—she knew how to handle a 1911 Colt—and there wasn't much ammo for it anyway. She could use it if she needed it, but it was his job to keep that from happening. Instead of the 1911, Silva still carried his cutlass, and a long-barreled flintlock pistol he'd taken from the Company assassin Linus Truelove. Silva expected, with some satisfaction, that Truelove had been reduced to a few floating ashen specks, when Silva had contrived to blow up *Ajax*, but the pistol was a dandy. It would shoot only once before reloading of course, but they had plenty of ammo for it.

He took the opportunity to fish a whetstone from his pouch and run a few swipes down each side of his cutlass blade. He then offered the precious whetstone to the others, and when they took it, he watched keenly while it made its rounds before being returned. Dropping the stone back in his pouch, he carefully secured the flap. He took a deep breath and resumed his attack on the shoots.

They continued moving slowly under the sweltering sun, through the rest of the morning and into the early afternoon. Eventually, finally, it appeared that the stalks were beginning to thin. After a little longer, Silva was sure of it, and he slew the final shoots like the helpless stragglers of a routed army.

Before him now stretched a virtual savanna, filled with long grasses of various types. Some looked like "normal" grass, like coastal Bermuda, but there were large, almost islandlike clumps of taller stuff that reminded him of kudzu, complete with blue and purplish foxtail blossoms congregated near the edges. Strange birds (real birds, it seemed) flitted and swarmed around the clearing on strange wings, almost like dragonflies. There *were* a few of the now ubiquitous lizard birds, which occasionally streaked in to snatch one of the inoffensive-looking things, but even the birds nearest the victims didn't appear to give them any heed. Perhaps from within the apparent security of their multitudes, the weird little birds just didn't notice.

"Every time I turn a corner on this goofed-up world, I see somethin' even more goofed up," Silva mumbled. He surveyed the expanse of the savanna for several moments, trying to divine if it represented a threat of any kind. There were few large animals on the island, and most of those behaved aggressively only within the bounds of their apparently single-minded desire to be left alone. They were retiring and extremely heavily armored in the manner of giant land tortoises, even if any physical resemblance was remote. The smaller ones could be killed, with the Doom Whomper at least, and their flesh was fat and wholesome, but they'd learned that killing *anything* on this island came with a dose of risk. They'd met an interesting variety of smaller predators and scavengers that were far more capable and dangerous than they appeared. All were smaller than a man and most were fairly skittish. Some were not, and those were usually more than happy to contest them for the meat.

So far, they'd encountered only one type of really large,

dangerous animal during their brief, limited forays—and those didn't exactly *live* there. Silva now knew from experience that they had to be particularly watchful for the occasional, early-arriving "shiksak." He called them "shitsacks"; of course, "shiksak" was a Tagranesi word and he tended to prefer his own names for things. No matter what anybody called them, the damn things gave him the creeps.

Once, if anybody had ever told him he'd run across anything scarier than a "super lizard" on land, he'd have called them a liar. Now he knew better. Shiksaks were almost as big as super lizards, and although generally slower moving, they were actually quicker in a sprint. Maybe "lunge" or "leap" was a better term. They struck him as kind of a twisted cross of a crocodile, an eel, and a frog. They had big, fat bodies with long swimming tails with a ridge or finlike arrangement beginning behind their heads that ran the length of their backs, all the way to the ends of their tails. Their forelegs were little more than stumpy, clawed "flippers," but they had long, powerful hind legs with heavily webbed "feet" like those of a frog or toad. Add long, broad heads full of lots of teeth to the mix, and they even looked sort of comical in a way, like a giant pollywog that had swallowed most of an alligator. The young, towheaded Abel Cook, who'd once been fascinated with the dinosaurs of their "old" world, believed they were a type of mososaur that had evolved an amphibious capability to lay their eggs on shore, away from this world's more treacherous seas. Maybe so. "Mosey-saurs" they may once have been, but Silva was only concerned with what they'd become.

Individually, they weren't really *that* bad, he admitted to himself. A *single* shiksak wasn't as scary as a *single* super lizard. Unlike super lizards, which seemed to possess a kind of creepy cunning, shiksaks apparently weren't any smarter than pollywogs. Also, even if their thick, croclike skins made them practically bulletproof to the Imperial muskets, nothing was immune to his treasured Doom Whomper. No, so far the most pressing menace represented by the usually lethargic "early bird" shiksaks was that the sneaky bastards could change goddamn colors! That just wasn't fair. They crept ashore, made a nest, and plopped down to lay their eggs. Sprawling there, in the dense Yap, or "Shikarrak" Island jungle, they were difficult to see—and they would gulp down anything that came wandering by. Fair or not, even that wasn't an insurmountable problem: be careful, watch where you're going, and stay in pairs. Simple enough. The really big, scary problem—according to what they'd squeezed out of Lawrence ("Larry the Lizard")—was that within a month the whole island would be working with the damn things like maggots in meat, and nothing that wasn't armored like a tank, couldn't climb a really big tree or squirm down a tiny hole, would survive.

No human or 'Cat would fit down a hole small enough that the shiksaks couldn't dig it out, and the trees . . . would be full of other dangerous things. Larry had been here before when things got like that, during his "trial," and he'd survived. That was the point of the trial—to test his wits. But he'd been all alone, with only himself to look after. Dennis Silva had to make sure nothing happened to Princess Rebecca, Lieutenant Tucker (the Skipper's dame), the Lemurian Captain Lelaa, Sister Audry, and the gawky but gutsy Abel Cook. Maybe he would concern himself a *little* with a few of their Imperial companions who didn't like him very much—or maybe not. As he saw it, his plate of responsibility was pretty damn full.

Larry hadn't been willing to "blow" about the danger at first, even though he blamed himself for their presence there in the first place. He'd sworn an oath. He finally agreed to tell Rebecca and Miss Tucker, since no female was ever expected to undergo the trial. Even that might have been stretching things, but he just couldn't bear to let his precious Rebecca face the dangers unprepared. Silva was still a little put out that Larry hadn't just told him. He had to know the girls would blow. Oh, well, at least this way Silva got the word without Larry having to technically break his. One way or another, he'd learned what he was up against, as far as looking after the girls was concerned, and ultimately that was all that really mattered. Larry could look out for himself.

Dennis examined the tall grass a little longer, then shrugged. He couldn't *see* anything dangerous, but that didn't mean much. He thrust his cutlass into the scabbard tied to his belt and unslung the Doom Whomper. The big, heavy thing had been strapped diagonally across his back to keep it out of the way. "All right, fellas, come on out, I guess," he said. "If there's any boogers out there, I can't see 'em. Just keep your eyes peeled."

Abel Cook emerged first from the bamboo forest. He'd also secured his cutlass and was awkwardly carrying an Imperial musket in what he seemed to consider a proficient and vigilant manner. He managed a relieved, tired smile as he joined Silva. Midshipman Brassey of the Imperial Navy appeared next. The dark-haired boy was no older than Cook, and even if he was more accustomed to his cumbersome musket, he seemed just as relieved to escape the oppressive, confining thicket.

Captain Rajendra was close on the boy's heels. He was the only one of the marooned survivors with skin darker than Silva's, and whereas all the color had been bleached from Silva's, Rajendra's hair, bushy mustaches, and short, thick beard remained jet-black. In Rajendra's case, it was probably racial, but Silva had never asked and didn't care. Courtney Bradford might have been fascinated to learn more about Rajendra's genealogy, but God knew where Bradford was now. He might be in Baalkpan or points west. He might even be ironically near, with the Skipper, searching for the castaways. It was ironic because even if that were true, they would never find them. The Skipper had no way of knowing that the survivors of *Ajax* had become castaways and *Ajax* herself had literally ceased to exist. Silva usually enjoyed irony to a certain degree, even if he'd only recently learned the word. He even managed to glean a small measure of amusement from it in the current situation. He recognized irony for the bitch she could be and tended to be philosophical about it when she turned around and bit him on the ass.

Rajendra didn't appreciate irony at all, as far as Silva could tell. Apparently he didn't appreciate much of anything. Even after all these weeks, he seemed able to summon only a scowl when his eyes fell upon Dennis. Silva was philosophical about that too. He'd saved the man's life. He'd saved all their lives. But the way he'd gone about it . . . He supposed it was inevitable there'd be a touch of resentment. Like the others, Rajendra went armed with a musket, but he also carried a brace of pistols and a sword. Occasionally, absently, Silva wondered if the man's desire to use the weapons on him had waned at all. He didn't lose sleep over it, but it could be distracting to know he really needed to watch his back as well as his front.

At least one other "person" looked after him besides the well-intentioned Abel Cook. Larry the Lizard may not have been willing to technically spill the beans about the island, but he was Silva's friend. Larry was a Tagranesi, a species strikingly similar in appearance to the hated Grik. He was colored differently and not as big, but those distinctions hadn't been particularly clear when they'd met.

There's irony for you, Dennis thought, remembering that he'd actually shot Larry, thinking he was a Grik, but the little guy didn't hold it against him. *Hell of a lot more forgiving than Rajendra. I didn't even* shoot *him.* Irony again. Of course, having now seen the Grik and participated in the Battle of Baalkpan, Larry understood why Dennis had shot him. That had been a different time. The "lizards" were the enemy. All the lizards. They now knew not all Grik-like beings on this world *were* Grik, and that added even more confusion to an already screwed-up situation. *Just like folks*, Dennis thought, *hell, even Japs. There's all different sorts. Things sure were a lot simpler back when. you could just kill 'em all without needin' to sort 'em out first.* Oh, well, those days were over and it was probably just as well. Even Silva never thought in quite such simple terms anymore. He was glad Larry liked him—and that he always seemed to bring up the rear when one of their Imperial co-castaways was behind Dennis in the bush.

Appearing last, as usual, Larry was also armed with a musket. The weapon didn't really fit him—he just wasn't built for it—but he'd probably had more practice with one than most of the Imperials on the island.

"There you are, you little runt," Silva said. "I figgered I'd have to go find your lost ass . . . again. You been chasin' butterflies or bugs or something? Find a worm to eat?"

"I not lost," Lawrence grumped. "I thirsty, though."

"Shouldn't have drank all your water so fast then."

"I 'ound 'ater. I al'ays do."

"Even if it leaves you draggin' ass along like a one-legged toad?" Silva accused.

"I not draggin' ass. You draggin' ass. I go slow to stay 'ehind you. I don't need to hack a hole to get giant, useless ass through here."

"Mmm." Silva looked at the Tagranesi, who stared back with his head cocked slightly to one side. According to Bradford, the young darkening and lengthening crest atop it meant he was nearing adulthood—if he hadn't already reached it. Whether he was actually there or not, he increasingly acted like it, and joking aside, Dennis knew exactly what Lawrence had been up to. Oddly enough, his almost orange, tiger-striped, downy-furry hide afforded him considerable camouflage, even against the dark green, hazel, and almost bluish foliage of the dense jungle covering most of the island. As usual, he'd been hanging back to make sure he'd spot anything that went after the main party so he could give warning before it was upon them. He had a musket and he could shoot it, but his formidable claws and teeth were probably a better deterrent to anything sneaking up behind them.

"Well," Dennis said when the group had gathered around him, "let's see if we can get across that patch yonder in one piece." Without waiting for comments, he started across the clearing, entering the ever-deepening grass. Behind him, Rajendra slung on his musket and pulled out his pistols—the better to engage close-up threats. Silva was mildly impressed that the usually puffed-up Imperial did something he approved of without being told.

"Mister Silva?" Abel asked. "I notice that you are avoiding the large clumps of colorful foliage."

"Yep. If there's any dangerous beasties out here, I'd expect 'em to live in the thicker crap."

"May I approach one closer?"

Silva stopped. Abel was kind of Bradford's protégé, and was apparently just as interested in strange critters and bushes as the Australian "naturalist" was. "Well, I suppose," he grumped. "You're the next thing to grown-up, and I can't nursemaid you forever. Just be careful." He raised his voice. "Larry, Mr. Cook's gonna gawk at them weeds. Keep an eye on him, will ya?"

Larry nodded without complaint. He'd learned to "kid around" with Silva and others, but an order was still an order. Besides, he liked and trusted Abel.

"We don't have time for this," Rajendra grumbled. "We've wasted more of the day in that dreadful bamboo than I care to contemplate. What if we reach this dubious destination of yours and then can't make it back to our beach camp before dark? We may be forced to make camp out here somewhere. I don't relish that thought."

"Oh, quit moaning. It'll be clear sailing from here. The sea can't be far beyond that little stretch of jungle past this plain. Hell, I can *hear* it. We won't get stuck out here; all we got to do is scamper back down this cut we made. It may have taken us all day to make it, but we can be back at camp in an hour or two, I guess. Why don't you ever look on the bright side? We done thrashed a damn road through here, like fleas marchin' across a dog's back."

"Where you are concerned, Mr. Silva, the only 'bright side' to anything I seem able to imagine involves fire and destruction," Rajendra said darkly. "You must forgive my lack of enthusiasm."

"Gloomy, pessimistic, *and* touchy," Silva replied cheerfully. "How you ever survived childhood, ugly as you are, is a myst'ry to me."

Rajendra's face clouded, but he didn't respond. Dennis knew the man hated him for a number of reasons, not least because Silva was very good at pointing out Rajendra's real failings. The problem was, Silva was irrepressibly irreverent by nature, and friendly banter was as necessary to his survival as food and water. Particularly now. The worse things got, the more he joked around. It was his way of dealing with stress. If it helped keep his and the others' spirits up, that was a bonus. He'd begun to suspect that Rajendra just couldn't take a joke though, especially from him, and probably took his banter as calculated taunts and insults. Oh, well. He couldn't help what folks thought. Maybe, if he was lucky, he'd finally goad the Imperial captain into giving him an excuse to kill him. Then he wouldn't have to watch his back so much.

He eased a little farther to the left while Abel and Larry approached the nearest mound of "kudzu" so he could cover them a little better.

"Goodness gracious!" Abel exclaimed, reminding Silva of Bradford again, and causing a grin to split his face. "It's full of bones!"

"Bones?" cried Midshipman Brassey, hurrying to join Abel. The two boys shared many interests and were becoming friends. "What sort of bones?"

"Well, big ones! They're difficult to see through all the foliage, but they're perhaps comparable to those of a small whale." He stopped, looking at Brassey as the boy joined him. "Do you have whales? I mean, are there any where you live?"

"We have creatures we *call* whales," Brassey admitted thoughtfully, "but they may not be precisely the same. I've seen drawings in books of the whales from . . . our old world—from the time before the Passage—and we have similar things . . ." He grew silent as his eyes sought out what Abel had seen. "Look! There! I see them too!" He moved slightly forward, pushing some of the purple flowers aside. "It may well be an entire skeleton, fully articulated!" He gestured around. "It's as if all this viny grass has grown up around it."

Abel slung his musket onto his shoulder and began parting the flowers as well. Larry crouched, sniffing, staring into the shadows beneath the grass around the bones.

"Come on, boys," badgered Silva, growing impatient. "So there's some old bones. Quit foolin' around."

"Wait," said Abel, "there's something— Ow!"

"What? What is it? Are you all right?" asked Brassey.

"Yes, yes, I'm fine. Something poked my finger. One of these little thorny things, I believe. I thought for a moment I saw something moving in there. You may think me mad, but it looked quite like a fox!" He held up his hand and examined it, finding a tiny thorn in his left pinky. "You see? It's nothing. It doesn't even hurt." He removed the thorn and cast it away. Just before a tiny drop of blood welled up, he thought he might have seen a dark speck within the wound, but he shrugged it off. "Come on, Brassey, we mustn't anger Mr. Silva. Perhaps we can look again when we return this way."

Reluctantly, Brassey agreed and the two boys moved back toward where Silva and Rajendra stood. For a moment longer, Larry continued to stare at the kudzu, until Silva whistled at him. Tossing his head, he bounded back through the tall grass to rejoin his companions.

"Next best thing to a dog," Silva said, laughing. "Next best."

"What is a dog?" Larry asked, suspicious.

"Man's best friend," Silva said, his grin fading. "If you saw a dog you'd prob'ly chase him down and eat him, but dogs are the best. I guess you'll just have to do for now." Larry looked at Silva as if unsure whether he was being mocked or complimented. His uncertain pose provoked another laugh and Dennis ruffled his crest. "Don't worry, you make a pretty good dog substitute. You can't help what you are any more than I can. Just wag your tail now and then and you'll be close enough as to make no difference. 'Specially if you don't talk so much."

Larry glanced at his slightly feathery tail and twitched it experimentally.

"Can we please resume our march now?" Rajendra demanded exasperatedly.

"Why, by all means!" Dennis said. "In fact, why don't you lead the way, Captain Rajendra? With them two pistols, you can pro-tect us from the boogers."

Meeting the challenge, Rajendra stepped off and led them across the remainder of the clearing. They passed several more clumps of the strange kudzulike grass, and it looked like there were more bones in at least a couple of them. Abel and Brassey chatted excitedly about what it might mean, clearly hoping to crawl all through the things as soon as they could. The little thorn that had pierced Abel's finger was already forgotten.

As Silva had predicted, the stretch of jungle was not very wide, and though they traversed it with care they soon saw the sea through dwindling brush. Without a word, Silva resumed the lead and stepped out from the cover of the jungle alone. Intently, he scanned the beach in both directions for some time, looking for telltale tracks or marks in the sand. They saw them sometimes, even near camp. When they did, they knew they had to be extravigilant that day. Who knew what improbable, screwy, terrifying damn thing might have squirmed up out of the sea during the night? God knew the island was dangerous enough without the shiksaks it was beginning to draw.

A mighty bolt of lightning seared the guts of a distant, spreading thunderhead and lashed the sea behind a black curtain of rain. Except for that one squall, however, the sky remained mostly clear and the fierce sun baked the sand around him. Silva saw no evidence that shiksaks or anything else had come ashore nearby, and he motioned his companions to join him.

"Well, here we are, Mr. Silva," Rajendra growled irritably. "I do hope you haven't had us thrashing about for most of a day merely so you might view yet another beach—that looks quite identical to the one we left this morning, I might add."

"As a matter of fact, that's exactly what we're doing here." Silva waved out to sea. "You're a sailor. You've seen the beach we came ashore on. There's breakers, coral heads or something like them, for a mile or more offshore. No way we're gonna get the boat back through that even after we're done fixin' it. It was some sort of biblical miracle we came across in one piece the first time. I guess the tide was running and them big waves helped a bunch, sort of tossed us over the reef, or something. Anyway, like I said, we're going to have to break out somewhere." He nodded beyond the beach. "This might not be it either. If you look over there, the breakers seem to run even farther out to sea." He pointed southwest along the beach. "That might not be too bad over there, though, see? The tide's not out, but it's on the ebb. I don't see anything but happy beach waves there. We take the boat out at high tide, we might just make it."

Rajendra spluttered. "Are you suggesting we attempt to move the boat through . . . I don't know, *miles* of terrifying jungle, full of even more terrifying creatures? I consider you an evil man, Mr. Silva, but not an idiot. It simply can't be done."

"It ain't 'miles,' an' not that much is even jungle. Did we just come the same way? Besides, there you go about 'evil' again," Dennis said, shaking his head in frustration. "It's been maybe a month since I blew up your ship! Give a guy a break! You blew up Cap'n Lelaa's ship first, and helped start this whole mess, but she doesn't whine and moan about it on and on like you do. She'll probably kill you someday when this is over, but for now she's put all that aside to get the princess and Miss Tucker off this damn bump. Why don't you do the same?" He paused, reflecting. "I never said I ain't an idiot, though. If you can think of a better idea, maybe we'll give it a shot. Ain't you been thinking about anything? Larry says this joint's gonna be jumpin' with shit-sacks soon, and we can't be here when that happens."

Rajendra surveyed the apparent passage in the breakers. "Perhaps we could launch the boat where it is and sail it around to this point," he speculated.

"Might work," Silva admitted. "I've walked the beach this far a couple of times, and the patch this side of the breakers is real calm in places. The rough stuff's just too damn close in others. We'd have to land the boat and cart it around a few times. Amounts to about halfway. I'm not sure if that would be easier or harder. I've walked a lot farther in the other direction, north, and it's the same deal, except I bet the breakers run two miles out to sea, and I never saw a hole in 'em. This is the only place I've found so far. We can keep looking, but anything we find is just going to be farther and we're runnin' out of time. Unless you can come up with a better stunt, moving the boat, one way or another, to launch it here is what we have to work on.

"Now, one other possibility might be to break it up and wag it over here in pieces, since we've got it apart to fix it anyway. Bring it across a piece at a time and rebuild it here. It's either that or try to move it in one piece. Float it and drag it, or drag it all the way. Personally, I'm for bringin' it overland. Less complicated. All we have to do is clear a bigger trail and use rollers or somethin'. I know it's too heavy to carry, push, or drag without rollers." He shrugged. "Those are the schemes I've come up with. You conjure up something better, we'll do it."

Rajendra was silent for a long moment, staring at the shoreline, the breakers, and the waves. Absently, he twisted the ends of his mustache probably out of what was an old habit. He sighed. "The shattered planks on the bottom of the launch have been removed. Sadly, there were quite a few. Like you, I confess to believing only a miracle delivered us across the breakers. The carpenter has been shaping planks from what he hopes will be suitable trees—it is so difficult to tell with these unknown woods—but even with the existing repairs, he fears an inadequacy of fasteners. Nails. I don't see how we can disassemble the boat further without damaging or destroying even more fasteners. That's one thing we didn't think to carry away much stock of."

"Carpenter forgettin' nails is like a gunner's mate runnin' off without bullets," Silva accused. "Dumb-ass."

"He does have tools," Rajendra said in defense of the carpenter. "A drill and some bracing bits. Perhaps he can use dowels instead of nails, but I don't think we dare break the boat down into pieces small enough to carry." He looked at Silva. "I also agree, if you're right about the obstacles, that the combination of floating and portaging the boat would be more complicated and potentially more dangerous." He sighed. "So for now it looks as though your tedious and laborious plan is our best chance after all."

CHAPTER 4

Talaud Island

Lieutenant Irvin Laumer felt the tremor through the hull of the old submarine, S-19, even over the vibrating rumble of the big starboard NELSECO diesel. The battered submarine was entirely afloat now, in the sandy pit they'd carved around it, which meant the tremor must be bad indeed if he felt it through the water. He looked at Machinist's Mate Sandy Whitcomb, who was tinkering with the diesel, adjusting it. Sandy glanced back at him, catching his eye. He felt it too. Together, they just stood there in the engine room, sweating in the dull glare of the electric lights that glowed with the power the generator was packing into the batteries. The tremor continued. Radioman Tex Sheider stuck his head into the compartment through the forward hatch. His bearded face was flanked by a pair of 'Cats, and it would have been a comical scene if not for Tex's expression.

"You better get a load a' this, Skipper," he said.

"On my way," Laumer replied. "Where's Midshipman Hardee?"

"Topside."

Laumer exchanged another tense glance with Whitcomb and hurried after Tex. The almost bare aft berthing space had been converted into a workshop where many of the boat's systems were undergoing repair, and they had to weave their way among the various ongoing projects before reaching the even more cramped control room. Climbing the forward ladder, they exited onto the deck, just in front of the conn tower and aft of the boat's four-inch-fifty gun.

For just a moment Laumer looked around. The excavation around the boat had filled with water during a small storm the week before, which meant any remaining repairs below the waterline were out of the question. It was just as well. The boat was as tight as they had any reason to expect after wallowing on the Talaud Island beach for the better part of a year and a half. The rudder, shafts, and screws seemed relatively straight. The only thing they hadn't been able to fix was a warped starboard diving plane. They'd managed to straighten it a little, so it shouldn't cause a problem on the surface, but it had little range of motion. Of course, the last thing any of them ever wanted to do was take S-19 underwater again.

He quickly noted that their tender, perhaps whimsically named USS *Toolbox*, still floated where she should a couple of hundred yards offshore. As an auxiliary, she carried only a few guns to save weight for things Irvin's project might require, but like so many Allied ships, she was a highly modified Grik prize captured after the battle of Baalkpan. Even as he stared at her, Laumer began to feel a little dizzy and her masts almost seemed to blur.

"At the mountain, sir! Look at the mountain!" Hardee blurted. Laumer turned to see and automatically looked up. And up.

"Jumpin' Jehoshaphat!" exclaimed Shipfitter Danny Porter, joining them from below. Far in the distance, a massive mushroom cloud of dark ash piled high into the otherwise clear late-afternoon sky above the volcanic mountain that dominated the island's landscape. The ash resembled a titanic, roiling, spreading blot in the heavens.

"What do you think, sir?" Tex asked. "Maybe it's just a fart, like all them others."

"Bigger this time," Porter said. "Might be just clearin' its throat for something *really* big." That was the closest anyone had come to suggesting that the Talaud Island volcano might "pull a Krakatoa" since Laumer's own long-ago ill-considered comment.

"Shut your hole, you mindless monkey turd!" Tex demanded. "You'll jinx us for sure."

"Maybe not," Laumer said thoughtfully. "According to reports from Mr. Ellis, and now General Alden too, Krakatoa hasn't 'pulled a Krakatoa' on this world. They said they saw it, and it's a humongous mother, but all the 'Cats who hang out around there say that aside from spewing a lot of red fire, it never does very much."

"Well," Porter said, "just because Krakatoa hasn't 'pulled a Krakatoa' doesn't mean Talaud's not fixing to pop its cork."

"If you don't shut the hell up, I'm going to feed you to the spider-lobsters if they come back," Tex declared.

Laumer put his hand on Tex's shoulder. "Skip it," he said. "You're both right." He looked at Porter. "You *do* need to lay off. You'll upset the fellas." He forced a laugh. "Shoot, you'll upset *me*. You're right, though; I don't know anything about volcanoes, but that thing's starting to give me the creeps." Even as he spoke, the tremors slowly subsided and the relief he felt around him was palpable. He sighed. "Anyway, we've got to find some way to pick up the pace. Adar hasn't come right out and ordered us off the project, and neither has the Skipper, but I guarantee *Toolbox* has already reported this latest burp. Her captain isn't any happier about hanging around here than we are, and I can't say I blame him. If we don't wrap this project up pretty quick, I expect we *will* be ordered out."

"Maybe the transmission didn't get picked up," Tex said. "Comm's been pretty spotty."

"Maybe not," Irvin agreed, "but they'll send it again. It usually does get through at night."

"Well, so what's left?" asked Porter. "We're afloat and the starboard diesel's up and running. We could get the boat underway . . . well . . . today, for that matter, if only . . ."

"Yeah," agreed Laumer, gazing at the beach-locked puddle the submarine floated in. "If only."

"Sid has six boats, nearly a hundred 'Cats, and the whole *Toolbox* dredging us a channel. They're going as fast as they can," Hardee defended.

"I know. They're all doing a swell job." Laumer looked back at the mountain and rubbed his face with his hands. "We're going to get some ash tonight. Make sure everyone's under cover. Bring them on the boat if you have to. Maybe we can get an early start in the morning."

"Aye, aye, sir."

Irvin took a last look around at the battered submarine that he was determined to deliver—intact—back to Captain Reddy, and the 'Cats working so hard to help him succeed. Then he glared at the mountain in the dwindling light. He was on the very brink of accomplishing his mission—and the almost more important mission he'd set himself: to prove he was worthy to join the "Captain's Companions," those who'd been with Reddy from the start. To be considered worthy of that, he'd do whatever he had to—even if it killed him. To accomplish so much only to have it threatened by a volcano, a force of nature, seemed wildly unfair, but he would manage. Somehow, he would succeed. Pacing to the hatch, he prepared to descend the ladder and go back to helping Whitcomb. Before he did, he stood up straight and shook his fist at the distant smoky peak. "You won't beat me," he warned. "By God, you won't."

CHAPTER 5

Yap Island (Shikarrak)

"How much longer do you suppose they'll be?" Princess Rebecca Anne McDonald, daughter of the Governor-Emperor of the New Britain Isles, asked anxiously; her large jade eyes narrowed with worry. Her sun-lightened blond locks had gone horribly astray under the constant battering of the stiff sea breeze, and finally getting some growth, she'd also suddenly begun to sprout from the battered Imperial dungarees she wore. Her waiflike appearance did much to undermine her "princess" status. She glanced fretfully westward, where the sun was making its final rapid equatorial plunge.

Nurse Lieutenant and Minister of Medicine Sandra Tucker's bad sunburn was beginning to turn tan, but her normally sandy blond hair had gone peroxide. She looked at the bedraggled and somewhat gangly royal teen. "Don't worry," she said with a smile. "They'll be along."

"But it's nearly dark!"

"I assure you, my dear," insisted Sister Audry in her precise Dutch-accented English, "Mr. Silva would be far safer in any wilderness you chose to drop him than any poor creature he might happen upon." Sister Audry's words were meant to reassure, but there was a subliminal thread of condemnation in her tone as well. Like the surviving Imperials, she harbored a deep suspicion that Silva was at least mildly psychotic. She stepped from beneath the sailcloth shelter they'd rigged against the daily rains and stood beside Sandra and Rebecca. She wore dungarees now too, although her practically destroyed habit was kept safely stowed in a bundle of oilcloth.

"I'm concerned about poor Lawrence as well," Rebecca said, "and perhaps ever so slightly about Messers Cook and Brassey."

"And Captain Rajendra?" Sandra asked dryly.

"Him too, I suppose," Rebecca conceded. "I really should be, shouldn't I?" she asked Sister Audry. Rebecca had learned to respect the nun's moral authority, even if most of the other Imperial castaways still considered her some form of Roman witch. Rebecca knew better. She knew there was no more similarity between Sister Audry's "Catholic" faith and that practiced by the "Holy Dominion" than there was between night and day.

"One should always try to think charitable thoughts about all people," Sister Audry replied, but it was clear by her tone how difficult even she found that at times.

A panicked cry arose near the shoreline, where Captain Lelaa and Carpenter Hersh were wrapping up their day's repairs to the boat. Three other men, armed with muskets, raced to the spot from where they'd been posted along the beach to provide security for the laborers and their important charges. A loud *thump* and a jet of fire flashed in the rapidly deepening gloom.

Captain Lelaa, the Lemurian commander and possibly only survivor of the destroyed sloop USS *Simms*, raced past them, tail curled high in alarm, toward the ranks of muskets they kept loaded and under cover. "Shik-saak!" she shouted breathlessly as she passed.

A large shadow, almost indistinguishable from the color

of the sea behind it, lunged up onto the shore, barely missing the overturned boat where it lay chocked and supported on the sand. The carpenter was on his back, frantically scrabbling up the beach on his hands and heels, shrieking as he went. The security detail raced to that side of the boat and fired a volley directly into the monster before fleeing as fast as they could, reloading as they ran. It was a tactic they'd practiced before; get the shiksak's attention, then lead it away from the boat and camp. They had no real hope of killing it with their muskets, and wouldn't have wanted to kill it *there* in any case. Its carcass would only draw more predators. Their intent in this instance was to preserve the boat, protect the camp, and—hopefully—save the carpenter by provoking the beast into chasing them. It worked.

With a mighty froglike leap, the shiksak lunged after them, absorbing its fall with its semi-rigid front legs, or flippers, and the mattresslike cushion of fat on its belly. It emitted a kind of croaking wail when it struck the ground, but immediately gathered itself for another hopping leap. In a flat-out sprint, the security detail avoided being crushed beneath the massive body or taken by the gaping jaws, but they'd learned in a previous encounter that *only* a flat-out sprint would save them—and they'd practiced the technique against a considerably smaller shiksak. They'd discovered then that the slightest misstep, fall, or stumble would spell their death. It looked as though this larger, more powerful beast would render their tactic moot. Without a word among them, they split up.

Lelaa snatched a pair of muskets and raced into the jungle that paralleled the beach. With a glance that encompassed Rebecca and Sister Audry, Sandra did the same, following Lelaa as fast as she could.

"I must go as well!" Rebecca insisted, "I can handle a musket as well as any!"

Sister Audry grabbed her. "No, child, you must remain here. Those others are willing to sacrifice their lives to save yours. If any die and you are not saved, their sacrifice will have been in vain. It is a harsh and heavy burden to bear, but it *is* yours to bear."

They heard another thundering, croaking groan, this time accompanied by a shrill scream. Sister Audry muttered something and crossed herself with her free hand while holding Rebecca even tighter against her renewed efforts to escape. The night was punctuated by more musket fire and shouts. Evidently pausing to devour its victim, the shiksak did not immediately leap again, allowing the survivors to gain some distance. It was almost pitch-black now, and the musket flashes of a suddenly augmented skirmish line pulsed in the darkness a considerable distance up the beach.

"I would attest that that volley was comprised of more guns than Miss Tucker and Captain Lelaa alone would have added!" Sister Audry assured Rebecca hopefully. The shiksak leaped again and again, moving beyond their ability to hear the dreadful sounds it made or see any movement. Rebecca collapsed against the nun and began to sob. Even if she broke free now, the action had drawn too far away to join.

Sister Audry led the girl carefully out onto the beach, keeping a wary eye on the deadly sea, until they reached the traumatized carpenter. The scrawny man was standing now and almost blubbering with relief.

"I thought the bugger had me!" he gasped. "So big and fat, and yet so fast!" He calmed himself slightly and glanced apologetically at the princess. "Pardon the 'bugger,' if you please, Your Highness."

Through the tears that filled her eyes, Rebecca could still occasionally see the distant sparkle and bloom of a musket shot, but the hissing surf now drowned any report. Suddenly, to her surprise and almost infinite relief, she saw the muzzle flash of what might almost have been a cannon. A moment later, she did hear a muffled boom punctuate that shot. Shortly afterward, there came a veritable flurry of flashes, followed by another massive discharge. Then there was only the darkness and the surge of the marching sea.

"It would seem that your inimitable Mr. Silva has come to the rescue once again," Sister Audry observed with an apparent mix of relief and disgust. "I only hope his various schemes to save us don't cost a life with each attempt."

"What happened?" Sandra asked impatiently. Silva sat on a large fallen tree trunk, ravenously devouring a plate of stew. He brandished a spoon, delaying his answer while he chewed. Finally, he pointed the spoon at Rajendra.

"Things went pretty much the way His Surliness said, except it wasn't as tough a trip as he made out. Sure, hacking through all that bamboo stuff was a chore, but I had tougher days behind a mule when I was seven. Once we got through that stuff, wasn't anything to it. Might've found a good channel through the breakers too."

"Then what took you so long, and what's the matter with Mr. Cook?"

"He took to acting strange on the way back. Poked his finger on something in that kudzulike stuff. Went all silly on us. We had to throw together a stretcher, sort of, to get him back here. Even had to tie him down eventually. That's why we was dee-layed." He waved the spoon. "As for what's the matter with him, you got me. You're the doc. See for yourself."

"I can barely see *him* with just the light from the fire," Sandra said in frustration. "I certainly can't diagnose what's wrong with him."

Silva shrugged. "Look at him in the morning, then. He might live that long."

Sandra shook her head. "You *are* a heartless bastard," she observed, almost amazed.

"Nope. I like the little guy a lot. I'm just sick o' getting blamed whenever somebody croaks." He pointed his spoon at Rajendra. "Bastard said it was my fault another one of his guys got ate. What was I supposed to do? I wasn't even here."

"That's just the point," Rajendra snarled. "If we'd been here, it wouldn't have happened!"

"You mean if me and the Doom Whomper'd been here it wouldn't have happened. Another few muskets wouldn't have made a difference. You want me to sit here all day and guard everybody until we starve or I run out of lead to cast my bullets? What the hell good is that gonna do when there's too many of the damn things to kill? Look, I'm sorry you lost a fella, but sometimes bad sh . . . stuff just happens, an' it ain't always my fault!"

Sandra glared at Rajendra. "You know, he's right. All you've done is whine ever since we got here. You stood up and pulled your weight on the boat, but now all you do is complain and blame. That's not good enough! Do you want to save your princess? Do you want to *live*? Look, you don't like taking orders from a woman. I get that, but here's the deal: I already command my people, Rajendra, and your princess has placed me in command of you and yours. Our numbers are about even, with a dozen of us left, counting Rebecca and Larry. Even if this was a democracy, you'd lose. If more of you besides Hersh and Mr. Brassey don't pitch in and pull your weight, we aren't going to make it because we're just dragging the rest of you along. Well, I have the cure for that! By the authority vested in me by the United States Navy and Princess Rebecca Anne McDonald, and as Minister of Medicine for all the Allied powers, I'll consider any further dereliction of duty or refusal to obey my orders tantamount to mutiny and punishable by death. Do I make myself perfectly clear?" Her voice had risen to a roar that her small frame seemed incapable of producing, but it would have made the Bosun proud. In a quieter voice she continued, "Mr. Silva and I have discussed his plan and it seems the most viable option. If we all work together, we can get it done with hands to spare. If I were you, I'd try very hard not to give the impression that I was a spare hand. I'm completely, deadly serious about this, and I advise you not to test me."

She took a long breath and continued to glare at the darkened faces as if measuring each one. "Tomorrow we start moving the boat. We'll need rollers, and plenty of them. Those not actively cutting rollers will be widening and clearing the path Mr. Silva and Captain Rajendra's party made through the bamboo today." She looked at Rajendra. "Now, I know you've been saving back some candles and at least two lanterns. I want them. All of them." She allowed only the slightest hesitation, as the Imperials glanced at their commander, before she pulled the .45 from its holster and racked the slide.

"Captain Rajendra," she said very softly, "must I repeat myself?"

"Princess?" Rajendra asked.

"Obey her this instant, you fool!" Rebecca demanded harshly. "I have told you she alone commands! If you ever ask my approval for her orders again, I swear I'll shoot you myself!"

"Very well, Your Highness. Please accept my apologies. I was only trying—"

"What you were trying to do, what you've *been* trying to do, is quite clear! The traditions of the Empire have no bearing here, and you will obey this woman as you would me."

"Brassey," Rajendra said stiffly, "please fetch the items Miss Tucker requested." Brassey leaped to his feet and raced to the pile of supplies the Imperials had kept somewhat segregated.

"A wise choice, Captain Rajendra," Sandra said as her thumb pushed upward on the pistol's safety and she thrust the weapon back into its holster. "You might be interested to know that I was counting to myself and you had less than three seconds to live." She smiled, then moved off toward where Abel Cook lay.

Silva shook his spoon at Rajendra. "And here all this time you thought I was a bad man." He chuckled quietly. "You don't know doodly."

With the help of the lanterns and a couple of mirrors, Sandra was finally able to examine Abel's hand. The boy was conscious and even tried to cooperate with the inspection, but he had a fever and was acting almost euphorically drunk. He was still tied to the stretcher so he couldn't get up, but he sometimes almost desperately wanted to, as if his main goal in life had suddenly become to run off into the jungle as far and fast as he could. He alternated between begging them to turn him loose and apologizing for being a bother. Silva held his arm still when necessary, and Rebecca dabbed at his forehead with a cool, damp cloth. Most of the others had gathered around to watch interestedly, but they kept a respectful distance. Only Sister Audry and Captain Lelaa remained in attendance to hold the mirrors and reflect the best light.

"Good Lord!" Sandra said when she at last got a good look at the wound. "What on earth did he get into?" She could see where the initial puncture had been. The area around it was almost black, and the finger had swelled to three times its normal size. The skin was mostly pink and seemed stretched tight enough to burst. The boy should have been in agony instead of acting, well, like he was. On closer inspection, she thought she saw tiny bluish-green filaments radiating outward from the blackened region as if they were following the capillaries and veins within the finger. She'd never seen anything like it.

"Uh, he was pierced by a thorn," Brassey supplied. "It was just a little thing, and we gave it no thought at the time."

"A thorn? What did it look like? The plant, I mean."

"Well, Mr. Silva said it looked like something he called 'kudzu,' but I don't know what that is. We have plants with similar blossoms at home, and they even have thorns, but they don't cause anything like Mr. Cook's reaction."

"It's the damnedest thing I ever saw," Dennis murmured. "One little poke. It's almost like it left a seed in there and it sprouted something fierce. Already putting out roots!"

Sandra felt a chill. "My God, I think that's exactly what it's done! You say these plants were growing up among and around skeletons of some sort?"

"Yes . . . ah . . . ma'am," Brassey confirmed. "Great big ones."

"Say," Silva muttered thoughtfully, "they ain't no big critters running around on this island! Not most of the time, anyway, except for them big lizard-turtle things, and if these were them, they'd've left big old shells layin' around!"

"You're saying that the skeletons must have been these shiksak creatures?" Sister Audry asked.

"No way around it," Silva replied. "I bet those big old shit-sack toad boogers go hoppin' through that kudzu stuff, get poked, and eventually wind up fertilizin' a whole new patch of them nasty weeds! God . . . dern! I always hated kudzu!"

Sandra sighed and laid Abel's hand down. "If you're right—and I'm afraid you are—that finger will have to come off. Immediately. In just the few hours since he was infected, the 'roots' have spread nearly to his hand. Those are just the filaments I can see. Deeper down, they might already be *in* his hand."

"We better get crackin', then," Dennis said.

"Right." Sandra looked at Sister Audry. "Would you and Lawrence please boil some water? Mr. Silva, you still have a small amount of polta paste in your shooting pouch, do you not?"

"Are you absolutely certain we have no other choice?" asked Rebecca. The tears in her eyes reflected the candlelight.

"I don't know that we can be certain without waiting," Dennis answered her gently. "But if it does what we think it does, I don't reckon we have time."

Later that night, Dennis was one of the last to arrange his bedding in the sand. It had been a long day and he was exhausted. As usual, there were plenty of biting, stinging insects to pester him, but he doubted he'd notice them tonight. Captain Lelaa and Lawrence had the guard and he knew he could sleep soundly with them on duty, so he arranged his weapons around himself, scrunched down, and pulled his wool blanket up to his chin. There was often a chill before dawn. Almost as an afterthought, he pulled off the patch that covered his ruined left eye and stared at it for a moment. Hell, a pinky finger ain't much, he decided. The kid was already resting easier. He laid the patch on his shooting pouch and closed his other eye.

From somewhere nearby he heard a strange sound. Opening his eye again, he rose up to listen. Over there. Sighing, he replaced the patch—no reason to disgust folks—and pulling his cutlass out of the sand, he crept over to where the sound was emanating. He sat.

"What's eatin' you, Li'l Sis?" he whispered. "You know you can tell ol' Silva."

The muffled crying continued a moment longer before Rebecca managed to control it. "It's just so awful," she said at last. "Not just Mr. Cook's poor hand, although that is bad enough. It's just . . . everything! This whole day has been dreadful! I don't know how much longer I can bear it!"

"Now, now. You're doin' fine. I bet Abel'll be just fine too. We're gonna get outta this jam, I promise." He cocked his head. "I'm glad Miss Tucker finally laid down the law, though."

"And that's another thing! She seemed fully prepared to shoot Captain Rajendra! That can't sit well with her. She is so kind and gentle! Do . . . do you think she would have done it?"

"Yep. Lookie here, she may be kind and gentle, but she's a tiger when it comes to you and the Skipper. Hell, when it comes to *any* of us she thinks of as her kin."

"Do you think it will matter?"

"Yep."

"Why?"

"'Cause Rajendra and the rest o' his people . . . *your* people, believed her. Believed you too. You and her is so much alike it spooks me now and then, honest to God. You look alike, act alike, you both got plenty o' brains, but you got even more guts." He snorted. "A time or two, that's got you both in trouble."

"You think I have 'guts'?" Rebecca asked, incredulous.

"Yep. Big, long, heapin' piles of 'em, and you're gonna

need 'em too. I'll tell you somethin' else. Havin' guts is one thing, but bein' too sleepy to use 'em is another. So why don't you just squirm on down there an' shut them little eyes. Ol' Silva'll be right here." He paused a moment, looking out at the surf and the hazy moon beyond. In a quiet, gravelly voice he started to sing:

"Once upon a time the goose drank wine.
The monkey chewed tobacco on the live steam line.
The steam line broke, the monkey choked,
And they all went to heaven in a little tin boat."

Rebecca snorted a giggle. "What's that supposed to be, a lullaby?"

A little embarrassed, Dennis shrugged. "Nope," he said. "Just a stupid song."

CHAPTER 6

Andaman Island

General Pete Alden, former sergeant in USS *Houston*'s Marine contingent, stood in USS *Dowden*'s captain's quarters staring at a map on the bulkhead. Captain Greg Garrett of *Donaghey* and "Commodore" Jim Ellis sat at the table behind him with General Muln Rolak, Safir Maraan, and several other officers. How times had changed. Jim had originally been Matt's exec on *Walker*, and Garrett had been the gunnery officer. Rolak and Queen Maraan had been bitter enemies, but were now as close as a father and daughter might be. All were waiting for Pete to speak.

"You know this is nuts, right?" he finally pronounced, raking his dark hair back from his forehead. He still kept the hair burred short everywhere but on top.

"I thought it was possible you might think so," Ellis said, grinning through his light brown beard. "That's why I wanted your opinion."

"Well, there it is. I just don't see how we can run along and leave that nest of snakes at our backs, sitting right on top of our supply lines."

"But they are not," Safir Maraan pointed out, her silver eyes reexamining the map. "With Aan-daa-maan as our forward staging area, we can watch this Raan-goon place closely enough. As long as we control the sea, the forces trapped there can do nothing but slowly starve. They cannot affect our campaign against Ceylon."

Rolak grunted. "I fear I must agree with General Aalden," he said. The scarred old warrior pointed at the Malay Peninsula. "With a little initiative—something we have learned the enemy leadership, their Hij at least, is capable of—this force at Raan-goon might attempt to threaten our new base at Sing-aa-pore. We know that when we took it from them, some Grik managed to escape from there as a cohesive force. They were not all 'made prey,' as they call it. They may have traveled as far as Raan-goon by now. With no other purpose, they might even attempt to return."

"Right," Alden agreed. "We know at least some didn't break, and according to Okada and some other stuff we've seen, we know they aren't 'destroying' all their troops that chicken out anymore." He shook his head. "Still don't know what to think of that. I wish we could've figured out a way to talk to those goofy Griks that Rasik was using for bodyguards."

"Evidently we *could* talk to 'em. They just couldn't talk to us," Jim pointed out. He shrugged. "We sent 'em back to Baalkpan hoping Lawrence could figure out a way to communicate—but he'd already been swiped with the rest by that bastard Billingsley. I'm sure the pointy heads back home will keep working on it, but I don't know that it'll make any difference to us. They were just Uul warriors, and I doubt they were privy to the grand strategy of the Grik High Command!"

"Maybe so," Pete agreed, "but we *have* learned one important thing from them. We always assumed that when they went nuts, or experienced Bradford's 'Grik Rout,' they were just ruined. Maybe they are for a while. Over time, though, it seems like they kind of get over it. Worse, when they do, it's like they're smarter somehow, like somebody flipped a switch and turned their brains on. Like . . . whatever happens to turn Uul into Hij . . . happens." He shook his head in frustration. He knew his words were inadequate, but the meaning should be clear. "That really gives me the creeps," he added.

"A 'Hij' switch," Garrett said thoughtfully. "You know, there's a precedent for that." The others looked at him. "Lawrence himself," he said. "Remember his story? He told how he was 'raised' on an island separate from 'Tagranesi' society, where he and all his young lizard buddies just ran loose for a while. He didn't know how long. All they had was a kind of cadre of instructors or mentors to keep them in line and teach them stuff and try to guide them out of savagery. Their final exam was a trip to some other scary island where they faced their primal fears and learned self-sufficiency." He shook his head. "He never would talk about it."

"I have heard Mister Braad-furd propose a similar theory," Rolak said, "but you present it in a . . . more understandable way."

Garrett grinned, and for a moment he looked like a kid again instead of the experienced Naval officer he'd become. "Well," he admitted, "Courtney did influence my thinking. He probably has the whole thing in his head, but it can be tough to keep up with what he's saying sometimes." Everyone laughed at that.

"He does tend to tack back and forth," Rolak agreed. "A brilliant mind, but there may perhaps be too much in it at once, on occasion." There was more laughter at Rolak's tact.

"Okay, so we call it 'the Hij switch.' I don't care," Alden continued, relentlessly returning to the subject at hand. "My point is, we can't ignore it. That makes things even spookier if you ask me. Bad enough that a Hij captain or colonel or whatever they are might have reached Rangoon with a coherent report of the tactics we used to seize Singapore. Add in some wild Griks that might've flipped their switch. If they're not killing 'em anymore, what if they just throw 'em back in the pool with a bunch of regular Griks? That might be bad enough, but what if a Hij general actually listens to 'em? They might wind up with a lot more insight about us than we have about them, and we'd be right back at square one again."

Commodore Ellis leaned forward. "You're right," he agreed reluctantly. "That *is* a spooky thought. So far, they've always had numbers on their side, but their inflexibility and predictability has been their greatest weakness, while our flexibility and initiative have been our greatest strength. We've never been more than a step or two ahead of them technologically—the Japs see to that—and there's no reason to think any advantage we have now will last very long. That's been my reason to keep pushing as hard and fast as we can." He interlaced his fingers on the table before him. "But. Right now we're in kind of a holding pattern. We're consolidating our position here on Andaman." He paused. "Ought to call it something else," he said absently. "On our world, this one big island was several smaller ones that used to be, basically, a British prison." He shook his head and went on. "Anyway, we're building fortifications and warehouses and generally setting up shop, but we're not really pushing just now. We don't have the forces to move on Ceylon yet, not until *Big Sal* and the other new ships and troops join the fleet. The whole show'll be Keje's after that." He sighed. "You know, it's tempting to leave him with it. I always wanted the Navy for a career and dreamed of being an admiral. Now I'm not so sure. It's a lot easier to command a ship and fight her than send others out to do it."

"You've already proven you can fight a ship superbly," Safir said quietly.

"Yeah, if you don't count losing her in the end," he said with a brittle, false cheerfulness, "and I didn't do too well at first. I had a good teacher."

"We all did, Jim," Garrett reminded him. He scratched his chin, looking at the map. "I've got to say that Pete's convinced *me*, though. We're just spinning our wheels, aside from stomping on the occasional Grik supply ship. Not many of those anymore. I think they've finally figured out that somebody's beating up the mailman. We can't move on Ceylon until the rest of the fleet arrives, but we can do something about Pete's nest of snakes. If we leave them alone too long, maybe they will just wither on the vine, but they might cook up something behind us instead."

Jim Ellis looked around the cabin at his commanders. Not all were present, of course, but these represented everyone. Pete still stood beside the map, but the rest were nodding, as if to themselves.

"Okay," Jim said. "We'll do Rangoon. I never really *wanted* to leave it for Keje to deal with, and you've presented good arguments. Actually, I have another, maybe even better, one. We've developed a lot of new tactics and equipment since Singapore. Not everybody has 'em yet, but this'll be our first action with the new muskets in any numbers. I also hope, if Keje gets close enough by the time we're ready, we might use a little of his 'air.' We might *need* this to work some of the bugs out of things before we hit something like Ceylon. That's going to be the biggest thing we've ever done, and I'd personally like to be confident that everything works like we hope it will before we jump in with both feet." He looked at Pete. "This'll have to be different from Operation Singapore Swing. We need a lot more than a raid, but we don't want to get 'stuck in,' if you know what I mean. We don't need the territory right now."

"Yes, Commodore," General Alden replied. The relaxed discussion among friends was over. "It just so happens that I've been working on a plan." There were a few chuckles. "Again," he continued, "owing to the somewhat different topography we often encounter . . . here . . . the depot, outpost, fortress, or whatever they call it that we've been referring to as Rangoon isn't exactly where the 'old' Rangoon was. The main river empties out a little farther down the coast, closer to what we'd call Kynonkadun. Weird, I know, but that's where they are and it's a pretty good anchorage.

The problem we ran into with Singapore was that we just assumed the strait would block the enemy from escaping—not that we were that worried about it at the time. Trouble was, while the strait's still there, it's narrower than it ought to be, due to lower sea levels, but it's also deeper, cut out by a hell of a tidal rush. Turned out there wasn't a causeway, but they'd strung barges across for their hunting parties and such."

"But what does that have to do with Raan-goon?" Ro-lak asked.

"Just this: this time, we don't want any of the bastards getting away."

Garrett whistled. "Tough fighting."

"Maybe. Definitely at first, as always, but my . . ." He paused. "Well, my spies say we might actually have them outnumbered this time. If we can sneak upriver, land, and then push them south, they'll only have two places to go—the sea, or that nasty, swampy country west across the mouths of the Irrawaddy."

"What is that?" Safir asked.

"A maze of tributaries that open into the Western Ocean," Jim explained.

"Are they still there . . . here?"

"Oh, yeah," said Jim. "Before I sent Chapelle and *Tolson* to join Mr. Mallory's expedition to Chill-chaap, he cruised off the Burma shore to map it and see if we *wanted* Rangoon. That's when he discovered the Grik outpost. He said the place was a primordial, miserable, swampy hell with, quote, 'absolutely Gi-Goddamn-Gantic brontasarry-like things romping in the shallows.'" He stopped and looked at Pete and Garrett. "Our first look at continental creatures," he said, arching an eyebrow. "Well, we'd already 'taken possession' of Andaman and confirmed Port Blair was still a decent anchorage, but with water shallow enough to keep the mountain fish away. It didn't take a lot of thought. Disease-ridden swamp, full of God knows what, swarming with Grik, or beautiful tropical island with white sandy beaches. There's a few weird critters here, and lots of gri-kakka in the channel, but plenty of room and, for some reason, no Grik."

"But these 'trib-u-taaries' are still there?" Safir asked again.

"Oh. Yeah. Sorry if I didn't answer your question clearly. My point was that they are, and they're even worse than they 'ought' to be. More of them, worse terrain, and full of scary monsters even the Grik can't relish tangling with."

"Good," Safir Maraan replied with satisfaction. "It sounds like an excellent place to drive them!"

Rolak looked at her. "Yes, and a dreadful place to *chase* them. Do not let yourself grow overenthusiastic, my dear."

CHAPTER 7

Baalkpan

Alan Letts, redheaded, with fair, peeling skin, stood up from behind Matt's desk in the "War Room" office of the Great Hall when Adar swept into the chamber. Perry Brister and Steve Riggs also stood from their stools and faced the High Chief and Sky Priest of Baalkpan, and chairman of the Grand Alliance. Despite his new, exalted status, Adar still wore only the trappings of his previous occupation: a hooded purple robe with silver stars embroidered across the shoulders. It was the vestment of a Sky Priest of *Salissa* Home, or *Big Sal*, as the Americans had practically rechristened her. A Sky Priest was all Adar had ever wanted to be, but like everyone, his American friends in particular, he'd been forced to become much, much more.

"Your Excellency!" the three men chorused.

"This is certainly an unexpected pleasure, sir," Letts continued. "What can we do for you today?"

"First, you may cease calling me 'Excellency,'" Adar grumbled, blinking frustration. "I don't feel particularly 'excellent' at anything these days." He stepped to a more traditional Lemurian cushion in a corner of the room and collapsed tiredly upon it. "If you simply must call me something official, I assure you 'Mr. Chairman' is sufficiently lofty and undeserved to spoil my appetite, but it does not imply that I have actually accomplished anything."

"You've accomplished a great deal, sir," Riggs assured him. "A lot more than anyone else could have, guaranteed."

Adar waved his hand. "Captain Reddy did most of the 'accomplishing,' I'm afraid. I am merely a 'Cat wrangler." He chuckled. "What a delightful term! I have never seen one of these small cats that inspired your diminutive of my people, but I gather from descriptions that, in addition to a barely measurable level of intelligence, they are extremely independent, maniacally self-centered, and virtually incapable of concerted action. Not so?"

Letts, Riggs, and Brister couldn't help chuckling in reply. "I assure you, Mr. Chairman, the diminutive was never meant as an insult, but you know that. It had more to do with what your people looked like to us than how they act."

"Well, then," Adar said, "imagine how coincidental it seems to me to discover how like your 'cats' my people actually are!"

"More trouble in the Allied Council?" Brister asked.

Adar sighed and his ears flicked back irritably. "Of course. What else? More and more of the 'runaways' return all the time, now that it is 'safe,' and they somehow manage to get themselves selected to the People's Assembly of Baalkpan regardless of their past behavior. They are but an irritating minority for now, and have no real voice, but our allies fear they may subvert Baalkpan's commitment to the cause." He shook his head and blinked again in a series most of the humans had learned represented reluctant acceptance. "The People do grow weary of war and all the demands it makes upon them. When we fought here, to defend our Home, the war was much easier for them to understand. But now we are raising and equipping armies and navies for expeditionary campaigns. You would think that would reassure them, but all it does is make them feel that the war has become distant enough for them to safely ignore it."

Adar had learned enough about human face moving to recognize the concern his words brought, and he raised a placating hand. "Oh, don't worry. I apologize if I have alarmed you unduly. As I said, the elements that believe thus are still few, but the longer it takes to defeat the Grik, the more difficult that task becomes—not only militarily but politically." He sighed again. "That filthy Billingsley creature could not have struck at a worse strategic time. He caused us to divert Captain Reddy and *Walker*—two of our most precious assets—in an entirely different direction. I do not begrudge the mission they have undertaken. I still blame myself for its necessity. I also believe it may be essential for our long-term success. I just can't help thinking, however, that it has delayed our offensive in the West."

"So," Letts asked carefully, "why exactly have you come here? Is there something you'd have us do differently?"

Adar chuckled. "Of course not! This little room is part of my residence after all, but it is the one room that is secure from office- and favor-seekers and petty, self-interested functionaries."

"Like Laney used to do," Riggs said, rolling his eyes.

"Well, yes," Adar confirmed, "but he was not the only one, nor the worst. He sought advancement, but he did contribute to the greater good in his own way. He still does. He may even be happier on this trip with Major Mallory." There were chuckles. Riggs would certainly be happier without Laney and Chief Electrician's Mate Ronson Rodriguez feuding over resources and personnel all the time. With Spanky gone, Riggs had been feeling singularly picked on. "No, it is the others," Adar continued, actually showing his sharp white teeth in a grin, "that have sent me scurrying here to hide among trusted friends!"

When the relieved laughter died down, Adar asked a serious question. "So, what is the latest news? I assume Mr. Riggs has brought you the most recent communications?"

"Yes, Mr. Chairman," Letts replied. "We were just going over the message forms. Do you want east or west first?"

"I admit I am most anxious to hear the latest from Captain Reddy," Adar replied.

"Very well. As you know, *Walker*, *Achilles*, and their 'prizes' safely arrived at an uncharted atoll. They're completing repairs. Captain Reddy says he has sufficient fuel to reach Respite; that's the first Imperial possession they're heading for. We have the coordinates and he intends to await the arrival of the squadron of tankers Saan-Kakja has dispatched before pushing on into the heart of the Empire. That squadron is making good progress, by the way, and should reach Respite within a month of the Skipper. They're taking a more direct, northerly route, and should be able to expand the search for *Ajax*, in case she stopped anywhere along the way." He frowned. "The Skipper hasn't seen any sign of her yet and assumes she's still ahead of them. Anyway, the Y guns are scaring off the mountain fish, and the big brutes haven't been much of a problem for the tankers. I wish we had something better because I still worry about nighttime encounters and the crews have to be able to *see* the devils before Y guns can do any good." He shrugged.

"Our communications with Lieutenant Laumer on Talaud Island are still intermittent, even though they've got a new transmitter up and running." He shook his head. "It's got to be atmospheric interference from that damn volcano they're sitting on top of. Laumer's still confident they can get that old sub off the beach, but as much as I'd like to have it, I almost wish Captain Reddy would order Laumer and his people out of there." He looked at Adar. "Maybe you should do it," he suggested hesitantly.

Adar shook his head. "I will not second-guess Captain Reddy or Lieutenant Laumer. Mr. Laumer is 'on the spot,' as you would say, and believes he can accomplish his task. Captain Reddy must trust his judgment or he would have ordered him to abandon the project. I too worry about Mr. Laumer and his people. The smoking mountain on Talaud

Island has long been known to be irritable, but when the world grumbles, not even Sky Priests can divine the reasons for its complaint. Apparently Talaud is complaining most bitterly about something, but there is no way to tell what it will do. It might return to sleep as it has often done, or it might bellow its rage as the scrolls record it has also done before. Mr. Laumer is there. He must decide."

He leaned forward. "Now, tell me what Colonel Shinya has to report. How go things in Maa-ni-la?"

"Swell," Letts said. "As you know, the first thing he did when he got there was turn that goofball Jap, Commander Okada, loose, and see to it he had passage to Honshu—you know, Jaapan?"

"I still do not understand why he wanted to go there," Adar said. "He could have been of much assistance had he chosen."

"No telling," Riggs replied. "He did tell us quite a lot about the Grik and that damn Kurokawa. A hell of a lot more than we would've known otherwise. Shinya's a Jap too, but he's gotten to know us. He's a friend. He also spent time in the U.S. before the war, in California, so he might be more prune picker than Jap nowadays, anyway."

"I doubt that," Brister said. "But he's a good guy, and he isn't nuts. He knows what this fight is about. Okada just doesn't seem to get it. Shinya said he even recruited some oddball 'Cats and started teaching them a bunch of crazy samurai stuff!"

Letts sighed. "Not much we can do about that, and according to Shinya, it's probably not a bad idea. The Fil-pin colonists on Honshu aren't soldiers. There are some pretty strange creatures there that can be really dangerous. That's where the me-naaks, or 'meanies,' originally come from, as I understand it, and there's a lot worse stuff there too. Manila has always had trouble getting folks to move there. They actually need soldiers, and who knows? If a Grik probe or scout ever penetrated that far . . ."

"Yeah," agreed Brister, "and besides, it gives us a place to ship the Jap prisoners we 'rescued' from the Grik on Singapore. A couple of them want to help us out, and that's swell, but what were we going to do with the other ones? I don't think Okada'll rebuild the Japanese Empire with a handful of Japs and a few kooky 'Cats."

"I'm sure you are right," Adar said. "I hope they may find happiness there. But what else has our illustrious Colonel Shinya been up to?"

"Training Saan-Kakja's army, mostly. We left a few Marines to begin the process before we went looking for the sub in the first place, and judging by the quality of the troops Saan-Kakja has already sent, they've done a pretty good job with the basics. Shinya's been training them in larger unit tactics so they'll be more prepared to step right into line as fully formed, independent regiments once they get here. That's what's taken the most time in the past; they show up with excellent basic infantry skills such as those we've taught our own troops, but their officers and NCOs don't have any experience. In other words, Shinya's trying to teach them all the stuff we've had to learn the hard way."

"What of the Fil-pin industry? How does their shipbuilding proceed?" Adar asked anxiously.

"It's not up to our level yet," Alan Letts replied, "but I expect it will be pretty soon. No offense, but the Fil-pin Lands had already outstripped Baalkpan as an industrial trading center before the war even started."

"You certainly do not offend me." Adar chuckled. "Remember, I was but a lowly Sky Priest when this war began. I had no notion or concern regarding the relative industrial capacity of Baalkpan or Maa-ni-la. Any disparity may have troubled the great Nakja-Mur, but my only interest lies in what our combined capabilities might accomplish."

"Well, as I said, their production of ships, weapons, and heavy equipment hasn't quite matched ours just yet, but their fundamental industrial base and capacity is greater. Baalkpan had one large foundry when we arrived. It was mostly devoted to casting huge anchors or 'feet' for your humongous floating homes, but we turned it to pouring large cannons easily enough. We have upwards of half a dozen even larger foundries now, some pouring iron, but Manila had that many to start with. Once they hit their stride, I think we'll be in pretty good shape. They've already blown us away as far as leather implements, canvas, grain production, even leather body armor are concerned. They had a bigger labor pool to begin with, and when everybody began fleeing there in the face of the Grik, that labor pool grew even more." Letts's expression was philosophical. "We'll catch back up to some degree as people continue returning. In the long term, Baalkpan has much greater potential than Manila. Borno is a *big* island. Lots of space and raw materials. There's no reason why Baalkpan and Manila ever need to become rivals, if any of your people are worried about that."

Adar waved his hand. "That is the least of my worries, although I must admit the possibility is a concern to some. As you know, I ultimately seek a greater, more permanent union than our presently strong but potentially fragile Grand Alliance represents."

"I think he was asking 'How many ships have the Maani-los built so far?'" Riggs supplied, sotto voce.

"Oh! I'm sorry, Mr. Chairman." Letts shook his head. "I guess I'm a little preoccupied today."

"Quite understandable under the circumstances," Adar allowed. "Our people share far more similarities than one might ever imagine just by . . . looking at us. There are profound differences, of course, but our unity and friendship feed upon a number of fundamental commonalities." He grinned. "Such as our devotion to mates and younglings, it would appear. I have watched how the mid-age younglings you rescued from the Talaud submarine behave, and that behavior is somewhat consistent with that of our own young of like age. Your mate's youngling is due to arrive at any time, I understand, and I am most anxious to observe the behavior of a human infant!"

"Trust me," Riggs jabbed, "the behavior of the human parents is far more bizarre!"

"Say—" Letts grinned. "Steve's probably right. Anyway,

Shinya reports that the Maa-ni-los have only finished two steamers, but they're close on a couple more, and they have ten that'll be in the water within a month. He says the wood isn't as good—they weren't drying it like we were—but they've set up kilns. Hopefully, that'll work. Their hardwoods are a little different than those around here too."

"Maa-ni-lo-built Homes and feluccas last just as long as those built here," Adar mused. "As in all things, 'different' may not mean 'not as good.' "

"Of course, Mr. Chairman," Letts replied. "I think he meant it wasn't as good in the sense that it wasn't as 'ready.' Maa-ni-la was building two or so Homes a year, and their hardwood supply has moved away from the city. It takes them longer to cut it, move it to the construction area, and lay it up for drying. That's why they're setting up kilns. Aside from the hardwood we'd already laid up when we cleared the jungle away from the city, the people here only used to build a Home once every couple of years, so there was a lot more suitable wood nearby. A Home takes at least ten times as much wood as one of our new frigates. Don't worry," he said soothingly, "they'll catch up pretty quick, and probably surpass us in shipbuilding."

"How is our dear Saan-Kakja holding out?" Adar asked. Saan-Kakja was a remarkable High Chief in many ways. Like so many of the "youngling rulers" or commanders this war had created or "brought of age," Saan-Kakja had "stepped up to the plate" with poise, resolve, and a singular dedication to "the cause." They'd been fortunate in her, and others as well: Tassana-Ay-Aracca, Safir Maraan, Chack-Sab-At, Princess Rebecca—arguably even Matthew Reddy himself. He was no "youngling" at thirty-three, but he was awfully young for the responsibilities heaped upon him. So was Pete Alden. He'd been just a sergeant in USS *Houston*'s Marine contingent, and now he was General of the Armies and Marines. Alan Letts himself had been a lazy, freckled kid from Idaho, marking time as *Walker*'s supply officer. Now he was Adar's and Captain Reddy's chief of staff. It was like that for most of the men and women who'd ridden *Walker*, *Mahan*, and S-19 through the Squall that brought them here.

Of them all, however, Saan-Kakja was burdened with the greatest responsibility for her age. While in Baalkpan, she'd passed her fourteenth season and, as High Chief of all the Fil-pin Lands, she ruled over the largest single territory claimed by any one High Chief. Even Adar didn't claim all of Borno. He ruled only the inhabited settlements thereon, and then only until they were independent. Most of the many islands of the Fil-pin Lands were populated to some degree or other, and all were "daughters" of Ma-ni-la. Only her brother's settlement on southwestern Mindanao, Paga-Daan, had been close to independence, and now that brother was dead—killed by Walter Billingsley and the HNBC.

In addition to the difficulties of overseeing a painful and somewhat resentful industrial revolution in a land that was rapidly becoming the "arsenal of freedom," Saan-Kakja had to deal with an even larger population of malcontents and antiwar "runaways." The guilds were more entrenched there, and she hadn't even had the support of her own Sky Priest, Meksnaak, at first. Her iron will had finally co-opted Meksnaak and the council members she hadn't fired, and with Shinya's help and the devotion of her army and the majority of her people, she'd steamrolled the guilds. Adar—and most of the chiefs of the allied Homes and cities—worried most about the "runaway" faction. With Maa-ni-la firmly in the Alliance, they had nowhere left to flee, and it is always remarkable how violent some "pacifists" can become in order to maintain their status.

Adar worried for Saan-Kakja, with her mesmerizing golden eyes. He worried for Matt and *Walker*. He worried about the fate of Princess Rebecca, Sandra Tucker, and even Dennis Silva. He feared for the safety of his own new realm and the exposed distance of the 2nd Allied Expeditionary Force. He couldn't help it. All were beyond his help and all were people he cared about a great deal.

He glanced through the small shutter at the world beyond the War Room. The rain that had come with the dawn was over, and as though the Heavens had exhausted themselves early that day, the sky was suddenly clear and bright.

"I am, of course, well informed regarding those events that have transpired in Baalkpan today," he began. That was certainly true. He'd been at the docks himself when his old Home, *Big Sal*, finally rebuilt and completed as the allies' first "aircraft carrier," or more appropriately, "seaplane tender," got underway and steamed slowly out of the bay under the command of his oldest friend, Keje-Fris-Ar.

Watching that had been a bittersweet experience. His old Home had risen from near destruction to become the most powerful warship known to exist, but she was no longer his Home. Baalkpan was his Home now; he'd made that choice. But *Salissa* epitomized the changes his society—his world—was undergoing at such inexorable speed. No longer did she stand to sea under her lofty, mighty, beautiful wings. Instead, she belched smoke, and two massive engines turned a single giant screw propeller. She would never be fast, like *Walker*, but she would always be faster than she'd ever been, and in any direction.

Adar knew *Salissa*'s conversion was the only way she would ever survive this new kind of war. It was the only way she could really contribute. Other High Chiefs had volunteered their Homes as well: Tassana had offered *Aracca*, with the consent of all her people. Geran-Eras's *Humfra-Dar* was in the dry dock, with work already begun. Still, it made him sad.

"But what news is there from the AEF?" he asked. "I noticed the messenger from the telegraph office seemed more heavily burdened than usual. Has there been a major action?"

"No, sir," Letts replied. "If there had been, that would've been the first thing I told you when you came in." He shook his head. "No, it's mostly just a bunch of logistical stuff. Alden and Mr. Ellis are gearing up to jump on that Grik force at Rangoon." He stood and paced to a map on the wall. "Mr. Ellis was inclined to bypass it at first, but General Alden changed his mind. He thinks a bunch of the Grik that abandoned Singapore might have wound up there by now. Some didn't break. We still don't know what to make of that. We've got those Grik 'guards' Rasik-Alcas had, and I wish we could understand them. They seem to understand 'Cat but can't speak it. You ask me, I think they're too young. They act crazy to please, like dogs, but don't seem to really know what's up." He scratched his nose. "I sure wish Lawrence was here."

"As do we all," Adar agreed. "I sincerely doubt he speaks the same language, though. He had no idea what the aboriginal—I think Mr. Silva called them 'Injun Jungle Lizards'?—had said to him during their encounter. Perhaps he would be better able to learn their language, or teach them his, however."

"Yeah. Anyway, it's starting to look like being on their own for a while kind of 'wakes them up' a little, or something. Pete says that gives him the willies."

"Do you think they might influence this Grik force at Raan-goon?"

Letts shook his head. "Not really, and neither does Pete. Chances are, the Singapore Grik will never even make it to Rangoon. Alden, and Mr. Ellis now too, see the campaign more as a chance to test new tactics and equipment before the bigger push later, than anything else. But face it, Mr. Chairman, our 'tame' Grik aside, meeting Lawrence has forced us to realize that the Grik probably aren't all nuts. They may be born nuts, and the Hij may do their best to keep their Uul that way, but that doesn't mean they just naturally have to stay that way."

Adar stroked his whiskers in thought. "A most disturbing . . . speculation."

"You said it," agreed Brister.

"I suppose that leaves only Mr. Mallory's expedition to discuss," Adar said.

Riggs looked at the other men, then back at Adar. "Mallory's little squadron has passed through the Bali Strait and should reach Tjilatjap—'scuse me, 'Chill-chaap,' within a few days. They picked up another transport and two hundred more troops and laborers at Aryaal." He shook his head. "That whole deal is going to be complicated as hell. I really wish we didn't have to spend the resources on it just now."

"I agree with you on that," Brister said, "but think of the payoff if he succeeds! I wish I was with him. He's going to need a good engineer, and time isn't on our side. The longer we wait, the more deterioration there will be."

"He's got Mikey Monk, Gilbert Yeager, and Jim's dispatching Isak Rueben to help out."

Letts laughed. "Both original Mice back in one place, working together! Ha!"

"An effective combination, surely, but who will 'wrangle' them?" Adar asked.

"Well, they're all 'chiefs' now, but Monk's a lieutenant. He worked with Mr. Mallory throughout the development of the Nancys. At least he knows something about airplanes, and Ben Mallory likes him."

"Yeah, but he's almost as screwy as the Mice, and all of them will be under the command of a hot-pursuit jock who's just been given the greatest Christmas present of his life," Riggs pointed out.

"No, I sent a message to General Alden and he talked Captain Ellis into giving *Tolson* to Russ Chapelle. Russ has earned her anyway. He'll take *Tolson* down to Chill-chaap for two reasons: first, it'll give the expedition some real defensive firepower if they need it, and second, Russ will assume overall command. *Tolson*'s current skipper will get one of the new steam frigates when it arrives."

"Russ Chaap-elle," Adar mused. "An interesting choice," he continued delicately. "He has always struck me as a most formidable man, but perhaps a little . . . too much like Sil-vaa? In some ways."

"He *is* like Silva in some ways," Letts agreed. "But Silva—if he's alive—is like a lone marauding wolf that might take on protecting a cub now and then. He's loyal to the Skipper and damn handy in a fight, but otherwise, his most predictable personality trait is to 'kill whatever worries you so you won't have anything to worry about.'" Letts shook his head. "Honestly, regardless of the fate of the other hostages Billingsley took, I expect Silva's dead. I can't imagine even Billingsley being crazy enough to let somebody that dangerous live."

There was silence in the War Room for a moment while those present reflected on the probable loss of a bold and valuable warrior, as well as what his death might mean for the other hostages under Billingsley's control.

"Anyway," Letts continued, "Chapelle is sort of like Silva. He's a wolf, but he can lead a pack—or be part of one." He glanced at Adar. "Sorry for all the human euphemisms. What I mean is that he can be aggressive as hell, but he can also be counted on to follow explicit orders and lead others in carrying them out. He started out as a torpedoman, so he's got some engineering smarts, but he's also been exec of two square-riggers now, so we know he can sail, lead, and organize men and 'Cats. With him riding herd on Ben Mallory, I'll feel more confident that the mission will proceed in an efficient, timely fashion than if the 'euphoric pursuit jock' was running the show."

"Does the 'euphoric pursuit jock' know all this yet?" Riggs asked.

"Sorta," Letts hedged. "He knows he's in charge of recovering and/or preserving the airplanes, and he's already done a good job preparing for that. He's mixed up a quantity of what we hope will serve as high-octane fuel with all the ethyl alcohol we could cook up in so short a time. He says if we mix it with the gas we're running in the Nancys it ought to work; it'll just be inefficient as hell."

"And I still don't think it'll *stay* mixed," Brister objected, continuing an apparent argument.

"Maybe not," Letts allowed with a sigh. "I'm not the guy to ask. There's no way, under the present circumstances, we can come up with tetra-ethyl-lead—that's the stuff Mallory and Bradford told me they usually add to the gas. Anyway, we've got an airstrip started north of the shipyard. If he and

Russ decide to try to fly the things out, we'll have a place to land them. God knows who'll fly them, though. He's got a few of our new pilots with him, but as I understand it, learning to fly a P-40E is about as far beyond flying a Nancy as brain surgery is beyond picking your nose." There was general laughter at the analogy, but Adar clearly didn't quite understand. Hopefully, he would one day.

"Personally," Brister said, "I'd rather they try to get the ship out, with the crated planes on board."

Letts nodded. "That's my hope too, and one of the main reasons Russ will be in charge. Ben won't give a hoot about the ship; he'll just want the planes. I'd rather have it all, and if there's any way that can happen, I bet the Mice and Mikey Monk will figure it out."

"Captain Ellis said the area the ship's in, this . . . swamp, is a really spooky place," Riggs pointed out.

"Yeah, well, if it was easy, we wouldn't have to send as much to do the job." Letts looked at Adar. "I know you've been a little reluctant about this. You think 'we've got airplanes, why do we need these?' All I can tell you, until you see one fly, is that they're even further out of our Nancys' league than *Amagi* was out of *Walker*'s."

With an exhausted grunt, Adar stirred himself from the cushion and stood. "Oh, I believe you. I just hope the gain will be worth the effort—and the cost as well, I fear." He sighed. "I have been hiding here long enough, however, not to mention interfering with your meeting." He bowed to Alan Letts. "Please do convey my kindest regards to your mate, Nurse Kaaren. I know nothing of human birthing customs, but among our people it is expected that the male should be nearby, to render support and protection to his mate during her time of helplessness." He blinked, and Alan Letts shifted uncomfortably.

"Another similarity our cultures share," Riggs proclaimed. "It's not like a fellow is supposed to be in the *room* or anything, but he ought to be there. That's pretty much what we told him when we showed up for this meeting."

Letts cast a scathing look. "Pam and Kathy said they'd send word when . . . you know, the . . . water thing . . ."

"I know you are busy," Adar said. "You have great responsibility over momentous events, but the first human youngling born in Baalkpan is momentous as well. The city stands still in anticipation! Perhaps you might consider that, as well as the possibility that the war might manage to muddle along without you for a short time." He turned to the others. "Mr. Riggs, Mr. Brister, good day."

CHAPTER 8

Jaava Sea

Admiral Keje-Fris-Ar honestly still could not decide if his colossal ship's new configuration made him ecstatic or morose. Certainly he had spells when one emotion or the other predominated. The unavoidable sight of his beloved Home from her new "bridge" constructed from the abbreviated "battlement" made him sad. Gone were *Salissa*'s three great pagodalike structures, the apartments of the wing clans. Gone as well were her towering tripod masts and vast "wings," or sails. All that, almost her very identity, her soul, had been demolished in the great Battle of Baalkpan. *Salissa* Home, or *Big Sal* as his human friends called her, had been altered forever by that cataclysmic day and night. She was not dead, however, and difficult as it sometimes seemed, he still believed he sensed a soul within the pounding, vibrating body beneath his feet. *Salissa* now had only a small offset superstructure and four large, equally offset funnels, venting gray smoke from her eight oil-fired boilers where once the Body of Home clan and her vast polta gardens and fish-drying racks occupied her main deck. She looked like nothing Keje had ever seen before—squat, in a way, but longer somehow, even though he knew she wasn't.

What Keje believed was still *Salissa*'s "soul" tasted of a different purpose now as well. She'd lost the benign, passive essence that once so mirrored the great Galla tree that had grown upward from her very keel to bask in the glory of the light let through the shutters of the Great Hall. In its place, her soul was now an avenging spirit, sustained by the pounding, steam-driven heart deep within her body. She was a thing of heat now, of passion, no longer content to move with the wind. Now she harbored an urgent anger, a drive to return to the fight and avenge her people who'd been taken from her by the Grik.

Keje considered his Home formidably enough armed, particularly if her planes were as effective as the destroyermen predicted. Dozens of the ungainly but oddly familiar "Nancys" she'd been rebuilt to accommodate were secured to her high, flat deck. Even more were stowed below, where they could be serviced and assembled and moved up to the main deck by means of ramps that dropped to accept them. Far below, in *Salissa*'s magazines, were bombs that would give teeth to the fragile-looking craft. The planes weren't her only weapons. She now boasted a broadside armament of fifty 32-pounder smoothbores, twenty-five to a side, and they'd breeched and mounted a section of one of *Amagi*'s ten-inch naval rifles on a pivoting carriage forward, beneath the "flight deck." They'd designed a muzzle-loading projectile for the gun with copper skirt and bearing bands, and the nearly two-hundred-pound bullet could reliably strike a target the size of a small felucca at a range of fifteen hundred tails. No "gyro" was required because the massive Home was so stable in most seas. All they needed was a good range, course, and speed estimate of the target. There were also a couple of longer-range guns aboard, fore and aft of the superstructure. These were five-and-a-half-inchers salvaged from the sunken Japanese battle cruiser. They could have installed more of *Amagi*'s guns, and they might still, but Matt, Spanky, and Brister had other plans for them.

That was some consolation. *Salissa* was back in the fight, one way or another, and though her splendor was gone, Keje had long recognized that form and function often possessed a beauty of their own. He couldn't entirely suppress the elation he felt over the fact that his altered Home could now move in literally any direction he desired. Also, with her mighty engines throbbing at their maximum safe rpm's, she could do so at the almost unimaginable speed of twelve knots! Before, his ship had been capable of achieving ten knots on occasion, when the sweeps were out, but the speed could be maintained only until his people were exhausted. Now *Salissa* could steam at "high" speed almost indefinitely. Her fuel bunkers were immense, easily large enough for her to replenish other ships. Combined with her two huge, relatively crude but extremely reliable reciprocating engines turning a single shaft, there was sufficient mechanical redundancy to make him confident that his ship could steam to any point in the known world. He'd often wondered why *Walker* was so utilitarian, so devoid of the decorations his people loved so much. Now he knew. Just as had now been done to his own precious Home, aesthetics had been sacrificed for capability.

Fortunately, *Big Sal* was still large enough for some amenities. The "battlement bridge," which was quickly becoming simply "the bridgewings," still sported decorative awnings to protect her officers from the sun and the occasional swirling soot. There were no cushions on the bridge, but there were stools for the watch to rest upon. Speaking tubes were clustered here and there, connecting the bridge with every part of the ship, from the "crow's nest"—a dizzying hundred tails above the centrally located "pilothouse"—to the "ordnance strikers" stationed in the dark, gloomy magazines far below the waterline. Matt had told him that *Salissa* now most resembled a ship from his own world he'd called *Lexington*, and he insisted *Salissa*'s hull was probably much tougher and her aircraft nearly as capable as the ones *Lex* first sailed with. He'd shown Keje a picture of *Lex* in one of his books, and Keje had to agree the comparison was not without foundation.

Striding across the wide bridgewing, Keje reached his own favorite stool. The rest of the stools were ornately carved, but not his. His was old and creaky and somewhat battered, but he and it had been through a lot together. The faded wood was even liberally stained with his own blood. He wasn't about to abandon it—and woe was he whom Keje ever caught sitting on it! There'd been several occasions now, enough that he suspected his new officers had begun a tradition of hazing their juniors as they rose, when "newies" had been told they had to "start out" on the ugliest stool, only to have the "aahd-mah-raal" descend upon the unlucky candidate like a roiling Strakka. Instead of being angry with his officers, he played along, pleased that they too seemed to recognize the need for many new "traditions" in this new Navy to replace some of those they'd lost.

Settling upon the protesting stool, Keje leaned on the rail before him and watched the labor far below on the forward "flight deck."

"Aadh-mah-raal," said Captain Atlaan-Fas, "we have received a wireless message from Lieutenant Mark Leedom, Tikker's executive officer. He will arrive within two hours with our new medical officer, Nurse Lieutenant Kaathy McCoy. Captain Tikker has been working his flight crews very hard and begs you to allow him to fly a sortie to meet Lieutenant Leedom's plane."

"Outstanding," Keje replied. "I assume that if Nurse McCoy is joining us, Nurse Theimer's—I mean, Letts's—youngling must be thriving." He shook his head. "Most curious that human females change their names when they mate."

"Not terribly curious," Atlaan objected. "Our younglings often follow the names of their fathers." He grinned. "It is certainly not the most significant difference between our peoples!"

Keje huffed a laugh. "No concerns for the mother?"

"Surely not, or Nurse McCoy would not be joining us."

All Allied transmissions the evening before had been virtually dedicated to the happy news that "Allison Verdia Letts" had been born into this world at last. Congratulations were returned from the far reaches of the world, from Commodore Ellis in the Western Ocean to a late-night message from Captain Reddy in the Eastern Sea, relayed through Manila. Chairman Adar had proclaimed that this day, October 3 by the American calendar, would henceforth be "Allison Verdia Day," in honor of the first human youngling born among the Lemurian people. May there be many more.

"Very well," Keje replied. "It is time we tested the new launching system, at any rate. Captain Tikker may take a single flight of planes. We will have plenty of time to recover the aircraft before dark." Keje grinned, and glanced port and starboard at the two new steam frigates pacing his Home. One was USS *Kas-Ra-Ar*, named for his lost cousin and the first frigate of that name destroyed during the Battle of Baalkpan. The other was USS *Scott*. Everyone believed that a frigate was a far better monument to the heroism of *Walker*'s lost coxswain than a motor launch. "You may also grant his request to 'play' with our escorts when he returns!"

"Aye, aye, Aahd-mah-raal."

Captain Jis-Tikkar, or "Tikker" to his friends, glanced to his right, over his shoulder, to make sure the rest of the ships of "B" flight were still where they were supposed to be. He was mildly amazed to see that they were. Somehow, in the twisted way of things that seemed to have become the norm, he was *Salissa*'s "Commander of Flight Operations," or "COFO," in general, and commander of *Salissa*'s air wing of, eventually, forty planes, in particular. Officially, the wing was the "1st Naval Air Wing," composed of the "1st and 2nd Naval Pursuit Squadrons," and the "1st, 2nd, and 3rd Naval Bomb Squadrons." Evidently, the officious, confusing, multiple names of the elements under his command were the result of a compromise between Major Ben Mallory and the Navy types that predominated. If it didn't make much sense to him yet, he presumed that it would eventually, when other "wings" were operational.

His own lofty new status was gratifying, he supposed, but it still struck him as astounding. Granted, he'd become a good pilot and had learned he actually had a gift for teaching. He was also the most "experienced" Lemurian aviator in the entire world. But it hadn't been that long ago when Ben Mallory had actually forbidden him to touch the controls of the battered PBY Catalina they'd finally lost in the Battle of Baalkpan. Well, he'd improved. Everyone had. This first draft of "Naval Aviators" from the growing "Army and Navy Air Corps Training Center" outside of Baalkpan was composed of raw but competent pilots. Tikker was proud of them, proud of the role he'd had in training them.

Calling the group of four aircraft he now led "'B' flight, 1st Naval *Pursuit* Squadron" didn't make any sense at all, however, and Tikker wasn't sure it ever would. He and Ben both *hoped* it would, eventually, but at present, each of his "Nancy" flying-boats was identical, regardless of its designation. Of course, even if some planes were ultimately specially designed to chase something down and shoot it out of the sky, as far as they knew, there was nothing else in the world's skies for them to "pursue." Yet. Tikker and Ben both worried that that wouldn't always be the situation, and Ben, at least, wanted some kind of organizational structure already in place. Just in case.

Tikker was a "believer," but he shrugged mentally. Right now he didn't really care. He was flying, and that's all that mattered. The "improved" Nancys, or "PB-1Bs" as Mallory preferred to call them, were showing themselves to be pretty good little airplanes. They were easy to build and maintain and the ridiculously simple power plant was reliable and powerful enough for anything they would ever need a Nancy to do. They weren't fast (by Ben's standards), but they were maneuverable—while being forgiving at the same time—something Ben always said was hard to achieve. Tikker had the flying bug in a big way, and if they could only invent a seat that was comfortable for a 'Cat with a tail, he would have no complaints about the planes at all.

He was also pleased that he could report that the new hydraulic catapult worked even better than anyone expected. The fundamental mechanism was simple—if leaky and extremely messy—but the means of launching aircraft without landing gear had required unexpected imagination. They'd settled on a wooden "cradle truck" that accelerated forward, supporting the fuselage of a Nancy until it reached the end of the flight deck. At that point, the truck slammed to a stop and tripped a release hook. Tikker had to admit, it scared him half to death when the machine literally flung his plane into the air in front of the ship. The acceleration was extreme, and he was amazed it didn't break any of the planes. The contraption might need a little adjusting to take some of that initial jolt out of it, but it beat lowering the planes over the side one at a time with the big crane and then having them take off in possibly dangerous seas. They still had to land on the water, but they could then simply motor into one of the huge bays that opened in *Big Sal*'s sides, from which she'd once launched her gri-kakka boats. If they ever launched every plane on the ship, that wouldn't work, but they could still hoist out the extras with the crane.

He glanced again to make sure his flight was keeping up, then spoke into the voice tube beside and a little behind his head.

"Hey, Cisco," he called to his copilot/engineer/observer in the aft cockpit. Cisco's real name was Siska-Kor, but like nearly everyone in the Naval Air Corps, she had a nickname now. "We're going to gain some altitude. Send that we'll climb to five thousand and maintain formation."

"It will be cold up there," came the tinny, windy reply.

"Not that cold," Tikker assured her. He realized they were going to have to get some proper flight suits for the air crews. Right now they wore little more than the regulation Navy kilt and T-shirt, with goggles for the primary pilots. They needed goggles for everyone, but the glass industry in Baalkpan was having fits and starts and they were still using salvaged glass from *Amagi*. Cisco was right, though—it would be chilly. He'd never really known what cold was until he flew. He wasn't even sure what the Nancy's "service ceiling" was, since he'd always been too cold to reach it.

"Besides, Lieutenant Leedom is a 'hotshot.' A natural. Strange for a sub-maa-reener, I guess, but he's liable to try to intercept *us*, and I bet he and Nurse McCoy are wearing warmer clothes!"

Slowly, the flight climbed. All the planes bobbled a little in the unruly air, but the formation held together. Tikker scanned ahead, below, above, and even behind, but the early-afternoon sun was too bright to stare in that direction for long. The west coast of Borno lay before them, but the blue-green shore would make it difficult for them to pick out Mark Leedom's blue-painted Nancy. "No signal yet?" Tikker asked unnecessarily.

"From Leedom's plane? No, sir," Cisco replied.

Well, that was good, Tikker guessed. If Leedom had engine trouble, Nurse McCoy would have sent *something*. She didn't know the code, but she'd been instructed to transmit a single long blast if they ran into trouble. Tikker hated the idea that anyone might ever be forced down in the unexplored jungles of Borno. The thought frightened him even more than the prospect of setting down on rough seas. "So. Wherever they are, they're still airborne."

"That would figure."

"Then they're either still ahead of us—" Tikker abruptly had to grab the stick more firmly and fight for control against a surge of sudden turbulence as a blue and white shape flashed down in front of him. For just an instant he was frightened and confused, but he already knew what had happened. "Or above and behind us!" he grated bitterly. Looking around, he saw that his flight's formation had disintegrated like a flock of akka birds. When he looked down, he recognized what could only be Leedom's Nancy pulling out of its steep dive and beginning to rise once more. "Send for the flight to reform on me," he said irritably. "Now that we've 'found' Lieutenant Leedom, we'll return to the task force and begin our other exercise." He shook his head and allowed a grin to sweep away his annoyance. "I guess Lieutenant Leedom fancies himself a 'pursuit' pilot, even if all he has to pursue are his friends. Let's hope it stays that way."

Captain Tikker, Ensign Cisco, Lieutenant Leedom, and Nurse Lieutenant McCoy appeared, as ordered, at the door to the admiral's quarters directly below the bridge. Marine Captain Risa-Sab-At awaited them in the passageway, grinning hugely. Without a word, she knocked on the door and ushered them inside. The "admiral's quarters" were Keje's personal staterooms, and served the same purpose now as his larger Great Hall had once done. Many of the same intricate tapestries that had survived decorated these walls, and if the space wasn't as expansive as before, there was still plenty of room for quite a large gathering, and the furnishings were far more decorative than any human carrier had probably ever boasted. Keje stood as they entered, along with Atlaan-Fas, *Salissa*'s nominal captain, and Atlaan's executive officer, Lieutenant Newman. They were indoors, so no one saluted, but there was an unspoken exchange of respect.

"Welcome aboard, Lieuten-aant McCoy!" Keje said. "I have missed you. The youngling is well?"

"Very well," Kathy replied.

"Excellent! I wish I could see it!"

Newman grinned. "Human babies aren't nearly as cute as 'Cat babies," he said. "They always look a little like grubworms."

"Nonsense!" Kathy protested. "Allison is utterly precious!"

"I'm certain of it," Keje declared. "Please be seated, all

of you." The stools in the stateroom were all quite ornate, even Keje's. His favorite stool having been taken permanently to the bridge, he considered it pointless to try to "replace" it here. "Nurse McCoy," he began when all were comfortable, "I presume you are now prepared to begin your duties as chief medical officer? Excellent. I apologize for the uncomfortable necessity of flying you out to join us."

"No apology necessary." She glanced at Leedom. "It was quite exhilarating."

"Yes. Well, I'd like to hear about that before we're finished." Keje turned to Tikker. "It would seem Mr. Leedom surprised your flight quite badly."

"Indeed," Tikker replied, "and that lends further credence to what Major Maallory has been saying. He has always wanted the Air Corps, Naval and otherwise, to be prepared for pursuit activities. Right now, we're not. We're not armed for it in any way, and we haven't practiced pursuit tactics to any real extent. Mr. Leedom graphically demonstrated how devastating that unpreparedness might someday prove."

"But the Grik, and even the Imperials, don't have any airplanes!" Atlaan protested. "Practicing against threats that do not exist is dangerous and possibly wasteful of pilots and machines."

"The Imperials don't have airplanes *yet*," Tikker conceded. "Now that they know they are possible, I bet they will someday. They are not my immediate concern, however. We have no idea what the Grik may have by now. We know they have *one* airplane, the observation plane that bombed Baalkpan. We know from Commander Okada that it was damaged, but we haven't recovered it at Aryaal or Sing-aa-pore. They have taken it with them, somewhere. Even if they aren't copying it as we speak, all they have to do is fix it, and it can sweep every plane we have from the sky. It is faster and, unlike our own planes, armed." Tikker glanced at Leedom. "I now believe we must be prepared to meet *it* someday, if nothing else."

Atlaan was silent and Keje grunted. "I see your point," he said. "We must consider some sort of air-to-air armament for our aircraft, and yes, our pilots must at least practice a little of what to do if they are attacked in the sky. 'Evasive maneuvers,' I think you called them. Very well. You and our new 'pursuit pilot extraordinaire' will formulate tactics and begin integrating them into the training flights." Keje's voice lightened. "At least we know the dive-bombing tactics you have been working on are effective!"

Tikker cringed. He'd expected a chewing-out over the exercise his flight performed just before they set down in *Salissa*'s lee. Keje sounded pleased, in a way, but Tikker knew the admiral enjoyed irony and he might fly into a rage at any moment. "Uh, well, yes, Aahd-mah-raal. They do seem to work well, at least against . . . unsuspecting targets."

Keje and even Atlaan laughed out loud. It was a strange sound to humans, but all those present had learned that what sounded like a hacking cough to them was the height of mirth for a Lemurian.

"Unsuspecting!" Keje managed at last. "I actually *told* them to expect an attack from the air! I wanted them somewhat prepared so they could practice some 'evasive maneuvers' of their own! Trust me, you are not the only one who has sleep-terrors of Grik aircraft, or torpedoes or other unrevealed capabilities!" He barked another laugh. "Cap-i-taan Cablaas-Rag-Laan of USS *Scott* actually *complained* to me regarding the successfulness of your attack!"

Tikker cringed again. Evidently, Keje wasn't mad at him; most of his people enjoyed practical jokes, but he hadn't meant to make enemies of the new steam frigate captains! And *Scott* had actually dodged a few of their "bombs"! What must Captain Mescus-Ricum of USS *Kas-Ra-Ar* think of him? His ship hadn't escaped a single hit!

Captain Atlaan produced a creditable imitation of the slightly imperious commander of *Scott*. "Aahd-mah-raal, I must protest! An exercise is all well and good, but have you any idea how messy a large, putrid, flasher fish can be when it strikes my clean new deck from such a height at such a speed?" Keje and Atlaan roared again, joined by Risa and Newman.

"It was just like that," Newman said. "It came over wireless, but you could still almost hear the indignation!"

"Wha—what was your reply, Aahd-mah-raal?" Tikker asked, and Keje's tone became more serious.

"I told him that bombs make a far bigger mess than rotten fish, and that he might try a little harder, in the future, to avoid them. I had intended to tell you not to use fish again because I suppose someone might be injured if struck, but I have changed my mind. For the next few days, you will bomb the frigates with rotten fish unmercifully, until you can't hit them anymore, understood?"

"Aye, aye, Aahd-mah-raal."

The room sobered and Keje nodded to Newman, who stood and uncovered a map on the wall. "Now, gentlemen—and ladies. That brings us to another issue. This task force is still some distance away from . . . well, we've been calling it 'First Fleet' because like as not, we'll have more than one before this is over. Anyway, First Fleet, for various reasons, is going to hit Rangoon"—he pointed—"here, in a couple of days. Commodore Ellis now believes it essential that we remove this possible threat to our forward-most base on Andaman. For the same reasons he made that decision, Admiral Keje now agrees as well. The thing is, we want in on the scrape. Commodore Ellis is the man on the spot, and he and General Alden will run the show, but this will be a good opportunity for our pilots to rack up some combat experience before we move against Ceylon."

"I thought it was our intention to keep this ship and our aircraft secret from the enemy as long as possible," Tikker said.

"It is," said Newman, "and everyone's pretty sure we can operate against Rangoon and still accomplish that. Nothing's getting in or out of there by sea, and if they try to send a message overland, we hope to have Ceylon long before it could arrive."

Tikker looked at Leedom and scratched his ear around the hole with the highly polished 7.7-millimeter cartridge case thrust through it. The hole and the ornament were souvenirs of his first "solo" flight, and also served as a reminder of just how incredibly lucky he'd been. His was a risky job by definition, but he preferred that his risks be as calculated as possible nowadays.

"Sounds okay," he said guardedly. "We need to know what they will expect of us, and how big an effort we should make."

"As of now," Keje said, "they don't *expect* anything from us. Commodore Ellis has made the request, and I told him I wanted to discuss it with you before I agree. Schedules will have to be revised to coordinate our participation, but that participation ought to be advantageous to all concerned, I should think. Commodore Ellis might have to delay his attack until we get within range of your aircraft, but he should agree that a full-scale aerial assault by our entire wing can accomplish numerous objectives. First, I feel certain that such an attack would have a disastrous effect on enemy morale, and General Alden could take advantage of that and control the battle with far fewer casualties. Second, of course, I believe the wing should inflict a substantial number of casualties itself. Finally, and Captain Reddy would certainly appreciate this, I'm sure, your timely observations of the battlefield from the air should help General Alden shape his battle with much greater certainty."

"The entire wing?" Atlaan asked softly.

"Yes. Captain Tikker needs to practice organizing such an assault, just as much as the fliers need to practice making one, and this seems the best, least risky way to do it." Keje regarded Tikker once more. "What is the farthest distance you feel comfortable striking from with such a force?"

"We need to keep everyone together," Tikker said, "which means the first to take off will be burning fuel until the last ships join them." He shook his head. "That is too long. We should probably attack in two waves."

Mark Leedom was nodding. "That makes sense. If the first ships only have to wait for the last ships in that wave, each wave should have a couple of hours' flying time to reach the target, hang around long enough to find somebody to bomb, and still make it back to the ship. I'm assuming this ship will be a little closer by then?"

"Of course," Keje assured. "Possibly by as many as fifty miles or so."

Tikker was silent a moment, then sighed. "Well, as I said, it sounds okay. Fifty miles is a nice buffer as well. Coordinate the timing with Commodore Ellis based on those numbers, and I'm as confident as I can be that *Salissa*'s first action as an aircraft carrier will be a success. Remember, though, we are all new at this, and no matter how well we plan or how carefully we prepare; regardless of how good our pilots are, or how well made their aircraft, I fear some lives will be lost."

"You suspect the Grik may have developed some defense against aircraft?" Risa asked, speaking for the first time.

"No," Tikker answered. "Not yet, and if so, not at Rangoon. Honestly, I don't much fear we will lose many planes and pilots in action . . . yet. I am more concerned about our own inexperience and ignorance." He shrugged and looked around at the others. "Bear in mind that all of us, even our human Americans—our 'original' destroyermen—have no real experience with this kind of war. We still, essentially, make it up as we go."

CHAPTER 9

Eastern Sea

When *Walker* sounded her "drowning goose" general quarters alarm for pre-dawn battle stations, Matt was surprised to hear the thunder of drums on the ships nearby, sending their own crews to action stations. He remembered that Jenks had expressed interest in the practice several times. Evidently, Matt's explanation that they did it because dawn was a dangerous time of day when enemy ships—and in their "old" war, submarines in particular—might see their silhouette before they saw the enemy, had made eminent sense to the Imperial commodore. It looked like Jenks was beginning to institute the practice among all the ships of his command. That was certainly for the good—if they all became true allies someday. Matt realized, however, that he might have given away a serious advantage if the Empire and Alliance ever found themselves on opposite sides. Oh, well, it couldn't be helped. Right now, they had the same cause and they needed their friends to be prepared

That morning, instead of standing down into a morning routine, Matt gave the order to "make all preparations for getting underway." Sparks began to rise from nearby stacks, and black and gray smoke curled into the air as *Walker* and the "squadron," consisting of *Achilles*, *Icarus*, and *Ulysses*, raised steam and prepared to pull their hooks. Their immediate destination was an old Imperial outpost—probably the first. Jenks said the island, called Respite, was the first hospitable place his ancestors had encountered on their voyage to the East, and it was there they'd rested, victualed, and taken on fresh water before continuing in search of the most remote place they could find. Some few had stayed, tired of the seemingly endless journey, and Respite had been almost constantly inhabited ever since. Over time, it became the regional capital of all the surrounding islands and, until recently, the western frontier of the Empire. It had been to one of the newer, slightly more northwestern outposts under Respite's jurisdiction that Rebecca's one-armed protector, Sean O'Casey, had been fleeing the Imperial hangman after an unsuccessful rebellion against Company usurpation of Imperial authority. It had been only wild coincidence that Princess Rebecca Anne McDonald had been dispatched aboard the same doomed ship by her father, the Governor-Emperor himself. In his effort to provide for her safety from increasingly dark Company machinations, he'd set the wheels in motion that left her marooned and presumed dead these two long years. In the end, the Company had snatched her anyway.

The best thing, from the perspectives of Matt and Jenks, was that Respite's inhabitants had become increasingly dissatisfied with the arbitrary policies enacted by the distant Imperial government—particularly as the Courts of Directors and Proprietors fell increasingly into the hands of the Company. The "Respitans" had always been a self-sufficient, individualistic lot, and Jenks suspected they would have supported O'Casey's rebellion if they'd caught wind of it in time. He was sure that when USS *Walker* and her consorts arrived with news of the fight that *Walker* and *Achilles* had had with Company and pressed Imperial warships bent on murdering the princess, they would find themselves among a sympathetic population and territorial governor. A perfect place for the Allied supply ships and tankers to head for.

Icarus flew her Imperial flag once more, and Matt noticed with interest that *Ulysses*' new Imperial flag flew above her old Company flag. He wondered what the next Company ship or official they encountered would think of that. Bosun's pipes twittered similar or familiar calls on every ship, and the special sea and anchor detail on *Walker*'s fo'c'sle sprayed the anchor chain with hoses as the steam capstan sent it dripping and clattering into the locker below. Finally, the anchor was aweigh and the little crane forward hoisted it into its cut-out storage space forward. Matt watched while the other ships' anchors were raised and secured, and was struck by how primitive his own ship was in many ways. The stocks on Imperial anchors were wood and *Walker*'s was iron, but the overall shape was virtually identical. His ship was probably the last class in the U.S. Navy to use the old-style anchors, a design completely unchanged for a hundred years, but the Imperial model was even older.

He shook his head and strode from the bridgewing to the chart table. No one aboard was really sure where they were headed anymore. Somewhere in what they remembered as the Carolines, he supposed. It seemed the farther east they steamed, the less relevant their charts of the "old world" became. Courtney Bradford took the disparity between their charts and the actual locations of the various islands of the "Eastern Sea" as a matter of course. He still insisted that the larger, exposed surface area of the atolls was consistent with his Ice Age theory, and Matt had to agree there might be something to that. The fact that, according to the charts Jenks had loaned them, *these* Carolines were larger and more substantial than Matt remembered, or the old charts indicated, seemed to follow. What didn't make any sense to Matt and many others was why the atolls, or actual islands, had been so shifted around. They'd discovered quite a few islands in—call them the Marshalls for lack of anything better—where there shouldn't be anything at all. The island where they'd made their emergency repairs was one example. According to Jenks's charts, other substantial atolls such as Kwajalein didn't even exist. Bradford maintained that it was all perfectly understandable. Matt only wished Courtney would find some way to make it just as easily explainable. In the meantime, and for the foreseeable future, he would have to trust Imperial charts of the region.

"All ahead one-third," Matt said. "Make your course one, one, five."

"Ahead one-third," Staas-Fin, or "Finny," replied. "One, one, five, aye!" The blower rumbled contentedly and *Walker* gathered way. Juan arrived with his battered carafe and a tray of cups and Matt accepted one with thanks. Juan's coffee was terrible, even using the ersatz beans of this world, but it was coffee of a sort and that's all that matters sometimes.

"Thanks, Juan," Captain Reddy murmured as he brought the green foam–rimmed brew to his lips.

"My pleasure, Cap-tan! Would you like breakfast? A haircut perhaps? A hot towel and a shave would do wonders for you," he hinted. Matt's razor had about given up the ghost, and he'd finally relented and begun growing a beard like the rest of the men under his command. "I traded a case of rusty cans of 'scum weenies' for a new Imperial razor!" he declared in triumph. "It is quite sharp!"

Matt scratched his itchy chin and winced. He'd love a shave—but he had never let Juan shave him despite the Filipino's incessant attempts. Now . . . he had the only razor. Matt was convinced that if he ever relented, Juan would be shaving him for the rest of his life. On the other hand, he'd always believed that keeping himself well-groomed was important. It was just his little way of showing defiance in the face of the odds against them. "No matter how bad it gets, the Skipper always shaves." Something like that.

He sighed. "Well, can we do it right here? I mean, can I just sit here in my chair?"

Juan beamed. "Of course, Cap-tan! In fact, it would be best, I believe. The chair is just the right height! I will return in a moment!" With that, Juan darted away and Matt looked around the bridge. Finny was trying to suppress a grin and the lookouts diligently studied the horizon. Norman Kutas glanced at the chart and stepped around the chart house—probably so Matt wouldn't see him crack up. True to his word, Juan returned quickly. He had two 'Cat mess attendants in tow, one with a basin of hot water, the other holding some damp, steaming towels. Juan immediately removed Matt's hat and draped a towel over his face.

"Oh, for God's sake, Juan! I thought you were just going to shave me!" he muttered under the towel. "I can't conn the ship like this!"

The shipwide comm suddenly blared. "Now hear this!" It was Chief Bosun's Mate Fitzhugh Gray's voice. He was in on it too! Gray was around sixty, barely shorter than his captain, but the man who'd once grown flabby and jaded on the China station of the U.S. Asiatic Fleet had transformed into a lean, powerful pillar of moral authority within the Alliance. He was no longer a "mere" chief bosun's mate; there were plenty of those in the rapidly expanding American Navy. He'd become something much more, still ill-defined. Officially, he commanded Matt's personal security detail, the "Captain's Guard," and was "chief armsman of the supreme Allied Commander." Unofficially, he was often referred to as "The S.B." (Super Bosun), but most, even Chief Bosun's Mate Bashear, still just called him "the Bosun." To Matt, and probably Matt alone, he was still just "Boats."

"Now hear this!" Gray repeated. "Lieutenant Steele to the bridge! The exec will take the conn while the captain endures his mornin' toy-letty!" A roar of laughter echoed through the ship, amid the stamping of Lemurian feet.

"Oh my God, Boats!" Matt groaned, but he couldn't help laughing. "Put yourself on report! And . . . whoever else is responsible for this stunt!"

"Aye, aye, Skipper," Gray said, "but beggin' the Skipper's pardon, your beard is startin' to look a little scruffy." He lowered his voice. "That, and with all the stuff that's been goin' on, the fight, the chase for the girls . . . me and a few of the fellas figured you could use a laugh. Besides, you've always stayed shaved through a lot worse scrapes than this. Don't want the fellas to think you're lettin' yourself go."

For just an instant Matt tensed. Gray couldn't see his face under the towel, but it might actually be best. Suddenly, Matt reached out and grabbed Gray's sleeve, pulling him down closer.

"They don't call you Super Bosun for nothing, do they?" Matt whispered huskily. "You're right. I need a laugh, and so does this crew. Let's make the most of it."

Freshly shaved, trimmed, and with his face tingling with whatever refreshing soap Juan had been able to create or procure, Matt sheepishly relieved a grinning Steele and resumed his watch. Cheerful voices and snatches of good-natured banter rose to his ears from the fo'c'sle forward, and the weather deck aft. It suddenly struck him that his crew was happy—not because they'd pulled a stunt on the Skipper, but because they'd managed to do something for him. He felt embarrassed and a little ashamed that he hadn't noticed a growing cheerfulness aboard the ship. He'd been too lost in his own duty, and his ongoing misery over Sandra's unknown fate. The rescue of the princess might be the primary diplomatic reason for the mission, but to him it was personal. He had to have Sandra back, for the very survival of his soul. He needed to rescue the young princess too. She'd trusted him, relied on him to keep her safe, and he loved her too, he supposed, much like a daughter. His recent mood must have been a terrible drag on the ship.

All the crew felt his anger and they'd do whatever was necessary to make things right, but these were extraordinary times as well. The humans under his command were almost giddy with the prospect that they were nearing lands where actual human *women* dwelt, and each of them harbored happy fantasies of how they'd ultimately break the "dame famine" that had plagued them ever since the Squall. The 'Cats were happy too. They'd steamed much farther into the vast Eastern Sea than they'd ever believed possible. They'd always known the world was round, but they also *knew* that the force humans referred to as "gravity" pulled down. It had simply followed that if one went too far from the "top" of the world, one would plummet off the side into the endless heavens. They'd *believed* the human Americans, *hoped* they were right that gravity pulled down wherever on the world one stood, but only now had it become a demonstrated fact. Matt knew this "fact" flew in the face of some very long-held religious dogma, and regretted that they'd upset their friends yet again in that respect, but the contradiction didn't seem that important to his Lemurian-American crew right now. Just the fact that they hadn't fallen off the world and were free to continue their important adventure satisfied them at present. Later, they might contemplate the religious implications. Matt knew from the messages relayed through Manila from Baalkpan that Adar already was, but right now, *Walker* was a happy ship and his own serious, intense mood had been like a . . . wet towel on the humor of the crew. He would have to try harder to conceal his anxiety and concern. He'd had a lot of practice at that—but then, of course, he'd always had Sandra to help him.

He glanced at his watch. Almost 0800 and time for the watch change, so this was as good a time as any. "Mr. Campeti," he said, addressing *Walker*'s new gunnery officer, "I assume you've managed to standardize the drill on the number four gun?" The number four was a dual-purpose, 4.7-inch gun they'd salvaged from *Amagi* to replace the four-inch-fifty that had been badly damaged in the Battle of Baalkpan. The respectable quantity of ammunition for it that they'd salvaged as well was still high-explosive, cordite propelled, as opposed to the black powder–loaded four-inch-fifty's they had for the other guns. Until they perfected their own cordite using the indigenous materials, they couldn't "regulate" the 4.7-inch with the others, and they'd decided to keep it in local control.

"Aye, aye, sir. The drill's mostly the same, and the fellows have it down pat."

"Very well. They no longer have any excuse to be late, then, I take it?"

"No, sir."

"Good." Matt grinned. "With all this 'nervous energy' everyone seems to have today, we should be able to break some records!" He turned to the bridge talker. "Sound general quarters, if you please. The watch is ticking!"

The "drowning goose" began gasping for air, and Sonny Campeti raced up the ladder beside the chart house, to the fire control platform above. Other men and 'Cats quickly appeared, laden with belts of ammunition and shoving two heavy Browning .30-calibers up the ladder to waiting hands.

The Bosun paced the fo'c'sle, bellowing at the crew of the number one gun in his inimitable fashion, while Chief Gunner's Mate Paul Stites assembled his gun's crews atop the amidships gun platform.

Ensign Fred Reynolds and his copilot/observer Kari-Faask dumped their breakfast in the can under the amidships deckhouse, despite Earl Lanier's ranting, and raced toward where their Nancy's "deck crew" was clearing and securing its cover, and preparing the hoist davit that would put the plane down in the water alongside. The same "deck crew" would also serve as a "plane dump detail" if the aircraft was ever damaged in action or became a deck hazard in any way.

Chack's Marine drummer sounded a long roll, and the Marines not assigned to gun's crews abandoned their ordinary seagoing duties and scrambled to one of the old vegetable lockers aft of the number three stack, to grab their leather armor and bronze "tin hats." The company armorer issued their muskets from a new locker beside the galley, and they assembled on the weather deck, port and starboard of the numbers one and two funnels. First Sergeant Blas-Ma-Ar quickly called the roll over the racket.

On the rebuilt aft deckhouse, where the auxiliary conn was located, Frankie Steele took his post and Gunner's Mate Pack Rat and Chief Bashear roared at the crew of the number four gun, as well as the depth charge handlers on the fantail below.

Matt watched this activity with growing satisfaction. He knew Spanky, Miami Tindal, and Tabby would be sorting things out below. The drill was unorthodox by prewar standards, but it was efficient, and it worked well for their purposes under the circumstances.

Chief Signalman Lieutenant Ed Palmer was the talker at the moment, repeating the readiness reports as they came in. "Wireless comm gear is under continuous watch," he finished for his own division. "All stations manned and ready, Captain."

Matt glanced at his watch. "Not quite a record, but not bad," he remarked. "Not bad at all." He made himself grin at those around him. "All stations may secure from general quarters. Continue steaming as before under condition three alert. Chack's Marines may commence their morning exercises."

Courtney Bradford and Selass-Fris-Ar, Keje's daughter and currently *Walker*'s medical officer, ascended to the bridge. As usual, Courtney wore his wide, battered "sombrero" and had to remove it before entering the pilothouse. It was a standing order for him alone. His red, balding pate was shiny with sweat when he snatched the thing off.

"Well, we're off again at last, I see," Courtney said, glancing aside at the atoll slipping away off the port quarter. "Just as well. Of all the mysterious lands we've encountered, that one had absolutely the least to recommend it!"

"You mean to tell me you didn't discover anything unusual?" Matt asked.

"Well, not as you would say 'unusual' . . . now. A few odd crabs, I suppose, but nothing astonishingly peculiar, if you know what I mean? Of course."

"You're getting spoiled, Mr. Bradford. When we first met, a strange twig would've kept you enthralled for days."

"I'm *not* spoiled, sir! I merely have . . . higher expectations now. With good reason!"

Matt looked at Selass. With his human preconceptions, it was always a little tough for him to accept that she was even related to Keje, much less that she was his daughter. She couldn't have looked less like him. She was sleek and thin where Keje was thick and muscled. Her fur was almost silver, while her father's was a reddish brown. Keje's eyes were about the same color as his coat, but Selass's were almost as startlingly green as Saan-Kakja's were . . . goldish—whatever. Lemurians had no photography of course, so Matt had never seen a picture of Keje's lost mate. He'd have been willing to bet anything that Selass took after her mother.

He also knew she and Chack had a "history." Given his understanding of what 'Cats considered attractive, he could understand it. Male Lemurians were drawn to physical beauty, just as men were, and Selass was stunning even to his eyes. Exotic rarity also seemed to enhance perceived attractiveness, and that was probably why Saan-Kakja, Safir Maraan, and even Selass were viewed almost as icons of Lemurian beauty. Saan-Kakja with her amazing eyes, Safir Maraan with her jet-black fur and silver eyes, Selass with her silver fur and green eyes . . . Shoot, maybe it was just the eyes. Matt mentally shrugged. There was no doubt about it, Lemurians were handsome creatures. He wouldn't dwell on the fact that some of his men, including Silva, apparently considered them more than just "handsome." He supposed the only thing 'Cat women got out of such hypothetical relationships was the exotic rarity of humans. He thought he felt something squirm down his back.

Chack's history with Selass. That's what he'd been thinking about. He'd almost refused to allow her on the mission because of that . . . but then, he really couldn't have refused, could he? With Sandra gone, Jamie Miller with the fleet, Karen pregnant, and Pam Cross a nervous wreck after Silva's abduction with the others, he couldn't have taken Kathy McCoy. For such an important mission, though, he did need a "high-profile" medic. Selass was it. She was good with human and 'Cat physiology, and she'd earned her "nurse lieutenant" status. She'd changed dramatically from the self-centered, spoiled brat teenager Matt first met, and she was utterly devoted to Sandra. She'd grown up. The war and the loss of her first mate, Saak-Faas, had finally made something of her. If Matt had refused to take her, it might have been seen as a slight by some of his very best Lemurian friends. The problem was, no matter how well she hid it, Matt and Sandra had long known that Selass was still hopelessly in love with Chack.

Chack was virtually mated to Safir Maraan, Queen Protector of B'mbaado. They'd planned to announce their betrothal and perform their nuptials after the liberation of Aryaal and B'mbaado, but after what they found there, the time just didn't seem right. Now Matt had dragged Chack thousands of miles from his beloved and he felt really bad about that, but damn it, he needed the kid! He was a veteran of vicious combat now and a steady leader. He'd earned his post, and Matt couldn't have taken anyone else. What he didn't need was Chack getting all a-twitter and confused around his old flame, though. So far, it didn't seem to be a problem, and Matt hoped it wouldn't be. Probably wouldn't. Chack was "engaged," and he and Selass had their duty. They'd both amply demonstrated how important that was to them.

"Good morning, Selass," he said, nodding at her.

"Good morning, Cap-i-taan," she replied. She'd begun accompanying Bradford to the bridge after the two of them prepared her "battle station"—the wardroom—which would become a surgery in the event of battle. It certainly wasn't due to any policy or anything; she just did it—like Sandra always had before. It probably even made sense in a way that the medical officer would want to come to the bridge and see for herself what was happening, so she'd have some idea what she might be about to face in the way of casualties. Matt hadn't liked it when Sandra did it—at first—but as time went on, he couldn't change it and didn't really want to. She'd always known when it was time to leave. Now . . . to chase Selass off when there wasn't any need would be hypocritical.

"Coffee?" Matt offered. Selass blinked distaste. Most Lemurians hated coffee, or "monkey joe," as the destroyermen had dubbed the local equivalent. They considered it a medical stimulant, not a staple of daily life.

"Don't mind if I do," Bradford said.

Juan had returned with another carafe and he happily poured a steaming cup. "At least someone appreciates the labor necessary to render the strange seeds I get into something almost as good as the coffee I used to make!" he proclaimed piously.

Matt was glad he hadn't been taking a sip just then, or he'd have spewed it out his nose. "Trust me, Juan, everyone appreciates it," he interjected truthfully.

"That vile, bloated cook, Lanier—he just incinerates the beans and grinds them up! Sometimes he will even waste an egg!"

Matt's brows furrowed. That explained a lot. Vile and bloated as Lanier certainly was, his monkey joe was actually better than Juan's. And it didn't have green foam on top.

"You know, I always kind of liked an egg in my coffee, Juan," Matt experimented delicately.

"Nonsense, Cap-tan! If you want lizard-bird eggs, I will cook them for you, any way you like! Why eat disgusting green eggs, full of grounds?"

Matt sighed. "Oh, never mind." Maybe he could drop another hint later. Juan was good to him, to all the officers. To come right out and tell him *Walker*'s greasy cook made better coffee was out of the question. "Maybe I'll have an egg sandwich, then, after all."

"Good!" Juan approved. "You did not eat before GQ. You need to eat! You get too skinny!" The little Filipino—who probably didn't weigh ninety pounds—scampered down the stairs behind them.

"That was close!" Bradford said. "For a moment I feared you might have gone too far! If Juan ever got his feelings hurt and went on strike, I know *I* would starve." He shuddered. "Has Lanier ever actually bathed?" he asked. "Or even washed his hands, perhaps?"

Matt grinned sheepishly. "I had to try." He turned back to Selass. "How's everything in your department?"

"None are sick, oddly enough. I think they are too excited about our next landfall to malinger. All the injured have returned to duty but one, and he will recover."

Matt remembered a striped, mustard-colored machinist striker who'd taken a rivet in the chest like a bullet when one of the thirty-pounders punched through the engine room. It had looked bad. Again, he was amazed by the curative properties of the Lemurian polta paste. "Glad he'll be okay," he said sincerely, then winced. "No, ah, screamers?" He asked, using Silva's universally accepted term for diarrhea.

"None, Cap-i-taan. We seem to have arrived at a proper mix."

The reason for Matt's wince was that in spite of his best efforts to maintain Navy traditions and regulations, the U.S. Navy on this world was no longer exactly "dry." One of Sandra's longest-held concerns was that some bug in the water might annihilate the crew. This concern was not without foundation. For the longest time she'd insisted that the crew drink only ship's water that had been either boiled or manufactured by the condensers. With personnel now spread so far apart, that was no longer always practicable. They'd consumed the various nectars and spirits produced by the Lemurians with no ill effects, but every time somebody even accidentally drank a little "local" water, they wound up with a bad case of Montezuma's revenge. Even the various 'Cat clans had a few problems along those lines. The massive, lumbering seagoing Homes collected sufficient fresh water to keep them independent, but they almost always got a little sick when they visited the Homes of land folk. Before the destroyermen had arrived, they'd had no idea what germs were, but they'd settled on the simple expedient of making a sort of grog by mixing water with highly alcoholic "seep."

Seep was a spirit made by fermenting the ubiquitous polta fruit that gave the Lemurians food, juice, and the fascinating curative paste. When seep was further refined and distilled, it produced a high-grade alcohol. Alcohol could be made from other things, such as certain grains the 'Cats used in the production of their excellent beer. A beetlike tuber worked well, and their efforts to boost the octane of their gasoline had resulted in the discovery of other things that could be used to produce ethanol. Seep, or its distilled version, still remained the preferred ingredient in Lemurian grog. Matt didn't know if they'd come up with the idea on their own or if Jenks's ancestors let it slip, but under the circumstances, necessity dictated that some form of grog—the weakest effective mixture—be reintroduced aboard U.S. Navy ships.

Matt was certainly no Puritan, and he'd considered prohibition a useless, stupid, harmful political stunt, but as far as *his* Navy was concerned, he'd done his absolute best to maintain its traditions and regulations. He wouldn't have a bunch of drunks running his ships. Fortunately, the mixture required to purify water could barely be tasted, much less felt, and the condensers still provided enough fresh water to dilute the mixture even further. At least on *Walker*. She utilized an open-feed-water system, with seawater going straight to the boilers. This hadn't worked as well on some of the new boilers they'd made. Corrosion and sediment in the steam lines were already becoming a concern on USS *Nakja-Mur* and USS *Dowden*. The closed systems they were using on some of the newer steam frigates about to join the fleet when *Walker* left Baalkpan were fresh-water hogs. They'd have to keep fuel *and* water tenders trailing behind them wherever they went. *Big Sal*'s massive engines were open systems, so maybe they could replenish from her. He shook his head. Ultimately, he wasn't bothered nearly as much by the result of the policy as he was by the principle of the thing.

"How long until we reach this 'Respite' Island, Captain?" Bradford asked. "We'll be there for a while, I take it?"

Matt refocused and shifted uncomfortably in his elevated chair. "A week and a half at this pace. Maybe more," he said grudgingly, glancing out to port, where *Achilles* steamed. She'd set her fore course, topsails and topgallants, as well as her fore staysails. Soon, she would draw her fires and proceed under sail alone. She'd be just as fast, and didn't have the fuel to keep her boiler lit for the entire passage.

"I say," Bradford said, "couldn't we just go on ahead without her? We could be there in a matter of days! If we dawdle along awaiting Mr. Jenks and his prizes, our oilers and other ships will most likely beat us there!"

"Oh, Courtney, come on. You know that's ridiculous. I wish it were true, but our supply convoy from the Fil-pin Lands must travel under sail alone, and I'm afraid our stay at Respite will be longer than even you would like." He didn't say that he was far more anxious than Bradford to reach their destination and then be on their way. Billingsley, *Ajax*—and Sandra—drew ever farther from his grasp with each passing day.

"Well . . . but surely there will be some emergency that will prevent me from properly studying the biology there! No doubt something will derail my first opportunity to gaze upon the wonders of an utterly isolated land! It happens all the time, as you well know. Poke, poke along, and then 'Do hurry up, Mr. Bradford! We must get underway!' "

Matt almost chuckled. In a way, he envied Bradford's ability to set aside their primary objective, even for a while. At the same time, he kind of resented it too. A lot of people were counting on them, not only to rescue Sandra and the princess but to forge an alliance with a powerful seagoing nation. All in the midst of a cataclysmic war. To even contemplate other priorities at a time like this struck him as at least mildly selfish. He knew Bradford well enough by now to understand that the man just couldn't help it though. It was just the way he was. What he was.

"We can't go any faster," he said, with a trace of lingering bitterness. "We don't know these seas like we used to, and it might not be a good idea if we arrived at our first Imperial outpost without Commodore Jenks to smooth the way. Besides, if we don't wait for our resupply, we won't have the fuel to reach New Britain with any reserve."

"Well . . . then I do have your word that I may spend at least some time exploring?"

"As far as it's in my power to let you. The local authorities might not want you running wild. They're not the most trusting folks with strangers, if you'll recall. At least not until you get to know them." Matt reflected on the real, growing friendship between Jenks and himself. They hadn't liked one another at all when they first met. Jenks and the Bosun had probably actually hated each other. But the exigencies of war, a shared battle, and a common cause had erased their earlier animosity.

"Perhaps they are not all quite so standoffish and paranoid," Courtney speculated.

"Hard to say. Our sample of their society's been pretty small. All of Jenks's people were—some more than others—and before that, all we had to go on was O'Casey and the princess. Even they seemed awful protective of their nation's whereabouts."

The pilothouse was quiet for some time after that, except for the rumble of the blower. Juan appeared with an egg sandwich and Matt wolfed it down under the Filipino's satisfied gaze. Eventually, possibly sensing that Matt wanted to be alone with his thoughts, everyone not actually on watch in the pilothouse filtered away. The sea to the east stretched wide and empty, and the sky was clear except for a lonely squall, possibly lashing yet another unseen, uncharted atoll.

CHAPTER 10

North of Tjilatjap (Chill-chaap)

"Lawsy, what a creepy place," Isak Rueben mumbled softly.

"You said it," Gilbert Yeager agreed. "Gave me the willies when I was here the first time. Didn't 'spect 'em ta send me back."

"We need you," Major Benjamin Mallory called back from the front of the boat. "You and a couple of the Marines are the only ones who've been here before."

"So I'm kinda a guide?" Gilbert asked.

"That, and our resident expert on conditions at the site," Mallory replied.

"That mean you'll take my advice?"

Mallory paused before answering. Gilbert and Isak, both of *Walker*'s "original Mice," were capable of some of the most . . . unusual . . . thought processes he'd ever encountered. "Within reason," he said at last.

"Then keep yer damn voice down . . . sir," Gilbert hissed. "They's some nasty boogers in this here water!"

Mallory nodded. He would try. The problem was, he was so excited he could barely contain himself. Ever since Mr.

Ellis and his expedition discovered the wreck of the *Santa Catalina* in this swampy estuary north of Tjilatjap, or "Chill-chaap," he'd been so anxious to salvage her—and especially her miraculous cargo—that sometimes he thought he'd burst. In his excitement he'd mentally dismissed or disregarded the dire warnings of Ellis and Chack. They'd been very specific about the terrible nature of the few threats they'd actually encountered. Both were certain that other, possibly more dangerous creatures lurked in and around the wreck. Gilbert was certain of it too, and he took every opportunity to remind anyone who'd listen.

Mallory looked around, taking in the water, the shoreline, and the dense jungle that bordered it as his large steam-powered flat-bottomed barge towed several other heavily laden barges upstream. The jungle did look spooky, and he noticed several big swirls in the murky black water as they proceeded. Other than that, however, it was an unusually beautiful day. Even the humidity wasn't quite as oppressive as usual. Lizard birds and other flying creatures capered ceaselessly above, defecating all over everything and everyone, but that happened everywhere he went. Despite all the warnings, he just couldn't summon enough anxiety to displace his eagerness to get there and get started.

He did recognize the possibility that he was being just a tad rash, and perhaps even irresponsible, but everyone—Adar, Letts, Ellis, even Captain Reddy—knew he would be. That was why he wasn't in charge! Lieutenant Commander Russ Chapelle was in overall command of the expedition, and it was his job to do all the worrying. That suited Mallory just fine. He had a specific, important job, and the less he had to worry about other things, the better. He knew he'd have to take care, though; he had quite a few people under his personal direction and enough of the warnings had seeped past his enthusiasm for him to recognize that *Santa Catalina* and her environs were a dangerous place.

Russ Chapelle stood beside Mallory in the lead barge. USS *Tolson* was his first command, and leading this expedition was his first truly independent mission. For a former torpedoman aboard USS *Mahan*, he had a lot of responsibility heaped upon him. It may have seemed odd to those who didn't know him, but while he was highly conscious of the responsibility, it didn't really worry him that much. In an infant but growing Navy that had already seen so much desperate action, he'd seen more than his share on land and sea. He'd earned a level of confidence in himself that comes only with experience. He knew some people often compared him to Silva, and the thought amused him. He liked Silva, and he did have a lot in common with the maniacal gunner's mate. There was a profound difference, however. Whereas Silva had learned little from his own vast experience except how to be a better warrior, a better killer, Chapelle had learned to temper his boldness with caution. On a steamy, bloody, chaotic night, not yet a year ago, Russ Chapelle had learned that the reaper wouldn't take IOUs forever. Despite all his injuries, Silva still hadn't figured that out.

In any event, Chapelle was fully aware of the dangers the expedition faced, and he was mentally prepared for other things as well, even worse than they knew about. Chill-chaap had once been a thriving city, much like Baalkpan, before the Grik came and literally exterminated it. According to Keje and many of the other 'Cats he'd spoken to who'd once traded there, even less was known about the jungle surrounding Chill-chaap than was known about the area around Baalkpan. Doubtless there'd been Hunters, like the one Silva called Moe, who'd agreed to accompany them here, but to the land folk who once inhabited the city, the jungle beyond it was a mystery. Now, only about two years after Chill-chaap was sacked by the Grik, the insatiable jungle had reclaimed it. The dwellings were covered with greenery and the pathways were impenetrably choked with vines and briars. No one could live there now without burning the entire area to the ground and starting over from scratch. He knew how hard the people of Baalkpan worked to keep the jungle at bay, how difficult it was for them to maintain the open killing field beyond the ramparts. He had a sudden mental image of what Baalkpan would look like now if they'd lost the great battle there. It wouldn't be as bad as Chill-chaap had become—yet—but within a few years it would be impossible to tell it ever existed.

He frowned. That reminded him of something else that was bothering him. As soon as the discovery of the ship had been reported, a small contingent of Sularan troops was immediately dispatched to the ruined city. They'd landed with a pair of heavy guns, their only duty being to keep an eye on the river mouth and drive away any snooping Grik ships that came nosing around. They were to remain concealed and not reveal themselves to any passersby, and only fire on anything that tried to enter the river itself. They hadn't been on station very long, a little over a month perhaps, and a Navy ship had resupplied them just a couple of weeks before. Yet when *Tolson* arrived accompanying Mallory's flotilla, after they rendezvoused east of the Bali Strait, there was no sign of the Sularans. Their guns remained, strategically placed but with vines already crawling up the carriages. A few things had been found lying about—a sword, the implements for the guns, a few personal items. That was it. He couldn't believe the Grik had taken them. The guns had not been fired; their bores were clean. The powder kegs and shot crates were scattered and broken, but nothing had been taken. Most telling of all, if the Grik had come, they certainly wouldn't have left the guns. The loss of the Sularans was a tragedy, but the mystery of what became of them loomed menacingly over the entire expedition.

"We're gonna be openin' the lake purty soon," Gilbert warned. "Maybe you'll get to see some o' them big-ass duck critters!"

"What duck critters?" Dean Laney demanded grumpily, showing some mild interest for the first time since he'd set foot on the barge. The big machinist's mate was still angry about being sent on the mission in the first place. He'd had a cushy berth back in Baalkpan, running one of the machine fabrication factories, but Laney's biggest problem was that he was universally considered a jerk. He'd lorded it over the 'Cats in his division to such an extent that, war and all, there'd nearly been a strike. Adar and Letts hoped if they got him back aboard a ship, back within a recognized Naval hierarchy, he might settle down. He was too distracting to keep around and too useful to shoot. The scheme had worked—a little. He wasn't throwing his weight around quite as much, but he was bitter about being equal to or outranked by men and 'Cats he'd once had under his thumb.

Gilbert stood up, pointing. "Them ones, over there! See? Hey! Mr. Chapelle, we might wanna either speed this tub up or slow it down. I don't know which. There's some critter here in this water that eats them things!"

They were all looking at the "ducks" now. They were huge, goofy-looking things, maybe as big as a giraffe. Gilbert knew their legs were about as long as what was visible above water. A couple had reddish wattles dangling from their very ducklike bills and bluish crests on their heads. Most were a mottled brown all over, not unlike the drowned trees and other vegetation protruding from the surface of the widening swampy lake. Still several hundred yards away, the entire herd or flock or whatever it was looked directly at them, their long necks stretched out like turkeys trying to get a better view, heads bobbing almost comically from side to side. Most of the men and 'Cats on the barges were doing the same.

"I guess we should slow down," Gilbert decided. "Last time, the thing that got one didn't make its move until after we scared the ducks and they took to hurryin' off."

"Very well," Chapelle agreed, and nodded at Bosun's Mate Saama-Kera at the throttle. The black and white Lemurian, unavoidably known as "Sammy" now, tightened the valve with an "Ayy, ayy, sur," and the train of barges began to slow. "How much farther to the wreck?" Russ asked.

"Yeah, where is she?" demanded Mallory anxiously.

Gilbert was flustered. He'd only recently begun *talking* to officers. Having them ask him for guidance was utterly beyond his experience. He retreated a step and looked at Isak, who wore a face that seemed to say, "No good'll ever come of puttin' yerself forward." Of course, it was too late for that advice. Besides, he suddenly realized he'd just now provided guidance without even thinking about it when he suggested they slow down . . . and they had! "Uh," he managed, "we was a little further along when Mr. Ellis asked that damned Rasik that very thing . . . sirs. The ship was almost growed to the west bank, yonder, maybe a little around that bend." He stared hard for a moment, concentrating, trying to recall. "As a matter o' fact, I don't remember that there bend. I b'leeve the jungle's growed out an' plumb gobbled up the ship!"

Gilbert was right. The closer the barges chugged to the "point," the clearer it became that the jungle had indeed engulfed *Santa Catalina*. They caught occasional glimpses of rusty iron, and even a vine-wrapped cargo boom was identified, jutting from the mass. Only near the waterline were the old hull plates somewhat visible. The vines grew down to within a few feet of the water and abruptly stopped, as if something in or on the water fed on them, keeping them trimmed as high as they could reach, like trees in a goat pasture. Then again, maybe the vines couldn't abide salty water. This lake had obviously once been smaller—and fresh—until something, an earthquake or a flood, caused a break into the estuary. Now the tide rolled in, poisoning the rotting stumps that lined a much smaller beach.

Laney was peering over the side into the brackish water as they neared the old freighter. "What about flashics?" he asked, suddenly nervous. He had a right to be. One of the few truly heroic deeds Dean Laney could claim was his work to replace *Walker*'s screw with one of *Mahan*'s. The dreaded flasher fish had nearly beaten him to death even through a sail they rigged to protect him.

"Cain't be many of 'em," Isak said with just a trace of

sarcasm in his reedy voice. "I don't think them duck-o-saurs'd just wade off in amongst 'em. Maybe the water ain't salty *enough* for 'em." He grinned. "Or maybe whatever eats duck-o-saurs cleaned 'em out! Glad *I* ain't a diver!"

"God damn you, Isak!" Laney snarled. "I guess we'll find out when I tie a line around your scrawny neck and throw you in to see what eats you!"

"Silence on the barge!" Chapelle growled. "I'll decide who gets eaten around here!" He made sure Ben Mallory wasn't paying any attention. The Army aviator was fixated on the ship ahead. He looked at Laney and lowered his voice. "I may be an 'officer' now, with my own ship and everything, but except for Mr. Mallory, every human on this trip is a 'chief' now. Whether they're new chiefs or ex-chiefs, it makes no difference. You know what that means. If you've forgotten, you better remember right quick. There's rules, Laney, and you've been on the edge of breaking one of the most important ones for a long time! Why do you think you're here? Real officers have fancy words for it, but I call it the 'everybody hates his guts and wants him dead' rule. Officers have fancy charges, sentences, and lots of different punishments for it too. Chiefs only have one. Do I make myself clear?"

Laney gulped and Chapelle raised his voice just a little so the nearby 'Cats could hear as well. "That reminds me. A lot of you guys are 'new,' and don't know what a real hero Major Mallory is. You're Navy . . . men. Destroyermen and Marines. You make fun of the Allied armies, and that's fine. They make fun of you. That's the way it works. But as we go aboard that ship, remember we're all *here* for Major Mallory. Our reason for being here is the cargo on that ship, and that cargo belongs to him. Is that understood? He may not be 'Navy,' but he's the 'Air Minister,' and that means he even commands the Naval Aviators, God save us. In fact, they're the Naval Air Corps now. That means even though I command this expedition, he outranks the hell out of me." Russ paused and glanced at Ben. He was surprised to see the flier looking back at him. He hadn't realized he'd been talking that loud.

"Thanks, Captain Chapelle. No need to puff me up in front of the fellas, though. I'm sure we're all here for the same reason. To win the war." He gestured up at the ship that now loomed above them, dripping vines like a vast green waterfall. "It's been kind of a secret, I guess. Mr. Ellis tried to keep it one for a while. I don't know how many of you have heard, but this old ship, out here in the middle of this crummy place, might just help us win the whole damn war."

The steam barge pulled the others as close alongside the ship as possible. Gilbert could tell there was no way they could board on the side closest to the shore as they'd done previously, and he said so. The jungle had already taken a hold on the ship to a remarkable degree when he'd last seen it, but he was amazed by how much worse it was now.

"The Marines will go first," Chapelle said to Lieutenant Bekiaa-Sab-At on the next barge. Bekiaa was originally from *Big Sal*'s forewing clan and was yet another one of Chack's many cousins. She was brindled like her relatives and had trained under Risa. She wasn't as . . . free-spirited . . . as Risa, but she'd seen action at the Baalkpan docks at the height of that terrible battle.

"Be careful," Gilbert warned. "There was some sort of Marine-eatin' booger in the aft hold." He gestured up at the tangled mess. "No tellin' what's moved in since."

"Charlie Company!" Bekiaa called to the Marines on the second and third barges. "Prepare to grapple!" She waited briefly while the thirty-odd 'Cats that had accompanied them from the ship prepared. "Execute!" Heavy treble hooklike implements arced upward, trailing stout lines, and disappeared into the foliage. Raucous, indignant cries filled the air as flocks of lizard birds exploded from the mass and swirled above them, along with a cloud of flying insects. Most of the hooks caught something when they were pulled taut, and after heaving the barges closer, the Marines scampered up the lines. Many had to hack their way through and over the bulwark to the deck, but when a sufficient number had managed the feat and there'd been no cry of alarm, Bekiaa grabbed a dangling rope and scurried up after her troops.

Chapelle grinned at Ben Mallory. "Now we just wait a little while for them to check things out. It won't be long before you can kiss your prizes!"

Something big jostled the barge from below, spilling the men and 'Cats to the deck.

"Whoa there!" chirped Isak, grabbing for the bulwark. The barge tilted and creaked as whatever it was slowly scraped along its bottom. All the men had Springfields and a couple of the 'Cats had Krags. All went for them at once, snatching them up or unslinging them from their shoulders.

"Goddamn!" bellowed Laney. "It's one o' them pleezy-sores!"

The barge righted and something cruised away from it, rough, pebbly back, streaming water. There were big swirls alongside like it had very large flippers, or maybe feet like an alligator. An extremely long tail slithered through the water behind it, probably providing most of the propulsion.

"What *is* that thing?" Mallory asked. Already, seven rifles and a pistol were aimed at it. Moe, the Lemurian Hunter, had his massive crossbow leveled at the beast. "It's too damn big to be a croc. . . . Isn't it?"

"Hold your fire!" Chapelle ordered. "We might just piss it off. Maybe it'll leave us alone."

"Nothin' *ever* leaves us alone," Gilbert predicted darkly.

"It come back!" Moe exclaimed.

"What is happening?" Bekiaa shouted from above.

"There's some big beastie down here, Lieutenant!" Chapelle replied. "You stay right where you are!"

The creature described a long, leisurely arc, settling on a heading that would bring it back to the barge. It didn't accelerate or anything, so maybe it was just curious. Of course, they could see only a small fraction of its mass and they already knew it was big enough to overturn the barge. Its curiosity might kill them. 'Cats on the other barges had clustered near the middle, clinging to the heavy machinery, tool crates, and supplies. The few Marines who'd remained behind aimed muskets at the thing as it approached. It slowed.

"Ugly devil," Laney said.

The head was fairly clear now and it didn't look like a croc. It was huge, about four feet wide and maybe seven feet long, but it was broader and more rounded and there were no grotesque, interlocking teeth. The eyes, while mounted like a croc's, were even larger in proportion to its body and possessed an almost mesmerizing, alluring quality. If Courtney Bradford had been there, he would have been fascinated, but he also would have told them that the shape of the head was cause for greater concern than any crocodile.

"I think he's kinda cute," Mallory said.

With an erupting spray of water, something pink, shiny, and rather bulbous darted from the creature's suddenly gaping mouth and slammed into Sammy, knocking him back against the hot, exposed boiler. Just as quickly, the 'Cat was jerked toward the bulwark. He hadn't even had a chance to cry out. For an instant, everyone was too stunned to react—everyone but Moe. The powerful old Lemurian dropped his crossbow and clamped onto Sammy's legs. The blur of motion slowed just enough for the others to see what was happening. Sammy was still sliding toward the open mouth, with Moe along for the ride, but now realization had dawned.

"Shoot it!" Russ yelled. Seven rifles cracked almost together and Ben's pistol barked quickly, filling the sudden silence while the others worked their bolts. Muskets roared from the other barges and heavy lead balls slapped into the monster's body while the riflemen fired another volley into the thing's head. Both its eyes were reduced to spattered, gelatinous orbs, and white bone glared around a ragged, bloody gash between them. It started to convulse.

"Grab Moe!" Russ shouted, and Isak and Gilbert dove on the 'Cat. The creature in the water jerked backward and began to flop and roll. Sammy shrieked in agony as the massive "tongue" was torn away, leaving his entire arm and shoulder naked of fur. The terrible beast continued to flail with wild, mindless abandon, sometimes lunging almost entirely out of the water and drenching the barges when it splashed back down. Once, its whipping tail nearly swept the Marines in the second barge over the side, but eventually the convulsions ebbed. Finally, the mighty lake monster floated still, the brackish water around it turning black with blood under the afternoon overcast.

Bekiaa's corpsman had crossed from the adjacent barge and was tending Sammy's wound. A lot of skin had come off with the fur.

"You okay, Moe?" Gilbert asked.

"Swell," the nearly toothless 'Cat replied, using the term he'd heard Silva use so often. It sounded strange coming from him.

"Well, you done good," Gilbert said. "You know, I bet that was the booger that got Chack's Marine in the aft hold of the ship! Chackie said he was there one second, standin' on some ammo crates to stay outta the water and then"—he snapped his fingers—"pop! He was gone."

"Stands to reason," Chapelle replied. "If it wasn't the same one, it was probably something like it. That thing was damn big, though. I hate to think there's a hole in the ship big enough for it to come and go."

"Maybe it growed some since then," Isak said hopefully.

"There not be many monsters like that, big as that, 'round here," Moe said judiciously. "Be like too many super lizards in one place. I bet they no agree so well. We git off boats quick now, though. Bloody water, big food, other things come soon, I bet too."

CHAPTER 11

Rangoon

The plan had seemed so simple, so clear, in *Dowden*'s great cabin riding at anchor in Port Blair. Now, in the vast, thick, reeking darkness of the misplaced river the Amer-i-caans still called the "Ayarwady," nothing whatsoever was clear. There was no moon to speak of, and what little there was, was heavily smothered by an oppressive, visible humidity, almost a fog. As reported and expected, there were no channel markers of any kind and leadsmen in *Dowden*'s bows constantly tossed their lead as the steamer crept slowly upstream against the moderate current. *Dowden* made just enough steam to keep steerageway and continue her advance with her heavy burden of troops and the long train of troop-packed barges behind her. If she'd been a coal burner or a side-wheeler, this would never have worked. Telltale sparks from her funnel or the noisy, churning white water alongside would have betrayed her to anyone watching from shore. As it was, commands were kept to a minimum and muted, and even her engine had been muffled with blankets, wrapped around what was accessible and otherwise hung as baffles in the engineering space. *Nakja-Mur* was under the same discipline, with much the same burden. USS *Haakar Faask*, another new steamer that had arrived a few weeks earlier, had the newest, most powerful engine, and behind her trailed *Donaghey* with her sails all furled, as well as her own allotment of nearly two dozen barges filled with troops, field artillery, and a short company of the 3rd Maa-ni-la Cavalry with their silently purposeful "me-naak" mounts. The paalka teams to pull the guns were kept inconveniently muzzled and stowed belowdecks on the frigates to prevent them from causing alarm with their shrill cries.

General Safir Maraan, Queen Protector of B'mbaado and representative to the Allied Assembly, was immaculately groomed for battle, as always. In fact, she was practically invisible on *Dowden*'s quarterdeck in her black cape with her almost blue-black fur. She wore a silver-washed helmet, though, that complemented her form-fitted, matching breastplate, and that was how Lord General Rolak picked her out of the gloom and the milling throng of nervous, excited, whispering warriors.

"This creeping around in the dark always makes me uneasy," he confessed quietly, joining her by the rail.

Safir grumbled a chuckle. "An admission I never expected from you, O valiant opponent."

Rolak chuckled back. "I will never be your 'opponent' again," he said. Then his voice turned serious. "You are the daughter I always wanted of my one mate who passed into the Heavens too soon."

Safir touched his scarred, furry arm. "And you have become as my father, as the noble Haakar-Faask did before you." She paused. "Do not make me mourn you today as I still mourn him—and my true sire."

Rolak grinned in the darkness. "Fear not. I am already too old to die properly, bravely, on an honorable field against respected foes. That time is gone." His tail drooped. "There is no honor in this war, as I have said many times. It is not fun."

"It is not fun," Safir agreed, "but there *is* honor." She

huffed. "You know that. The honor comes with the cause, a cause far greater than any we had before: the very survival and freedom of our people—even if it is just the freedom to choose 'fun' wars!"

They both chuckled then. They knew that few of their allies would understand. They also knew that for them to succeed, for the Alliance to endure, "fun" wars were over forever. Things could never be as they'd been before, with Aryaal and B'mbaado remaining apart from others of their kind. Any wars of the future would always be like this: desperate wars of last resort.

"But why are you uneasy?" Safir asked at last. She gestured at the southwest bank of the river. There had been lights there, obscured in the riverside wood of unfamiliar trees ever since they'd entered the river mouth. Most were probably lingering cook-fires, left unattended by sleeping Grik. A few rough structures eyed the river with lights from within, but there was no sign that the stealthy squadron had been detected. They'd seen only two Grik ships moored near the once impressive harbor facilities they'd passed, and one appeared half-sunk. The garrison here had clearly been abandoned, and the Hij in charge understood that the remaining ship represented suicide, not escape.

"Oh . . . you know. These night antics of the Amer-i-caans still disturb me," he admitted. "Just on the off chance that this battered old sack of bones was to manage a noble deed, or even die an honorable death . . . I'd like for the Sun to see it."

Safir slapped the admittedly old but still rock-hard arm this time. "Shortly we will be in position, I hope, and the Sun will not be long in coming! If you die *any* kind of death today, the Sun will watch me taunt your corpse! Do you understand me, 'Old One'?"

Rolak patted her shoulder. "Yes, my Queen!" he replied lightly.

"Besides," Safir added, suddenly somewhat concerned for Rolak's state of mind, "you *cannot* die. You still owe your life to Captain Reddy! I was there when you made the pledge, remember? You may only die in *his* service, you know!"

"This is not?"

"Absolutely not! You must be at his side, protecting him from something ridiculous and foolish!" she declared.

The deck shuddered beneath their feet and the apparent motion of the ship, slow as it was, came to an abrupt halt, spilling quite a few soldiers and Marines to the deck with a clatter of equipment. The curses that followed were almost as loud. Runners came and went, barely visible, and there was a muted discussion near the wheel. Rolak and Safir looked on with interest. After a short time Commodore Ellis joined them.

"We've hit a snag or something," he said. "Who knows, maybe we strayed from the channel. The lead showed deeper water. . . . It doesn't matter. This is as far as we go. I'd hoped to take you another mile or so, but we knew it was dicey. No friendly pilots on *this* river."

"Is the ship in danger?" Safir asked.

Jim Ellis shook his head. "Nah, we'll back her off okay once the troops and equipment are off her. We could probably back off now, but we're running out of night anyway." He regarded the two generals, his friends, in the gloom. "Just keep an eye on that right flank," he reminded them. "Especially now. We've got no idea what's out there and we won't be able to cover you much with the ship's guns for a while. At least until daylight shows us the channel better." He paused. "Be awful careful, both of you. This whole thing is . . . different. We've never done anything on a *continent* before. Pete's scouts saw nothing on the northeast side of the river, and the enemy you'll be facing was kind of strung out. Like in the plan, if they don't get wise, you shouldn't have much trouble establishing a strong beachhead anywhere along here. The forest opens up a lot past the shore . . . supposedly." Jim shook his head. "Captain Reddy's right. Being blind is sure a pain. I'll be glad when *Big Sal*'s planes show up and tell us what they see! Anyway, if they stick to their usual routine, they'll run around like chickens with their heads cut off for a while until they get sorted out. Use the time to dig in and wait for 'em to come at you, then slaughter 'em!"

Safir blinked amusement in the dark. "We have done this before, Commodore, and we know the plan well. We will 'watch our flank,' and I have high confidence in that aspect of General Alden's strategy. It *should* work, and it might well be the only way to prevent 'seepage.'" She grinned predatorily.

"I know," Jim agreed. "I guess I just wish I was going with you." He turned to his exec, who'd drawn near during the conversation. "Send: 'This is it. All forces will immediately disembark and proceed to their relative positions according to General Alden's plan. There is no geographic objective other than the shipyard, and that needn't be taken intact. The only real objective is to kill Grik and practice new tactics. Maintain maximum communication and physical contact with adjacent units. Nobody is to go running off on their own.'" He took a breath, wondering if he'd forgotten anything. He started to add "be careful," but decided that, like Safir, the various commanders would probably think he was carrying on too much about the obvious. "Send: 'Good Hunting,'" he said instead, then turned back to Safir and Rolak. "Just promise you'll remember: just because the Grik have always done things a certain way doesn't mean they always will. I guess I don't really expect anything fancy—this time—but keep reminding your NCOs particularly to expect the unexpected. Someday they're liable to get it."

The landing was discovered fairly quickly, but that didn't mean surprise was totally lost. Guttural shrieks and excited, high-pitched cries echoed from the trees along the shoreline in the vaguely graying, predawn haze. One of the strident Grik "battle horns" brayed insistently. Only a few barges actually made it to shore before the Grik in their area knew something was up, but the commotion arising along the roughly three-mile shore upstream of the Rangoon docks appeared to confuse the enemy far more than it rallied them to any sort of coordinated effort. Several companies piled ashore in the face of headlong Grik counterattacks, but these were poorly timed, terribly executed, and totally unplanned. Each may have been composed of anywhere from a dozen to two hundred warriors, and they simply attacked what they saw. In other words, they behaved in a perfectly predictable fashion. So far. Except for a couple of companies of the 5th Baalkpan that took some casualties from one of the larger attacks that met them right in the water between the barges and the shore (and the short, greenish "flashies" drawn by the splashing), the rest of the Allied troops brushed aside the ad hoc enemy efforts. Immediately, the army began to expand its foothold all along the shore.

To encourage further disarray among the enemy, at least at first, the big thirty-two-pounders of the steam frigates, and *Donaghey*'s eighteens pulsed with fire, flashing on the dark water of the Ayarwady through the mist and gunsmoke like the most intense cloud-to-cloud lightning imaginable. The thunderous booming of the guns was muffled some by the dense air, but the pressure of each report seemed even more intense. The fused case shot that had worked with such surprising efficiency and reliability at Singapore had long since been replenished and then some. Now it flashed over the landing troops like meteors, trailing short, luminous, sparkling tails. Half a mile inland, it detonated unseen except for periodic brief stabs of light that rained fragments of crude iron down through the trees and among the rudely awakened camps of the enemy. Rolling booms reached the ears of the army several seconds later, and droplets of moisture shivered from the leaves.

Safir Maraan strolled slowly along in the rapidly brightening dawn, hands clasped behind her back. She uttered no orders. She'd come ashore with half her personal guard, her Silver Battalion of the Six Hundred, and they had things well in hand. For organizational purposes, the Six Hundred was considered a regiment with two battalions, Silver and

Black. Unlike the rest of the B'mbaadan and Aryaalan troops who'd adopted their own distinct colors, the Six Hundred still clung to their old black and silver livery. They also trained right alongside Pete's Marine regiments and were crack troops. They knew exactly what they were doing and needed no distractions from her. Thrashing, hacking, chopping sounds reached her from the front as the perimeter was expanded. For just an instant, she allowed her thoughts to stray to her beloved Chack, and as she'd expected, his presence, his very scent suddenly filled her heart just as quickly as she opened it. The Sun and the Heavens only knew what unthinkable distance separated them, but for a moment he was with her, beside her on the field that day. Back where he belonged.

A paalka squealed behind her and she coughed loudly to stifle the sob that had risen to her lips. Consciously, she restored the stones to the wall that protected the Orphan Queen from herself at times like this—times she'd never known before she'd met the "re-maak-able" wing-runner-turned-warrior. Times when she didn't want to be a queen or general or even a warrior anymore, but just a mate to the one she loved.

The paalka squealed again and she shook her head, turning to see a pair of the heavy beasts, their palmated antlers bobbed and capped, being dragged from a barge and taken to a picket line. She still marveled at the creatures. They were infinitely better draft and artillery animals than the stupid, lumbering, dangerous "brontasarries," as the Amer-i-caans called them. They were really too broad and large to ride, but except for their annoyingly high-pitched cries they were among the greatest gifts the Allies had yet received from Saan-Kakja and the Maa-ni-los. She watched as the barges withdrew, headed back to the ship for more troops or equipment, and another barge landed to disgorge its cargo of two more paalkas and four light guns under the anxious, tail-twitching glares of the gun's crews. None too soon.

"My Queen," cried a "lieuten-aant," rushing to stand before her. "Cap-i-taan Daanis begs to report a substantial Grik force marshaling to our front!"

Safir peered upriver. The coming day had actually made it suddenly, if likely briefly, more difficult to see in the haze. "Are we well connected to the 3rd B'mbaado and the rest of Lord General Rolak's command?"

"Yes, my Queen."

"What is Cap-i-taan Daanis's definition of a 'substantial force'?"

"Perhaps six or seven hundreds so far. There may be many more on their flanks. It is . . . difficult to tell."

Safir nodded. "Of course." She glanced around at the beachhead they'd secured. She would have preferred it bigger, deeper at least, but it was sufficient. As long as they had a contiguous battle line and enough room to land their subsequent waves in relative safety, it would be enough for the time. "Very well. Tell Cap-i-taan Daanis that his company may lay aside its garden tools and prepare to receive the enemy!"

"Yes, my Queen!"

Safir paused while a squad of signalmen raced past, unspooling a long roll of wire with little red ribbons tied to it at intervals of about a tail. They had to stop a moment and wait impatiently while the gun's crews moved their pieces forward by hand. She turned to Colonel Anaara, who'd been pacing along beside her. "The Silver Battalion will 'stand-to,' if you please."

The drums—another of Captain Reddy's imported innovations—thundered in the gradually fading morning mist as youngling drummers blurred their sticks. Even as the battalion fell in, preparing their bows and spears and locking their shields; while artillery crews rammed fixed charges of canister down the mouths of their gleaming bronze six-pounders and gunners sighted the tubes, the raw, visceral roar of the first mass charge of Grik warriors fell upon them. The Battle of Raan-goon had begun.

Lord General Rolak heard the sound of the Grik charge, the *whoosh* of arrows, and then the stuttering *Ka-burr-*

Burr-aak of a battery of guns on his left. He could see little, but he wasn't much concerned. There'd been none of the raucous, thrumming horns, calling and answering like skuggik cries on carrion, so even though he doubted that Safir was completely ready, he expected her to handle this first thrust with little difficulty. The distinctive sound of Grik "infantry" crashing against a shield wall confirmed his confidence that the Silver Battalion had made ready for the charge. The odd trees of the forest muted the sound, of course, but he could tell from experience that the blow had not been a heavy one. Arrows and canister had certainly blunted it as well.

So far, the 5th B'mbaado was not involved, which meant the charge had fallen either on Safir's center or left. Rolak hoped she'd had time to deploy the follow-up regiments between herself and Captain Garrett's forces. Even if she hadn't yet, he doubted she'd have too much trouble. Runners had just reported stiffening resistance—in the form of sporadic attacks—against Garrett's landing at the port facilities. He *had* heard horns from there. With any luck at all, most of the enemy was being drawn to those horns even now. Garrett's landing had been the first, most exposed, and by far the largest in apparent size. He had to make the deepest penetration against the largest known enemy concentration and establish the biggest beachhead. He had two full Baalkpan regiments, one Aryaalan regiment, and one fresh, unblooded Maa-in-la regiment to accomplish this, but he also had the most mobile artillery and mortars. Additionally, General Alden's 1st Marines would follow on Garrett's heels and he could call on them if he had to, but supporting him was not their main objective.

Rolak snorted. They'd already discovered one major weakness in the Allied military organization: logistics. At least as far as large-scale expeditionary efforts were concerned. Previously, they'd noticed an annoying disconnect between naval and land forces regarding what equipment and troops should be loaded on what ships and barges, and where those barges should land. A lot of it had to do with preparation and simple sequencing, but the Lemurians (and a few humans) weren't that good at those tasks yet. Particularly on something of this scale. They had a lot of work to do to improve that situation, and hopefully this "live fire exercise" would highlight the most egregious discrepancies. The worst so far today was that the 1st Marines, which were supposed to land here on the right flank, had instead been mistakenly loaded on barges towed behind *Donaghey*—towed behind *Haakar Faask*!

Discovering the error after it was too late to repair had resulted in radical last-minute alterations to the plan. Rolak was glad he hadn't been there when General Alden learned of the foul-up. A few officers had doubtless become privates or seaman's apprentices, but really it was not unexpected. They were all amateurs at this sort of thing. They'd practiced numerous landings and even faced a few hostile ones now, but as Commodore Ellis had said, this was different, and their next landing would be even more different still. In any event, now the Marines would have to double-time nearly three miles behind the—hopefully by then—contiguous beachhead, to reach the point where their real mission would begin. In the meantime, there was that right flank Jim had warned them about, just hanging out there.

There might be nothing beyond it, and if there was, he was confident he could refuse the flank with the forces he had. The entire 9th Aryaal was wrapped around, anchored to the river, deployed to do just that, even if it deprived him of close to a third of his own front. The one good thing was that some of the Maa-ni-lo Cavalry meant for Garrett had already arrived here. He would keep it and use it to warn of any threat gathering on his right.

Grik horns blared almost directly to his front. The naval bombardment had paused while the ships sought to maneuver in the clearing morning light, and it sounded like the horns were coming from the area they'd recently been "pasting." He grinned with the certainty that the guns would resume firing with the same elevation once the ships had rearranged themselves. He glanced at the river and saw that *Dowden* had finally cleared the snag and was working her way a little farther upstream. While he watched, he saw a cart being wheeled into position beside the tent that had been established as his "See-Pee" (what a strange term, if he translated it correctly) and a small group of 'Cat signalmen began stringing wires from the grotesquely heavy "baat-eries" in the cart to the transmitter already inside the tent. Another haggard, filthy crew of signalmen raced up, panting, with their spool of wire unrolling behind them. Still another crew was hoisting a pole with an aerial attached. Good. If all worked properly—he snorted again—the entire Expeditionary Force would not only have hard communication within itself but wireless communications with the ships—and eventually *Big Sal*'s planes.

The sound of battle to the left had faded, but the horns thrummed again. This time there were more.

"Lord General!" Colonel Taa-leen of the 5th B'mbaado spoke as he returned. He'd gone to try and view the action. "The assault against the Silver Battalion has failed."

Rolak nodded. "Did you speak to the Queen Protector?"

"I did, briefly. The enemy came on in 'the same old way,' but they did not break as they were slaughtered." Taa-leen blinked uneasily. "All but a handful were slain, but the Silver sustained heavier than expected losses. Not *heavy*," he hastened to add, "but . . . more than would usually be expected. I personally viewed the Grik corpses heaped before the shield wall and they do look poor. Not starved necessarily, but ragged and lean."

"They have a wider range to forage here than was the case on Singapore," Rolak speculated.

"My assessment as well, Lord General, but the Silver recovered one of their diseased standards. It was the same as some of those taken after the Battle of Singapore."

"So. We knew they were attempting to evacuate that place before we blockaded it. I would presume they took the better troops first, perhaps even before we cut them off.

Some of those may not have been taken all the way to Ceylon, but deposited here instead."

"Indeed. Which makes it likely we face still more of the vermin responsible for the . . . atrocity . . . committed against our homes, General, as well as all Jaava."

Perhaps a dozen horns were sounding now, more stridently than before. They would soon be ready. *Dowden* and *Nakja-Mur* opened fire again, and as Rolak watched, mortar teams prepared their tubes. Case shot shrieked overhead and thunderclaps pealed through the trees. Orders swept up and down the line and the three regiments under Rolak's command, far better prepared than the Silver had been, readied for a much larger test.

"Indeed," Rolak said, "but that only means they know us better—and even their insane youngling minds may comprehend that fleeing will do them no good."

The "Raan-goon" harbor facilities were a dismal wreck by anybody's standards even before *Haakar Faask* and *Donaghey* started in on them. They'd been something once, before the Grik planted their next outposts at Singapore and then Aryaal. Nobody really knew much about how the Grik ultimately expanded behind their frontiers. Ceylon was fully integrated into the "Grik Empire," and evidently so was much of India. It was like they'd stopped there for a while, until it was nearly filled up, before pushing on again. Still, Rangoon had been big once, apparently for quite a while. Now it looked a little like the rats were taking over. At least it had. Most of the strange city was now ablaze.

General Pete Alden hadn't been to the American southwest before, but Grik architecture, at least here, reminded him of a Mexican border town in a western movie. Everything was wood and adobe, though how they kept the adobe from melting under the nearly daily rains was beyond him. Maybe they'd developed some kind of cement? They might mix it with their nasty spit for all he knew. Whatever it was, the adobe didn't burn, but there was plenty of other stuff that would. Cannon fire still rumbled from the ships, but it was mostly ranging longer now, exploding in the jungle or among the crumbling dwellings that probed into it. A few Grik guns still responded—that had been an unpleasant surprise—but the ones that remained seemed intent on shooting at the ships. Grik gunnery had been notoriously poor ever since they revealed their first cannons, and judging by the relatively light shot they were throwing, these were probably some of those early weapons. They might have been left here or offloaded from the partially sunken ship. It didn't matter. As long as they were shooting at the ships, they couldn't do much damage even if they managed to hit one—and the Grik weren't using them against his infantry anymore.

Pete took a huge chew of the yellowish "tobacco" leaves and trotted down off the dock where he'd been observing the action. Greg Garrett's troops had a lot of the crummy city near the docks already, but the 1st Marines were still waiting for him to solidify the link with Queen Maraan's forces upstream. The Marines had a long trot ahead of them on what promised to be a miserably humid day. They could fight a battle, run three miles or so and fight another, but he didn't want them to if it wasn't necessary. Besides, the end-around maneuver might wind up being a lot more than three miles. He joined his troops where they were strung out, resting on the shore under the protection of a high embankment.

"That's it, fellas," he said and spat. "Rest up while you can. One of the most important combat skills a Marine can ever learn."

One of the somewhat dreaded and always poorly trusted me-naaks, or "meanies," charged down among the Marines, sending several of them scattering. It loped right up to Pete and came to a mud-spraying halt. It stood there, glaring insolently with its tightly trussed, saliva-oozing jaws and reptilian eyes. The damn things always reminded him of a cross between a horse-size dog and a crocodile. He looked up and goggled a little to see that the rider was none other than Captain Greg Garrett.

"What the devil are you doing on that monster? I can see it now; when the history of this war gets written, your story'll be like ol' Albert Sidney's, who rode around all day while he was bleeding to death—except in your case, it'll end with you getting ate by your horse! Don't you have more important shit to do?"

Garrett chuckled and patted the animal affectionately. "Gracie's no monster! You'll hurt her feelings. She's kind of sensitive. As for what I'm doing on her . . ." He shook his head and grinned. "I *am* from Tennessee! I've been riding since I was a kid. Shoot, I was in the Navy before I learned to drive a car! Besides, while I was recuperating and getting back in shape playing Devil Dog with you and your boys, I was also hanging around the Manilo Cavalry learning the monkey drill!"

One of the crudely cast Grik cannonballs moaned overhead, then kicked up a geyser of spray about halfway across the river, just short of *Donaghey*. Greg didn't even flinch. Of course, commanding the veteran *Donaghey*, he'd probably had more Grik cannonballs fired at him than anyone else in the Alliance.

"But what are you doing here . . . now? You talked me into letting you command ground troops. Fine. Everybody's done it but you, and I get it. All the higher-up Navy guys need it on their résumé and we'll need you at Ceylon, but your troops are over *there*, and you probably don't need to be making such a target of yourself."

"I could make the same argument about you," Greg warned. "You're our MacArthur—sorry, make that 'Black' Jack Pershing. You're supposed to be moving the chess pieces, not running around like a rifleman." He looked pointedly at the '03 Springfield slung on Pete's shoulder.

Pete rolled his eyes. "Don't start that again. I've got to be with my Marines to evaluate the new tactics. Rolak and the Queen have done this sort of thing more often than I have. They'll do fine. All they have to do is hold. I have to *see* what the enemy does when we change the rules!"

"*I* didn't start it again," Greg reminded Pete. "I came

here to report that my guys and gals have everything under control. The battle line's secure for the moment and we have comm from one end to the other. Your Marines won't be needed here, and you're free to go ranting off on your own. You might want to hurry, though. General Rolak says things are starting to build on his right—like you figured. I don't know if we drew as much down on us here as we'd hoped. Apparently they don't think much more of their port than we do. Rolak thinks they're trying to do unto us what we're planning to do unto them."

"Well . . . why didn't you just *say* so?" Pete demanded, turning to his lounging troops.

"One other thing—may be nothing," Greg said, regaining Pete's attention. "These buggers we've been fighting here are pretty scruffy. Practically skeletons. They fight, but there's not much fight *in* 'em. Rolak and Queen Maraan both report the ones they're up against are skinny, but fit. I don't know what it means, but I thought you should know."

Pete Alden nodded thoughtfully. "Form up!" he bellowed, and the drums began to roll.

"Very much as expected, only somewhat more so," Rolak replied to the signalman who'd requested a status report for Queen Maraan. The signalman ducked back into the tent and the "tele-graaph" key began to clatter. A most remarkable invention, he mused again; instant communication on a battlefield. Throughout his life, signal flags had served well enough, but before this war, his people had never fought battles on such a grand scale. They still used signal flags, but now distance, gunsmoke, and intervening terrain and foliage made them unreliable. He loved the tele-graaph.

The last of the Maa-ni-la Cavalry scouts he'd sent to investigate their flank leaped back over the hastily constructed breastworks. The rider was winded but unharmed, although the me-naak had two of the wickedly barbed Grik crossbow bolts embedded in its right quarter. The scout dismounted, handing his reins to a pair of cavalrymen who'd already returned. With a regretful backward glance at his suffering mount, he raced to stand before Rolak. The me-naak snorted shrilly through its nostrils and tried to smash one of the cavalrymen against its flank with its head when she jerked the first bolt free.

The scout saluted in the Amer-i-caan way he'd been taught, and Rolak returned it.

"Beg to report, sir," he said. "Our troop encountered a few Grik as we set out, but most seemed to be running for the port in response to the earlier horns. We left them alone, as ordered, and found a place where we could spread out a little, beyond the thickest jungle, and observe a large enemy camp. The commander there sent out some scouts of his own, and we tried to kill them all in the woods, but I fear we failed. After a while, horns began sounding from the camp itself—you must have heard them—and they just seemed to suck Grik out of the jungle. I presume, with the isolated nature of this Raan-goon, the enemy has dispersed most of his force to forage for itself. That seems consistent with the fact that we encountered almost nothing in the way of wildlife. In any event, a surprisingly large enemy force has assembled on your right front."

"An excellent report, ah, Corporal," Rolak said, glancing at the stripes on the hem of the trooper's black and yellow kilt. "What is your estimate of the size of this force?"

The corporal blinked uncertainty. "Perhaps two thousands, Lord General. More? It was impossible to tell for sure, and our presence was discovered, interfering with our estimate. They pursued us very near." He paused. "We lost two troopers to their crossbows."

"Very well. Thank you, Corporal. It is not their nature to linger overlong when their prey is in sight. Tend your mount. We might expect their full attention at any moment." He turned. "Colonel Taa-leen, Colonel Grisa, you heard?"

"Indeed," replied both officers. They'd arrived nearly as quickly as the scout.

"Signalman," Rolak called, "acquaint my dear Queen

Maraan that we will likely have visitors shortly. I may call on her Black Battalion of the Six Hundred as a reserve if she has no objection and General Alden does not arrive in time."

"Lord General," the signalman replied, "General Alden and the First Marines have left the port at the double time."

Rolak's response was interrupted by braying, thrumming horns, quite close. An expectant roar thundered in the trees. "Send to *Dowden*," Rolak yelled over the sudden cacophony. "'Concentrate fire two hundred tails—I mean "yaards" forward of our position.'" He took a breath. "Mortar teams, make ready! Archers and artillery will commence firing at my command. Lock shields!"

Several *Hoosh-KAK!* sounds split the incoming tide, and the veterans who'd heard them before called out "Firebombs!" or "Grik-fire!" in two tongues.

"Cover yourselves!" roared Colonel Grisa, and he and Taa-leen attempted to tackle Rolak to the ground and cover him with their own bodies.

Rolak twisted away. "I will stand," he said. "My old hide is not so valuable that I must squirm in the dirt to protect it."

Taa-leen got another grip and roughly pulled him down. "With respect, Lord General," he growled, "your 'old hide' covers the mind that will preserve *our* hides, and mine is quite important to me!"

Rolak was laughing when the first bombs struck.

"Grik-fire" was little more than a clay vessel wrapped in coarse cloth and painted with flammable resin. The contents were a mixture of other things, not necessarily always the same and still a little ill-defined. More resins, mostly. Some kind of tree sap. Maybe some petroleum. The result, however, was an effective incendiary that created an impressive fireball when the jar ruptured on impact and exposed the contents to the flaming wrap. There was no explosive force to speak of, but enough to blow the burning sap in all directions, and the stuff was incredibly hard to put out.

The bombs streamed in, trailing smoke, and erupted

with large mushrooms of roiling flame. One fell directly on an open ammunition chest for the six-pounders, and the combination went up with a dull *fwump* and a towering column of white smoke. Droplets of burning sap spattered the paalkas and they screeched in agony. Another bomb fell in the water and had little effect, but one ruptured in the trees over the shield wall and dozens of Aryaalan troops were burnt to death beneath the descending curtain of fire. Others scrambled to quench themselves either by abandoning their posts and leaping into the river or by rolling in the loamy sand.

Rolak staggered to his feet. "Signalman! Please ask *Dowden* to hurry her barrage! Mortars may commence firing!"

The Allies had done away with their original mortars, basically small bronze Coehorns that launched a copper shell with a powder charge. Now they had "real" mortars, the "drop and pop" kind, as Bernie Sandison called them. They were larger and shaped like an egg, with a finned tube protruding from the rear. They had to be handled with care, but in action all one had to do was drop them down a much-improved mortar tube and they launched themselves with an integral percussion-fired charge. A rod protruding from the nose of each "egg" fired another cap inside and detonated the bomb on impact.

Two dozen mortarmen each removed an egg from a small padded box, gently inserted the rod in the nose, and poised their weapons over the mouths of the tubes. The tubes had already been adjusted for elevation by other mortarmen. There, they awaited the orders of their section commanders. The wait was short. The command to "drop" spread down the line, and with a rippling *paFWOOMP*, two dozen mortar bombs leaped skyward, trailing smoke from their expended launching charge. The resulting stuttering detonations in the jungle didn't sound like much through the overall din, but the screams, and at least one secondary explosion, indicated the range estimate was good.

"No change, no change!" Taa-leen bellowed. "Fire for effect!" Even as the mortars began coughing independently, *Dowden*'s guns sent heavy case shot flying as high overhead as elevation would allow, and the six-pounders positioned at the hasty breastworks bucked backward, sending canister scything through the vines, leaves, and bodies of the Grik front rank, finally visible through the trees.

"Archers must wait for targets," Rolak declared. "It is some denser here than the ground before the Queen. The trees will soak up too many arrows!" Grisa passed the word.

Another salvo of firebombs dropped behind Lemurian lines, but there were only three this time. One wiped out an entire squad hurrying forward from the barge they'd just left, and their screaming antics were horrible to behold. Another fell in the water again, and the third fell close to the command tent but didn't go off. By the look of it, it hadn't even been lit.

"Keep at it! Keep at it!" Rolak chanted aloud. "Punish them! Kill them!"

The jungle pulsed with explosions, filling the air with hideous wails and acrid smoke. A huge fireball vomited into the sky, and after that there was no more Grik-fire.

"We run low on mortar bombs!" Taa-leen observed.

"Send to *Donaghey* that we need more ammunition!" Rolak shouted at the beleaguered signalman.

"I already did. They have no more to send us. Most of our reserve was sent to the left by mistake!"

"Then tell them we need it *here*!"

The light guns spat another load of canister into the smoke-shrouded woods, and then the crews pulled them back so the shield wall could close the gaps where they'd been. With a stunning crash, like the one they'd heard to their left near dawn but much, much louder, the Grik slammed into the interlocked shields in front of Lord General Rolak.

The shield wall bowed inward alarmingly in several places, but nowhere did it break. The front rank merely hunkered down and heaved against the blow, with the second rank pushing against them with its shields. Over their heads, the spearmen of the third rank probed and stabbed at the attackers. Rolak had seen it many times now—the determined wall of people, his people all, now standing and struggling against the vicious jaws and curved talons of purest evil. Individually, hand to hand, Grik warriors had no equal. Braad-furd had once called them "perfect killing machines." "The top of the Darwinian predatory heap." But individually, mind to mind, the Grik simply couldn't cope. They carried wicked swords, but used them poorly. They had crossbows, but often fired them indiscriminately. Some were better than others, of course, and though not up to Allied standards, their gunnery was improving, so they *could* learn. They might even be cultivating specialized elites within the ranks of the Uul. That was an unpleasant thought. But only the Hij, the "elevated ones"—probably naturally elevated, if allowed—could devise and implement a strategy, or even a more involved tactic than "up and at 'em."

But Hij didn't fight in the line. Regardless of their ferocity and physical superiority, the average Grik warrior stood no chance against the skill, discipline, and training of the average Lemurian soldier. The problem was, they never fought "one on one." When given time to think about it, they did seem to understand the principle of "mass" as Captain Reddy taught it, and they knew where and when to apply it. Crossbow bolts streaked by, mostly overhead but in almost continuous sheets. Nearly as continuous were the stretcher bearers carrying wounded to the barges. Corpsmen worked frantically near the beach, in a little muddy recession, but many would have to be carried to the ship for a proper surgeon—Jamie Miller—to look at. Jamie had started out a mere pharmacist's mate on *Walker*, but everyone was filling bigger shoes nowadays.

"Lord General!" cried the signalman, rushing from the tent. "The B'mbaadan Queen asks if we can hold a little longer. She has observed how closely we are engaged, and though she is pressed now as well, she will gladly send the Black Battalion to our aid. Scouts from her left have determined we face the deepest enemy reserves . . ." He paused as one of the signalman's mates joined him, speaking quickly. "Lord General, the first elements of the First Marines are passing behind the Queen's position!"

"Excellent. We would hold regardless, but send my—" A Grik bolt nailed the signalman's helmet to his head and he dropped instantly, his tail quivering. Rolak paused for the slightest instant, then looked at the other "comm-'Cat," staring down at his companion. "Send my appreciation for the Queen's gracious offer, but we will hold. The enemy is gutting himself on our spears." The signalman's mate saluted shakily and dashed for the tent.

"Colonel Taa-leen, your B'mbaadans are heavily engaged, but you have some reserves yet. Grisa does as well, but his are still coming straight from the barges into the fight. They plug holes. Can you move anything behind him?"

A triumphant roar built on the far right and spread across the front. A suddenly unmasked four-gun battery spewed double loads of canister, and the distinctive yellowish smoke drifted back across the shredded landing zone between the battle line and the shore. The roar of battle slowly dwindled, as did the flurry of bolts overhead. Another battery, closer to the center, unleashed its own swath of canister, lunging back until the double-pole trails buried in the loam. The cheering grew.

"Thank you, General," Grisa said, "but that is not necessary! We have repelled them!"

"They will be back," Rolak assured him. "The question is, will they strike the same place again, hoping they have weakened it, or somewhere else, hoping *we* have weakened it?"

"Surely you give them too much credit?" Grisa asked. "I was at Baalkpan, sir."

"I give *most* of them too much credit," Rolak agreed, "but the 'strata-it-gee' at Baalkpan nearly succeeded. I will never be guilty of giving too *little* credit to their ones who design battles."

A troop of six me-naaks loped near, out of the smoke.

One of the yellow-and-black-uniformed riders noticed Rolak and steered the rest of his troop toward the old Lemurian. The me-naaks were clearly restless in this environment of smoke and noise, and though they'd been exposed to cannon fire as often as possible, they still flinched a little when the guns boomed again, bidding the fleeing Grik farewell. They were also drooling buckets, probably due to the smell of so much blood.

"Lieu-ten-aant Saachic, General," announced the trooper, saluting. "Third Maa-ni-lo Caav-alry. I have the honor of informing you that Gener-aal Aal-den and the First Maa-reens will be at your service presently."

Rolak returned the salute. "That is excellent news, Lieutenant. Now, if you might ride back to the general and give him a message for me, I would be most appreciative."

"Of course."

"Tell him if he can manage to arrive and position his troops within the next one, perhaps as much as two hand-spans of the sun, I believe I can promise him exactly the battle—the 'test'—he seeks!"

The Grik did nothing for the next hour, but horns continued sounding in the jungle. All the vegetation except the larger, harder trees in front of the fighting position had been sheared away by the coming and going of the Grik horde, and the canister that had churned all the vines, small trees, and low-hanging branches to mulch. Equally mulched were the countless Grik dead heaped at the base of the breastworks and scattered on the ground as far as the eye could penetrate into the once dense foliage. Many had already been buried by the falling leaves. Visibility was good now, with the sun well up in the midmorning sky. Scattered cottony clouds had begun to form. *Dowden* continued a desultory barrage, a round or two every quarter hour, as if to goad the Grik into remembering and concentrating on this supposedly exposed flank.

Garrett reported that the "city" was secure at last and his cavalry was busy chasing those who had fled toward the mouths of the Irrawaddy. Behind them, Garrett dug in beyond the city with a Baalkpan regiment while the rest of his troops went to bolster his connection with the center line and reinforce Queen Maraan. A few squads still roamed the city, torching anything that would burn. Most important, Pete Alden finally arrived at Rolak's position with eight hundred of the 1st Marines. He was breathing hard, but not exhausted after his slog through the calf-high sand. He'd lost a few Marines to straggling and injuries along the way, but those who made it were ready to fight. Company commanders and NCOs were already deploying the Marines when Pete went to find Rolak.

Rolak saluted him when he appeared at the command post and Pete waved back.

"I could use a drink," Pete said, grinning.

"Water?"

"Not unless it's ship's water, boiled—or maybe mixed with something stronger. The last thing I need right now is the screamers. I still have my canteen, so something stronger would be nice."

"Orderly," Rolak called, "bring chilled beer for the general." He huffed apologetically. "I fear 'chilled' will be a relative term, General Alden."

"Anything below eighty degrees will be plenty refreshing, Lord Rolak. Could you send a few water buckets to my Marines so they can drink and refill their bottles?"

"Of course. Colonel Grisa?"

Grisa called one of his own orderlies to delegate a detail.

Pete gulped the sweet Lemurian beer that was brought to him. "My God, but that hits the spot! War's getting downright civilized around here."

"It was not so 'civilized' a short while ago, I assure you. We held well enough, but it was costly."

Pete nodded grimly. "Sorry about that. You did swell." He shook his head. "Logistics was a goose-screw in a sack. We have to sort that out."

"We must, or those who died here today will have done so for nothing."

"Not nothing. We've already learned a lot. I hope we learn a lot more. Weird fight, though. Going by what Captain Garrett's faced and what you've been facing here, it's almost like we've got two entirely different Grik tribes."

Rolak nodded. "Yes, I 'got the word.' The ones he faced were . . . less healthy, it seems."

"Yeah. You had it tougher. Glad we got here during a lull. You think they'll hit the same place?"

"I am as certain of it as one can be about such things," Rolak replied. "Our scouts, and those attached to the Queen, say they are massing everything that faced us both into a single concerted effort against us here. The fighting was fiercest here, so they must believe us the weakest." The grin that stretched across his teeth was feral. It faded. "I do wish *Salissa*'s planes would arrive and confirm that, however."

"Another hour or so, according to the report I heard from Queen Maraan's command post."

Rolak nodded. "We heard the same. We can hear the planes themselves report, but they cannot yet hear us."

Pete pointed at the aerial. "Not enough antenna, I guess. Too many trees too. Too much interference. The ships can talk to 'em."

"That will have to do."

"Maybe it'll get better when they're closer. It'll be tough coordinating everything through the ships."

Grik horns brayed in the woods, interrupting their conversation. Many horns. More than before, Rolak thought.

Pete finished his beer and wiped his lips. "Here we go again," he said, turning for the front.

"Do you mean to stand in the line?" Rolak asked accusingly.

"Yep. I have to, to see what happens."

"Unfair!" Rolak protested. "You ordered me to stay back and I spent the entire last fight strolling about with nothing to do!"

"That's your job. Normally, it'd be mine too, but I have to see this."

"Then perhaps I 'have to see' it too!"

"Well . . . what if I get knocked off? You know the plan. You can still carry it out."

"Everyone here knows the plan, General Aal-den. But if you *are* 'knocked off,' who else here has my experience in war? Who else would be better to observe the enemy reaction than I?"

Pete shook his head and shifted the sling of his Springfield. "Aww, hell. C'mon!"

The Lemurian "phalanx," as Captain Reddy had helped create it, worked much like its historical predecessors on that other earth. No physical activity ever conceived could possibly be as exhausting as prolonged hand-to-hand combat over a shield wall. The tactic was therefore designed to allow periodic rotation of combatants from the front rank to the rear, where they might manage a little rest until they started forward in the rotation again. Ideally. The trouble was, Grik assaults were usually so relentless and chaotic, there was rarely a "good" time to rotate troops. In this war, the 'Cats had learned to do it by "feel" and fleeting opportunity more than any other way. The system worked after a fashion, but some fought, by necessity, until they were nearly dead from fatigue, and that often resulted in them being completely dead. The fighters in the front ranks relied on the spearmen behind them to give them the break they needed, and woe was he or she who did not learn spearwork well, because in this business, what went around came around . . . literally.

Rotation must have been fairly steady in this fight, Pete thought, looking at the blood-spattered troops. "Okay, fellas," he shouted, his words echoed by NCOs down the length of the line. He always used the term "fellas" inclusively, whether his troops were male or female. Here, with B'mbaadans and Aryaalans predominating, there were still few females in their ranks, although that was changing. It was impossible to ignore the fact that Pete Alden's Marine Corps ran about half and half, and it was composed of volunteers from every "nation" in the Alliance. It was equally clear that even the best-trained, most-conservative Aryaalan regiment would never want to tangle with the Marines. Queen Maraan's Six Hundred were on a par with them, but it also accepted females now. Nobody was really *happy* with that arrangement, least of all Pete and the human destroyermen, but the Baalkpans, Manilos, and various sea folk insisted on it. It was their way. It also worked.

"You've had a tough fight and killed the bastards like proper devils," Pete continued over the growing tumult of the Grik horns as the enemy prepared for its next attack, "but this time we're going to play something new. At my command, the first and second ranks will remain in place. Third and fourth ranks will step to the rear, behind the First Marines!" He waited while the order was relayed. "Execute!"

The two rearward ranks, gore-streaked spears on their shoulders, about-faced and marched through the waiting ranks of Marines. "First Marines! Take positions . . . March!"

The two ranks of Marines that stretched the entire length of the line, except for the most extreme right, stepped forward in near unison, their blue kilts and largely unblemished white leather armor a stark contrast to the troops they'd replaced.

"Load!" Pete roared.

Eight hundred of the new muzzle-loading Baalkpan Arsenal muskets were removed from shoulders and placed butt down on the ground. Almost in unison, each Marine shifted his or her black leather cartridge box around, closer to their front, and proceeded to load their weapons by silent but endlessly practiced detail. Finely woven, almost silk cartridges made from the webs of some kind of long-bodied spider were handled and torn open with sharp teeth—the Alliance still didn't have any real paper—and the gunpowder within was poured down eight hundred 36-inch barrels. The remaining silky stuff at the base of the "service load"—consisting of a .60-caliber lead ball with three roughly quarter-inch balls stacked atop it—was wadded up and the whole thing was seated on top of the charge with a glittering flourish of eight hundred bright ramrods. The weapons were then brought up to an almost precise forty-five degrees, hammers placed on half-cock, and tiny copper caps were pushed onto the nipple-shaped cones at their breeches. Again, with a simultaneity achievable only after long, repetitive drill, nearly every musket landed back on its owner's shoulder.

Pete climbed to the top of the breastworks, looking back at his creation. The Marines were his, of course, but even the various national regiments were "his" in a way. The tactics were Captain Reddy's, but he was the one who, with—now Colonel—Tamatsu Shinya's help, had formed the Armies of the Alliance. Currently, Shinya was still doing the same job in Maa-ni-la. For a moment, oblivious to the growing tide that prepared to thunder down upon it, he took time to admire what he'd achieved. Ostentatiously, he unslung his own M-1903 Springfield, with "S.A. 1—21" stamped prominently near the muzzle, and pulled his sixteen-inch bayonet from its scabbard. The bayonet was dated 1917. Strangely, it suddenly occurred to him that he'd been nine then. Thirteen when his beloved rifle was made. *Odd, the sort of things that go through your mind at times like this.* He shook his head. The Grik tide had been released.

"First Marines! Fix . . . bayonets!"

Weapons came back off the shoulders they'd been resting on, and the twenty-inch, triangular-bladed socket bayonets were jerked from their scabbards. Adding an historical flourish that Captain Reddy had thought of and Pete just loved, every Marine brandished his bayonet with a roar, as if showing it to the enemy. Then, with a satisfying clatter, the wicked weapons were affixed to the muzzles of eight hundred muskets.

There was no Grik-fire this time. It had all apparently been destroyed by the earlier bombardment, but swarms of crossbow bolts filled the air. Pete stepped down, grinning, from the breastworks, and rejoined Rolak, who'd been watching him with interest.

"You are a most unusual creature, General Aal-den," Rolak said. "In some ways you remind me of Cap-i-taan Reddy. Even as I grow to dislike this war, I believe you are learning to enjoy it!"

"God help me, Rolak, I think I do—but not the way you think. I purely do enjoy killin' the literal hell outta those nasty Grik bastards, and I'm proud of the tools we've put together to do it. But you got the Skipper wrong if you think he likes all this. He doesn't, really." Pete paused a moment, thoughtful, while the Grik horde swept down upon them. "Not usually, anyway," he said at last. "It does bring out the best in him, though, doesn't it?" He glanced quickly over the breastworks. It was time. "You may employ your artillery now, General Rolak!"

Firing off the muzzle blast of the next gun in line, one after another, two batteries of five light six-pounders each sprayed canister into the face of the charging mass of Grik. Again the distinctive yellowish-white smoke accompanied the thunderclaps, and through the smoke the roar became mixed with the wails and shrieks of countless wounded. The guns pulled back and the shield wall closed before them once more. With a momentous crash of bodies, weapons, and shields against shields, the Grik slammed into the wall. Again, the wall bowed, but with all the might of the first two ranks, doing nothing but pushing against the enemy, the wall regained its place.

"First rank, First Marines, pre-sent!" Pete bellowed. Youngling Marine drummers, ranged behind the line, relayed the command with a staccato tattoo.

"Fire!"

Four hundred loads of buck and ball slashed into the gaping jaws of the Grik warriors. Through the smoke, a perceptible cloud of downy fuzz from the feathery-furry bodies mingled with the misty red spray from so many simultaneous impacts. The shield wall almost collapsed forward into thin air when the pressure against it abruptly lifted.

"Second rank, First Marines, pre-sent!" Pete called, even as that rank stepped forward to the right and the first rank stepped back to the left and began reloading. Pete waited a few moments to let the first rank get well underway with their task and allow the enemy to press forward once again.

"Fire!" Horizontal jets of flame lit the lingering, choking smoke of the first volley, and again the pressure against the wall fell away. A collective loud, keening moan had replaced the anticipatory roar.

"First rank!" Pete yelled relentlessly. "Present! Independent, fire at will." The drummers altered their cadence. "Commence firing!"

The ensuing shots were almost desultory. A volley would have been wasted, since there was little left to shoot at. A few Marines got to practice their new combined drill, skewering Grik from behind the protection of the shield wall with their bayonets, just like spearmen would do, but then being free to shoot other enemies when none were directly in front of them or within reach. That was the real test Pete had hoped for: the bayonet as a primary weapon and the musket fire just the music before the dance—as well as an added "killer of opportunity" that spearmen could never indulge in with their bows. He'd hoped the initial volleys would provide a psychological effect, but they'd been unable to really evaluate that. The Grik hadn't had time to "break" into Courtney's Grik Rout. A lot did run, but most of the Grik force in front of the shield wall had been eviscerated before it had a chance to make up its mind *what* to do.

"Marvelous! Utterly marvelous!" Rolak chortled, yellowed teeth showing in a genuine, delighted grin. "I *did* enjoy that! We will pursue them now, of course?"

"Yeah. As soon as we kill the enemy wounded in front of us. Even if they are Grik, it ain't decent to let the damn things suffer. Besides, some might still be dangerous."

"Generals!" cried a runner from the command post tent. "The aar-plaanes from *Salissa* Home draw near! They report seeing smoke from the city, and smoke from this fight.

The wing commander, Cap-i-taan Jis-Tikkar, asks how his force might best be employed."

"Tell 'em to bomb the hell out of any large collection of Grik they see southwest of our current position. Try to herd 'em toward the swamplands. I'd also appreciate a look at our far right, northwest along the river, to make sure there's nothing else out there. Mainly, though, advise Captain Tikker that we'll be pushing forward momentarily, so he should watch where he drops his eggs! Oh, and give my respects to Queen Maraan, and tell her we're about to advance. I want the shield wall to stick together as much as possible, just like in the plan."

Tikker yawned hugely. The steady, reliable, workmanlike drone of the Nancy's engine had a lulling effect, and after staying up most of the night going over last-minute details and sorting through maintenance issues with the crew chiefs, he'd had to get up early and meet with the pilots for a final, redundant briefing. *Salissa* hadn't been commissioned into the U.S. Navy; she was still an independent Home, but all her pilots were duly sworn "Navy men," and therefore "Americans." As an "American" now himself, with somewhat unprecedented responsibility, Tikker had finally solved one of the great mysteries of his human clan-mates: their addiction to "coffee." Despite its vile taste, he'd actually become as dependent on the stuff as any American. So had most of his pilots. They'd virtually emptied *Salissa*'s "medical lockers" of coffee the night before. Aahd-mah-raal Keje promised to send across to his other ships for more, but his human officers dipped into their own "stash" so Tikker's fliers would have enough to "get their blood moving" before the mission.

This would be the First Naval Air Wing's maiden combat operation, and the first almost entirely Lemurian and Lemurian-led air operation in all of history. Thirty-two planes would participate. Sixty-four young lives, not to mention endless months of training, preparation, and the very concept of naval aviation on this world, were on the line—on Tikker's shoulders. If he'd felt a little overwhelmed in the predawn hours, that was understandable.

This morning, Tikker commanded "A" flight of the 1st Naval Bomb Squadron, while Mark Leedom led "A" flight of the 1st Naval Pursuit Squadron. Only the names were different. All the planes were identically loaded with one fifty-pound bomb under each wing, and a crate of mortar bombs in front of the observer's stick. Mark's was the lead flight in the lead squadron and Tikker brought up the rear. Not long after takeoff, they'd lost a couple of planes to mechanical problems, but there'd been no issues since then. The planes that had to fall out of the formation had headed back to *Salissa*. The sea was flat and calm, so if they couldn't make it, they would set down and wait for pickup. With most of four squadrons of the blue and white Nancys still in the air ahead of him, Tikker felt a flush of pride and accomplishment at the sight.

The voice tube beside his head whistled.

"What have you got, Cisco?" he shouted into it.

"There's a big fight at Raan-goon," Cisco said. Her voice sounded tinny and remote. Riggs had contrived a set of earphones that sort of worked on Lemurians, so the observer/wireless operators could actually hear signals in flight. "Big fight," she continued. "Yasna-At, with Lieutenant Leedom, says they can see plenty of smoke." Tikker could see the jungle peninsula ahead, the swampy marshland receding in the west, but couldn't see any smoke yet. The overland sky was hazy, and almost the same color smoke would have been. "Commodore Ellis says that we must fly to the north end of the battle. He will place *Dowden* in the river there for a waypoint. Our new orders are to sweep west-southwest from there, and engage any substantial force but one. There is an enemy camp of some sort about a mile from the river, in front of Generals Alden and Rolak. Commodore Ellis says to leave it alone for now, but to save enough munitions and fuel to 'paste' it at his command!"

Tikker wondered what that was about. "Very well. Reply 'Understood. Entire First Bomb Squadron will orbit area and remain at his service.' Inform Lieutenant Leedom he will command all other attack elements and pursue the enemy. Make sure we have confirmation from all ships."

"What the hell is this all about?" Pete growled when a lone Grik warrior stepped forward from the mass that had fallen back in front of the enemy camp the scouts had discovered. He watched in astonishment as the Grik poked its sword through a piece of white cloth and held it high, continuing forward. "No way!" he said, incredulous.

Lord General Rolak was equally shocked. The sounds of battle still seethed on the left, where Queen Maraan's forces were pushing forward, but here, for a moment, except for the occasional shell from *Donaghey* detonating well forward of their position and just beyond the Grik, there was only stunned silence. "If I understand the meaning of such gestures—we have used them among ourselves and the Imperials before—it would seem the Grik Commander would have a parley."

"Well . . . How in God's name can he expect . . . It's not like they ever . . . What makes him think . . . Well, he ain't getting one!" Pete roared. Raising his Springfield, he shot the warrior directly in the snout at a range of about seventy yards. The back of the creature's head erupted crimson clay and one of the warriors behind it squealed and fell when the bullet continued on and struck it in the torso. The Grik with the white rag collapsed instantly.

A strange sound, like an anxious moan, escaped some of the eight hundred to a thousand warriors still blocking the camp, but there was no other reaction. A few moments later, another Grik strode from the mass, again bearing a rag. Perhaps even more disconcerting and . . . well, creepy . . . the frightening creature showed no more hesitation than the last one. Pete swore and raised his rifle again, but Rolak stopped him. "I must confess a most profound, almost morbid curiosity, my friend," he said, "to discover whether they would keep sending them regardless of how many you shoot—but let us see what we shall see."

"Shit, Rolak," Pete grumped, picking up his empty shell

and putting it in his pocket. "What's he going to say? We can't talk to the damn things! Besides, how come they wait until we're fixin' to wipe 'em out before they want to talk?"

"Indeed," agreed Rolak. "But they've never done that before. They could still flee—or attack and die. Indulge me, please. I am interested."

"Well . . . okay." Pete relented and ordered: "Hold fire. Pass it down!" He waited until the order was picked up and began to spread.

They waited expectantly while the lone warrior approached. The creature didn't look like a Hij "officer"—its dress was too utilitarian, too drab. It did have an impressive crest flowing from beneath a hard leather cap, however. Probably an older NCO or something. Unlike the other, this one wasn't armed—besides its natural battery of lethal teeth and claws—and merely held the rag above its head. Finally, a few paces short of Pete and Rolak, who'd moved slightly forward, it hissed and spat something that sounded like a piece of steel slapped against a grinding wheel. Tossing a piece of the heavy Grik parchment on the ground, it turned and stalked off. It was all Pete could do to keep from shooting it in the back.

"Fetch it," he told a Marine nearby, and the 'Cat trotted the few steps and stooped, distastefully retrieving the object, like one might pick up a turd. Returning, he thoughtfully held it so Pete could see it without touching it himself.

"Son of a . . ." Pete snatched the parchment and turned it right side up. "You can read, can't you, Rolak?" he asked in a strange tone.

"I've learned to read *English*," Rolak stressed, ignoring what he knew was not meant as an insult, "fairly well. Quite an accomplishment, considering my years."

Pete held the parchment for him to see.

AMARKON JENRAL>>>

YOU FITE GUD. WE FITE GUD. WE EET YOU IF NOT FORGETED BY SELES-CHAL MUTHUR. YOU NOT

PREY. WE NOT PREY. WE DISKUS TERMS WE JOYN YOU HUNT. STOP SHIP BOMS WE NO FITE.

"Runner!" Pete demanded, as if expecting one to materialize out of nothing, and he scribbled something on the back of the parchment. A young 'Cat Marine raced to his side and he passed the note. "Get that to the CP, PDQ, see?"

The 'Cat saluted. "Aye, aye, Gen-er-aal!"

"What was that? What did you write?" Rolak asked, still stunned.

"Request for *Dowden* to cease firing. Also, those brand-new Naval Aviators'll be swarming around here pretty soon. Might as well find out what the deal is with these guys before our flyboys bomb 'em."

Tikker couldn't believe his eyes. His squadron had been the last to use *Dowden* for a waypoint, and he'd easily caught her flag signal reinforcing the signal they'd received by wireless. Alden was talking with some Grik! When his eight-plane squadron buzzed over the Grik encampment, there'd been some evident confusion on the ground, but there stood two distinct forces—the Marines and a numerically roughly equal mob of Grik warriors staring at one another across a clearing about a hundred tails wide. From his plane, he could see Queen Maraan's regiments proceeding past the "situation" to the south, followed by most of Rolak's troops that had moved from line into column and were picking their way along in the Queen's wake. Basically, all that remained facing this enemy concentration was the Marines, and they were more than a match for it. Tikker had received a final addendum to his orders: if the Marine guns began to fire, he was to bomb the enemy with everything he had. He glanced at his fuel gauge and hoped the standoff wouldn't last long, one way or the other.

Rolak had placed his force under Colonel Grisa and remained with Alden. He couldn't help it. He had to see how this was "sorted out." Grisa would report to Safir Maraan and offer his regiments to her. Now Rolak stood with Pete Alden and a couple of Marines facing what was certainly the most formidable-looking Grik he'd ever seen alive. It was taller than most Grik, something they'd expected after examining dead Hij before, and it was dressed in relatively ornate, if garish, bronze armor over its chest, shins, and forearms. It was armed with one of the sickle-shaped swords favored by its kind, but the weapon remained sheathed and the pommel was well crafted if, again, somewhat grotesque. In contrast to the shining armor, the cape and kilt it wore were a somewhat battered red and black.

The creature called itself "General Arlskgter," and the reason they knew that was because it was accompanied by three other Grik, one of which was stooped with age and not attired as a warrior. That one named itself Hij-Geerki. The very first thing they established was that Hij-Geerki had been liaison to a party of Japanese who'd been sent in search of undisclosed raw materials for the Ceylon war machine. For different reasons, English was the technical language of the Grik and Japanese, and though they couldn't actually converse, Hij-Geerki could understand spoken English and the Japanese technicians had learned to understand some spoken Grik. Both could read the written words. Through a quick series of notes, Pete and Rolak learned that Hij-Geerki understood nearly everything they said and could form a very few words. Mostly, however, he would write English translations of what his master told him to say. In a few short minutes, they'd already confirmed everything Commander Okada had told them about how the Grik and Japanese managed to cooperate.

"Well," Pete said, "let's get on with this. We haven't got all day." He gestured up at the eight aircraft circling the clearing, their droning engines and passing shadows still clearly disconcerting to all the Grik, even their general, who glanced up at the planes each time they flew by, high behind Alden. He gave the impression it was all he could do not to stare at them continuously. "What do you want?"

"Terms," Hij-Geerki wrote again in reply. "My General

Arlskgter and all his Hij and Uul warriors would join you in the hunt."

"Which 'hunt'?" Rolak asked. "What does that mean?"

"The war hunt you wage against the . . . Ghaarrichk'k . . . others of our kind."

"I'll be damned," Pete muttered. "They really *do* call themselves something like 'Grik.' And all this time, the Skipper always thought that was just somebody else's rude name for 'em, kind of like the names we always got for Indian tribes—from other Indians." Rolak looked at him questioningly, but Pete shook his head. "You, Geeky; you mean to tell me your General Alski-gator would just switch sides? That's nuts."

"The wise hunter joins the strongest pack," Hij-Geerki wrote. "It is the same when we wage the war hunt among ourselves. It is true that no Ghaarrichk'k . . . no 'Grik' . . . has ever joined other hunters against Grik before, but the Grik have always been the strongest pack."

When Rolak read this last, his tail went rigid with indignation. "General Alden," he said formally, "I respectfully insist that you must entertain no notion of any . . . alliance"—he spat the word—"with these vermin!"

"Cool your guns, Rolak," he said. "I'm just picking my way through this. You're the one who wanted to talk to 'em. I'm just talking." He looked at Hij-Geerki. "You seem like a smart cookie . . . ah, Grik. What would you have done if Alski-gator was dead?"

"I would have made the same offer," Hij-Geerki wrote in reply. "It was my idea. I am no general, no warrior. I am Hij, but just a . . . procurer of supplies. My general requires that I obey him, so obey him I must while he lives."

"Holy smokes," Pete whispered to Rolak, realization dawning. "Geeky's a *civilian*! I didn't even know they *had* civilians!"

"It would seem they do, after all. It makes sense. We know they must have females, though we've never seen one."

"Yeah, but we're starting to knock on their own door for a change. This might make a big difference when we move on Ceylon." He turned back to Hij-Geerki. "What about the other Grik, the ones around the town, or port? By all reports, they seem like a whole other command. Weaker. Can he make them switch sides too?"

Hij-Geerki spoke with his general before replying. "Why? They are of no use except for fodder. They believed the Celestial Mother would not forsake them and remained overlong near the harbor where there was little food. We foraged and remained strong. Eventually, we came to feed on them with almost no resistance. Do you not now easily drive them like prey yourselves?"

Pete shuddered. He'd begun to suspect something like that. He could almost understand a rebel force, in this situation, separating itself from some Pollyanna leader who couldn't read the writing on the wall, but to then *prey* on former comrades, to eat them like cattle! His skin crawled. The Grik were like Martians or something, totally unlike anything he could imagine, unworthy of existence. When he spoke again, his tone was wooden.

"We've heard your general's terms. Here are mine. He and all his warriors will surrender at discretion, unconditionally, and take whatever I decide he has coming. That's it."

Hij-Geerki was practically wringing his hands. He could barely hold them still enough to write. The general spoke harshly to him and he made some sort of reply that didn't seem to mollify his master. "He will not accept that!" he wrote. "He cannot accept that!"

"Sorry," Pete snarled. "We don't allow cannibals in my Marine Corps. We don't even let 'em in the Army. Besides, if he changes sides once, he'll do it again, and I don't keep copperheads in my shirt pocket!"

Rolak looked at Pete. He knew what was about to happen, and knew it would happen fast. He agreed completely with the decision, but also feared losing an opportunity. "Hij-Geerki," he said quickly, almost interrupting Pete's last words, "you are not a warrior and you make no decisions here, correct?"

Geerki responded with a large, hasty "NO" on his tablet.

"You seem like a sensible creature that does not want to die, yes?"

"YES!"

"Then I suggest you lie down."

Hij-Geerki flung himself to the ground just as Rolak drew his sword and slashed across the throat of one of the Grik guards in one continuous motion. General Arlskgter opened his terrible jaws in a shriek of fury and had his sword half out when Pete fired two shots with his .45 that came so close together it was difficult to distinguish the reports. He still carried standard military ammo, and the empty shells dutifully ejected high and to the right amid the smallest wisp of brown smoke. Both 230-grain copper-jacketed slugs struck within two inches of each other, punching deeply recessed round holes in the general's polished breastplate. At least one bullet must have severed the spine because General Arlskgter crumpled to the ground like a marionette with its strings cut. Both of the Marine guards had driven their long bayonets into the remaining Grik, and it squalled hideously as they twisted their triangular blades and jerked them free.

For just an instant the Grik horde seemed stunned. This whole activity had been beyond their experience from beginning to end, and a little confusion was understandable.

"Come along quickly now, Hij-Geerki," Rolak said. "You will live, but you are *mine*, understand?"

Hij-Geerki croaked something unintelligible, but punctuated it with a definitive nod. Together, the four "delegates" and their new, possibly priceless acquisition scampered back to the Marine lines, just as crossbow bolts began thrumming past. Each of the eight light guns of the 1st Marines fired double canister off the muzzle flash of the closest gun on the right, creating a rolling, booming thunder, punctuated by the shrill screech of projectiles and the horrible screams of the enemy.

"Well," Tikker said, sighing theatrically to himself when he saw the gouts of smoke belch from the Marine line, "I knew it would never last." He shifted his face so he could speak more directly into the voice tube. "'A' flight to form on us," he instructed. "Send 'Apparent failure of "diplomatic" effort. Will proceed with final instructions to "kill them all," unless ordered otherwise. Inform Commodore Ellis we are only a little over half fuel level anyway.' "

"Roger," Cisco replied, again reminding Tikker that someday he'd have to ask why they said that. It was a name, wasn't it? There was a *Mahan* destroyerman in Ordnance named "Roger." Maybe he would know? He banked a little left and pulled back on the stick until his compass indicated north. He'd gain a little altitude, then roll out on a reverse course and align his attack on a north-south orientation. He didn't want to risk hitting any Marines, and he'd still have to be careful not to release too late, or he might drop an egg on the force moving past the target to the south. He glanced around, confirming that the flight was with him—including a stray he'd picked up from "B" flight. He shrugged. There was too much comm traffic as it was, with everybody stepping all over one another. He'd let the pilot's flight leader deal with it later.

Judging that his distance was just about right, he banked hard left and gave it some rudder until his nose started to drop, then he leveled out and pushed the stick forward. Ben Mallory had passed on what he knew of dive-bombing attacks and the information was good, but Nancys were a little different. With their very high wing and considerable engine and radiator drag, one had to be careful with the rudder so as not to release one's bombs into one's own plane. Steadying up, he concentrated on the target below. For once, he didn't check behind him to make sure everyone else had executed the maneuver properly. He was going in hot, and there was nothing he could do about it. Either they had or they hadn't.

The dingy sailcloth tents and rude makeshift shelters grew rapidly in size. The Grik were running in all directions: toward the Marines, away from them, and into the surrounding jungle. Smoke still drifted downwind from the

Marine line, and it even seemed as if some of the enemy were trying to hide in it—from him! That was it. The air attack *was* panicking them! Whether it started the panic or not was unclear, but it was definitely making it worse. A large jumble of Grik gathered near the center of the camp, either for protection or for orders from some leader. Tikker aimed for that.

Their altimeters were always slow, but they were taught to compensate. Judging his altitude, he pulled back on the stick, counted "one, two, three" to adjust for the relatively low angle of attack, and yanked back on the lever attached to two cables that in turn pulled the pins that held the bombs secured to the hardpoints under the wings. It was a ridiculously simple release. Bernie Sandison had actually been a little ashamed of its lack of ingenuity, but it worked every time they tested it, and it worked again now. The Nancy literally leaped upward when the bombs fell away, and Tikker continued climbing, bleeding off the airspeed he'd gained in the dive. Finally, he banked left again and turned to see the show.

His bombs had already gone off, unheard and unfelt. Smoke and debris filled the air around his target and pieces of bodies were beginning to fall back to earth. As he watched, the next plane in line performed an almost identical attack, and this time he witnessed the impressive effects of the fifty-pounders going off. They weren't in the same league with *Amagi*'s ten-inch guns, but they appeared at least equal to *Walker*'s four-inchers. They were far more destructive than the little mortar bombs. He whooped with glee when two plumes of smoke and earth rocketed into the sky a third time, and a fourth. So far, the pilots were being careful not to drop on the exact spot he had. They were trying to saturate the clearing with the heavy explosions and lethal, whizzing fragments of crude cast iron. He'd almost reached the point where he first began his dive when he watched the last ship go in. He was preparing to make another pass, low and slow, so Cisco could hand-drop mortar bombs on the enemy, when he realized the last plane was still barreling in.

Even as he watched, knowing with sick certainty what had happened, he saw the plane lurch upward, apparently dropping its bombs at last, but it was too late. Against a floating target on the open sea, the air crew of the last Nancy might have had a chance, but here . . . there were trees. Even so, miraculously, the plane almost made it, clearing the first trees by the width of a whisker. Tikker had never believed in anything like the human concept of "luck" before he became an aviator. He did now, with good reason, and thought he had it in spades. But he also knew "luck" was a fickle phenomenon. Just when it looked like the Nancy below might actually survive, it clipped a treetop with its fuselage and created a small explosion of leaves. The contact slowed the plane just enough to force it into another treetop, then another. It collided head-on with the fourth tree, the pilot's compartment crumpling under the engine, the wing wrapping around the trunk. The ruptured fuel tank ignited almost instantly with a hungry rush of flame, and the tangled wreckage of the fragile plane tumbled to the jungle floor, leaving a dwindling fire in the treetops and a chalky black pall of smoke.

Tikker blinked rapidly with sadness and irritation; his lips were set in a grim frown. Target fixation. Ben had warned them, and they trained hard to avoid it. They'd even lost a couple of pilots and ships in training, and he'd known it was going to be a problem. He blinked again, and surveyed the field below. Their target had evaporated. The Grik gathered there had either fled or died, and there was no point in wasting the little bombs.

"Cisco," he said, "send to 'A' flight: 'Well done, but let that be a lesson to us all. Never forget it.' " He sighed. " 'This squadron's going home, unless we receive further orders from Commodore Ellis. "B" flight will withhold ordnance for targets of opportunity. That is all.' "

The squadron re-formed and together made a low-level pass over the field. Unheard over the engines, the Marines cheered them; Tikker saw their gestures and the waving banners. Without orders, every ship in the 1st Naval Bomb

Squadron waggled its wings at the 1st Marines. The squadron had done well in its first action, no doubt about it. The outcome of the fight below had been a foregone conclusion, but the squadron had saved a lot of lives. A lot of highly professional and experienced lives. It was a heady moment. Tikker knew their success would have been proclaimed even more exuberantly in the air and on the ground if not for the already dwindling black column of smoke.

The squadron climbed to a thousand feet. That was high enough to see the jungle panorama below and avoid the eruptions of lizard birds and other flying creatures that flushed, panicked, into the sky at their passing. Larger flying things, like nothing he'd ever seen, with half the wingspan of his plane, didn't seem too alarmed and even tried to climb and pace them. Whether they were driven by hunger or curiosity was moot because the Nancys easily outpaced them. The port city, "Raan-goon," still burned, and they flew east, over *Donaghey*, to skirt the smoke and updrafts.

There were wounded on the docks, waiting to be carried out to the ships. There weren't a *lot* of wounded, compared to the depressing throngs he'd seen after other battles, and he supposed they were getting better at this business of war. The battle wasn't over, though, even if it had essentially degenerated into a general chase; it might last many hours more. Whatever it had become, there would be more wounded before it was done. More dead. He hoped this exercise would be worth the price.

CHAPTER 12

Eastern Sea

Walker had averaged eight knots during the last week, a respectable speed given the generally light airs the other ships relied on. Sometimes she sped up, steaming a wide circle around her plodding consorts. Occasionally, she hove to and let the Nancy down into the sea and Reynolds flew. Matt forbade him to fly out of sight, but one of the flights did warn them of a basking mountain fish, several miles farther out than they would have detected it with lookouts. This allowed them to give it a wide berth. Fred Reynolds saw nothing else, no islands or ships at all. If they'd been in the Carolines before, they must have left them behind. Otherwise, the sea was calm, the weather pleasant, and if not for the antiquated sailing steamers they kept company with and the Lemurian heavy crew, it would have been easy for the men aboard USS *Walker* to imagine that they'd somehow returned to the world they'd left behind.

Beginning the third week out of the nameless atoll where the ships refitted after the fight, the sky grew dark and the sea began to dance. A cool wind pushed rolling swells out of the south, and *Walker* started rolling sickeningly, as was her custom. A pod, or herd, of gri-kakka, a form of plesiosaur they'd grown uncomfortably accustomed to, crossed their path and blew among the swells. The creatures veered away and plunged for the depths as the ship's sonar lashed at them. They used the sonar to frighten mountain fish—or "leviathans," as the Imperials called them—away, and it seemed to work extremely well. *Walker*'s crew was glad to learn it worked on gri-kakka too. They'd taken some damage once by just striking a young one.

That night *Walker* ran under running lights and the other ships hoisted lanterns. The wind and sea continued to build, veering out of the southwest. The quartering swells made *Walker*'s crew, particularly the Lemurians, even more miserable as the roll took on a swooping, corkscrewing motion. Even the 'Cats who'd been on the sea all their lives had a hard time with it. Except for the ones who'd made their living on the fishing feluccas, none had ever noticed any except the most severe storms. Riding heavy seas on a Lemurian Home was like doing so on an aircraft carrier. *Walker*'s relatively small and slender round-bottom hull made for a far more boisterous ride. With the dawn came the realization that they were unquestionably in a typhoon, or possibly a Strakka—something even worse that this world's different climate managed to conjure. They'd never experienced a deepwater Strakka before.

Ever eastward they struggled, in the face of the mounting sea. Waves crashed across *Walker*'s narrow bow, inundating the forward four-inch-fifty and pounding against the superstructure beneath the bridge. During her refit, they'd replaced *Walker*'s rectangular pilothouse windows with glass salvaged from *Amagi*, but there hadn't been much to spare. To protect the new glass, as well as the people behind it, plate steel shutters had been cut and installed that could be lowered into place over the windows. The shutters retained only small slits to see through, and all but eliminated visibility, but they had the compass, and soaked lookouts stood watch on the bridgewings. Chack stood watch-on-watch high above in the crow's nest as well. He had the longest experience aboard the old destroyer of any Lemurian, and had probably developed the strongest stomach of any of his farsighted peers. Still, the wildly erratic and exaggerated motion of the crow's nest would have made the post hell for anyone. As the storm built, he was the very last to report visual contact with the lanterns of the other ships.

Even then, they maintained wireless contact with *Achilles*, but her signal grew weaker with every passing hour. The growing distance between the ships wasn't to blame. The problem was that they hadn't been allowed time to install and regulate one of the virtually "Allied standard" 120-volt, 25-kilowatt generators in *Achilles*' engine room when they left Baalkpan. She still relied on one of the portable six-volt wind-driven generators used by Allied sailing ships. The wind had grown much too violent to continue operating it, though, and the batteries were beginning to fade. *Icarus* and *Ulysses* had only lanterns, flags, guns, and rockets to communicate with, and by late afternoon even *Achilles* couldn't see them anymore over the mounting crests of the tortured sea.

"Jeez, this is awful!" protested Frankie Steele through clenched teeth, struggling with the large polished wheel. Water beaded in his beard. Everyone on the bridge had been saturated by windblown rain and spray. "I remember steering *Mahan* through that big Java Sea Strakka on one engine, but I don't think it was this bad."

"If you'll remember," said Matt, "*Walker* only had one engine at the time as well, and I believe you're right. The water's a lot deeper and the swells are more organized, but the troughs are deeper too." He braced himself against his chair, bolted securely to the bulkhead, when the bow shouldered through another high peak and then tilted downward at an alarming angle. With a rushing crash, it pierced the next enormous wave and the sea boomed against the pilothouse. Through the slits in the shutters all Matt could see was a swirling white vortex, and water gushed into the pilothouse over the bridgewing rails, nearly sweeping the lookouts aft and down onto the weather deck. Somehow, they managed to hold on, and climb hand over hand back to their posts as the rush of seawater drained through the bridge strakes. Slowly, reluctantly, the bow came up again and the ship heaved sharply over to port.

Kutas, clinging to the support pole near the chart table, watched the clinometer pass twenty degrees. "A lot deeper," he muttered nervously. "Skipper, the wind's come around out of the northwest, and these waves are getting harder to crawl up at an angle. I recommend we change course to one, two, zero. We might take them harder over the bow, but maybe they won't tump us over!"

Matt hesitated. If they turned away, they might get separated even farther from their consorts. But the Imperial ships couldn't steam forever in these seas. Sooner or later, they'd have to run with the wind. "Very well. Mr. Steele, make your course one, two, zero. Mr. Kutas, please have Mr. Riggs inform *Achilles* of our course change. According to their charts, there shouldn't be anything out there we need to be concerned about running into."

"Aye, aye, Skipper," Steele replied, "making my course one, two, zero."

The Bosun staggered up the stairs aft, and gasping, joined Kutas at the pole.

"What are you doing running around in the rain, Boats?" Matt quipped.

"Oh, just checking on things."

"How's she holding up?" Matt asked.

"Swell," Gray replied breathlessly. He'd pulled the decorative strap on the front of his sopping, battered hat down under his chin to keep from losing it. He didn't add "so far." That might jinx them. On the other hand, maybe just thinking it was bad enough.

"Skipper!" cried Reynolds, who as usual joined the duty roster as talker when he wasn't flying or tending the plane in some way. Right now, the Nancy had been disassembled and secured as well as possible.

"What is it?" Matt demanded.

"Lookout, ah, Chack, says there's a whopper coming in! It just keeps getting bigger! He sounds . . . scared!"

Chack scared? Oh, hell. "Mr. Steele?"

"Almost there," Frankie replied, straining against the wheel.

Matt joined the starboard lookout on the bridgewing. At first he couldn't see anything through the darkness and the blinding spray. Then he heard it. Even over the screeching wind that moaned hideously through the foremast stays and the wireless aerial, over the blower and the groaning hull and thrashing sea, he heard a sound like mounting thunder. What he could see of the horizon beyond the gray-green foam had become as black as night. He looked up. And up. "Oh, Lord," he said. Then he spun. "Sound the collision alarm!"

In spite of the situation, Tabby was actually pleased with herself. This was the worst storm she'd endured yet on *Walker*, but for the first time, she hadn't been transformed into a heaving, retching, practically lifeless wreck. *Must be the 'sponsibility*, she decided. She'd never seen Spanky look even mildly ill when the sea kicked up. He'd been through the aft fireroom just a few moments before, moving carefully along the rail with the motion of the ship. The hull seemed tight, and though brackish water gushed back and forth in the bilge, the ship didn't seem to be taking much on as she worked. At least the hull repairs had been properly handled—of course, they'd had more time on them. The boilers had been a hurry-up affair. She didn't mind. She'd finished the work on number three, and it was roaring away contentedly despite the turmoil outside. She was satisfied.

She glanced around and wrinkled her nose. Just because *she* wasn't sick didn't mean there wasn't a powerful lot of puking going on. She'd been the first Lemurian fireman and had suffered her baptism alone, except for the somewhat disinterested solicitations of the "other" Mice. Now the whole fireroom was full of her people—none of whom had ever endured anything like this. She felt sorry for them, spewing wretchedly on the deck plates, trying to reach the one they'd left open to the bilge as a "puke hole," but she felt slightly superior as well. She *was* superior. She was a *chief*, wasn't she? The others would come along, just as she had, and at least most still seemed able to function.

Suddenly an alarm blared in the compartment that she'd only heard a couple of times in drills. Her spine stiffened and her eyes went wide.

"Everyone! Grab hold of something!" she screamed. "Get away from the boilers and hold on!" She embraced a feed line and clenched her teeth. Something struck the ship like the hand of God. One instant, *Walker* seemed to be climbing a swell like so many others, and the next, the old destroyer was practically on her beam-ends. Deck plates were uprooted and went sliding or tumbling to port, and the air was filled with loosened condensation, followed by a flood of bilgewater . . . and screams. Tabby's feet fell out from under her, and she held on to the heavy pipe for dear life as others in her division did the same, or fell screeching amid the clattering tools and other debris. A few must have fallen against the boilers themselves—suddenly the air smelled of burnt hair and flesh. She watched as one of her water tenders, motionless against the port-side hull, was impaled by a plummeting deck plate that struck her with its sharp, pointed corner. The water tender never made a sound. A thundering vibration added to the din, and whether it was water coursing over the ship or the starboard screw running away, she couldn't tell.

Another sound began that she'd never heard before. It started as a whooshing, drumming hiss, and quickly grew to a pounding rumble, and she knew—*knew*—that water was pouring down at least one stack into the smoke-box uptake! For what might have been only moments but seemed like forever, the ship just hung like that, heaved over, as if trying to decide whether to right herself and struggle on, or roll all the way over and go to sleep at last.

"No!" Tabby screamed. "You NOT give up! You NOT!"

Over and over she shouted, "You NOT! You NOT!" until she no longer knew if she was screaming at the ship, herself, or her weakening arms. Slowly, slowly, the angle grew less extreme. "Pleeeese, ship!" she begged, almost sobbing. "You got too much to do! You got too many who love you!" Almost as if in response to her plea, *Walker* practically lurched upright and her screws bit again. There were more screams when firemen fell into the jumble of iron that slid deckward with them. Then came a terrible roar, and Tabby remembered the water in the uptake. Later, she could never exactly describe the sound she heard when warm seawater coursed down into the number three boiler. Maybe her ears were already shot from all the noise, and her own high-pitched wail. The best she could remember was a "crackling, thundering *BONG*!" before the aft fireroom filled with scalding steam.

CHAPTER 13

North of Tjilatjap (Chill-chaap)

The expedition's first task had been to clear off just enough of *Santa Catalina* to construct a camp for those who'd be remaining, and then hoist their tools and equipment aboard. The heavy work was accomplished with the old ship's own cargo booms and plenty of hard labor by men and dozens of 'Cats, heaving on lines with a high-ratio block-and-tackle. Once there was nothing left on the barges that some monster might eat, they were sent back downriver for more supplies, equipment, and personnel. The ship was an ungodly mess. Her decks were tangled with roots and vines, and some had even gained purchase between the very planks. There were nasty, biting insects, and feces of every imaginable shape, smell, and consistency was smeared all over everything. A large proportion was lizard-bird droppings, but a lot—perhaps most—was from something else, bigger, that dumped turds the size of ostrich eggs. Either whatever left those things rolling around pooped more than anything had a right to or there were a bunch of them.

That first night they camped with a heavy guard. They'd

closed every hatch leading to the interior of the ship they could find, so hopefully all they had to worry about was creatures from the water or shore. They couldn't build an open fire, of course, but Lemurian tinsmiths had come a long way with directional gri-kakka oil lamps, inspired by the shape of Navy battle lanterns. Plenty of these were rigged facing outward. They'd brought a gas-powered generator, based on one of the four-cylinder airplane engines, and intended to eventually power some of *Santa Catalina*'s lights if they weren't too corroded.

Plenty of spooky, ill-defined things crept around in the dark that night, and nobody really got any sleep. Nothing attacked them, though, except bugs, some of which had a painful sting. Unlike the giant "gekkogator" (Isak, of all people, coined the name, in honor of the Philippine geckos he remembered), they were familiar with most of the insects. As for the shadowy creatures that lurked and screeched indignantly just beyond the lights, Chapelle was still inclined to leave things alone as long as things left them alone. The benign visitations probably wouldn't last. Their presence couldn't be welcome, and once they started clearing the ship properly, they were bound to aggravate the various denizens that had claimed it as their home.

With the dawn, the clearing began in earnest. Work parties, flanked by armed Marines, hacked away the vines that seemed to clutch the ship to the shore. One Marine blew a splintered gash in the wooden deck with a musket ball when he saw the first snake any of them, 'Cat or human, had ever seen on this world. In his initial panic, he missed the snake, but then managed to poke it with his bayonet and pitch the writhing thing over the side. It was colored kind of like a coral snake, with purple, orange, and lime green instead of yellow, red, white, and black. Several spectators gathered and watched it try to swim to shore. When it was almost there, something slick-skinned, like a catfish, but blotchy-colored with bulging eyes, rose and gulped it down.

Other parties started clearing the ship's decks, and Major Mallory was having kittens to get a look inside the large crates arranged there. All the containers were about six feet wide by ten feet tall, but some were thirty-five feet long, and others forty. They were darkened with mold, and roots had invaded a few seams, but even after all this time they were largely intact. Even the one Gilbert said he and Commodore Ellis had cracked open to identify the contents didn't appear to have deteriorated appreciably. Having seen crates just like these at Pearl Harbor before he'd shipped for Java, and then again aboard the old *Langley*, Ben knew exactly what was in each one. If it was possible, his excitement only grew. He was like a kid staring at the presents under the tree, waiting for his parents to wake up on Christmas Day.

"Hurry up, fellas," he murmured now and then to the party that was clearing debris from around the once opened crate, not really caring if they heard him or not. When that box and the one just next to it were completely exposed, and the deck around them was clear and swept, leaving only the damp, dark, mushy wood, he finally advanced on the crate with a wrecking bar. Ellis had opened it carefully before, and once he discovered what was inside, he'd closed it up as best he could. To Ben, it looked like the seam had survived okay. If anything, the constant humidity might have swelled the crate even more tightly shut. He hoped so, anyway. He jammed the wrecking bar between the reinforcing planks and then drove it in deeper with a heavy mallet somebody handed him. He soon had a gap, and he worked the iron bar up and down, wrenching the nails from their holes.

He didn't want to damage the crate too much. One way or the other, he'd decided he wasn't leaving this place without its contents, but regardless of how he managed it, the salvage party would eventually have to off-load the crates and so they needed to be structurally sound. He decided to use the same method Ellis had before, simply pry one panel away far enough to form a gap he could squeeze through. Gilbert appeared at his elbow, offering advice on how they'd done it before. He also brought one of the lanterns and set it down protectively beside him, implying that he intended to get a look inside this time as well. With a final, rending *scree!* the left panel released enough to allow one of the 'Cats to hold it aside for them. Mallory knocked a few of the nails out, just as Ellis had done before, and after the slightest, rueful hesitation, allowed Gilbert to precede him into the crate.

"Je-hoshaphat, there she is," came the muffled exclamation. "First time I seen one o' these babies since those stupid Army A-A goons guardin' Cavite shot one down by mistake. Like that *really* looks like a goddamn Zee-ro!" Unable to contain himself any longer, Ben shoved his way through as well. Inside the crate, the air smelled musty, and there was definitely some mildew, but the strong scent of fresh wood, oily steel, aluminum, new rubber, and fresh paint still predominated. Gilbert was flashing the lantern in all directions, almost spastically, creating a kaleidoscope of images. He seemed most intent on surveying the dark reaches of the crate to ensure that no vermin waited to spring at them.

"Here," Ben said, snatching the lantern, "give me that!" He focused the flickering beam on the nearest shape and experienced a sense of almost religious joy. Dark grease still covered a bright steel prop shaft. More surface rust than Ellis had probably seen when he was there had taken hold where the grease was thin, but it wasn't nearly as bad as he'd feared when he saw the ship. For this crate at least, the expedition seemed to have arrived just in time. Any longer and the roots would have opened it to the salt air and the tropical rains and heat; just a few weeks of such exposure would have ruined everything. He knew some of the crates in the hold were actually *in* the water and the submerged aluminum and steel would be corroded beyond repair, but some spare parts would be salvageable. Maybe even more than that. Regardless, a huge grin split his bearded face as he gazed at the shiny Curtiss green color, the flared exhaust stacks, the distinctive intake and lack of nose-mounted guns that confirmed the fuselage as that of a P-40E—the most advanced fighter he'd ever flown—instead of a B, which had still been the more common aircraft.

He knew the P-40s, and especially the Es, had been getting a bad rep out of the Philippines, but they were heavier than the Bs, and the guys there had just received them when the war started and hadn't had time to get used to them. He'd flown both, and knew the E was better. *Hell, Claire Chennault's AVG had been kicking Jap ass with Bs in China, while the poor guys in the Philippines were cracking up more planes trying to take off and land in clouds of dust than they were losing in combat.* He stroked the intake fairing like he might caress a woman's chin. *They just weren't used to them. They'd never had a chance.* He took a piece of chalk out of his pocket that he'd brought to mark the crates and drew something on the plane.

"What's that?" Gilbert asked.

"An M."

"What's it for?"

Ben shrugged. "M for 'Mallory.' M for 'mine.' Whichever. But that's *my* plane!"

Ben didn't open any more crates that day as the clearing proceeded, but he did find a couple that were damaged and he marked them accordingly. Presumably those would need the quickest attention when they were off-loaded to determine if they could be salvaged as planes or parts. By midafternoon, most of the ship's upper works were cleared, and the work party almost wished they'd waited, since the sun beat down on them unmercifully. Chapelle was right, though. Once they went belowdecks, they didn't want to leave any hiding places up top for anything they flushed from below. Hopefully, if they encountered anything and it made it past them, it would see the lack of cover and abandon the ship for the water or the jungle. After all the ruckus and banging around they'd done during the day, they expected something akin to a disturbed hornet's nest when they cracked the hatches, so everyone was prepared for anything when the first party entered the superstructure.

To their surprise, nothing flushed out of the pilothouse, radio shack, or the officers' quarters but a few of the "lizard bats" Gilbert had told them to expect. The interior furnishings were considerably more deteriorated than when he'd been there before, but as they cleared away the rubbish and filth, they discovered a number of useful items. They'd taken some long guns with them after their first visit, mostly civilian models, but all worthwhile specimens for Bernie Sandison's guys to look at for ideas. This time they discovered a few handguns in drawers or other places that were in various stages of preservation. There was an old Mauser that something had dropped a turd right on top of and Chapelle was tempted to just throw it over the side. It was so badly corroded, he doubted it could even be disassembled. Laney found a pitted but serviceable 1911 Colt between a pair of rotting mattresses and Chapelle said he could keep it. The real prize, from a technical, and perhaps sentimental perspective, was a nickel-plated single-action Colt "Frontier Six Shooter," in .44-40 caliber, that they found wrapped in oilcloth inside what was probably the captain's desk. Chapelle figured it would make a good pattern for simple revolvers they could make at Baalkpan, as well as a fitting gift for Captain Reddy. The Skipper was a Texan, after all.

The ship's radio equipment was all badly corroded, but some of the components were probably salvageable. Riggs and Rodriguez would be happy just to get their hands on the resistors and capacitors. Even Bakelite knobs and insulators would be welcome. A work party entered a large compartment in the aft superstructure, just at deck level, that Gilbert said they'd never explored during their brief prior visit. Chapelle was summoned and Mallory joined him in what appeared to be a dining room or lounge of some sort. As a freighter, *Santa Catalina* would have had at least limited accommodations for passengers. With her cargo of aircraft, she'd probably been transporting air crews, and possibly ground crews, for the planes. The earlier expedition had been unable to even speculate upon the fate of those people or the crew of the ship. The presence of firearms, still locked in a cabinet, argued that not only had no one ever made it off the ship, but they hadn't even known they were in danger before "something" got them. Now a little better explanation emerged.

"Say," Russ said, looking around the ruined lounge, "that solves one mystery, anyway."

In the center of the compartment, partially concealed beneath overturned chairs, rotting rugs, and the detritus of marauding denizens, were a number of short, still vaguely olive-drab crates. A 'Cat kicked one open; inside was nothing but a heap of crinkled brown wax paper.

"Tommy gun boxes," Ben observed. "Ten each. And there's four crates that size. That's about right. These other boxes had ammo and twenty round sticks in 'em."

"So they left," Russ said. "Well armed. No wonder they left the civvy stuff. You know? I bet those poor guys pulled in here, ship taking water, and figured their navigation was off. They might've thought they missed Tjilatjap somehow and went up some other river. Maybe they set out to reach where they thought it was overland and... just didn't find it."

Ben gestured around. "It doesn't look like they came back, so either they found someplace better to hole up, or something *did* get them." He sighed. "Either way, at least they weren't helpless!"

"Yeah," Russ agreed. "Somehow that makes me feel better too. Say, I wonder if there's any more of those tommy gun boxes around. If they were freighting them into Java to fight the Japs, I bet they would've had more than four crates!"

By the end of the day, the ship's upper works and most of her superstructure had been cleared away and Chapelle thought the *Santa Catalina* looked like a new ship. Well, not a *new* ship, of course, but certainly a *different* one. She was utterly hideous with rust and most of her deck was already badly rotted, but she did look like a ship again instead of just a bump in the jungle. They'd exhumed several machine guns, a five-inch dual-purpose, and a three-inch antiaircraft gun, but all had been disabled, probably by the crew before they left. The cannon's breechblocks were missing and the bolts had been removed from the machine guns. Maybe the missing parts were hidden aboard, but it didn't really matter. All the guns were badly corroded.

Gilbert, Isak, and Laney had poked their heads below during the day, accompanied by a heavy guard. Much remained as it had been when Gilbert was there before. The forward hold was a little more flooded and the aft hold was full to the outside water level. The engine room had more water in the bilge, but nothing serious seemed submerged. The fireroom was still full up to the bottom of the boilers. The entire salvage crew moved into the now cleared but still moldy and reeking lounge and the hallway beyond, except for two squad-size guards left outside to provide security for their generators, pumps, and other heavy equipment. It seemed like a good idea. Since all the internal hatches closed, nothing could get to them from below, and they should have plenty of warning if anything tried to crawl aboard. With nearly everyone together as the sun began to set, Chapelle decided it was a good time to determine their next course of action.

They'd arrived prepared for three possibilities. The one Mallory favored at first hadn't involved any restorative work to the ship itself, beyond possibly getting her cargo cranes operating again. They were steam-powered, and despite the flooding it looked like they could probably return the boilers to their duty. He'd envisioned using most of *Tolson*'s crew to clear an airstrip in the jungle and simply setting the crates over the side, assembling the planes, and flying them out. There were several logistical problems with that plan, not least of which being that he was the only one who knew how to fly a P-40. The other pilots he'd brought along would require extensive training just to get one of the hot ships off the ground. They'd also discovered that, of the twenty-eight planes aboard *Santa Catalina*, only twelve of the crates were actually in the water. It depended a lot on which ones they were—for example, if they were all fuselage or all wing crates, that was twelve planes that were almost surely write-offs to start with. If they were evenly distributed, that could mean only six were ruined. Then there were the extra engine crates, the tires, spare propellers and drop tanks. . . . There was just too much to leave behind, even if all his pilots could fly. Best case, they'd probably get four planes out and flown to Baalkpan, and then have to ferry the pilots all the way back to Chill-chaap. Even if they managed to salvage only sixteen planes, the process might take months. The final coup de grâce was administered to that plan when Ben went ashore and inspected the ground.

"What's the deal?" Chapelle asked.

"There's no way, that's what the deal is. Look, even if the ground was flat enough—which it's not—and even if we could clear enough of the jungle—which I don't think we can—the dirt here will never make an airstrip. Even if we had heavy equipment, bulldozers, rollers, you name it, there's nothing to pack down but a billion years of rotten loam. Even if you could pack it down hard enough to get a plane off, it would rut the stuff up so bad you'd have to start all over for the next one."

"So basically that's out?"

"Afraid so," Ben replied. "The only interesting thing we found was a bunch of crunched-up 'Cat bones with a few weapons lying around." He looked at Gilbert. "Didn't you fellas turn Rasik-Alcas loose near here?" Gilbert nodded. "Well, it doesn't look like he made it very far."

"A shockin' tragidee," Gilbert said matter-of-factly. "An' he was such a *nice* fella too. I s'pect ol' Rolak an' Queen Maraan'll be plumb heartbroke ta learn o' his dee-mise."

Nearly everyone looked at Gilbert. Most had never suspected the "mouse" was capable of such . . . profound sarcasm. He returned their stares with raised eyebrows. "Hey," he said, "he was alive an' happy as a clam last time I seen him. What's his name, Koratin, put him ashore with food an' weapons. He didn't kill-eem either."

"Well . . . anyway," Chapelle continued, "that leaves us with Plan B. We off-load the crates onto barges and float them downriver. You say they're about four tons apiece? We should be able to put two crates, a complete plane, aboard *Tolson*, and take it to Baalkpan. Certainly not my first choice either because of the time involved, not to mention I'm not positive we can even hoist them aboard. The heaviest thing we've ever lifted is cannons. The crates weigh a little over half again as much. Then there's the trim to consider. The ship'll be top-heavy as hell."

"Yeah. I'm not keen on that one for a lot of reasons," Mallory agreed. "It might be quicker than building an airstrip and flying them out two or three or four at a time, but it's even more dangerous to a lot more people."

"So that pretty much leaves us with Plan C," Chapelle said, looking speculatively around the compartment at the others present, mostly 'Cats. They had the manpower and the knowledge to do the job. Most of those present had been involved in salvaging *Walker*, and there were a lot more workers still with the squadron waiting to come upriver. But it would be dangerous. His gaze settled on the Mice and Laney. It would be up to them, and Lieutenant Monk when he arrived, to figure out if it was mechanically feasible. "We refloat the ship and steam the whole damn thing the hell out of here."

That night the "natives" grew restless. They'd been restless the night before, but hadn't been prepared to do anything about it. The weird creatures with glowing things had slain the Great Mother, after all, so surely they were stronger than they appeared. The death of the Great Mother frightened them, but stirred no desire for revenge; another female would eventually rise to take her place out of necessity. None ever aspired to, for those that bred grew to such proportions they could never leave the water again except to lay eggs. Besides, she couldn't help but eat her young just as readily as any other predator, so her social life was inevitably somewhat limited.

No, the natives were not particularly angry, though the strangers had disturbed their repose. But during the day, while they swam the shallows, hunting mud-grubbers, walking birds, bugs, and small shore creatures, the visitors didn't go away. The natives assumed they would. Some were old enough to remember the strangers that had brought the Warren to this place. They had looked much like some of those now here and *they* had gone away. Others that came later went away as well. It was expected that these would also leave. Instead, in a single day these had completely remodeled their cozy home! They'd destroyed much long and careful labor; the redirection of vines and limbs that had ultimately formed the lush, comfortable, life-sustaining canopy that allowed the natives to move about upon the surface of their Warren even while the moisture-sucking orb traversed the empty sky. That *did* anger them, and collectively they decided they must *make* these strangers go. Or destroy them. Besides, perhaps they tasted good.

~

Moe heard something. Kind of a *slurp-thump* in the gloom. None of the other guards nearby seemed to have noticed, but then they hadn't spent their entire lives listening to the dark, straining to hear things that would eat them. They were good warriors, he knew that. Show them something to fight and they would do well. But they were often far too "civilized" to notice things on their own. He heard the sound again and tensed, more firmly grasping the musket he'd been given. He liked the musket for the dark. It didn't reload much faster than his heavy crossbow, but the wicked bayonet on the end might be quite handy. He strained his ears and heard more *slurp-thump*s in quick succession. Numerous . . . things were coming aboard, and they weren't coming to stare. The sounds the night before had possessed a tentative, skittish quality. These were deliberately stealthy, purposeful. He knew the difference well. One was the sound of uncertainty, fear. The sound of prey. This was the sound of a predator.

Quietly, he hissed, drawing the attention of the other guards. "Show no fear. Move slow, but not scared-like. Stand-to careful."

Lieutenant Bekiaa-Sab-At nodded and motioned for the others to rise. The guard here consisted of 2nd Squad, with six Marines—not counting Moe and herself. They were basically protecting the doorway to the lounge, while 4th Squad was forward, guarding the equipment just aft of the fo'c'sle. "Bayonets fixed?" she whispered. "Very well. Slowly bring your cartridge boxes around to the front. You two"—she gestured at a couple of Marines—"pick up a couple of lanterns, but don't point them aft until I give the word. Also, no one is to fire without orders. Understood?"

There were nods, and the Marines hefted the lanterns almost casually. Bekiaa noted that one was shaking just a little. "Mr. . . . ah, Moe?" she asked. No one knew what Moe's real name was—least of all Moe. Before Silva started calling him that, he'd simply been known as "the Hunter."

Moe nodded.

"Now!" Bekiaa said.

The Marines pointed the directional lanterns aft, and the first thing Bekiaa saw was a swarm of bright yellow eyes that not only reflected the light but almost seemed to intensify it. There was a collective shriek that sounded like the big circular saw at the Baalkpan shipyard hitting a knot, and slim, webbed, almost grotesquely clawed hands moved to protect the brilliant eyes. The whole aft part of the ship was working with the things! She couldn't see much, but they were shaped like a cross between the huge monster they'd killed the day before and some kind of furless, slimy-skinned Grik! They weren't as large as Grik—they didn't seem quite as big as she was—but they'd gathered with sufficient stealth that clearly even Moe hadn't caught on for a while.

"What do we do, Lieuten-aant?" a Marine nervously asked.

"Hold your fire!" The things had recoiled from the light and for the moment just stood there, blinking huge eyelids. Her own vision was clearing a little. The sudden glare of the lanterns and the even brighter yellow orbs had left afterimages swimming through her sight. Like Grik, she concluded, but not. Webbed feet and hands; a longer, slimmer tail with something like a fin down its back. Their coloring was dark, with lighter splotches, and they weren't as heavily muscled as Grik. Their handclaws were even longer, as she'd first observed, but their teeth not as wicked.

"What are we going to do?" the Marine demanded again.

"I don't know!" Bekiaa almost shouted. The creatures stirred at her harsh voice, but didn't advance.

"I think, of a sudden, they not know either," Moe said.

Bekiaa took a deep breath and advanced a single step. "Hello," she said, hoping her voice was firm but nonthreatening. The creatures babbled excitedly among themselves in a croaking, grunting gibberish, punctuated with high-pitched exclamations.

"Maker!" Bekiaa hissed. "I wish Mister Braad-furd was here!"

The door behind them opened suddenly, and Dean Laney came out, groggy eyed, already fumbling with his belt. Apparently he'd been awakened by a call of nature. Noticing that the guard was all silent and standing, he looked aft at the scene illuminated by the lantern. "Jumpin' Jesus!" he practically squealed as he pulled his "new" .45 from his pocket.

"No, Laay-nee!" Bekiaa yelled.

"Help!" Laney screeched over his shoulder, at the lounge. "There's Grik-toads takin' over the ship!"

"No!" Bekiaa screamed again, just as Laney began firing as fast as he could pull the trigger.

Lieutenant Bekiaa-Sab-At was a veteran of fierce fighting; she had to be to have become a Marine officer. She'd never *led* before, however, beyond an NCO level. She'd never been "in charge." Still, she knew Captain Chapelle would back her up regardless of her decision, and she couldn't possibly screw things up any worse than Laney had just done. Over the next eternally long split seconds, she contemplated several alternatives. With Laney's shots, several of the creatures fell writhing on the deck and quite a few others simply leaped over the side in panic. Most seemed stunned. A few crouched and advanced purposefully, either armed just with their amazingly long, curved claws or clutching a stone or jagged piece of bone.

Feeling the heft of the musket in her hands, she was sorely tempted to shoot Laney down, or at least bayonet him . . . a little. She'd established that the creatures could communicate among themselves, and she might have been able to make some kind of nonviolent contact with them. If they saw her kill or wound the one who'd harmed some of them, the . . . opportunity . . . she'd sensed might be restored. That was a serious gamble. It was obvious the creatures had come to kill them. Only discovery and the bright lights had given them pause. Maybe a hasty defensive formation, strengthened by the others as they awakened and emerged from the lounge, would work? Perhaps the creatures would respect the threat and the reluctance to harm more of them implied by that? Impossible. That would leave the work group backed up against the superstructure with dwindling options. There was no telling how many of the things there were, how many more might come, the longer this confrontation lasted. If they could climb the hull—how did they do *that*?—they could climb amidships too, and drop on them from above.

A ragged volley from forward cinched her decision. Mere seconds after Laney's shots, they were coming over the bow as well. It no longer really mattered what difference Laney's shots had made, if any. The expedition to recover *Santa Catalina* now had an enemy all its own.

"Marines!" she shouted. "Pre-sent! Take care not to hit the crates," she reminded them. The first attackers, still visible in the light of the lanterns that had hastily been set on the deck, were only a few strides away. "Fire!" Tongues of flame stabbed out from the muskets and the building charge shattered under the onslaught of eight loads of "buck and ball" and a sudden cloud of choking smoke. Bodies flopped on the deck and writhed and thudded with spastic, distinct, fishlike sounds. An eerie groan swept through the attackers and more splashes were heard as others abandoned the fight. "Mister Laay-nee, get back inside," Bekiaa ordered. "No one is to come out in ones and twos. They must form squads of at least six or more and come out together. Everyone at once would be nice. Send squads to relieve the forward guard as well. We cannot let them inside." Forgetting Laney, she turned back to the front.

"Reload!"

"What the hell's going on out there?" Chapelle demanded when Laney staggered, wide-eyed, back into the lounge. Lanterns were being lit and Marines and Navy salvage workers were snatching weapons and clambering for the door.

"Monsters!" Laney declared. "Slimy, toadlike, Grik-lookin' bastards! There must be thousands of 'em!" They heard muffled firing from forward. "Oh, yeah, that 'Cat Marine said to send help to the other guards. They're attackin' all over the ship!" Amazingly, the big man seemed close to panic. "God a'mighty, all I wanted was a whiz over the side!"

Isak and Gilbert appeared, grimly holding two of the long, heavy Krags they always bitched about, and Ben had his pistol and an '03 Springfield.

"You, Gilbert, go forward with Jannik-Fas and two squads of Marines," Russ said. "They may need your help with a repeating rifle." Another volley crashed outside, punctuated by weird cries. "Isak, you come with me and the rest of the Marines."

"What about me?" Ben asked angrily.

"You stay out of it, hear? This whole trip's for nothing if you get yourself killed! Know anybody else that can fly a P-40? You stay back with the rest of the Navy 'Cats. Send a runner forward with Gilbert. You'll have to send reserves wherever they're needed."

"Goddamn it, Russ!"

"Just do as you're told, flyboy." Chapelle grinned. "Everybody knows you got plenty of guts. You can break your neck later in an airplane, and it's none of my business. Right now you're my responsibility!" He looked around. There were about seventeen with him, not counting Isak and Laney. Laney had an '03 now, bayonet fixed. "Let's go!"

They poured out the door yelling like fiends, just as Bekiaa, Moe, and the four remaining outside Marines charged, bloody bayonets lowered. Russ and his reinforcements flowed around her, firing independently as soon as their front was clear. Russ immediately saw that there weren't "thousands" of the bizarre creatures, as Laney said, but there were more than a hundred. Quite a few lay dead, and a steady trickle of the remainder was jumping over the side, but a cohesive mass was still fighting determinedly, even in the face of their assault. If they were similar to Grik in other ways, they apparently didn't panic en masse.

Russ fired his Springfield, careful of his shots in the dark with the precious ammunition. One of the creatures he'd thought was dead suddenly latched onto his foot with a long, sticky tongue, and he shook his leg violently as a primal revulsion coursed through him. He stabbed down with his bayonet, pinning the thing's head to the deck, and finally managed to pry his foot free.

"Watch out for their damn tongues!" he warned, perhaps a little shrilly. "They're just like the one that big monster had!"

"EEEEWWWWWW!" squealed Isak, as he started jumping in circles. He'd stepped on an entirely dead tongue that had glued his shoe to the deck.

Laney shoved him forward, out of his shoe and back

into the press. "This ain't no time for ballerina tryouts, you nitwit!" he growled. Apparently he'd gotten over his own initial shock.

The weight of the attack, and possibly the unexpected violence and remorselessness of it all, not to mention the now steady hail of bullets that shredded bodies far beyond the natives' ability to inflict any harm, backed the dwindling horde of slimy creatures up onto the fantail. They continued to resist, slashing at bayonets with their unnaturally long handclaws with an almost metallic *shkink* sound, but the steady fire and the bristling wall of bayonets kept those foreclaws from reaching much flesh. Russ did see one of the creatures dart its tongue out and snatch a musket right from the hands of a Marine—and then drive the bayonet through its own head when the tongue retracted. It was probably the most bizarre thing he'd ever seen, and he imagined the macabre humor of the image would stay with him the rest of his days.

From within the milling mass, a thrumming bellow arose, like the steady roar of a thousand frogs. The creatures fighting on the fantail seemed to pay it no heed, but suddenly there was firing from the direction of the lounge again! Behind them! Chapelle risked a glance, and there was Ben Mallory with about twenty Navy 'Cats armed with muskets, shooting at more of the monsters trying to clear the rail.

"Son of a bitch!" Russ murmured. "They sucked us in and tried to *flank* us!" He raised his voice. "Bekiaa, keep up the pressure! We got company!"

Lieutenant Bekiaa also risked a glance. "We will. Take that damn Laay-nee and a couple Marines. We can spare them here, but those things must not get between us!"

Russ pushed another stripper clip full of .30-06 shells into his rifle's magazine. The clip fell away and he closed the bolt. "Yeah," he said. "C'mon, Laney!"

Together with two lightly wounded Marines, reloading as they ran, Russ and Laney sprinted around the wide cargo hatch and the big crates cradled upon it. Yellow eyes peeked over the rail in front of him and Russ fired low, between them. The eyes disappeared. As he neared, Russ saw that Ben and his reserves were doing essentially the same thing. Few of the creatures were reaching the deck, and those that did died almost instantly. Ben was firing carefully, aiming his pistol with every round, each shot pitching one of the creatures backward as soon as it showed itself.

"I thought I told you to stay out of it!" Russ said breathlessly.

"I did stay out of it," Ben replied. "As long as possible. I decided I was perfectly happy to let you deal with these nasty frog-lizards, or whatever the hell they are." He fired again. "It *isn't* possible now. Sneaky bastards tried to come up from below! They *undogged* the hatches, Russ! I've got some guys watching them now, but it came as a hell of a surprise. I also sent half the reserves forward when I saw what they were trying to pull back here." He shook his head. "A hell of a thing. They aren't running either, not like Grik, and they don't really even have weapons. God help us if the Grik ever learn to fight like this!"

"God help us tonight!" Russ replied.

Ben shook his head. "They're about done, I think. Their scheme didn't work, and isn't going to. If they're as smart as I'm afraid they are, they'll figure that out pretty quick. Back here, we're just killing them."

Ben was right. A few moments later, the thrumming roar sounded again from aft, followed by another one forward. No more heads appeared over the bulwarks, and toward the fantail they heard almost continuous splashes as the creatures there suddenly jumped over the side. Ben dropped the magazine out of his Colt and pushed down on the remaining cartridges with his thumb. Taking a few loose rounds from his pocket, he refilled the magazine and shoved it back into the pistol. Only his slightly trembling fingers betrayed the fact that he'd been nervous at all. Flipping the thumb safety up, he dropped the pistol back in its holster. "It was a tough fight, Maw, but we won," he said softly.

Bekiaa, Isak, and Bekiaa's remaining Marines slowly, carefully, worked their way back across the corpse-strewn deck. Only now, in the light of more lanterns, could Russ see that nearly all of them were at least lightly wounded. *God*, he thought, *I hope those damn things' claws aren't poisonous!*

"Double the guard for the remainder of the night," Russ said. "No wounded, though. If you even got a scratch, get it looked at now. Pass the word." He sighed. "First priority tomorrow is getting the generator up and running; power every bulb on this bucket we can get to light up! We need to send a message to *Tolson* too. Tell them we need reinforcements and the rest of our salvage crew. . . ." He paused. "But what if those slimy devils gang up on the barges? Hell. Lieutenant Monk'll be in charge of the next bunch. He'll have to make sure they're ready for anything, that's all."

"What about the wounded, Cap-i-taan Chaapelle?" Bekiaa asked.

"I already said I want them looked at," Russ repeated tiredly.

"No, I mean the 'enemy' wounded."

"Maybe somebody ought'a throw some water on 'em," Gilbert said, looking at the half dozen "frog-lizards" gasping in the meager shade offered by one of the crates. "They're gonna dry out like a smushed toad in the road."

Isak shrugged. "Let 'em. Nasty bastards!" Isak was missing a patch from his scruffy beard on the left side of his face, courtesy of one of the sticky tongues the night before. He also had a bandage around his left hand where a couple of claws had "barely" touched him. He hadn't even felt the "scratch," but it nearly severed two of the tendons in his hand. A little polta paste and the company corpsman, or "corpscat"—whatever—had absolutely, positively assured him he'd be okay. Maybe. Twenty-odd Marines had worse injuries, and three had died. Two of the dead would be burnt in the Lemurian way. One would be buried, the "Navy" way, per his dying wish. All their names would be added to the growing tablet monument on the parade ground in Baalkpan. The dead frog-lizards had been thrown over the side.

"What're you two doin' here?" Laney snarled. "I been lookin' all over for ya. We gotta raise steam today and check for leaks."

"You ain't my boss no more, Laney," Isak declared. "Lieutenant Monk's over all of us. Far as I'm concerned, until he gets here—today, I hope—we're on 'official terms' only. I don't even gotta talk to you 'cept in the line o' dooty."

"This *is* duty, you moron. Cap'n Chapelle's orders. 'Sides, we're all still snipes, and I'm King Snipe . . . unless you want to strike for the job."

Isak took a step back. Laney probably had a hundred pounds on him. "I ain't goin' down there where them tongue-grabbin' buggers can get me," he insisted. He held up his hand. "And besides, my best flipper's wounded."

"Since when are you left-handed? Don't worry about it. A squad o' Marines has already been below, checking stuff out." He grinned savagely. "Found some more crates of them tommy guns too. Anyway, all the frog-lizards is gone—and there weren't none in the fireroom anyway."

They heard a splash near the "prisoners" and turned to see that someone else had had the same idea as Gilbert. Chapelle, Bekiaa, Jannik, Moe, and Sammy were standing near the dripping prisoners. Mallory was there too, but keeping his distance. Probably under orders. He had his pistol out, though.

"Oh, well," Isak sighed. "Since I ain't gonna get to watch them bastards desiccate, I might as well get some work done."

"Now what?" Bekiaa asked.

"You said you got the 'feeling' you might have communicated with them last night. Somehow. What made you think that?"

"I don't know if I 'thought' it, really," Bekiaa replied.

Her tail twitched in irritation, but from her blinks Chapelle knew she was irritated with herself. "Whatever it was, the feeling was gone as soon as Laay-nee started shooting."

"Shooting make no difference," Moe said. "They come to kill, not talk. No can talk. They come all over ship. Even we talk to these"—he indicated the area aft where his group had fought—"we not talk to others . . . ah . . . for-ord."

"He's right," Chapelle said. "Maybe you startled them, or even got the group aft wondering a little, but they hit the guards forward at the same time. One way or another, the fight was on. There was nothing you could have done. They *did* come to kill us." He paused, looking at the creatures. The dark color he'd noticed the night before was a brownish purple and the light was a yellowish orange. Weird, but probably well suited to the dingy water they lived in. They wore no clothes and had no implements, no ornaments of any kind. There was no physical evidence that they harbored any intelligence whatsoever. But last night they'd employed what could have been a damned effective tactic, and their "operation" had been well coordinated. "Throw some more water on them," he said, and when it was done, he watched the creatures' reactions closely. Four of the six didn't seem badly injured, and they continued staring at him with their weird, almost fluorescent eyes, but it seemed to him that the water did give them some relief. They weren't gasping as much, anyway.

"I wonder," Russ said quietly. There were still a few dead monsters on the fo'c'sle that hadn't been dumped yet. He called for one. When it arrived, carried between two disgust-blinking Marines, he had them lay it down in front of the prisoners. They showed no reaction, but of course there were several weapons pointed at them. "Jannik," Russ said, "I want you to poke your sword in that thing's tongue and make it flop around. Make it look like it's striking."

Jannik looked at him and blinked, but then did as he was told.

"Ben, shoot it in the head."

For a moment, Mallory didn't think he'd heard right, then he grinned. As soon as Jannik stepped back, he blasted away one of the still dully glowing eyes. The report of the pistol and what it did to the corpse caused the creatures to flinch, but that was all.

"Now, Jannik, grab its arm and make like it's clawing the deck." He did so, understanding beginning to dawn. Again, after he'd done it for a moment, Russ had Ben shoot it again, nearly blowing the dead skull apart this time.

Taking a breath, Russ pulled his own pistol out and pointed it at the creatures. He took a couple of steps forward, within easy range of their tongues, and squatted down to face them.

"Are you nuts?" Ben exclaimed, pointing his Colt, ready to fire if any of them even twitched.

"I think I know what I'm doing," Russ said. Still staring into the closest huge yellow eyes, he pointed the pistol away. For an instant, while the thing's eyes followed the pistol, he figured he'd just committed suicide, but then the eyes came back to rest on his and he *knew* it understood. "Well," he said, a little shakily. "Bring some polta paste. Sammy, let them see you smear some on your arm before you try to put any on them."

"You think they'll let him?" Ben asked. Sammy was clearly keenly interested in his answer as well.

"Yeah. Like I said, let them see you put it on your wound, then point at one of theirs. Do it slow and gentle. Easy does it."

"Easy does it, you betcha!" Sammy said sincerely.

After the wounded creatures were successfully doctored, Ben stepped over to Chapelle. "So. Now what? We've gotten them to let us smear some ooze on their oozy skins. You think that'll make a difference?"

"No." Russ shrugged. "I don't know. It would to *me*, but we can't think like that. Look, I ain't a philosopher, I'm just a torpedoman at heart. You're the one born with the big officer brain, but it just so happens I'm not a bad sailor, so they gave me a ship. That doesn't mean I feel qualified to speculate on stuff like this." He paused, still staring at the "frog-lizards." "You know, we never could really figure out how the Japs think, even with Shinya to try and explain it to us, and at least they were humans. We still don't have a clue what makes the Grik tick. I think it's pretty amazing that us and the 'Cats are on the same wavelength on most things." He nodded at the strange creatures. "For all we know, not killing them and doctoring them up might make them hate us even more."

"So what do we do with 'em now?" Ben asked. "It's going to be a hot day, as usual. We can't just keep throwing water on 'em. The guys have too much work to do, both guarding and trying to refloat this tub. I guess we could put 'em down in the forward hold, but I was kind of hoping, if we raise steam, we might get it pumped out a little."

Russ rubbed his eyes. "Let 'em go," he said.

"Let them *go*?"

"Yeah. We might have a whole other batch to deal with tonight. But we know they talk to each other . . . sort of." He shook his head and smiled. "Sorry. Tired. I'm rambling, I guess. Maybe what I'm hoping is that they'll think things over. They came at us and got creamed. We treat their wounded and turn 'em loose, maybe that'll at least confuse them enough to leave us alone for a while."

Ben chuckled. "So you *are* hoping they think a little like us?"

"I guess. At least on the basic, 'don't sit on the blowtorch twice' level."

~

The natives were still restless, but now they were afraid, and somewhat perplexed. The attempt to recover the Warren had gone horribly wrong. The strange creatures that infested it possessed inconceivable magic, and capable notions of the art of territorial conquest and defense. The natives considered themselves practiced students of that art. They used it every day to hunt and simply survive. How else had they managed to maintain complete control of such a vast body of water as their lake for so long? Now, after the terrible losses of the night before, their very hegemony over the lake itself might be at risk. They couldn't possibly mount another such attempt to retrieve the Warren. They'd be hard-pressed just to defend their territory from others of their own kind. They had no doubt they would succeed; they practiced the art well, but it would be difficult for a time—and they would, of course, require a new Great Mother sooner than they'd hoped. It was all so inconvenient.

Their perplexity had more to do with the behavior of the strange creatures after the combat was over than anything else. First, to their amazement, the strange creatures—clear victors in the contest—did not consume the dead, as was their right. Instead, they threw them into the water for the natives to claim, almost as an offering to a respected adversary. The corpses were duly retrieved. Food was food, after all, and it wouldn't do to refuse such an odd but flattering gift. The most perplexing thing of all, however, was that the strange creatures also released the wounded. This had almost never been done before. Ancient legends told of such deeds, often recounted when the natives gathered together in times of plenty to softly croak and wheeze their tales of mythic heroes. A favorite of these, and one of the oldest remembered, recounted the tale of a supreme Hunter and practitioner of the art who, after rending their own earliest ancestors in fair and honorable combat, displayed a barely remembered and vaguely understood virtue known as Mercy, before guiding their ancestors to this very lake and gifting them with its bounty.

Evidently, the strange creatures were not only consummate practitioners and students of the art, but they understood the mythic virtue of Mercy, even when they were the victors after a combat they did not start. Most odd.

That night, virtually every native of the lake gathered

around the Warren, their bright yellow eyes staring in wonder at the magical spectacle before them. The strange creatures had somehow literally brought the Warren to life! It gasped in the darkness with luminous smoke and sparks spiraling upward like the distant burning mountains! Many bright white eyes glared from it in all directions, and the strange creatures moved about beneath them, tending the living Warren's needs. Another string of floating things arrived, shortly after dark, bearing even more of the strange creatures, but the floating things were left in peace. The natives conversed in a muted rumble, so many voices at once, and came to the consensus that they'd been wrong to combat the strange creatures.

When the Warren first arrived, it had been sickly and wounded. The strange creatures had left it here. Presuming it to be a corpse, the natives had used it as they used all things in the world—for whatever it seemed best suited. They turned it into a shelter. It never occurred to any of them that it might be still alive, suffering the indignity of their trespass. Now the strange creatures had returned to what might even be *their* Great Mother, with the sole intention of healing it—as they'd attempted to heal the wounded natives that attacked them!

Slowly, as the night wore on, yellow eyes dipped beneath the surface of the water and disappeared. Food was not a problem, thanks to the benevolence of the strange creatures, but a new Warren, of a more traditional style, would have to be begun. It would not be as convenient or enduring, but it would be theirs. Most would begin the work in a somber, meditative mood.

CHAPTER
14

Eastern Sea

Nervously, Matt endured the one-handed shave. Somehow—even Juan couldn't remember exactly how or when—the Filipino had apparently broken his left arm during the terrible storm. He swore it hadn't been when the ship nearly capsized; he'd have remembered that. He was darkly suspicious that it happened when Earl Lanier fell on him sometime later. Now the arm hung suspended in a sling while Matt did his best to project calm indifference as Juan's shaky, unsupported razor scraped the stubble from his facc. The sea was almost calm at last. The morning sky was blue, with a purple-tinged fleece of clouds. The typhoon, Strakka, or whatever it was, had passed, and like other Strakkas he'd experienced, there wasn't any fooling around. When it was gone, it was gone. There was no lingering stormy aftereffect. In seas where land was near, there was always a tremendous detritus of shredded vegetation, trees, and tumbling corpses of fish and animals. Thc corpses never lasted long once the sea calmed down. At least within the Malay Barrier, flasher fish took care of that. Out here, in the broad Pacific, he didn't know. Lanier, who fished over the side whenever the ship was at ease, hadn't caught any flashies off their little atoll, although he caught plenty of other stuff. No, out here, the end of the Strakka had almost a cleansing effect; as if in its might it had absorbed and scoured the sea clear of all but the mildest weather.

They'd been lucky for once. The only thing that saved them, apparently, was that the monstrous wave hadn't actually broken over the ship, crushing her like a bobbing beer can. Evidently, it had risen in their path, moving in vaguely the same direction they were. There'd been no real warning as such—even Chack hadn't seen it in time for that—and all they'd been able to do was try to claw up its flank. They didn't make it. The thing was just too steep, and even now no one had any real idea how high the wave ultimately crested. In spite of the wind and the direction of the swells, the top of the wave must have split of its own accord beneath the titanic weight it had amassed. *Walker* simply dropped over onto her side when part of this avalanche of falling sea landed upon her.

Matt, like all seamen, had long heard tales of "rogue waves" that reached to the sky, "white squalls" made of almost solid, windblown water. He admitted that he'd always put both in the same category as mermaids and sea monsters. Now he knew there *were* sea monsters and "white squalls" weren't the most unusual squalls that one might encounter. Clearly, "rogue waves" existed too, and he wondered uncomfortably just how "rogue" they actually were on this world. The terror of the event still resonated within him, and even if the details of what he'd done and how he'd reacted had blurred, the overall sense of crushing, swirling hopelessness and failure wouldn't go away. It had been *that* close.

Grimly, he counted the cost yet again. They'd lost seven people, all 'Cats, over the side. Just gone. Both bridgewing lookouts were swept away. Most of the rest were lost while trying to secure the plane and boats and any number of other things that had been torn loose on deck. The sea had continued to run high for an interminable period, and the safety chains and lifelines simply hadn't been up to the task. One of the launches was a total wreck, and the Nancy had suffered some damage as well. Reynolds was surveying it now to see if it could be repaired. The number three boiler had burst when they took water down the stack. It hadn't been a catastrophic break, but the seams were blown and all the firebrick inside had exploded and practically shredded the tubes and tanks. Four more 'Cats had died in the fireroom and nearly everyone who'd been in there was injured to some degree.

Tabby was probably the worst. Somehow she'd managed to shut off the fuel and feed water to the damaged boiler in the smoke- and steam-choked compartment. She'd even closed the cut-out valve, ensuring that steam still reached the turbines from the undamaged boilers, before she'd finally been overcome. By so doing, she'd literally saved the ship and all those aboard her. *Walker* would have been doomed without steerageway. In the process, however, she'd burnt her lungs and been badly scalded. She was in the wardroom now, with half a dozen other bad cases. Her fur was coming off in bloody clumps and her labored breathing sounded like a sub's diesel exhaust when water washes over the vents. Matt had been to see her, to see them all, and he figured Tabby was done for. Oddly, Selass offered some hope. Not much, but some. Matt didn't know how she could, but he prayed she was right.

There were many other injuries, serious and light, ranging from broken bones, like Juan's arm, to the big, stitched-up cut running along the Bosun's jaw. Campeti had a concussion. One of the 'Cats, an ordnance striker named Faal-Pel, who'd previously been known as "Pall-Mall," had instantly gained a new nickname when he somehow contrived to lose half his tail. Matt supposed Faal-Pel would be stuck with "Stumpy" forever. Objectively, it could have been much, much worse, and looking back over their adventures and his poor old ship's many trials, he realized it usually had been. He had to concede that, in all honesty, this time they actually *had* been "lucky."

Achilles had been "lucky" too, in that she'd survived the storm, but otherwise, not so much. *Walker*'s wireless array had been damaged again, and they'd lost all contact with Jenks's ship during the storm. Even when the aerial was repaired, they couldn't reach *Achilles*. By chance, they found her the following day while crisscrossing their path to leeward. She'd been almost dismasted by the blow, and her starboard paddle wheel was a wreck. Matt was seriously concerned that the once beautiful, formidable ship may have endured too much. She'd been almost two years at sea, had fought a major action, and now had gone through the worst storm imaginable. He hoped she could reach Respite. With the same concerns, Jenks allowed *Walker* to take *Achilles* under tow. As if to show how fickle fate could truly be, they sighted *Icarus* later that evening, looking as though she'd missed the storm completely. Of *Ulysses* there was no sign.

"We can fix the boiler," Spanky said roughly, and coughed. His eyes were red and there were bandages on his forearms. He'd been one of the first into the aft fireroom and had sucked in some steam as well. He'd also personally carried Tabby to the wardroom, snarling "Don't touch her!" at anyone who tried to take her from him. "Actually, we can rebuild it. We're carrying more spare stuff than the old *Blackhawk* ever had for us." *Blackhawk* had been their destroyer tender in the Asiatic Fleet. "It'll take time and a lot of work, though. When I say 'rebuild,' I mean *rebuild*. Hell, even the casing's warped." He shook his head. "We've got a lot more water than usual coming in around the starboard shaft packing too, but otherwise, engineering came through okay." He paused. "I mean, other than a lot of people hurt . . . and the dead, of course."

"Of course."

The Bosun was gingerly feeling his jaw. "I never would've believed it," he said. "Thin as this old gal's skin is, I figured we'd have a thousand leaks after a beating like that, but she came through like a submarine."

"Hey," Spanky growled, "I was there when damn near

every new rivet went in. You weren't. She's tighter than a drum. And not all her steel's so thin anymore. We rolled the new plates out to original spec. That's why it sticks up in some places when your apes bitch about the paint scraping."

"Is that so? Well, *I* wasn't bitching."

Spanky looked almost accusingly at the Bosun. It was as if, having failed to rise to his argumentative bait, Gray had let him down. His next words, words they'd all been avoiding, confirmed it. "Then what are we going to do about the dead, anyway?"

Juan wiped the remnants of soap off the Captain's face and beat a hasty retreat. He wanted no part of this discussion.

Matt rubbed his face and took a deep breath. "Damned if I know. All the dead . . . still aboard . . . were 'Cats this time, mostly in the fireroom." He lowered his voice. "We can't cremate them the Lemurian way, and I don't know how they'll feel about burial at sea. Carrying them back to Baalkpan isn't even an option. Neither is waiting until we reach Respite. We're still at least a week out."

"Ask Chack," Gray suggested.

Spanky shook his head and looked away. "I'll ask Tabby," he said huskily. "Leavin' out Chack's Marine rank, she actually kind of outranks him now, anyway. Besides . . ." He couldn't finish.

Lieutenant (jg) Fred Reynolds looked at the PB-1D Nancy from every angle, still amazed that the plane had survived the storm in one piece . . . mostly. Kari-Faask imitated nearly his every move. She was just as concerned as he was about the condition of the plane, though she'd have been relieved if the damn thing had been totally destroyed or just washed over the side. She wasn't nearly as keen on flying as her friend and pilot was. Since the plane wasn't wrecked, she intended to make sure it was as well maintained as possible—as long as her precious hide might have to ride in it again.

"The motor plumb flooded," announced Jeek, the flight crew chief. "We take whole thing off, replace with spare. Gaas tank, all gaas lines, come out, dry out. Use big air blow!" he said, referring to air from the ship's compressor. "We take wet motor apart, dry out, new spare!" He seemed proud of his ingenuity. They had five spare engines for the Nancy, and an entire spare plane broken down and stowed in the aft deckhouse. Remembering that, Kari sighed. If they'd been down to the "spare" plane, that would have probably just left them making more dangerous flights.

"That's swell, Jeek," Reynolds said. "Any structural damage?"

"She wet inside and out," Jeek admitted. "Some glue come loose on inside." He brightened. "But glue dry again, pretty day!"

Reynolds looked at him. "You better clamp those places!" he said sharply, but Jeek grinned.

"Just joke. She tight. No water get inside. Only motor wet. It outside."

Reynolds stopped, noticing something he hadn't seen before. There were a lot of small patches in the plane's skin, where the flight crew had covered bullet holes. Most had been painted over and were barely noticeable. One, however, on the nose, right in front of the windscreen, had a circle around the patch with a big O and what looked like an upside-down N.

"What's that?" he demanded.

Jeek shrugged. "You bring plane back full of holes from bad guy guns, that fine. Lots of work to fix, but fine. You shoot hole in own plane"—he gestured at the nose—"not fine. From where you sit, numbers say NO. Maybe you remember not shoot own plane no more!"

Reynolds's ears reddened. "That wasn't my fault, damn it!" he said defensively. "They were shooting at us, I was shooting at them! All I had was a damn pistol!"

"You get 'carried away,'" Kari agreed. "You almost shoot us down yourself!"

"I did not! Get rid of it!"

"No!" Jeek said, grinning.

"Who's in charge here, you or me?" Reynolds demanded.

"You in charge of division," Jeek said, "but I in charge of plane."

Their argument was interrupted by a volley of musket fire aft, near the fantail. Kari jumped. "What's that?"

"Them Marines," Jeek said scornfully. "They shoot bullets at shields—see if bullets go through." He shook his head. "Ever-body shootin' holes in own stuff. Crazy."

"Well . . ." Reynolds hesitated. "What do I tell the Skipper?"

"Give me two, three day, this Naancy fly just fine." He peered at Reynolds. "You lucky you got me an' this flight crew 'stead o' those on big ship. We know shit."

"Yeah, lucky," Reynolds reluctantly agreed. "Just get that stupid sign off the nose, will ya?"

Spanky McFarlane stumped painfully down the companionway. He'd been to see Tabby several times, and each time she looked worse. He half expected to find her covered with a sheet. He met Chief Tindal in the passageway, returning from having the dressing on a badly bashed elbow changed. Both men made way for two 'Cat stretcher bearers carrying another 'Cat, swaddled in bandages, aft.

"He okay?" Spanky asked.

"Sure," Miami replied. "Just a few scrapes and some singed hair. Got a free pass from the doc to goof off a couple o' days." He nodded at the bearers as they passed. "They're just taking him to his rack in the 'guinea pullman.'" Gingerly, the Lemurians carried the stretcher up the companionway stairs.

"Actually, he ain't good," Tindal said when the patient was out of earshot. "He'll prob'ly look like he's got mange when his fur grows back, but he'll make it. Selass wouldn't have let him go otherwise. Wardroom's only for the worst cases left. We got to clear it out." He gestured aft. "His mates'll take good care of him now." Seeing Spanky's expression, he added, "Only two borderline cases left." He didn't need to say that Tabby was one of them.

Spanky sighed and nodded. "See what you can do about number three, will ya? Start tearing it down as quick as you can. I know we're short firemen, at least for a while, but it ain't like the old days, you know? Back then, if we had two good boilers, that meant we had a spare. Only two leaves us nothing extra anymore, 'specially with that Brit hulk in tow. Get with Bashear and shanghai some of his apes with boiler experience if you have to."

Tindal raised a brow. "He gonna squawk?"

Spanky shook his head. "Nope. Besides, we got all of Chack's Marines to help topside. Not many of them have ever even been in the fireroom." He started to move along, but Miami put a hand on his arm.

"Look," he said, "for what it's worth, everybody knows how you feel about Tabby." Spanky started to cloud up. News of the "kiss" Tabby had laid on him was all over the ship in a matter of hours. Miami shook his head. "And I, at least, know you ain't 'sweet' on her. She's a swell dish for a 'Cat, but she's a 'Cat, and some things just ain't meant to be. But I also know she ain't just a 'fireman' to you neither. I don't know what she is. She ain't nobody's 'pet,' unless she's 'teacher's pet' and you're the teacher. Maybe she's like a kid sister or stepdaughter or somethin'. My point is, whatever she is to you, let her see it for once. So what if she's sweet on you? God knows why she would be, but what difference does it make to you? Knowin' you care about her, in whatever way, might make a lot of difference to her."

Spanky nodded. This was a side of Miami Tindal he'd never seen. Maybe it was new. It seemed like everybody revealed new sides all the time these days. "Thanks," he said. "Now go get with Bashear." Turning, he advanced toward the embroidered wardroom curtain.

The next morning, *Walker*'s dead went over the side in the traditional flag-draped way, with the traditional service.

Tabby wasn't among them . . . yet . . . and only time would tell if there'd be another funeral service aboard the old destroyer in the coming days. Spanky's visit had seemed to perk Tabby up, despite the nature of their ultimate conversation. She'd been adamant that, if it came to that, she wanted whatever kind of service any other destroyerman would receive under the circumstances, and she was convinced that her Lemurian comrades who'd already perished would agree. Not for the first time, Matt wished they'd brought a Sky Priest along. He didn't feel right leading the brief Lemurian chant of supplication after the traditional service, but Jeek, of all people, had volunteered to lead a sort of "nondenominational" version. The chant was different for land folk and sea folk. Matt still found it odd when a minority of Lemurians, including a few of the Marines—such as Corporal Koratin—participated only in the Christian service. Once an Aryaalan noble, Koratin had been a convert to Sister Audry's teachings. The proceedings at an end, *Walker* increased speed, straining against the towline rigged to *Achilles*. During the brief pause, there'd been splashes alongside the Imperial frigate as well.

The weather remained fine, with a steady westerly breeze. *Icarus* easily kept company, and slowly, as *Achilles* pieced new masts and yards together from her remaining stores and as much as *Icarus* could spare, she bent new canvas and more and more of the drag came off the towline. On *Walker*, carpenter's mates built a new launch, scavenging as much of the wrecked one as they could. The little two-cycle engine seemed okay, but the propeller shaft was bent and they had to straighten it. Safety chains were rerigged and parted stays were spliced. Within a few days all the serious damage but the blown boiler had been attended to, and Gray, the ever-present, looming Super Bosun, even had details chipping and painting again. He was damned if *Walker* would steam into her first Imperial port with rust streaks down her sides "like wet makeup on a cheap Norleens whore." Even as evidence of the beating the ships took from the Strakka disappeared, however, hope that

Ulysses would turn up began to fade. She might well have been driven far off course and proceeded independently to their destination, but Jenks said her master, *Achilles'* own third lieutenant, would have made every effort to rejoin them. He feared she'd been lost with all hands.

They began to encounter land of a sort. Small, desolate, apparently lifeless atolls scoured of any vegetation were the first they saw. Wireless communications had been restored with *Achilles* and Jenks counseled Captain Reddy on the most beneficial bearings. Other islands began to appear, first with a few lonely trees, then with veritable jungles and even a few humps and hills that suggested more substance to their foundations. Courtney Bradford wanted to visit them, of course, but he lost considerable interest when Jenks advised that the main reason they sustained no settlements out of Respite was a lack of reliable fresh water. They'd already passed the island, far to the northwest, to which O'Casey and the princess had been bound, and Jenks, who was something of a naturalist himself, assured Bradford that it was the only place they'd neglected that might have truly interested him. The islands they steamed among did sustain life, however.

Birds began pacing the ships, swooping among the masts and generally, as usual, defecating all over the decks. For the first time since coming to this world, real "honest" birds not only predominated but seemed almost universal. They were strange creatures, with many of the characteristics of the "lizard birds," such as elongated, toothy mouths instead of beaks, and almost ridiculously long tail plumages like peafowl, but they were entirely feathered and had wide, broad wings. They seemed designed to soar for long distances and snatch prey from near the surface of the sea. They saw a few "regular" lizard birds like those they'd become accustomed to within the Malay Barrier, but they were oddly shaped, and ironically, some had beaks instead of teeth. They seemed more suited for stooping and diving for prey, which Courtney enthusiastically watched them do occasionally. Mostly, however, the birds they saw acted just as curious about the ships as Courtney was about them, and curses from the deck division competed with Courtney's chortles of glee.

One evening, Jenks suggested they anchor for the night in the lee of a low but expansive atoll. Far to the east southeast, a high, hazy shoreline could be seen. They'd raised Respite at last. Jenks said picking their way through the jumble of shoals from this direction could be hazardous in the dark, however, so Captain Reddy agreed to the pause and invited Jenks and his officers to dinner. To the frank amazement of everyone, Tabby had apparently turned the corner, and she'd finally been moved to her berth in the aft crew's quarters. She hardly got any sleep, to hear Spanky go on about it, what with everyone "carrying on over her so," but Spanky himself still visited her at least twice a day. In any event, the wardroom was finally clear and the ship's officers could gather there once again.

This was the first time there'd been a "social" meeting of the two commanders in weeks, and despite the carefully cleaned uniforms, all the Imperials looked tired and hard-used, with the possible exception of Ensign—now Lieutenant—Parr, who'd been given command of *Icarus*. When the Imperials were piped aboard, Matt and his side party returned their salutes with pleasure after each and every one of them first saluted *Walker*'s flag. Matt reflected that they'd certainly come a long way since their first meeting. He shook Jenks's hand, but had to raise an eyebrow at O'Casey, or "Bates," as Jenks called him. The one-armed former "rebel" now wore the uniform of an Imperial Navy lieutenant.

"Coming up in the world, aren't you, Sean?" he said with a grin.

O'Casey shrugged. "'Tis really a demotion, I fear," he said. "From beleaguered leader o' the resistance, to mere lieutenant . . ." He shook his head. "How the mighty are felled."

Jenks snorted. "I presume you prefer the fit of that uniform to a rope, do you not? Besides, you have converted me to your cause. At least you might still accomplish something without being shot on sight."

O'Casey grinned. "Aye, there's that! I've often heard it said 'tis better ta serve in hell than be led ta the gallows—an' then serve in hell!" That provoked a round of chuckles. Matt already knew there'd been some classic books aboard the ships of Jenks's ancestors. Matt had read many such books, and his ability to swap occasional literary references reinforced the common, if distant, heritage that his human destroyermen shared with the Imperials. In this instance, the deliberate misquote and O'Casey's and Jenks's banter confirmed that the two men were still getting along. After having once been friends, the two had become deadly enemies. Now, with Jenks's discovery that O'Casey's rebellion against the Company had been justified—if possibly premature—it seemed almost as if the years of hatred had fallen away. Matt knew Jenks hadn't needed to make O'Casey even a lieutenant. Essentially he'd evolved into Jenks's own version of Matt's Chief Gray—friend, discreet confidant, and personal protector.

O'Casey might not have the widespread, generally positive reputation Gray enjoyed, but he basically filled the same niche. Both men were large and powerful, but still considerably more than they appeared at first glance. O'Casey was the younger of the two, in his mid-forties. His hair had gone salt and pepper, including the wide handlebar mustaches trimmed much like the one Jenks wore, except in O'Casey's case the ends weren't braided but twisted and waxed. His skin was darker too, alluding to an ancestry mixed with the original "passage era" partial Lascar crews, or transportees aboard the eighteenth-century East Indiamen the Imperials had arrived in from the same world as the destroyermen. O'Casey himself professed to know little about his early lineage. His dark skin might even have come from other sources that Matt was just beginning to learn about.

"Well," Matt said, "why don't we adjourn to the wardroom? Mr. Marcos assures me that he's managed to put something edible together."

"Yes, thank you, Captain Reddy," said Jenks. He paused, glancing about at the destroyermen within earshot, the men in particular. He seemed a bit pensive when he continued. "Now that we stand on the brink of meeting more of my people . . . ah, civilians for the first time, there are a few things we should perhaps discuss so that there are no . . . misunderstandings, as it were."

"You've got to be *kidding* me!" Matt practically exploded. He half rose from his seat, nearly overturning his coffee cup.

Jenks made a visible effort to control his voice. "I am not. And though I do not personally approve of the . . . institution, I'm no crazed abolitionist either. It's a practice that has served the Empire well for many generations—the tool that ensured our very survival! On the other hand, I do believe its time has largely passed and I admit to certain . . . moral objections to its continuation. It's not a practice that can simply be 'shut off,' however. It's too ingrained, too much a part of our society. Arguably, the Company is largely responsible for that, and my hope is that once we've dealt with it, we can begin a gradual dissolution of all the immoral institutions it supports."

"Holy . . ." Gray breathed. "They *own* women like *pets*!"

"How do you buy one?" Campeti asked wonderingly, and Matt glared at him.

"It's *not* slavery—" Jenks insisted, but Matt interrupted.

"The hell it's not!"

"It is *not* slavery," Jenks continued determinedly, "and they're NOT property . . . as such. They *are* 'obligated,' however, and there's a value placed on that 'obligation.'"

Selass stood so suddenly that she upset the table again and did knock over a couple of cups. Matt was glad they'd waited until the meal was over before beginning the discussion in earnest, otherwise much of Juan's hard work would have wound up on the green linoleum deck.

"This is the most shocking, barbaric thing I've ever heard of!" she spat. "I can guarantee that my father, the

Great Keje-Fris-Ar, will be no party to this . . . abomination! There can be no 'alliance' with people such as you!"

"Ah . . . Madam . . . uh . . ." Jenks sputtered.

"The title's 'Nurse Lieutenant,' Commodore," Matt said icily.

"Nurse Lieutenant . . . Fris-Ar," Jenks continued. "You have my most abject apology for disturbing you, but it is not I who adopted this policy, nor, as I said, do I condone it now. That said, is it more barbaric than the Grik? You've heard me mention the so-called 'Holy Dominion,' but you don't know *them* yet. I assure you that 'barbarous' as the Empire may suddenly seem in your eyes, barbarity can be a very relative thing."

"But . . . to keep females in bondage . . . !"

Jenks sighed. "Believe me, I sympathize with your dismay. Please try to imagine mine. I have never been witness to *any* civilization in which women—females—are so fully integrated into the mainstream of society. Female warriors! Doctors! Leaders! It boggles the mind! Among the various cultures I've met, I've discovered a few—similar to that from which your 'Lawrence' springs, I have no doubt—where there is a matriarchy, but their queen is the only female who wields great power. Otherwise, our 'system' would seem to reflect the norm on this world. Regardless, after long association, I have managed to grow . . . accustomed to the way you do things." He turned to Matt. "Your Sandra Tucker, one of the very reasons for this expedition—you cannot imagine my surprise when I first divined that not only was she an important political figure, but you actually *consulted* her on matters of policy! Do you remember that day you took me on a tour of industrial works and your shipyard? That was the first time I fully realized . . . I was shocked and troubled, I admit, but she also made some quite excellent points about our mutual interests, if you'll recall. They certainly made an impression on me." He turned back to Selass, still standing before him. "Our females are not strictly in 'bondage,' as you say. Most are quite free. Some, such as the princess, even enjoy tremendous power. In certain circumstances, historically, her predecessors have even been the 'matriarchal' exception to the rule. Some females *are* 'obligated,' however, as I said, but there are strict laws concerning their treatment. They owe a debt and must 'work it off.' "

Matt suddenly understood a lot that had remained mysterious to him before; subtle comments or turns of phrase from both Jenks and Princess Rebecca returned to the forefront of his mind. He did remember Jenks's odd behavior whenever Sandra was around and openly voicing opinions and exercising authority in a way that he now knew Imperial females, no matter how highborn, simply didn't do. Evidently, of all female Imperials, *only* Princess Rebecca, as heir to the Governor-Emperor's throne, had real status and authority within the Empire.

"Indentured servitude, then," Spanky growled.

Jenks nodded thoughtfully. "Perhaps. A far more appropriate term than 'slavery,' at any rate."

"Not much different in practice, though," said Lieutenant Palmer. "Who do they owe their 'debt' to? The Company?"

"That depends," Jenks confessed. "Most do. Some owe it to individuals, some to industrialists, planters, and other commercial concerns. Some owe their debt to society as a whole, since in many cases it is purchased by the Imperial Government. The Company provides much of the 'supply' and profits in the 'trade,' however."

"The government *buys* them from the Company?" Matt demanded incredulously.

"No! The government buys their *debt*!"

"Same thing," Matt insisted. He was horrified as much by what he was learning as by the sick feeling that he'd embraced such people as "friends." Sure, women hadn't even had the right to vote in the U.S. for long—and sometimes he honestly wondered if that had been a mistake or not—but that aside, the ideal of "gentlemanly behavior" in the world he remembered was to protect and defend the "weaker sex," to guard their virtue and even, to a degree, place them on a pedestal of honor. Women were the guardians of civilization. They bore and raised children, made the home, and were often acknowledged as the "power behind the throne." Some, like the late queen of England, wielded considerable power from the throne itself. At any rate, it was women who protected the foundations of humanity even while men did their best to tear them apart. In a very fundamental way, regardless of the political reasons behind any war, men forever volunteered to fight to protect their women, their families, and their homes from the very horrors they marched off to meet. It was ingrained in men, particularly officers of any service he'd ever known, to protect, defer to, and be courteous to all women—not to *own* them.

It had been hard enough on Matt and many of his destroyermen to recognize the complete equality of the sexes among Lemurians. Sandra had already defiantly staked a claim to equal status aboard his ship before they ever really met the 'Cats, but she was different. She'd become the medical officer, and some measure of risk was inherent in that, as well as their overall situation. It wasn't as if they'd put her on a gun crew! But then, when they met the Lemurians, and began accepting Lemurian cadets aboard the ship, they couldn't discriminate based on sex, because it would have profoundly offended their allies. Over time, Matt guessed they'd grown desensitized. Female 'Cats aboard ship, in the Army or Marines, or working in the factories, became a matter of course. Some "traditionalists" like Spanky might still act scandalized, but they accepted the situation and the necessity behind it. There were always rumors of interspecies . . . associations, but in most cases they were still just rumors—with one glaring, possible exception.

Jenks looked around the table at the suddenly hostile faces. "Mr. Bates, would you care to give a history lesson?"

O'Casey glanced up from studying his spoon.

"Yeah, O'Casey, how about that?" Gray demanded. "How come you never said anything about this before?"

O'Casey cleared his throat. "Aye. Well, I could say ye

never asked, but I doubt that'd satisfy ye. To be sure, at first it wasn't an issue. When the darlin' royal lass an' I were marooned wi' yer submariners, it made no difference. 'Twas hand ta mouth an' little hope o' rescue." He bowed his head to those around the table. "Then, when ye came fer us in this lovely ship, ye might remember that ye had more immediate concerns than the domestic institutions o' the Empire. An' again, it didna' signify. Later, as we told ye more o' our situation, 'twas the princess herse'f who forbade me ta carry on aboot it. She was determined our peoples should be friends and cooperate against the evils o' the world, an' she feared this very reaction." O'Casey looked at Jenks. "As her father's only direct heir, an' a 'matriarchal exception,' she's quite the 'crazed abolitionist,' an' after such long association wi' the lass an' these fine folk, ye might now add me ta that list."

"I never doubted it," Jenks replied. "And yet you are an Imperial Officer once more." He glanced apologetically at Selass. "Might that at least gain me some credit as a 'flexible' barbarian?"

Selass huffed, but she did sit at last.

"In any event, Mr. 'Bates/O'Casey,' perhaps a more comprehensive 'history lesson' might build some slight mitigating context," Jenks said.

"Aye . . ." O'Casey paused, then took a long, slow breath. "Aye," he said more firmly, gathering his thoughts. "The commodore an' I, when once we were more 'equal,' used to engage in historical discussions, focused in the main upon 'post-Passage' subjects. I know you, Captain Reddy, are somethin' of an historian yerself." Matt nodded, a little self-consciously. "Anyway, when the Founders first came this way, they were in much the same position as ye. Admittedly, they dina' help the 'locals' with nearly the same zeal as ye, but in their defense, the threat wasna' so pressin' then. They chose ta hide from this terrible world. The rub was, even wi' their greater numbers, there were, proportionately, just as few 'dames,' as ye call 'em. None went west wi' the tragic ship the Grik managed ta take, but there were few enough. Ye an' I ha' discussed this oursevs. The ancient East Indiamen had many roles: part 'freighter,' ye call 'em, part warship—ta pertect themsevs—an' part passenger ship. They also transported convicts on occasion, as ye know.

"There were a grand total o' fourteen 'ladies' among the passengers, two beyond child-bearin' age, an' some mere children." He shrugged. "Well, the children grew up, but the 'stable' was still nearly bare, if ye know what I mean. By the by, descendants o' them first ladies, if they're ladies themselves, are not subject to the 'institution' bein' discussed. They're born free wi' no 'obligation' a'tall. That said, there were nearly twenty female 'transportees,' whose original destination was actually a series of isles, not the land o' 'New Holland,' or 'Australia,' as Mr. Bradford calls it. These women were bein' transported for crimes, an' that's what the 'System of Obligation' was founded upon. They had ta . . . 'work' their way through their terms o' transportation, but were then available fer honorable matrimony wi' the original crews. Their descendants were also 'unobligated,' as the child canna' be held responsible fer the crimes o' the parent. Here, I must point out that, despite some resistance, any crew member was ultimately granted equal status within the law, regardless o' ancestry." He smirked. "There were too many Lascars amongst the crews—Indians, Arabs, Malays an' the like—fer the officers ta do anythin' else, so long before yer own 'Revolution,' against the Mythic Crown, there was true racial equality wi'in Imperial society. I willna' say 'twas easy, or even bloodless, but it just had ta be. Finally, 'twas decided that any man who reached majority, swore ta hold fast ta Imperial law an' forswear heathern religions in favor o' the English faith, could enjoy full citizenship." He shrugged. "There were problems, but ye've had some o' those too, as I recall from our talks.

"Well, as ye can imagine, this didna' solve every issue. We still had our own 'dame famine' fer a time. Then, one day, a storm-battered ship was rescued at sea an' we first learned o' the 'Holy Dominion.'" He sipped the hot tea Jenks had brought aboard, still clearly savoring the flavor after subsisting so long on "coffee." A couple of the other men and Chack were just as glad to have the iced tea Juan had made from some gifted leaves.

"The survivors we took in were twisted souls an' devoted to a form o' popery we couldna' fathom, but were as yet not as foul as they've become. We met their folk an' traded wi' them. At the time, they seemed as much in flux as we, although they'd been 'here' a longer time. Their holdin's were confined to the central Americas an' they seemed a mix o' Spaniards from an Acapulco galleon an' some Indians that had landed there sometime much earlier. At first our peoples got along well enough. This world is just as big as the old, an' it can be a lonely place. They seemed as glad ta meet us as we did them." He looked at Jenks.

"As ye may know," O'Casey continued, "New Britain, or the 'Hawaiian' chain, has lovely, fertile ground, an' at least on this world, fast-growin' hardwoods ta support a respectable shipbuildin' industry, but it's poor in other resources. We'd come ta the same conclusion as ye, that this world had much the same structure as our old, wi' the exception of volcanic isles which appear inconsistent wi' what the Founders knew before. The great continents seem little changed, however, wi' a few strikin' exceptions, so we knew where ta look fer what we needed. The Americas were wi'in our distant reach, so we made colonies there, north o' Dominion territory, ta supply that need. As for the Dominion, the greatest surplus they had for trade was women."

"Despicable!" proclaimed Bradford. O'Casey eyed him for a moment, then nodded.

"Aye. But as the commodore has said, essential ta our early survival. The Company had re-formed by then an' become a separate entity under Imperial law, wi' broad autonomy much like before. It took advantage of the trade, an' understandably required compensation fer bringin' the lasses hither. Since the Imperial people an' government had little ta compensate wi' beyond fish, foodstuffs, an' increasingly modern manufactured goods beyond what the Dominion could produce, we supplied those goods fer trade ta the Dominion fer females. The goods 'bought' the women, but the Company demanded compensation fer the transportation, so the 'obligation system' was expanded ta include them. The Company brought the women, but held the obligation until it was purchased by individuals or the government. At first, those who bought that obligation, or indenture, did so for the good of all an' simply released the women among us. They married, bore children, an' became Imperial subjects. They weren't citizens, but their children were. There lay much of the incentive for them ta marry, ye see.

"Over time, however, once the immediate crises ended an' there was plenty of women fer all, the Company continued the practice o' bringin' 'em in, but increasingly ta sell their indentures ta those who wanted labor. There's now a permanent 'lower class' of women—called 'Lascars' again, I fear—who begat 'citizen' children with those holdin' their obligation. Strangely, it's they who support the Company more than any since it continues ta add ta their ranks and gives 'em a political advantage in the Court o' Proprietors, even while the ranks of those who canna' be citizens grows." He paused. "I fear some o' this may also stem from a . . . perverse reluctance ta dispense wi' their twisted faith as well. Unlike yer Sister Audry's approach ta convertin' 'heathens,' Dominion priests're more . . . insistent. Add ta this an even more burgeonin' 'trade' since, in recent decades, the Dominion's begun ta fear our numbers an' Imperial power. Their 'Church' has taken on more an' more of the pagan rituals o' the early Indian folk, an' e'en as the Company trade grows, it's become more costly since the 'Holy Dominion's' started . . . slaughterin' their 'excess' females in hideous rituals. . . . Now we have women bringin' their own daughters ta secluded shores an' *beggin'* the Company ta take 'em!"

There was silence in the wardroom as those present began to digest the enormity of the moral dilemma facing the Empire. The "trade" couldn't simply be shut down without condemning untold numbers to their deaths, yet the Company fed and grew and gained self-perpetuating power off that very trade.

"I think I'm finally starting to get it," Matt said quietly. "I see how the Company's growing in strength, and I understand why the government's concerned. I also see the moral and political mess the Governor-Emperor's in. What I guess I don't see is what the Company hopes to gain in the long run. They've saturated the market for marriageable women and they'll undoubtedly saturate the labor market at some point as well. It appears they also at least contributed to this new—and yes, *much* more barbaric—practice the Dominion has engaged in. What could the Company possibly hope to gain in the end?"

"Absolute power, for a start," Jenks said. "O'Casey saw it long before I did, but with the support the Company has gained in the Court of Proprietors, they can do almost as they please. And even as the Lascars empower the Company, they become dependent on it as well. It controls most jobs and industry, and by its actions it's provoked the Dominion, which besides its overwhelming numbers has a navy with numerical supremacy over and near technological parity with our own." Jenks snorted bitterly. "Start with a population that's dependent upon you for its livelihood, add an external threat to control those who oppose you, and you can do virtually anything you want. What *that* might be, I can only speculate."

"And I take it that the Governor-Emperor and his daughter are opposed to this?"

"Of course!"

"Wow," was all Palmer could manage.

"Yeah," grumbled Gray. "What a mess." He looked at Jenks. "Now I see why you're not an 'abolitionist,' but what the hell?"

"Well . . . but with all those extra women, they ought to be cheap, right?" Campeti asked.

Matt gave *Walker*'s gunnery officer another withering look, but then his eyes widened and he rubbed his chin. "Yeah. What about that? I never have gotten your monetary system straight. God knows ours is fouled up. What *do* they cost?"

It was Selass's turn to glare, but Matt held a hand up to her.

Jenks seemed confused. "Well, ah, our monetary system has largely returned to a foundation based on precious metals. We get ours from our colonies in the Americas, as does the Dominion. Of course, the Company gets a percentage of whatever they carry in their bottoms, but there at least, the Navy has some advantage since most is transported aboard Naval vessels. There is some piracy, after all."

"So you use what, a 'pound' system?"

"That's quite a simplification, but pounds, certainly. Twenty shillings to a pound sterling, at my last inquiry—some time ago—twenty-six shillings for a guinea . . ."

"In other words, just as confusing as, well, it still is. No paper money?"

"No. Except for lines of credit redeemable at Imperial banks. There is often a discount. . . ."

"But gold's gold, and a pound of gold's worth what?"

"Forty-four and a half guineas."

"And a guinea's worth twenty-six shillings—so a pound of gold would be . . . ah, eleven hundred and fifty-seven shillings, or . . ."

"Almost forty-eight pounds," Palmer supplied.

"Right." Matt looked at Jenks. "So what do they cost? How much is this 'obligation' worth?"

"Well . . . that varies. The value of the obligation depends on how much time a woman has been in service. Of course, their maintenance is added to the total, as are any extraordinary costs such as further transportation. . . ."

"You mean feeding, clothing, doctoring, and then transporting them, possibly against their will, to say, Respite, actually *adds* to their obligation?"

"Naturally. Any unobligated citizen would have to pay for those things. . . ."

"But they'd have a *choice*, Jenks," Matt pointed out. "And to then charge them for transportation to another place where they can be further enslaved for someone else's gain . . . !"

"I thought we'd moved past the 'slavery' dispute!" Jenks said.

"No, we haven't, because that's still exactly what it is! What's to stop an owner of an 'obligation' from just shifting a worker—a woman!—around as long as he likes, island to island and workplace to workplace, constantly adding to her 'debt' for her entire life?"

Jenks blinked. "I . . . I honestly never thought about it like that." He seemed sincere and . . . horrified. He straightened. "I'm a Naval officer, and until recently, I avoided politics as best I could."

Bradford grunted. "It sounds as though the vast majority of your people have as well. Most are probably as ignorant as you, if the majority of these—possible—abuses take place on your frontiers." He raised an eyebrow at the others. "Do remember that we're still dealing in conjecture here. We have no evidence that this 'perpetual obligation system' actually occurs, just a speculation that it might."

Matt almost laughed. He was still digesting some of Bradford's new theories regarding how they might have wound up 'here' in the first place. "Lack of evidence has never stopped you from 'speculating' away on every conceivable topic, Courtney!"

Bradford grinned and stroked a nostril with his forefinger. "Indeed. But let us leave off persecuting the poor commodore for now. The system he described does seem to have begun innocently enough. Through our own brief contact with these Company thugs—virtual Nazis, if I may make so bold—we do have ample evidence of their treachery and deceit. I do not find it at all difficult to believe that the ultimate result of this particular institution has been perverted, warped, and molded to fit whatever diabolical agenda the Company ultimately serves."

"Hear, hear!" exclaimed Lieutenant Grimsley, Jenks's exec. He'd remained silent, slowly sinking into his chair throughout the discussion. If Jenks "avoided" politics, he'd always tried to pretend they didn't exist. At least before Billingsley abducted the princess and the others. Emboldened by his voice, and the generally agreeable response to his words, Grimsley turned to Matt.

"Pardon me, Captain Reddy, but may I ask why you are suddenly so interested in the cost of these obligations?"

"Sure," Matt replied. "Gold isn't really money among our friends. Not yet, anyway. That said, we took on a . . . little . . . when we refueled at Mindanao—'Paga-Daan.' I'd like some idea how many Respitan women this ship can purchase out of bondage . . . and set free." He looked at Jenks. "You might want to think about that too. One way or another, we're going to *kill* this goddamn 'Honorable New Britain Company,' so the 'trade' is basically over, if I have anything to say about it. Consider this: all these women who've been under the Company and, yes, Imperial thumb for all these generations probably don't have much loyalty to either one. You say some still even adhere to this sick mix of Catholicism and . . . whatever else it is. Those I 'buy' will have the options of staying where they are, becoming free citizens of the Alliance, or maybe even joining the United States Navy, God help me. At least in noncombat roles. I'll bet most choose between the latter two."

CHAPTER 15

Andaman Island

Almost all the commanders of every force within what was now inclusively described as "First Fleet" were present in Aahd-mah-raal Keje-Fris-Ar's vast quarters aboard *Salissa Home*. The sole exception was Greg Garrett, who was patrolling the strait aboard *Donaghey*, dodging mountain fish and chasing the few Grik ships still trying to sneak past. The meeting began with a friendly meal, in the Lemurian way, and no serious business was discussed until the last plate was removed. It didn't take long for the diners to finish. All were anxious to discuss the outcome of the Battle of Raan-goon. Overall command of First Fleet had already been formally turned over to Keje, and he sat at the head of a long, ornately carved dining table. Formal dining tables were not the norm among sea folk, who tended to eat from plates on their laps while lounging on comfortable cushions, but that sort of arrangement was awkward when discussions involved so many. Somebody always had to shout to be heard. The vast table allowed a formal setting where discussion could take place with everyone at eye level and easy to hear—if Navy decorum was observed.

Keje had taken the idea from the hideous green-topped wardroom table aboard *Walker*, and he encouraged the same kind of free-flowing back and forth he'd witnessed there. His table wasn't green, however; it was a well-oiled, polished, inlaid thing of beauty; hand-carved with delicate raised relief and possessed of deep, dark, mysterious grains. It would probably never be used for surgery, but it served all the other necessary purposes. Those around it all sat on stools, an essential compromise, and one that didn't inconvenience humans or Lemurians. 'Cats and their tails always had a difficult time with human chairs.

Keje glanced around the table, listening to the gently rumbling conversations, and then wiped his mouth with a napkin. Pushing back his stool, he raised his large cup of seep.

"My friends, comrades in the Holy Crusade of our time, let all Fleet elements that participated now add the word 'Raan-goon' to the folds of their flags, to commemorate this great victory!"

There followed applause, foot stamping, and a little gentle knocking on the magnificent table amid the hoots of approval. Even the captains of *Scott* and *Kas-Ra-Ar* were pleased. They'd both initially been put out by the rumored proclamation, and Captain Cablaas-Rag-Lan of *Scott* even transmitted a protest to the flagship. He'd suggested that *Salissa* herself shouldn't claim the honor if they couldn't. Keje patiently replied that *Salissa* brought the planes and *Scott* and *Kas-Ra-Ar* escorted *Salissa*, so of course they had "participated."

"Let it be recorded on the flags," Keje continued, "and let it be set down in the very Sacred Scrolls! Let the Scrolls also reflect that Commodore Ellis led First Fleet to its first victory, and General Aal-den designed the battle that exterminated the Grik from the environs of Raan-goon!" There was more acclaim, and Keje poised his cup to drink. "My friend Adar, once Sky Priest of this very Home and now Chairman of the Grand Alliance, has received my report and asks that I offer these words: 'May we all pray to the Heavens above in whatever way we choose, that this victory will be the first of many, leading to that final, ultimate victory when the Grik vermin are no more!' " Everyone drank then, and the room thundered around them. Keje sat and motioned for more seep. "Now," he said, as the celebration waned, "tell me everything that went wrong." There was no accusation in his tone, only a genuine desire to learn what hadn't worked so they could fix it next time. Next time there might be no room for error at all.

"Your Excellency," Jim began, addressing Keje as the head of state he was, but Keje held up a hand.

"Commodore Ellis—yes, you will retain that designation for now—we have finally solved that . . . bureau-craatic . . . issue quite nicely, I believe. Mr. Letts struck upon the solution while holding his drooling new youngling, as I understand it." There was laughter. "It strikes me as . . . appropriate, and even elegant, perhaps." He looked around. "I have accepted a 'Reserve Commission' in the Amer-i-caan Navy! While I command First Fleet, I am aahd-mah-raal only. I still have a vote in the Allied Council, but as a different person, representing a different Home. I think Mr. Letts was pondering the profound contrasts between being both a father and Adar's chief of staff at the same time. He realized that the one duty need not preclude the other. In any event, *Salissa* has accepted a reserve commission as well, and for the purposes of First Fleet, she is the U.S. Navy Ship CV-1, *Salissa*!"

There was another round of enthusiastic acclaim and Ellis smiled. It *was* elegant. He knew it couldn't be "regulation," but sometimes they had to improvise. "Admiral," he revised, nodding with a grin. "We need to work on logistics—a lot. We're not exactly starting from scratch, as we learned quite a bit before Baalkpan, but we had Letts around to handle it. Besides, defensive and offensive *logistics* are just as different as defensive and offensive *tactics*. I wish Alan Letts was here now, but we've got to sort it out.

It could have been a lot worse at Rangoon, disastrously worse, but at least we had everything we needed. It just wasn't necessarily where we needed it."

"That chore will largely and necessarily fall upon you," Keje said, "and by extension, every executive officer of every ship, battalion, regiment, and company in this command. You are my 'executive officer' and chief of staff. You must coordinate this effort."

"Aye, aye, Admiral."

"It will become massive quite soon," Keje warned. "The troops, equipment, munitions, ships—all are 'in the pipeline,' as you say, right now. You must put yourself in front of this situation."

"I'll see to it," Ellis said, looking around the table with an expression even Lemurians could read by now that said, "There better be a continuous procession of 'execs' to see me ASAP."

"Next?"

"We need better contingency planning," Pete said. "My fault, this time. Jim asked me to add aircraft to the plan, but I didn't think things through well enough." He nodded at Tikker, sitting opposite and to the left. "A couple of times, we could have used close support again after Captain Tikker flew home. We didn't have any contingency for that possibility. I just came up with some guidelines and said 'do this.' Granted, it might not have worked anyway. Our communications are limited and I don't know if I could've even gotten through to him later. Things got really tangled up toward the end. Frankly, comm discipline went straight to hell, and we've got to fix that. As long as we're stuck with a single frequency, we're just going to have to work around it. Still, if I'd only thought to have Tikker put a squadron on the water, maybe carried some bombs and fuel on a couple of ships, we could've had air support and recon throughout the latter part of the fight."

"Excellent point," Keje said. "In fact, I think it should become policy that all ships carry enough fuel to resupply several aircraft—just as *Walker* and *Mahan* once did." He paused. "That brings us to another issue. Captain Tikker, all things considered, the Wing performed extremely well. You are to be commended. I would like for you to explain, however, the reasons for the number of aircraft and crews we lost in this action."

Tikker stood. He'd already discussed this with Keje, and he hadn't expected to be called out. "First of all, Aahd-mah-raal, the very nature of air operations is dangerous in the extreme. It is also new. Unlike many of the new things we learn, however, aviators are not standing on the ground or upon the deck of a ship when they try the 'real thing' for the first time. Everyone makes mistakes, but in the sky there is no room for them. It takes only one." Tikker looked down, then met Keje's eyes again. "One of the mistakes was one we have tried to train away, based on Major Mallory's cautions. He called it 'target fixation.' I know I witnessed it firsthand in one instance, when we lost a plane directly in front of General Aal-den's Marines."

Pete was nodding. "I saw it. I've seen it before too. It was a classic case. The kid clearly meant to drop on a particular group of Grik . . . and just followed the line a little too long. Hit the trees." He shrugged. "It's a terrible, wasteful, tragic thing, but it can happen to anybody if you're not careful. It happens on the shield wall! You get to paying too much attention to the enemy in front of you and the bastard next to him sticks you with his spear." He looked at Keje. "Hell, it can even happen to admirals."

Keje nodded. "That is exactly the point I wanted to make. To everyone, not just Captain Tikker. We lost three aircraft to this 'target fixation'—one each from three of four squadrons we sent to battle. A few of the planes had mechanical problems and returned to the ship, and one had to land in the river near *Donaghey* due to engine failure, but all their crews were safe. We had one plane and crew that simply disappeared. No one saw it go down or where it went. In total, we lost four crews and eight planes out of thirty-two! Granted, four of those planes and crews were recovered and will fight again, but they were out of this fight! That is a higher percentage of losses than any other force engaged! Do not let it be said that the Naval Air Corps does not 'pull its weight'! Still, the one greatest single cause of our loss was this 'target fixation,' and General Aal-den is correct; it can happen to anyone. My friends, perhaps the greatest example of this is what we planned for and did to *Amagi* herself! Let this thought linger in your minds as we prepare for the invasion of Saa-lon. Never let it be far from your thoughts as we plan. Think on it now as we discuss the mistakes of the enemy, and the things we did right!"

Lord General Rolak glanced at Safir Maraan and his eyes twinkled.

"Old warriors and their heroics," Safir bemoaned. The laughter lifted fallen spirits.

"Through the noble efforts of General Aal-den and myself," Rolak began, "as well as the superfluous presence of a pair of youngling Marines, we have gained a most useful asset for the Alliance! We will soon know everything there is to know about Saa-lon in particular, and the Grik in general." His tone lost its humor. "I expect we will learn more about our enemy, at last, than we can bear to know after a meal." He gestured to a pair of Marines, and together with Risa, they entered one of the inner chambers of the admiral's quarters. A moment later, they returned with a living Grik! Some of those present had been expecting this, but most hadn't known and there were a few gasps and growls.

"May I present my new pet, and special advisor on Grik affairs!" Rolak said with a flourish. "Hij-Geerki!"

With rapid, nervous glances around the room, the old but still ferocious-looking creature hesitantly bowed.

CHAPTER 16

North of Tjilatjap (Chill-chaap)

Gilbert Yeager leaned over the rail, staring down at the water and the bubbles gushing up from below. He was chewing some of the yellow tobacco leaves, and occasionally he'd spit in the tumbling, gurgling water. Laney was down there in a hard hat and diving suit, welding *Santa Catalina*'s open seams. The obnoxious bastard had guts; there was no doubting that. He was still an asshole, though, and it was fun to spit "on" him. Lieutenant "Mikey" Monk stood next to Gilbert, also looking down, as did a squad of musket-armed Marines. Apparently there were no flashies in the swamp, something they'd speculated on before, based on the less salty water and the "frog folks," who couldn't prosper here if flasher fish were around. Even if none of the voracious silvery fish were present, there were doubtless other things—and the frog folks themselves, of course. Ever since the "Battle for *Santa Catalina*," however, the slippery, sticky-tongued devils had left the salvage party alone. Chapelle wasn't sure how to take that. He was glad, no question, but he hadn't expected them to give up so easily. That indicated a level of intelligence beyond the Uul class of Grik at any rate. They'd taken a lot of casualties, sure, but there were a lot of them. Every night they surrounded the ship, croaking, thrumming, and chirping at one another, and the lights reflected hundreds of glowing eyes. Even now, in the light of day, eyes could be seen, barely above the water, peering at them like little crocodiles—or big frogs. They kept their distance, and the Marines were ready to shoot any that ventured too close to Laney, but after the previous violent encounter, they now seemed completely content just to stare.

"You got some more of that tobacco?" Mikey asked.

"Sure," Gilbert said, fishing a pouch out of his shirt pocket. He handed it over. "Didn't know you chewed."

"I didn't," Monk confessed. "Got to now, until we figure out some way to smoke this stuff." The "local" tobacco, a product of the environs of Aryaal, tasted like real tobacco and probably was, of a sort. The problem was, the leaves were coated in some kind of vile, waxy, resiny stuff that made people who tried to smoke it violently ill. It tasted terrible too, until one chewed through the coating and spit it out.

"Me an' Isak been workin' on that," Gilbert confessed quietly, looking around to make sure no one else heard. When they finally made their momentous breakthrough, they intended to keep the process secret and corner the market on "smokin' tobacco." It was common knowledge that the Mice had been experimenting, but there'd been no progress announced.

"Getting any closer?"

"Well, no," Gilbert admitted. "But we rule stuff out with every failure."

"Hmm. Say, where's Isak anyway?"

Gilbert gestured down. "He's in the aft hold, watchin' Laney work from the other side. There was a couple of places where the plates were buckled out a little and him and a bunch o' 'Cats are pryin' 'em back in place. Last time Laney was up, he said one more plate should finish the patch."

Monk nodded. "Yep. One more plate and we should be

able to pump out the hold. I just hope that'll float her. It's mighty shallow water hereabouts."

"Yeah," Gilbert agreed. "The engine *should* work. All the steam lines is fixed and most were tight to start with. This old tub's crew was nice to her . . . once. Course, we can't test the engine 'til the screw's clear of the bottom, but like I said, it should work."

"Then it'll just be a matter of steamin' this old bucket outta this creepy place," Monk said.

"Hopefully. Providin' the water's deep enough. Might have to lighten ship and take her out at high tide. Hell, them fellas got her in here somehow, didn't they?"

Monk pulled a small wad of leaves from Gilbert's pouch and stuck them in his cheek, grimaced, then handed the pouch back while he vigorously chewed to get past the initial foul taste. Gilbert grinned and aimed another splurt of tobacco juice at Laney's bubbles.

"You don't like Laney much, do you?" Monk asked, nodding at the water.

"No. Does anybody?"

Lieutenant Monk snorted. "Well, come to that, I guess not. Must get lonesome."

"Laney?" Gilbert asked incredulously. "He *wants* everybody to hate him. He likes it."

Monk didn't point out that Gilbert and Isak both acted like they didn't give much of a damn about anybody either, except Tabby. They'd finally established communications with one of the portable transmitter/receivers, a generator, and the ship's own wireless antennae array. The first news they'd heard was about the victory at Rangoon—and the storm trouble *Walker* had encountered. Included was a list of her dead and injured. Tabby's bravery had been mentioned, but so had her condition. Monk knew Gilbert and Isak would never show it, but they were both worried about the absent member of their strange little tribe.

"Do you *hate* him?" Monk asked.

Gilbert looked surprised. "Only when he's around. Otherwise, I don't think about him one way or another. An' it ain't like I'd go over there an' stand on his air hose or nothin'. Now, if somethin' swum up an' ate his sorry ass . . ." He paused, thoughtful. "Ya know, I guess it'ud be a shame, sorta," he admitted. "Not 'cause I like him or anything, but there ain't many of us 'born' destroyermen left, after all. Less than a hunnerd, from two ships now, not countin' them pig-boat pukes. 'Cats are swell, but they're, well . . . new. 'Sides, if Laney got ate, who'd put on that brass hat an' jump in the water? You'd probably make me do it an' I don't even know how!" He spat again. "Naw, Laney's a turd, but he ain't a useless turd. That's somethin', I guess. Biggest problem I got with him now is that just 'cause he used to be in charge o' me an' Isak, he thinks he still is."

"I'll fix that," Monk promised.

"Yeah? How? He thinks he's still in charge o' you too."

Isak was back on deck with the others when they hoisted Laney out of the water, and he, Gilbert, Sammy, and Monk helped him over the rail of the low-sided basket he'd been standing in and onto the ship. Monk undogged the helmet and he and Isak twisted it off.

"Chop the compressor," Monk called.

"Shit," Laney proclaimed when the stuttering drone subsided. "Somebody gimme a drink and a chew!" They eased him down on a bench they'd positioned near the ship's rail, and he sprawled on it while they helped him out of the suit.

"Did you finish?" Chapelle asked, offering a canteen.

"Best I could," Laney gasped after a long swig. "Water's murky as hell and the hull's covered with weed. Had to do a lot of scrapin'. No barnacles, though. Maybe the water killed 'em? Between that, the bubbles, the fire, an' all them creepy toad lizards gawkin' at me all the time . . ." He seemed to shiver involuntarily.

"You actually *saw* them?"

"*Saw* 'em! Hell, them slimy devils was on the *basket* with me before I was done! Didn't you hear me bangin' on the hull plates?"

"I did," Isak confessed. "Wondered why you was doin' that."

Laney glared at Isak, then at the Marines gathered near. "Fine lot of good any o' you did! They could'a been gnawin' my bones right now, and you'd all still be standin' here starin' at the water wonderin' how much longer I'd be!"

"We *were* startin' to wonder . . ." Gilbert said.

Chapelle gave him a warning look.

"You have my most sincere apologies, Mr. Laaney," Lieutenant Bekiaa-Sab-At said. "We watched them as closely as we could, but we only saw the eyes above water that they let us see. We had no idea any were that close to you. You continued to work, so we assumed you were safe."

Laney snatched Gilbert's tobacco pouch and furrowed his brow. "That's the weird thing," he said. "First one o' them buggers came driftin' into view, why, I was tempted to be a touch nervous. I hollered some, but I knew you'd never hear me over the compressor, so I waved the torch at 'em a little. They stopped, but didn't go away."

"There more than one?" Moe asked in his clipped English. He'd joined the group, as had half the crew who'd been working nearby.

Suddenly conscious that he was the center of attention, Laney nodded grandly. "D'rectly, there was swarms of 'em, just floatin' around me!"

"Why didn't you yank on your line?" asked Ben Mallory, who'd been drawn from his inspection of one of the damaged aircraft crates, aft.

"Yeah!" chorused others.

"We'd have pulled you up," assured Monk, looking at Gilbert.

"Well . . . that's the weird part. There they was, an' there I was, just lookin' at each other. Ugly bastards too, bobbin' there in the gloom. God knows what they thought o' me in the suit. Anyway, when they didn't eat me right off, I . . . I just got this funny feelin' they weren't going to. Don't know why." The suit was off his shoulders now, exposing his wet, hairy chest. He shrugged. "Maybe it was sorta like when a dog comes runnin' up to you. Sometimes you can just tell if he wants you to pet him or if he wants to eat yer hand."

"No dog'd ever bite you, Laney," Gilbert jabbed. "Might as well chew arsenic."

Laney rolled his eyes. "Two words, two syllables, mouse brain: Piss. Off." He looked at Chapelle. "So I went back to work. I guess, compared to them flashies that nearly got me that time, I got this *feelin'* these critters could *think*, you know? After that, it came to me that they could'a ate me before I ever even saw 'em, so they must'a *decided* not to." He shook his head. "Then came the weird part."

"You just said the other part was the weird part," Isak said accusingly.

Laney scowled. "It was, goddamn it! I'm tellin' this, so shove off! It was *all* weird, but it got even weirder, see? There I was, surrounded by giant 'toady-gators.' . . . Hey, that sounds pretty good! Toady-gators! Anyway, still surrounded by toady-gators, I finished up that second plate and signaled for you to move me an' lower down the last one. . . ." He stopped and glared at Isak again. "It just hit me. You *did* hear *that* signal!"

"That time it made sense," Isak replied defensively. "You used the signal you said you'd use. The first time I figgered you was bangin' on barnacles 'er somethin'."

"I just said there weren't any barnacles!"

"I didn't know that."

"Chief Laney—" Chapelle prodded.

"Yeah, well, I was havin' some trouble with that last plate. The curve was pretty good," he said, complimenting the 'Cats who'd formed it, "but it wanted to hang sorta bad. I couldn't tack the top and hold it against the bottom, if you know what I mean. Needed two fellas down there."

"Only the one suit," Chapelle reminded him.

"I know. But it was okay! Them toads must'a figgered out what I was tryin' ta do, and seen I couldn't do it by myself!" He stopped and shook his head again. "Couple of 'em helped me! Damned if they didn't!"

"You're telling me these creatures—the same ones we

fought a *pitched battle* against just a couple of nights ago—actually helped you patch this ship? Patch the very hole they probably used to get in and out?" Chapelle demanded.

Laney was nodding. "The last part of it, anyway. Not even the little ones could'a squirmed through there by then, but yeah, they did. Pushed in on the bottom while I tacked the top, then kept holdin' it while I ran a short bead on the bottom." He looked around defensively. "I just got this *feelin'*, ya know? That they knew what I was up to and had decided to help."

For a moment, except for the gentle whoosh of the boiler and the cries from the nearby jungle, there was utter silence on *Santa Catalina.*

"Well," Chapelle said at last, quietly, glancing over the side at the eyes in the water, "do you have confidence in your repairs, Chief Laney?"

"As much confidence as a fella can ever have in a weld, and an underwater weld at that," he said, hedging. "God-damn welded ships crack up and sink all the time, you know."

"It'll have to do until we can get her in the dry dock back home," Russ said. "We'll drill holes at the seams and use bolts too—if you don't mind going back in the water."

Laney deflated just a little, but nodded. "They didn't eat me last time. I guess they don't mean to. Them just bein' around probably keeps other things away. I'll go."

"You be sure an' tell 'em hi'dy for me, will ya?" Isak said with a snicker.

"I will," Laney grumbled. "Matter of fact, no reason you can't go next time. It'll just be slidin' bolts through some holes and backin' 'em up. The suit's no big deal. You can say 'hi'dy' right to 'em. Who knows, maybe you'll get a date."

Isak eased a step closer to Gilbert. That was what always happened whenever he tried to be friendly, talk to folks outside his "clan." Inevitably, things escalated to a point where they started expecting him to *do* things. "You go, Dean," he said, his voice subconsciously regressing to its flat, reedy, monosyllabic norm. "They're your friends. You need friends."

By that evening, with the assistance of the "portable" steam-powered generators from Chief Electrician's Mate Rodriguez's growing concern in Baalkpan, and the combination of his crude electric motors and the sophisticated Lemurian pumps, tons of brackish, ill-smelling water had already gushed out of the aft hold. Laney's patch leaked, but seemed to be holding well enough. Myriad bizarre creatures slithered or skittered in the emerging silt accumulated in the ship. The workers down there, occasionally tightening Laney's bolts or shoveling mucky silt toward a hose that reliquefied it so it could be sucked from the bilge, were constantly on alert for squirmy things. At one point, Isak emitted a most unmanly shriek, but then went after something that looked like a horseshoe crab with long, wickedly curved and articulated downward-stabbing forelegs, or "jabbers," as he later called them. It had come marching directly at him out of the gloom, and probably spurred by his own initial terror, he relentlessly pursued the thing with a wrecking bar long after it reconsidered its attack. He never found it.

At about 2100, *Santa Catalina* began to groan. She'd been glued to the bottom for so long, her sudden buoyancy was stressing her old bones as she tried to break the suction. Chapelle had everything they could spare thrown over the side—empty or damaged crates, chairs, beds. He insisted they save the springs out of the mattresses, but they were cut up and the dank, mildewed fabric and stuffing went. A lot of the once submerged crates in the hold contained spare engines for the P-40s. Many of the engines were probably ruined, but they could salvage parts and the steel was good. The crates around them went. Paneling was torn from the officers' and passengers' staterooms and went into the swamp. Most was too rotten to save anyway. *Santa Catalina* was Cramp made, in 1913, and everyone but Gilbert was surprised to learn she wasn't a coal burner. If she had been, Chapelle might have lightened her still more by transferring much of her remaining fuel to the barges alongside. The expedition, with the additional help of the rest of the squadron still anchored downstream, could have cut wood for her proposed voyage to Baalkpan. As it was, the ship had only about three hundred tons of fuel, and that was somewhat suspect. She could never make it to Baalkpan without a refill. It struck Chapelle that she never would have made it out of Tjilatjap with her original crew—back in their "old" world—and he felt a wave of sadness for their futile sacrifice. He transmitted the need for fuel oil from either Baalkpan, Aryaal, or First Fleet.

Considering her heavy cargo, Russ finally decided to pump out the ship's ballast. He knew he was running a risk, because with so many crates on deck, the ship might be top-heavy, but they had to break her hold on the bottom. After that, they still had to get her through the shallow swamp and closer to Tjilatjap without a tug, or anything but her own dubious, neglected power plant. He was afraid he'd have to lighten ship still more, and so he had Ben designate the crates most likely to have allowed the most corrosion to their contents. Even the worst-corroded plane was a treasure, but if they had to toss a few to save the rest, so be it.

Near dawn, with the tide pushing back against the flow of the river, the groaning hull suddenly stopped protesting. With a ponderous, swooping sensation, *Santa Catalina*'s stern finally freed itself from the muddy embrace that had clutched it for so long, and with an audible trembling moan, it swung a few degrees away from the jungle shore. Many of the expedition were asleep after a torturous night, but the unmistakable motion of the suddenly floating stern instigated a growing, exhausted cheer that soon included all the now nearly two hundred Lemurian sailors and Marines inhabiting the ship, as well as the half dozen humans.

"Pipe down, pipe down," Chapelle called benevolently over the newly repaired shipwide circuit. He himself had fallen asleep on the bridge, sitting on one of the few chairs they'd preserved. He glanced at his watch, realizing he'd slept through the morning watch change. He wondered briefly if there'd *been* a change. No reason to do it on the bridge of a beached ship, he supposed. Hmm. Monk should be officer of the deck. "Major Mallory, Lieutenant Bekiaa, and Lieutenant Monk to the bridge, on the double. Bosun's Mate Saama-Kera and Jannik-Fas will coordinate a detail to make sure we remain secure to the shore for now, but don't swing around and beach again either." He grinned. "The rest of you may continue to celebrate for one entire minute!"

The cheers resumed, punctuated by laughter, and the ship practically throbbed with stamping feet.

All around, in the water below, large yellow eyes popped up into the brightening day. The Great Mother of the Dry Folk had stirred from her sleep at last. They'd known she was alive, that she breathed once more for a couple of dark spans, but now she'd moved! They'd felt it in the water! All regretted their attack on the Dry Folk. They simply hadn't known. Would that their meeting had been different! They certainly respected the Dry Folk now, not only as warriors but for their medicine as well. The wounded they'd returned were healing quickly, and they seemed near to healing their Great Mother! They actually envied them that. Not that the natives would ever want to heal a Great Mother, but it might be nice to have a Great Mother that inspired such devotion—an actual desire to *heal* her in the first place. Most extraordinary creatures.

CHAPTER 17

Respite Island

Respite Island appeared to be all its name implied as the squadron approached it from the northwest the following morning. Doubtless volcanic, the island featured a pair of high peaks near its western coast, and the land around them was a mixture of dense, exotic jungles, interspersed with cultivated fields. Limestone cliffs jutted skyward along the north flank, heavily undermined by the relentless sea, but as the ships steamed east, they encountered a broad barrier reef that protected a vast anchorage on the northeast coast. *Achilles* was once more under her own power, but *Icarus* led the way, flying a large pennant to summon a pilot. Before long, a small, extreme, single-masted topsail schooner slashed its way toward them from beyond a point of land. It was a gorgeous little craft, Matt decided: around fifty feet long, painted dark blue with bright yellow trim and a white bottom. It was only about twice as large as one of *Walker*'s launches, but carried a truly magnificent spread of canvas. It was fast too, faster than anything Matt had ever seen under sail. He grinned at the sight of her.

"Pretty little thing," the Bosun commented.

"Yeah," Matt replied. "One of these days when all this is over and I get to retire, I want one just like her!" His grin suddenly faded. "I bet Sandra would like that," he murmured. Gray said nothing. What could he say?

Quickly, the little schooner raced to *Icarus*' side and the smaller Imperial frigate hoisted a clear signal to "follow me." As they steamed around the point and farther out to sea to avoid the reef, the schooner dropped back and paced *Walker* for a distance, its crew openly gawking at the sleek, freshly touched-up old destroyer that moved along so apparently effortlessly with her twin screw propellers. Matt doubted they gawked with envy; they had no reason to be envious, given their trim, beautifully appointed little craft, but he conceded they might have been struck with amazement.

Imperial shipmakers had developed crude screw propellers, but they were virtually unused. Paddle wheels were "tried and true" and required no underwater hull piercings, which tended to leak. Matt firmly believed that paddle wheels were far more vulnerable, not only to battle damage but to heavy weather as well, but he could understand why a ship without them might look strange to people so accustomed to their use. However inefficient they were, they worked, and in a very visible way. *Walker* could throw up quite a wake at higher speeds, but right now there was little more than if she'd been under sail. This, combined with her odd appearance and obvious steel construction, had to make quite an impression even on people more technologically advanced than the Lemurians had been at first. The little schooner certainly made an impression on him.

Many of the Lemurians held up their hands, palm out, in their traditional greeting, and the schooner's crew appeared to notice them for the first time. There was a sudden disarray among its sails, and then she was slanting away, back the direction she'd come. Some of the bridge watch chuckled, and Matt did too. He doubted the schooner was supposed to abandon her pilot—whoever she'd put aboard *Icarus* was probably throwing a fit.

After a long reach to eastward, the pilot must have indicated the channel, because *Icarus* turned and steamed back toward the island. *Achilles* made the same turn at the same point, and *Walker* followed suit. At their crawling pace, it would still be nearly an hour before they came under the guns of the looming limestone fortress overlooking the anchorage that Jenks had told them to expect. All the same, Matt summoned Boats Bashear.

"Another thirty minutes I should think, then line the sides, if you please."

"Aye, aye, Captain," Bashear replied and left the bridge, fingering his bosun's pipe. Exactly half an hour later, the pipe trilled insistently and the crew turned out in style. White T-shirts, blue or white kilts and dungarees, and the ever-present Dixie cup hats had become the standard tropical (as if they'd needed any other kind) dress, and as the mixed crew lined the rails, Matt was pleased by how good they looked. Maybe a little bizarre—with humans and 'Cats, tall and short, the 'Cats with their multicolored furs—but good. Behind him, Chack's Marines had lined the weather deck in full battle garb of dark blue kilts with red piping, white leather torso armor, and crossed black cartridge box straps. There were polished bronze greaves, sword hilts, and "tin hats" on their heads, and bright muskets on their shoulders with gleaming fixed bayonets. Chack paced among them, inspecting the troops for perfection, while he still wore his own battered American helmet, pattern of 1917 cutlass, and a Krag rifle suspended muzzle down by a strap over his shoulder.

Matt raised his binoculars. He hadn't expected much harbor traffic, and he'd been right. There were several ships at anchor, but none appeared to be warships, and a couple even looked like they'd been through the recent storm. They were weathered and washed out, as if they'd been too long at sea, and their lines were a little jagged with missing rails and spliced yards and masts. Only one was a steamer and it was rather small. They were close enough now to see the Imperial flag floating high above the fortress, and when a thought struck him, Matt studied the ships once more. Hmm. All but the steamer were flying the Company banner. He had to force himself to consider the probability that regardless of how corrupt the Company may be, chances were that the officers and crews of those ships were just honest sailors working for a living. He wondered what cargo they'd brought, however.

More small boats of every description darted to and fro, seemingly suspended on air. Now that they'd entered the vast lagoon, the water was utterly clear, almost crystalline in its purity.

"Skipper," Palmer said, "*Achilles* sends that she'll put in at the Company dock. It's the biggest one. There's no naval dock here. Commodore Jenks says he'll signal *Icarus* to take up a blocking station to prevent those Company ships from getting underway, and asks if we'll position ourselves to cover *Icarus* and *Achilles* with our guns. He . . . ah . . . begs that you'll give the people here the benefit of the doubt for now, and he's going to try to sort things out himself."

Matt watched a series of signals race up a halyard aboard Jenks's ship. "Very well," he said, then lowered his voice to a grumble. "What does he think I'll do? Just start blasting away?" He hadn't meant for anyone to hear him, but the Bosun chuckled.

"Prob'ly. And why not?" He motioned at one of the Company flags. "We may not be at war with the Empire yet, but the last thing we saw with one of those flags shot at us without warning. We *are* at war with the Company, ain't we?"

"The Company, but maybe not all Company ships. Yet," Matt said.

"Jumpin' Jesus!" Kutas almost chirped.

Bradford was on the starboard bridgewing, studying the island beyond the port, but at Kutas's words he looked back at the chief quartermaster's mate. "What?" he inquired. Kutas's face was practically purple.

"Them boats! The little ones . . . the fishing boats!" was all he managed.

Bradford redirected his glasses. "Goodness gracious!" he exclaimed. Many of the small boats Kutas had been trying to avoid running down were crewed almost exclusively by practically nude women. Some *were* nude, and their bronze skins and dark hair suddenly drew every eye. Even the men lining the rails had begun to lean incredulously forward, trying for a better view. To them, *Walker* had suddenly entered some magic, mythical paradise. It was Shangri-la without the snow.

"The joint's swarming with broads!" somebody shouted excitedly. It was true. Even if the island hadn't been exotically inviting enough before, the apparent abundance of dusky-skinned beauties lining the dock and the beach beyond was enough to send an electric thrill down every human spine. It was like a scene out of Gable's *Mutiny on the Bounty*. Many women working seines through the light surf along the shore were naked too, as best the men could tell—and they did their very best to tell.

"Stand those men to attention this instant!" Matt told the Bosun, and Gray bolted down the stairs and through the forward hatch onto the fo'c'sle. For a moment he paused, staring at the boats, as guilty as the rest of the crew. He shook himself.

"What's the matter with you . . . you . . . perverts?" Gray ranted with considerably less than ordinary zeal and imagination. "Them gals are practically *children*, fer God's sake! *Don't* tell me you devils never seen nekkid women before!"

"Can't," Stites breathed, "but it's been a long, *long* time!"

"Shut up, you! You're supposed to set an example!"

Paul Stites rounded on the Bosun. "What kind of example you want me to set, S.B.? Jeez!"

For once, even the Bosun was speechless. "Just grab yer eyeballs before they drop in the water!" Gray managed at last, "or by God, I'll kick 'em back in yer head!" He turned, glaring down the rail. "All you shif'less, useless bastards!

Try to be *destroyermen* a little longer, or you'll queer the Skipper's plans, and I *will* kill you for that! We make the wrong impression here, we might as well just turn around!" He whirled back at Stites. "And as for you, get back to your post on the number one gun! We're showin' up here all friendly an' such, but there might be a goddamn fight!"

Above, Matt rubbed his forehead. It had been a year and a half since his men had seen any women but the nurses and "nannies." The few women they'd rescued from S-19 who'd been . . . willing . . . had been a help, but this was like whacking a shark on the nose with bloody meat. He watched *Achilles* maneuver close to the dock as *Icarus* proceeded toward a place where she could supervise the Company ships. A slow roll of gunfire erupted from the side of *Achilles* as she saluted the fort's flag far above the harbor, and the smoke and report of the cannons drifted back across them. Perhaps that would have a sobering effect. Momentarily, an answering salute rumbled from the fortress.

"All stop," Matt said. "All astern one-third." He looked around at the others in the pilothouse. "I think we'll not go any closer for now. Kutas, we won't anchor either, so try to keep this position if the current allows." He turned to Frankie Steele, who'd just stepped into the pilothouse. "Rig out the launches and make preparations to take the Marines ashore. If Jenks needs a hand, I think Chack's 'Cats might scare the locals, but probably not as bad as those sex-starved men out there."

Ultimately, there wasn't any fighting. As soon as *Achilles* touched the pier, her own Marines swarmed ashore and three squads of red-coated troops swept into the city and along the docks. Another squad formed up on the dock itself, and a fifth rowed out to each Company ship in turn, leaving only when the Imperial flag had replaced the Company banners. It was that easy, and it all happened about that fast. Matt knew his own Marines were probably better infantry than Jenks's Marines, and Jenks knew it too, but the Imperials seemed professional and intimidating enough at the moment.

"*Achilles* wants us to come on in," Palmer reported. "Snug up to the Company dock just astern of her. Jenks has all the local cheeses gathered up for a talk."

"Very well," Matt replied. "Take us in, Mr. Kutas." To the Bosun down below, he called, "The crew will remain on parade until further notice. The first man who utters a sound will be transferred to the tanker squadron when it arrives. Do I make myself clear?"

Walker eased up alongside the dock, gray smoke curling skyward from the second and fourth stacks, blower almost sighing with relief. Boats Bashear trilled his pipe and Lemurian line handlers threw ropes at gawking men on the dock. One, dressed much like a thousand dockworkers the Bosun had seen in a hundred ports "back home," just stood there when a 'Cat expertly tossed him a line and it fell to the dock and dropped in the water.

"Catch the goddamn rope!" Gray bellowed at the man. "Ain't you never seen a rope before? It's called a *rope*! You're supposed to *catch* it, you imbi-cile!" Gray nodded at the 'Cat to haul in and try again. "Drop it this time, and I'll tie the whole damn ship off to you, since you ain't got the sense of a stanchion!" he warned the stranger.

This time the man caught the wet rope and took a creditable turn, although he still seemed shaken. "Dumb-aass," muttered the 'Cat, loud enough to be heard, and the man just gaped again.

Gray glanced from bow to stern. "Singled up, fore and aft, Skipper," he called to the bridgewing.

"All stop, finished with engines," Matt commanded and Pack Rat rang the engine room telegraph. He looked back at the dock. Men by the dozens, then scores, some dressed as laborers and others in their finery, were approaching the ship. Commodore Jenks strode among them, accompanied by a group of well- but practically dressed men with wide straw hats on their heads. Another man, rather fat, and easily the most elaborately dressed, rode at the head of the procession on the back of an honest-to-God *donkey*, fanning himself with yet another wide-brimmed hat. Matt suspected the donkey was a descendant of cargo carried by those early Indiamen. Jenks's Marines were still formed up at the *Achilles* gangway, and when Matt caught his eye, Jenks gave him a slight nod.

"Have Mr. McFarlane secure number two, if you please, but maintain pressure on number four." Matt turned to Bradford, who'd rejoined him on the bridgewing after rushing up to the fire control platform above to get a better view. He hadn't been gone but a minute or two, and seemed uncharacteristically nervous. "What's the matter, Courtney? You seem distracted. Looks like you'll be able to lay in a lifetime supply of those goofy hats you like."

"Indeed," Bradford replied, then allowed a small smile. "The 'matter' is, Captain Reddy, I'm a 'diplomat' in name only. I've only ever dealt with beings who I was relatively sure were being honest with me. I wouldn't count Billingsley, since he turned out to be . . . whatever he is, and besides, I never had to bargain with *him*. Perhaps dealing with Saan-Kakja's Sky Priest Meksnaak might count as a 'disingenuous encounter,' but he turned out fairly honest in the end. In any event, I've never had to negotiate with anyone who was practiced at it at all, and perhaps today—surely at some point, with this entire empire to draw upon—I'm bound to encounter someone who's been studying diplomacy and deceit their entire lives!"

"I wouldn't worry too much about it, Courtney," Matt said, and his voice went flat.

Bradford didn't notice. "Easy for you to say! You've had plenty of practice at what *you* do!"

Matt shook his head. "Notwithstanding this fine, clear lagoon, we're all in murky waters here. None of us really knows what will happen. I just mean that you shouldn't worry too much about what to say. Our mission's pretty straightforward: find Sandra and the princess, and make the people who took them pay." He shrugged. "Since it looks like those 'people' are the Company, *it* has to pay. In that respect, our mission and Jenks's new cause do overlap, and if we're both successful in achieving that, it might even help us gain another alliance of some sort as well. But make no mistake; we're not here to 'negotiate.' At least not for anything beyond what we discussed yesterday evening at dinner. Apparently, that's more of a business transaction"—he made a face—"and I'm sure you can handle that."

The procession had come to a halt alongside *Walker* and appeared to be waiting expectantly. "Pass the word," Matt said, speaking louder. "The Bosun, Stites, Chack, and two Marines of his choice will accompany me and Mr. Bradford ashore."

"Weapons?" Steele asked.

"You bet. From now on, always."

Marine Captain Chack-Sab-At proceeded across the gangplank, followed by two Marines with muskets on their shoulders. Matt was interested to note that he'd chosen First Sergeant Blas-Ma-Ar, whom the Bosun called "Blossom" for some reason, and the former Aryaalan noble, Corporal Koratin. Matt and Courtney followed them, dressed in their best, with 1911 Colts holstered at their sides. Courtney wouldn't wear a cutlass—he was more of a menace to himself with one than to anyone else—but Matt had his now somewhat battered but highly polished Academy sword. Bringing up the rear was the Bosun with his Thompson and Stites with a BAR—Browning automatic rifle. Together they stepped briskly up to the mounted official and Chack and his Marines stepped aside.

"Governor Radcliff," Jenks said to the man on the quite ordinary-looking donkey, "may I present the man who has made our arrival here, bearing this gloomy news, possible? There is no doubt that my ship and I, at least, would have been lost in the recent action without him, and had his people not previously rescued the Princess Rebecca, there would be no hope at all that she might yet live."

Governor Radcliff slid the short distance to the ground from the burro's back and peered intently at Captain

Reddy. The feat didn't require much in the way of physical exertion, but he managed it with a certain athletic grace inconsistent with his girth. He touched his immense graying mustache as if making sure every hair was in place. "Please do, Commodore. From our . . . abbreviated conversation, it would seem the Empire at large owes him and his people a great debt indeed."

"Very well, then." Jenks proceeded, bowing slightly and gesturing at Matt. "I present my excellent friend, Captain Matthew Reddy, High Chief of the American Clan, and Commander in Chief of all Allied Forces united beneath the Banner of the Trees."

Matt glanced at Jenks. They'd considered numerous possibilities regarding how they'd be received here. Apparently, Jenks considered this Governor Radcliff an ally—for now. Matt saluted. "Captain Matthew Reddy, United States Navy ship *Walker*. I request permission to come ashore, sir."

Radcliff looked at Jenks with a frown. "Well, what is he? A captain or a chief?"

"Both, Your Excellency. Ah, as I understand it, he prefers 'captain' while in direct command of his ship."

"And he's standing right in front of you . . . Governor." Gray growled under his breath. He too was still holding a salute.

"Boats!" Matt ground out.

The governor of Respite chuckled and Jenks quickly whispered something in his ear. "Oh! Of course!" He sketched a salute and Matt and Gray dropped theirs. "Permission granted, certainly—not that we could deny it, if the good commodore has been remotely accurate in his description of your ship's capabilities." He turned to look at Chack and the other Marines. "And what have we here?" An expression of genuine wonder crossed his face.

"They call them 'Lemurians,' Excellency," Jenks supplied. "Descendants of the ancient"—he glanced apologetically at Chack—"'Ape Folk' that the Founders described in their journals."

"If I may?" Matt said, not really asking. "As Commodore Jenks is likely about to inform you, they don't like the term 'Ape Folk' very much. I think they've figured out what an ape is by talking to us, even though they've never seen one. Jenks has told me you *do* have apes, descendants of pets aboard your old ships. Seeing those apes and being equated with them is likely to cause resentment. Trust me, sir, you really don't want to create resentment among my crew, and particularly among these Lemurian Marines."

"Indeed not, I assure you!" Governor Radcliff exclaimed. "These friends of yours seem rather touchy, Commodore," he said in an aside to Jenks.

"Still standing right here," Gray said. Matt rolled his eyes.

"Indeed. Please forgive me," the governor said. "I'm not accustomed to speaking so forthrightly with strangers."

"I believe you may find, as I have," Jenks stated in a neutral tone, "that is about the only way to communicate with Captain Reddy and his people. Perhaps it is time, and past, for a serious, forthright discussion about many things, Your Excellency."

"So it would seem," Radcliff agreed. "Captain Reddy, please do accompany us to Government House." He fanned himself with his wide hat. "We have much to discuss, and this heat is most tiresome. I would be honored if you would join me in some refreshment." He glanced at Chack. "And . . . charmed . . . if your Lemurian Marines and other companions would join us as well."

"Thank you, sir. We'll gladly attend. But maybe there are a few more pressing matters?" Matt looked at Jenks questioningly.

The governor clasped his hands behind his back and raised his chin. "Forthrightly, then," he said. "Captain Reddy, even as we speak, the Company Director and all his factors are being placed under house arrest by Commodore Jenks's Marines. I have personally ordered the territorial constabulary and militia to scour the island for any possible Company agents. My militia is ill-equipped, and while they may not be Marines, I expect they will be highly motivated." He paused and frowned. "I had never previously met Commodore Jenks before this day, but his reputation as a discoverer, a loyalist, and a man of irreproachable honor is universal within the Empire. With the few brief words we have shared thus far regarding this emergency, I have no doubt that the very existence of the Empire is at risk." He sighed. "Understand, something insidious has been brewing beneath the surface for a great long time, and the people here, and elsewhere, are not blind. I'm a loyal subject of the Empire, but even I can see that something has gone fundamentally wrong. Some will see this atrocity that you bring word of as the final spark necessary to ignite a powder keg of secession that has long been standing, waiting to explode. It may even be that Respite must finally split from the government over this event, if it does not suppress the Company at last. Perhaps I may repair the rift before the split becomes permanent, but I have a sick feeling that the twisted, almost incomprehensible agenda of the Company might shatter my beloved Empire forever."

CHAPTER 18

Yap Island (Shikarrak)

"Okay," Dennis Silva hissed, "don't nobody move! There's one o' them shit-sacks plopped square on our path ahead."

Instantly, the rest of the group ceased heaving on the boat and did their best to freeze in spite of the life-sapping heat. It was a good thing he hadn't told them to be quiet, because they simply couldn't have stopped their noisy gasping in the sodden air.

"Where?" Sandra Tucker wheezed, trying to clear the burning sweat from her eyes with the back of a grimy hand.

"Just ahead. Larry seen it first," Dennis admitted. Lawrence was poised, still as a statue, staring straight ahead. "Little booger's a good pointer. Make a swell bird dog someday." He was slowly easing the Doom Whomper from his shoulder.

"I still don't see it," Sandra said anxiously.

"I do, now that my good eye's turned thataway. Bastards is like camee-lee-ins. Blend right in. I never seen anything like it!" There was genuine admiration in his tone.

"My God!" Princess Rebecca exclaimed. "I see it! It's quite close indeed!"

"I see it too," Captain Lelaa commented. "It must have sensed our approach and positioned itself to intercept us. It takes them some time to blend in so well."

In recent days they'd all learned far more about shiksaks than they'd ever cared to know. There were more of them all the time, and Lawrence was growing increasingly nervous and upset, urging them on whenever they stopped to rest or sleep a very few hours. The boat was repaired, but it was big and heavy and the move was slow going, even with all of them pushing, pulling, or placing rollers in its path. They'd almost reached the end of the bamboo jungle and the going would soon improve, but their progress thus far could be measured in yards and sometimes feet per hour.

"Nothin' for it," Silva groused. "Larry, it's time for us to do our 'trick' again." Lawrence twitched his growing bristly crest and then, as fluid as mercury, flowed into the thick bamboo beside the trail. Silva looked at Captain Rajendra. "You stay here. If that sumbitch hops thisaway, you better already be dead if any harm comes to any o' these ladies, you hear?"

"I hear you, *Mr.* Silva," he snarled. "Such a thing goes without saying!"

"I hope so, but I feel better with it said." He was easing toward the trail Lawrence had already taken. "Whatever you do, though, *don't* shoot at it!"

"Mr. Silva?" asked Abel Cook, rising from within the boat and grasping the gunwale with his bandaged hand. His face was flushed. In spite of the polta paste they'd almost exhausted on him, he still had a persistent infection since they'd cut off his finger. Sandra was sure they'd gotten all the kudzu stringers out, but suspected that tiny particles may have entered his bloodstream. So far, it didn't look like they'd "taken root," and she doubted they could, but they must be toxic in some way and they'd clearly initiated a major response by the boy's immune system. "I would like to come," he said. "I can help!"

"No, boy," Silva replied in a gentler tone. "You and Mr. Brassey stay here and help protect the gals. I know *ya'll* will." With that, he was gone.

Lawrence could hear the thing breathing as he snaked through the bamboo or the strange cane alongside it. He'd never figured out whether the things had a well-developed sense of smell, either when he was here before or now, but he stayed downwind just in case. The breathing grew louder, more labored-sounding, the closer he came to the beast. With their immense bulk, shiksaks had to have a hard time sucking air during their annual venture upon dry land. He'd heard during his hatchlinghood and adolescent tutelage that the things sometimes ventured ashore on Tagran, his native isle, and were killed in a cooperative hunt, but here on the island that Silva called "Yap" was the only place they regularly did so. The others that occasionally menaced Tagran were probably lost or just old and wanted to lay their eggs in a place without so much competition for space and food.

Slowly, he eased closer, until all that remained between him and the massive, camouflaged flank was a single sturdy stand of bamboo. He glanced directly downwind, hoping Silva had had enough time to get in position. He took a breath. With a sharp, fierce cry, he lunged forward with the musket he carried, burying the sharp triangular bayonet deep into the monster's side. Twisting the blade and yanking it free, he fired the musket as directly into the gushing wound as he could, spattering the thin, slippery, almost watery blood all over himself and everything around him. Then he ran like hell.

With a thunderous, reverberating, outraged *groank!* the shiksak heaved its head and torso high and to the right. The bamboo splintered as the beast changed its direction and shifted its back legs to position them for a leap. The camouflage pattern rapidly drained away, replaced by a mottled greenish purple as the creature launched itself through the tall shoots. Lawrence was faster in a sprint than any human, but he nevertheless had to negotiate the rigid upright obstacles. All the shiksak had to do was smash them down. Still, he was clear before it landed with a crashing, earth-trembling grunt. He raced ahead, even as the beast gathered itself for another leap. A dense tangle of shoots appeared before him, and he reversed the musket, trying to use the butt to batter a way through. The bayonet end might have helped part the bamboo, but it might also get stuck. He had no choice. Lowering his head, he dug in with his claws and plowed forward. Behind him, he heard the crash of the shiksak's next hop and knew it would be close this time.

It didn't crush him, just barely, but the tall, heavy bamboo it knocked down fell across his legs and tail, pinning him to the ground. He struggled and squirmed, trying to slip out from under the trunks, but there were too many and they were too tangled. There was a gust of hot breath and he felt the strain building as the shiksak scrabbled quickly forward, keeping him pinned until it could seize him with its jaws.

"Hey, Larry," came a calm voice. Just ahead. Lawrence saw a ragged pair of go-forwards with two big feet stuck in them. His view traveled up past the battered cut-off dungarees and latched onto Silva, standing there with his bronze muscles tensed, his once black eyepatch faded and stained white with sweat, the huge rifle aimed, muzzle bobbing slightly in time with the motion of the shiksak.

The lock "clatched" and a cloud of white smoke "fissed" and swirled from the pan, but the gun didn't go off! Still, Silva continued aiming, steady as a rock. It probably took less than a second, but to Lawrence it seemed a lifetime. Suddenly an orange jet of flame gushed from the vent and a bigger jet vomited from the still gently bobbing muzzle amid a distinctive roar and gout of choking white smoke. In an instant, Lawrence felt himself grabbed by his proud new crest and dragged out from under the tangled bamboo. Silva was hauling him along the ground like a sack when Lawrence flailed at the hand and managed to scramble to his feet. Together, the big man and the smaller, ruffled Tagranesi bolted clear of the indiscriminate death throes of the mighty shiksak.

"Popped 'eem right in the noodle!" Silva chortled around great gulps of air as he and Lawrence finally wove their way to a stop. Behind them came the thundering, crashing, ground-shaking impacts of the thrashing, flopping—brainless—beast. They knew from experience that the shiksak might carry on like that for a quarter hour or so.

"I thought he had 'e . . . I," Lawrence admitted, gathering in his panting tongue to speak.

"Naw, ol' Silva wouldn't let that happen! You did good, you little scamp." He swabbed the Doom Whomper, wiped the lock with a piece of his shirt he kept in his pouch, then reloaded. Lawrence did the same with his musket when his hands stopped shaking. Silva held his weapon out, examining it. "She kinda hung-fired on me, though. I never get a chance to really clean her right, an' with all this moisture in the air, the fouling around the vent turns to soup."

"How did you know it 'ould still . . . shoot?"

Silva cackled. "Yep, I guess that must'a gave you a turn! I heard it hissin', see? I knew she'd go; I just had to hold her steady. Follow through."

"You sa'ed me," Lawrence said, a little resentfully. "Again."

Silva rubbed Lawrence's crest, then patted it down. "Hell, you saved *me*. All of us, likely." He pointed at his ruined eye. "Sometimes a fella don't notice as much when one o' his peepers is busted. I never saw the damn thing to start with. I prob'ly would'a marched straight down its throat if you didn't hit on it." He shrugged. "Let's get back. Them gals'll be worryin'. 'Bout you, anyway."

Lawrence was looking down, scratching the dirt with his toeclaws. Finally he exhaled noisily and looked up at Dennis. "This 'ill not 'urk," he said at last. "Us see too 'any shiksaks. They are here in . . . lots. Us take too long to go."

"Sure," Silva agreed, "we're seein' more o' them devils

every day—most we don't have to fight with, thank God. I figger we can dodge 'em a few more days till we can get the boat in the water, though."

"No!" Lawrence said adamantly. "I . . . should not tell you this, 'ut I ha' to. 'Ecky and Lieutenant Tucker are at stake." He paused. "There *lots* shiksaks here, 'ut not near all. They all get here, that is all there is."

"Sure, that's why we need to get off this bump."

"No. Too late. This . . . lots o' shiksaks on land, there hundreds—thousands? In sea near here, they get ready to co . . ." He shook his head irritably. "To get on land. No 'oat get out on sea until they are gone. Too late."

"Say," said Dennis thoughtfully. "You're probably right about that. Damn." He was silent a moment, thoughtful.

"Only thing to do, 'gals' get in trees, 'ig, tall trees. Us try to devend gals as long as us can. 'Orget 'oat. It no good. Us get gals in trees."

"You said everything else that can will get in the trees too. They might need a heap of defendin'."

"True. No choice."

Silva was scratching his beard. "Maybe not. Maybe so." He grinned. "I just had me a squirrelly notion. Maybe we can save the boat *and* everybody else too. Won't be easy, but nothin' else has been, so why whine about it? Maybe if all we save in the end is the gals, they're still gonna need that damn boat. I figger it's both, or what's the point?"

"You really ha' a 'notion'?" Lawrence asked.

"I *always* got notions. Some are better than others, I'll admit, but this just might work." He slung the Doom Whomper and started back through the forest of bamboo. "C'mon. You're gonna hafta help me sell this scheme. 'Sides, we still got a ways to heave that damn boat and time's a'wastin'!"

"I keep saying that!" Lawrence complained.

Silva's "scheme" almost killed them all. First, when he detailed it, it resulted in yet another near-violent confrontation with Rajendra and his remaining Imperials. Rajendra in particular thought it was insane, and almost had Princess Rebecca believing him this time. She'd thought their island ordeal was almost over, and she *so* wanted off the dreadful place. Young Brassey didn't remain silent this time, but openly sided with Silva and ultimately Sandra and the princess as Lawrence's clear certainty finally convinced them that, wild as it was, Silva's plan was their only hope. It was unquestionably Abel Cook's only hope, and Brassey had grown very protective of his injured friend. He knew Rajendra and the other Imperials considered the boy expendable, but he didn't, and he was beginning to suspect his princess didn't either. With Brassey, and eventually even carpenter Hersh, on Silva's side, that left only Rajendra, his engineer, and a single Imperial Marine objecting. There was no question of a democratic resolution, but the three holdouts doubted they could handle the "Mad American" by themselves, much less the rest of the heavily armed party. When Rebecca reluctantly decided to endorse the plan, the specter of treason reentered the dispute and open resistance melted away.

The second thing that almost destroyed them, despite the fact that they were molested by no more of the growing number of land-weary, lethargic shiksaks they saw, was the blistering, killing, physical pace Silva set beneath the murderous sun. The newly arrived shiksaks that had ventured so far from shore—probably staking an early claim to an ultimately less-crowded nesting area—would recover their "land legs" in time. They had to be finished by then. As the day wore on and they heaved the boat down the mild, much appreciated slope into the narrow savannah that Silva called the "kudzu patch," the apparent tension of the island itself began to grow. Lizard birds squawked querulously and the strange little birds in the clearing swarmed erratically from place to place, or burst their formations completely into chaotically buzzing individuals. The odd, purplish flowers of the kudzu seemed to dance and sway with the breeze, as though imitating live creatures grazing about. The prickly thorns, so small and difficult to see when the group had passed this way before, were now larger and more erect on the vines. They carefully gave them a wide berth, laying the wooden rollers to clear the menacing patches of the weed.

Odd, hoarse cries resonated from the tall trees ahead that separated them from the beach, and they saw many small—and not so small—creatures beginning to gather there. Shrieks exploded as fights broke out between different species. Lawrence warned that the fights would become general among individuals eventually, as the furry, gourd-like fruits in the trees were exhausted. Saying he had an idea, he sprinted back the way they'd come. A smallish shiksak thundered ashore, bellowing its arrival, beyond the massive trees ahead that they'd chosen for their size. It thumped and thudded directly beneath them, headed toward the boat at first, but then steered hungrily toward the coyly twitching kudzu flowers, crashing into the patch with a triumphantly gaping maw. It snapped voraciously at the flowers for several moments, but then seemed to grow sleepy, as if sated and now torpid. A little unsteady, it groped its way out of the kudzu in the direction of a distant shiksak that was still resting from its arrival.

"Young bull," Silva opined through gritted teeth as he reslung his weapon and took up his rope again. "Bet he don't get to be an *old* bull. Kinda sets a fella back, thinkin' 'bout all the times he's acted the same damn way." He gasped and heaved in time with the others. "Whoo-ee! Liber-tee! Where's the grub? Where's the broads?"

The raucous sounds of wildlife grew, birds erupted from the grass, the trees, everywhere, swirling madly and densely enough to create a kind of shade. Small shapes scampered in all directions to the extent that tripping became a concern. It was as if they somehow knew the full infestation was finally at hand. Even Rajendra quieted his objections and laid to with a will. It was late afternoon when, exhausted, panting, they finally placed the boat between the two trees they'd chosen, more by size, direction, and proximity than anything else. They rested briefly, gulping the rum-tinged water Brassey shared out with a tin cup. They'd already laid in plenty of water, and most of Silva's surviving "prize" rum he'd taken during their escape from Billingsley had gone to purify it into a kind of grog. Most, but not all. There were still medicinal purposes to consider. They didn't have a moment to lose, but they *had* to rest a little before they attempted their next pair of tasks. A misstep now or a mishandled line would doom them all.

"Are you ready for this?" Sandra finally asked.

Captain Lelaa nodded, looking at the trees, ears twitching appraisal. "I have been climbing masts since I was born," she said confidently. "These 'trunks' will be simpler."

"Them double-block falls are kinda heavy—an' you gotta make sure they don't get tangled up," Silva fussed. When they'd escaped, they unhooked the falls, thinking at least the rope might be handy. Now the heavy block-and-tackle arrangement might prove their salvation. They never could have built a set in time.

Lelaa practically sneered at Silva. "Mind your own business. Just keep those creatures up there away from me," she said. The creatures in question, a wild variety perched high in the tree's broad canopy above, had stopped squalling and now peered sullenly down at them.

Silva nodded, and setting down the Doom Whomper, he selected a loaded musket from within the boat. "You got it, Cap'n."

"What can I do to help?" Sister Audry asked, still somewhat breathless.

"Nothin' right now. Might not have to do anything a'tall 'til you climb aboard," Dennis answered, "unless you want to try your hand at shootin'?"

Sister Audry shook her head. She had no experience with firearms of any sort. She still looked concerned. "But the boat is so heavy! How will we lift it up there?"

"A double-block rig'll let you lift four times the weight as usual. I can hoist a thousand pounds easy as peein' with that rig . . . if you'll 'scuse me for sayin' so." He paused. "Just take my word for it. Five big fellas, two strong ladies—

countin' the squirt—a 'Cat that's prob'ly stronger than me, and a fuzzy, stripey lizard—I figger we can lift close to twice what that damn boat weighs. We oughta be able to manage without you and Mr. Cook." He looked around. "Say, where's that stripey lizard, anyway?"

Lawrence reappeared, trotting carefully around the kudzu with something almost as large as he was slung on his back. As he drew near, Sister Audry wrinkled her nose and Rebecca scolded, "What is that vile, revolting stench?"

Lawrence flung his burden down unapologetically, and Silva stooped to examine it.

"Yuk," Dennis said. "What the hell's that?"

"The scent glands o' that shiksak us killed," he said. There was a little blood around his mouth—he'd apparently paused long enough for a quick meal while he hacked the reeking things off with his cutlass.

"Aggh, they stink!" Silva exclaimed as the full force of the stench hit him. The glands were little more than pebbly, scaly slits in two large, dark patches of skin. "How's that work?" he wondered aloud. "I seen deer tarsals an' such, but you'd think a sea monster wouldn't do that."

"They aren't sea 'onsters on land," Lawrence pointed out.

"Well . . . what are you gonna do with 'em? Roll around on 'em an' pretend to be one?"

Lawrence actually seemed to consider it before shaking his head. "He 'ig 'ull," he said.

"Bull?"

"Yess. His scent keeph others a'ay. I tie these to trees, other 'ulls, at least, stay a'ay."

That made sense. Dennis had been a little worried about that. Big as these trees were, their roots weren't all that deep. He figured a really big shiksak might knock one over if he decided to whack on it.

"Good thinkin', twerp. Course, now you got that stink all over you, where are you gonna stay?"

"He can stay with us," Lelaa snapped, starting her climb. "If I can stand your stink, I can learn to put up with his."

For the first time since they'd been marooned on Yap

Island, Dennis Silva heard Rebecca's sweet, unfettered laugh. He grinned. "I guess I am gettin' a little ripe," he confessed, "but with mucho respecto, Cap'n, you smell kinda' like a hard-used hairball."

Lelaa snorted and scampered up the tree. About forty feet up, still short of the lower canopy, she stopped and began expertly rigging a seizing around the trunk. Something quick and leathery, with what looked like gliding wings stretched between its front and back legs, lunged down at her. Rajendra's musket flared, and light, fleshy bark sprayed at the creature's face. Never stopping, it leaped over their heads with a shrill cry, arrested its gliding fall on their other tree about fifty feet away, then raced into its darkening bower of leaves.

"Missed!" Silva said grandly, laying his musket against the boat and retrieving the Doom Whomper in case anything large chose to investigate the noise of the shot.

"So?" Rajendra said hotly. "I did my job!"

"Yeah," Dennis replied, looking back at the clearing, "about as well as usual. Half-assed. Spoiled *my* shot."

"Boys!" Sandra insisted, steel in her voice. "You *will* stop baiting each other and cooperate!" She knew she wasn't being quite fair to Rajendra. Silva had started it—as usual—but erratic as Silva sometimes was, he was a lot steadier than Rajendra. For Rebecca's sake, she wouldn't single him out. She was "playing favorites" and knew it, but Rajendra had proven time and again, once that very day, that her control over him was tenuous. He might be loyal to the princess, but not to the group, and his judgment had always been questionable. Silva couldn't be controlled at all, except through his loyalty to her and Rebecca, but the group as a whole was "under his protection," as he saw it. Also, his survival judgment might sometimes be extreme and disproportionate, but it had a good record of success. The last thing they needed right then was for him to go into one of his infamous sulks.

Dennis Silva actually thrived on adversity and Sandra suddenly realized that in that sense he was a lot like Matt.

Silva was over the top, where Matt was thoughtful—unless he lost his temper—but like it or not, their survival depended on the big gunner's mate, and for all their sakes, even Rajendra's, "over the top" was okay with Sandra.

Lelaa finished her knot and hooked on, then slid down the trunk, straightening the tackle as she went. On the ground, she hooked the bottom block onto the eyebolt at the boat's bow, leaving the fall rope dangling. She scooped up the second tackle and went up the next tree.

"Oh, please do hurry," Rebecca pleaded. "The sun is almost set!" It was true. The sun was falling rapidly now, as usual, and the trees and the clearing behind them were filling with gloom. Menacing shapes crashed about, and other creatures, much like bats—maybe they *were* bats—had joined the swirling birds.

"I shall, Your Highness," Lelaa assured her patiently. As before, she quickly finished her chore, with no distractions from above this time, and scrabbled her way to the ground.

"How we gonna do this, Cap'n?" Silva asked. "One end at a time, or climb in and try to lift her from inside?"

Lelaa glanced at Abel, alert and listening, but virtually helpless in the boat. "It will be dangerous either way, and from within, it will be more so. That is how it must be done, however. We will add weight that we must also lift, but some cannot climb. Besides, if we remove the provisions from the boat—which we must to lift it one end at a time—we will then have to hoist them aboard as well." She looked around at the twilight. "We must risk a quick ascent or we will be at this for hours. I do not think we have the time."

"That's it, then," Silva said. "Ever'body aboard!"

"This is madness!" Rajendra stated. "We would all be safer to lift from the ground!"

"Captain Rajendra," Lelaa said ominously, "we have worked together despite our differences, but do not imagine those differences do not still exist. You really *must* cease your constant objections and observe the obvious. Add to my earlier argument that we cannot secure the down-hauls within the boat if we raise it from the ground. Where would you have us secure them? To the trees here at this level, where any passing creature might gnaw them in two? All aboard."

Rajendra couldn't fault Lelaa's logic, and whereas Silva had promised not to "hurt" him, Lelaa had made no such pledge. She had simply swallowed her anger and done as she had to. Her reminder of a possible reckoning was probably more intimidating than Silva's harangues because it was the first she'd made in a long time, and she also had a more untainted claim on his honor as far as he was concerned. Besides, he harbored a real, secret . . . racial . . . fear of the physically diminutive but powerful—alien—Lemurian captain. He made no more objections.

Working together creditably enough—despite their differences, most of the "muscle" were seamen after all—they slowly, carefully hoisted the battered longboat into the sky between the two trees. There was a bizarre unreality about the whole situation that escaped none of them, but it was indeed their only chance. As the final rays of the sun surrendered to the sea, they saw the water beyond the trees, within the breakers, almost working with humping, splashing shapes, eerily void of color until they gained the shore, and then only briefly until they absorbed the darkening shades of their new surroundings. About thirty feet above the ground—high enough, they hoped—they secured the down-hauls to cleats on the boat's gunwales. Then they sat quietly, staring at the starlit transformation of the island they'd learned to hate but of necessity called home.

"God a'mighty," Silva whispered. "It's like you threw the manhole cover off a sewer an' looked down on a million man-eatin' pollywogs swarmin' in there."

As usual, he was exaggerating, but not by much. Lawrence had been right. Evidently, they'd made it just in time. They never would have survived another night on the ground. The shiksaks had come to Yap.

"It's a kind of hell," Rebecca said, and Sister Audry drew her close.

"How long will it last, Lawrence?" Sandra asked, also whispering. It seemed appropriate. All the creatures on the island, in the trees, had gone silent except for the bellowing, grunting, roaring shiksaks themselves.

"I don't recall," Lawrence hissed back. "I stayed in the trees, hungry, thirsty. . . . I don't know. Long days and nights."

CHAPTER 19

Talaud Island

Irvin Laumer leaned on the coaming of S-19's squat conn tower and cast a suspicious eye toward the brooding volcano that increasingly inhabited the expedition's thoughts. Nobody trusted it, and everyone felt convinced it was "up" to something, but the morning had dawned on a beautiful day, the kind that scoured away stress and fear with its simple charm alone. A brisk, cooling breeze, almost magically free of humidity, stirred the tree fronds and rippled the lagoon. High, wispy clouds moved across an otherwise brilliantly blue sky. The mountain near the center of the island seemed to have simmered down. Only the slightest trace of steam vented from the high, distant peak, and for once, its flanks weren't shrouded with mist and the workers could see the scars of its recent tantrums. The ground still moved, but not with the violent, jolting shudder it had for many days; now it was more like a steady, sullen grumble than anything else Irvin could compare it to.

"I think we'll have her refloated today," Tex Sheider predicted optimistically, appearing beside him. The shorter man scratched his nose with a kinked piece of wire, the braided insulation charred.

The day had clearly affected the man's mood, but he might be right, Irvin thought. "Technically, S-19's been 're-floated' for weeks now," he pointed out. "Ever since the basin filled up."

"Yeah, but I meant floating *free*," Tex explained. Irvin nodded. He'd known what he meant. He gazed out at USS *Toolbox*, securely moored in the lagoon. A pair of boats they'd lashed together with a flat deck between them, like a catamaran, was pulling for the beach laden with the big scooplike device they'd fashioned to dredge the sub clear of the sand. The scoop would be dropped near the submarine, and *Toolbox* would drag it into the lagoon with a pair of reinforced capstans operated by nearly her entire crew. A messenger line marked the scoop's position, and when it reached a floating platform, the scoop was hoisted and laid back upon the deck of the twin boats. The thing was a stone bitch to row, and it was hard work, especially against the wind like today, but the crews that rotated the duty didn't seem to mind that much. They were proud that their labor revealed the most measurable sign of progress toward releasing the sub from the beach. Irvin was proud of them, and by his estimate they were nearly done.

They could probably get the sub out now, by fending off aft and pulling her out nose first, but it would be dangerous work. The spider-lobsters had returned the night before, and they had no idea if any remained in the basin or not. The scary-looking half-skinny-lobster-half-spider critters weren't the menace they'd been when they first appeared. Now that the crew knew they couldn't climb up on the boat, when they'd come back a few times after the first terrifying battles, most of the crew on the shore simply took refuge on the sub. This time, they'd contented themselves with shooting a few that scuttled around on the beach, tearing at equipment, or some that seemed intent on wrecking the little "fitting-out pier" that Carpenter's Mate Sid Franks was working on. They needed the pier to finish preparing the boat for sea once they got her loose. Even now, 'Cats were boiling spider-lobster tails for lunch, and savory smells reached Irvin's nose now and then. The creatures had changed from terror to treat. They were still dangerous in the water, though, and the jet of seawater they "spat" could easily knock an exposed worker into the sea. It would take *very* exposed workers, standing in water up to their knees on the stern of the boat, to protect her delicate screws. Better to let the dredge handle it.

Irvin saw Franks wave at him from the pier, and he waved back. Franks and a detail were planking it now. If all went well, they might have S-19 free of her enclosure before nightfall. Once that was achieved, they'd inch her toward the pier with her electric motors, tie her up, and begin final fitting-out for their long-overdue and much-yearned-for departure. They might even get the port diesel up and running before they set out, but Irvin didn't consider it a priority compared to so many other ongoing projects. They had nearly a full load of fuel and the starboard engine ran fine, with every apparent intention of continuing to do so. Right now, it was a matter of "okay, propulsion works well enough, let's concentrate on what we need that doesn't work at all"—like sonar, comm, the stove, the crew's head, etc.

It would be nice to have the port diesel because, unlike newer boats that used four big engines just to charge their batteries, and had electric motors for all propulsion, S-19 cruised faster and more efficiently on the surface in direct drive. With her starboard engine in direct drive, she could still generate enough electricity to run the port motor, but the trip to Maa-ni-la would take longer, and with only two-thirds of her batteries after that long-ago depth charging, they wouldn't have much electrical reserve.

Still, Irvin Laumer didn't consider the port engine as important as getting the boat away from Talaud Island as fast as he could. Talaud was a perilous place, full of dangerous creatures, and if, on days like today, the dangers felt more remote, just a little dimmer, that damn volcano always seemed ready to focus them considerably. As quiescent as it was now, it *always* rumbled a little, so no one was about to forget it entirely. Besides, Laumer wanted back in the war. He wanted back among the men who'd have to consider him an officer of considerable resourcefulness now. An equal. He'd been set an almost insurmountable task, and he was finally on the verge of accomplishing it. Every day that passed was another opportunity for his success to slip away.

It *was* a pretty day, though, and even Irvin wasn't immune. The labor was strenuous, but it was good work with demonstrable results. There was a general feeling of accomplishment and a satisfaction that, hard as things had been, they were almost done. The dangerous chore of bringing fresh water from the interior, mixing it with seep distilled aboard *Toolbox*, and stowing it on the sub was complete. The even more hazardous task of laying in fresh provisions was almost done as well, and meat and fish were drying under several sheds on the beach. A work party was even mixing paint so they could "doll the old boat up a little" before she was "recommissioned" into this new United States Navy.

"Those tails are starting to smell good," Irvin said. He glanced at his watch. "We'll call all hands ashore to lunch in fifteen minutes. Make sure plenty goes out to *Toolbox*."

Tex nodded. He'd emerged as Laumer's de facto exec, even though he'd only been a radioman before. He had the aptitude, organizational skills, personality, and frankly, stamina for the job. Also, since S-19's radio would never work again, aside from his work on the electrical systems and a better wireless transmitter than Captain Reddy had been able to supply them with, he'd just stepped into the role. He knew the boat as well as Irvin did by now, and he could lead.

"Aye, aye, sir," he replied. "I'll announce lunch with the collision alarm!" he said.

"I thought it didn't work."

"It will now," Tex said, grinning.

Irvin grinned too. He didn't even ask what Tex had done to fix it. It might have been a loose wire or a corroded connection. They'd all gained a greater respect for the boat they'd been repairing than they'd ever had before. She was old and ridiculously obsolete, but she was a tough old girl, and most of her problems stemmed from age and the neglect she'd suffered since being stranded. "Carry on," Irvin said.

Tex was about to descend the ladder into the control room when the distant mountain emitted a great, rolling, cacophonous belch, followed by an earsplitting roar.

Stunned, Irvin noticed that 'Cats on the pier had already begun reacting to something they saw in the direction of the mountain, even as the terrible blast buffeted them. He turned and looked for himself. The sky to the south was black, except for a massive, roiling, gray cloud—headed right at them.

"Sound 'collision,' 'general quarters,' or whatever you can that's loud enough to hear!" he shouted. His voice seemed small, far away. He turned toward the workers on the shore and on the pier, waving his arms over his head and yelling as loud as he could: "All hands! In the boat! Drop whatever you're doing and *get in the boat*!" Sid Franks saw him, whether he heard him or not, and began shoving 'Cats off the pier in the direction of the submarine. Many were too stunned to move, fixated with horror. This was not another ash fall like they'd seen before; this was a dense, boiling, *wall* of ash, thundering toward them at an impossible speed. Irvin jumped down on the deck and raced across the forward gangplank that connected the boat to shore. As soon as he left it, he couldn't hear any of the alarms Tex had lit off on the sub.

He ran among the cooks and other work details on shore, rounding them up and gesturing at the sub. A new roar began to grow, different from the first but no less terrifying. His vision was growing dim. For an instant, he was alone. Midshipman Hardee grabbed his sleeve, tugging him toward the boat. His mouth was moving, but he made no discernible sound. Irvin looked around, saw 'Cats sprinting toward them from the pier, but everyone else was scampering across the gangplanks, tails high in terror, and disappearing down every open hatch. He let Hardee pull him along and soon they were both running. The gangplank bounced beneath their feet and they paused a moment while those in front waited to drop down the hatch. To the north, the day still seemed as before: a clear, almost cool blue sky, filled with patchy clouds. Turning to the south, they saw that the ash cloud, or whatever it was, had consumed the island. It was nearly upon them. Hardee got his attention; the hatch was clear. Irvin shoved Hardee ahead of him, then dropped down into the packed, sweltering control room.

"Franks and his detail are still outside," he gasped, surprised that he could suddenly hear himself. The roar was still immense, but muted now.

"Clear the control room!" Tex bellowed. "Fore and aft, off you go! Maneuvering watch, stand by your stations," he added. Just in case.

"Seal the boat, all but the forward hatch!" Irvin shouted. "That's where Sid's guys'll make for. Secure the starboard engine!" They'd been running it for the charge. "Close main induction!"

The 'Cat stationed in front of the telltale "Christmas tree" panel turned, blinking frantic apology. "Board not all green! I not know why not all green!"

"There's holes in the boat—we know that," Tex said. "The forward hatch is still open, for one." Sealing the boat for submergence had received even less priority than the port diesel, since no one had ever envisioned any eventuality that would make them take her down again. They still didn't want to do that, but they had to breathe. Nothing could breathe in what they'd seen coming.

Something banged dully against the conn tower above, and almost immediately other things began raining against the steel like hail.

"Up scope!" Irvin demanded. The undamaged number

one periscope slid upward and he grabbed the handles and twisted it south, peering into the eyepiece. "Oh my God," he murmured, flinching when something trailing smoke, about the size of a Buick, plummeted past the periscope and splashed alongside. Smaller objects were striking the hull continuously now. The world was gray-black. The roiling mass was *here*. Huge trees flew before it like grass clippings, igniting like matches as they tumbled in its path. He cringed at the sight of flaming meteors of debris. He'd known no one could breathe in what was coming, but he hadn't expected the sheer force and heat. He watched the shelters, tents, and other things they'd considered home on the beach simply disintegrate in fiery swirls as the periscope lens began to blur.

"Down scope!" he yelled. "Everybody hold on!"

The only audible blow was a massive rushing sound, but S-19 heeled over like a great hand had reached down and simply pushed her conn tower into the sea. Bodies fell atop one another, yelling, screaming, chittering in panic. Shrieks reverberated through the boat. The simple fact about submarines is that there are no soft, padded places anywhere in them. S-19 didn't even have rack cushions anymore. Irvin clung to the periscope chains—like those of a giant bicycle—as everyone on the port side tumbled to starboard. A 'Cat smashed against him, almost breaking his nose and his grip, before falling soundlessly away. The boat groaned and Irvin felt a juddering, thudding movement. The lights flickered, but never went out, except for those that were smashed by windmilling arms or legs. He watched it all in a kind of surrealistic daze. Somehow, he knew the boat was moving; he expected her to roll all the way over and tumble like a log, but she didn't—quite. He became too disoriented even to speculate on what was happening outside—how they were moving, where, and how fast. With a sudden sickening sense of loss, he thought briefly about the scoop boats and *Toolbox*. The hail-like sound against the hull grew louder, heavier, and the boat heaved again.

More shrieks reached his ears, cries of panic and surprise joined those of pain, and he realized it had jumped way beyond "sweltering" in the control room. *Of course it's hot*, he thought. The ash cloud had obviously been propelled by a massive burst of gas from the volcano! "Flood the trim tanks!" he cried, knowing he couldn't do it himself and hoping someone could who knew how. They'd had the boat riding high and empty of all but fuel as they worked on her and cleaned her out. The fuel in her bunkers was probably the only reason she wasn't rolling right now. "Flood auxiliary, flood fore and aft!"

"Flooding all variable trim, aye!" came a pained response. Shortly, even as the hail continued, S-19 began to right herself. God, it was hot! Irvin could barely breathe. The panting of Lemurians was almost as loud as the roar outside. He looked at the status board. Mostly green now.

"Flood her down," he said. "We've got to get her hull beneath the water before we cook!" He had no idea where they were, whether they were still in the depression they'd excavated around the sub or had been swept into the lagoon. Either way, they didn't have any choice.

"We can't take her to the bottom, sir," came a coughing voice from behind him. It was Sandy Whitcomb.

"No, but we can take her down until the pressure hull's under, at least." The deck was almost level now, and he lurched for the Kingston valves. "C'mon, Sandy. Flood main ballast two-thirds." He wiped blood from his eyes. Somehow, he'd conked his forehead. Maybe it had been the 'Cat that hit him? "We're going to have to guess at this a little," he cautioned. "She's not trimmed at all, and I never expected to let water in her again! We just didn't work on that stuff!" Theoretically, they should be able to partially flood the ballast tanks and hold the boat with the main deck awash, but with no reports from the rest of the boat, they had no idea if she was leaking or not. "Stand by to adjust the trim," he added. He saw a 'Cat who seemed to be recovering her composure. "Get a report from all compartments," he ordered. "See—" He started coughing and had to force himself to stop. "See if we're leaking anywhere!

Assemble damage-control parties. Damn it, this is the Navy! Shit like this happens!" He paused to consider the absurdity of his comment, but shook it off. "We've got injured in here! There'll be injured everywhere. Tex? Where's Tex?"

"Here, Skipper!" Tex appeared in the hatchway to the forward berthing space. "I got swept along with the tide. Jesus, what hit us? The whole boat looks like a stock trailer flipped."

"Any leaks forward?"

"Torpedo room's taking some water, but it won't sink us. Everybody's pretty banged up, but they're shaking it off. Lots of injured. What hit us?" he repeated.

Irvin shook his head, wiping at his forehead again. He wished he knew. He hated not knowing what was happening outside. That was one thing about submarine duty in general that he'd never been keen on, but in this case, that limitation had doubtless saved their lives. It was still incredibly hot, but as the boat settled, she righted, and at least it stopped getting hotter. "I have no idea. I've never seen anything like it. That wall of ash, sure, but it packed a hell of a punch."

"What about *Toolbox*?"

"I don't know," Irvin said, but he was pretty sure. He coughed again and noticed for the first time a kind of haze filling the compartment. "Did Franks's guys make it?"

"Some did," Tex reported tonelessly. "Franks didn't."

Irvin nodded. He'd known that too, before he even asked. Sid Franks would have been the last down the hatch. He might have shut it himself.

"Okay," Irvin said. "We've got work to do. We *had* three corpsmen—if they're not casualties themselves. Try to get things squared away with the wounded and see if you can get some air moving in here." He motioned to the 'Cat he'd been about to send to check the boat. "Lay aft and hurry back with a report. Check the comm in each compartment. After that, if you see anything you can fix that needs fixing, do it, and tell everyone else to do the same. We may be sitting here for a while." He sighed. "I know you weren't expecting it to be like this, but everyone aboard just became submariners today. That's what we spend most of our time doing: fixing stuff."

The wounded still cried out and others tried to treat them, but for the most part a quiet calm had settled over the rest of the panting 'Cats. Many were busy, mechanically performing repairs and other chores they'd been assigned. Others merely sat and waited. The boat was badly overcrowded and after almost six hours of being buttoned up, the hot air was growing stale. The "hail" had long since stopped outside and the roar had died away. Strange rumbling sounds, like a momentous stomach growling, still came through the hull from the island, propagated by the water that virtually covered them. Everyone had a fair assumption, based on their experience, of what had happened to everyone and everything not "fortunate" enough to have endured the hell aboard the submarine, but it was time to have a look. Irvin had put it off for a number of reasons, but he also believed the high-velocity ash and sand had actually begun scoring the periscope lens before he lowered the instrument. Now, the logy rocking of the hull and the comparative silence above convinced him it was time to take a peek.

"Up scope number one," he said at last, and when the eyepiece rose, he looked first to the south, now almost directly astern. Judging by the compass, "south" was no longer on the port beam, and that had been his first confirmation that the boat's position had been radically altered. He was stunned to see an almost clear sky where the black shroud had been before. The brisk prevailing wind had swept away the atmospheric evidence of Talaud's catastrophic but apparently brief spasm, as if the fit had gone unnoticed by the rest of the world. Irvin somehow doubted that was the case. The blast had to have been loud enough to be heard in the southern Fil-pin Lands, at least. Still, the now evening sky seemed to have returned to normal, for the most part—if one didn't count the smoke and streaming clouds of ash disappearing downwind of the moonscape that had once been a lush tropical island.

"God," he whispered. The lens had definitely been etched, but he could still see well enough to experience a stab of vertigo, looking at the now utterly alien landscape. Literally, the only remaining landmark was the eerily altered outline of the now naked mountain. Absolutely nothing remained between his scope and the volcano but millions of stripped, smoldering tree trunks lying in ordered ranks, radiating outward from its flanks. In some places, the ash was heaped so deep that the trees resembled rebar beneath an incomplete pour of cement. No single living thing could be seen—no creature, no bird, no tenuous speck of greenery.

Hesitantly, he followed the scope around to where the bearing *Toolbox* should have lain and was again stunned—this time to realize how far across the lagoon the boat had been pushed. Judging by the gray, dusty, billowing hump of land he saw just a few hundred yards away—it was impossible to judge distances accurately anymore—S-19 now wallowed near the spot where *Toolbox* had last been seen. Sick, he thought he saw the smashed, smoldering skeleton of their tender high among the splayed trees of the north point. He couldn't imagine any way any of *Toolbox*'s fine crew could possibly have survived. He gulped, realizing he'd done one thing right, purely by accident. Besides the heat, he suspected flooding her down was the only thing that had prevented S-19's blackened, half-buried corpse from joining *Toolbox* back on that other beach. His eye stung and he spun the scope back to the south. "Get a load of this," he said huskily, backing away and letting Tex have a look while he wiped his face with his bloody T-shirt again.

"Looks like the damn moon," Tex whispered, mirroring Laumer's own thoughts. Tex quickly relinquished the view to Hardee, who was cradling his left arm. The 'Cats in the control room went next, taking quick looks, their tails swishing rapidly in agitation.

The phone beside Irvin made its curious, distinctive, whirring *whoop*. Evidently they had internal comm again and he recognized the motor room circuit. He picked up the heavy Bakelite device and held it to the side of his face.

"Give me some good news, Sandy," he said.

"This no Saan-dee," jabbered the excited voice of the female 'Cat he'd sent aft so long ago now. "Maa-chin-ist Mate Saan-dee up to aass-hole an' elbow in hot water and no pitch hot for devil!"

". . . What?"

"Staar-board shaaft bearing packing pop cork, spew guts, blow chow . . . we wet! Motors wet soon. We go up soon? Saan-dee say we need go up soon . . . now."

Jeez. "We go up now," Irvin assured her, unconsciously mimicking her pidgin. "Maneuvering watch, resume your stations," he commanded loudly. "Blow main ballast! Prepare to open main induction." He paused. "Belay that! Stand by to *vent* main induction with high-pressure air." He peered through the scope again. "Tex, assemble a topside detail, bandannas for the ash. Take them up through the aft crew's berthing compartment with brooms—whatever you can think of. Make sure all other hatches and vents are clear before we open up the boat!"

"Aye, aye, Skipper."

S-19's tortured hull groaned around them as it lifted itself fully from beneath the protective water of the lagoon.

"Jesus H. Christ, Skipper!" Tex gasped, joining Irvin on the conn bridge. He'd finally removed his bandanna and the contrast between where it had been and the previously exposed skin was shocking. His eyes were red and streaming, leaving wet tracks in the pale dust around them. Gusts of wind created gray dust devils in the harsh, hellish twilight, but thankfully carried away more of the dark, dead ash coating the boat. All Irvin could do was nod appreciation for what Tex and his detail had accomplished. He was still too shocked to do much else.

Talaud Island, as he'd seen through the scope, had been incinerated. Thousands of fires smoldered upon it, brightening as the day faded, adding their choking smoke to the bitter ash that swirled and danced hotly across the unimaginable world that their island, their lagoon, had become. The lagoon itself was like a soupy mud wallow, heaving sluggishly with the dulled, exhausted waves that tried, even now, to cleanse it. Dead fish with poached, bulging eyes clotted the surface of the soup in their apparently endless millions, and charred, bloating corpses of land creatures bobbed in ghastly, unrecognizable clumps. Thankfully, they hadn't seen any remains of the scoop-boat crew or the hundred and ninety or so souls from *Toolbox*. . . .

S-19 had been sandblasted. Her rust streaks were gone, but so was all the remaining paint that had protected her. Even now, the exposed, dented, abraded steel was turning brown. All that remained of her rotten deck strakes were a few dangling, charred planks, still bolted to their supports. Even the top of the pressure hull, now clearly visible from above, had been blasted clean, and the dark, muddy water lapped against bright metal.

The starboard diesel rumbled and burbled to life, vomiting gobbets of mud from the exhaust ports.

"We can maneuver now," Tex gasped thankfully. "On the port shaft, anyway."

"Not just yet," Irvin replied wearily. "Sandy thinks we better let the lagoon clear a little first. Too much junk floating around. We'll stay anchored here until then." He grimaced. "He ran the port motor up for a few seconds, just to check things out, and that seems okay at least. He thinks the starboard shaft is *bent*! We must've whacked it when the . . . whatever it was—the ash blow? The shock wave?" He shook his head. "When . . . whatever it was tossed us out of the basin. Damned if I noticed it over everything else." He sighed. "At least the leak's under control, now we're on the surface. Man, oh, man! We're going to have to repack that bearing with *something* to keep the water out. Flooding her down didn't put any more pressure on the seal than a moderate sea!"

"*Toolbox*," Tex muttered after a long moment. "Poor bastards."

"Yeah," Irvin said. "Of course, that leaves us back on our own in a big, bad way—all over again—and I don't think we have much time. That damn mountain did all this and then just *quit*. Danny's started going on about Krakatoa again. He studied up on it some, it seems. Anyway, he said it pulled the same kind of stunt, throwing fits for a while and then clamming up. That's when it blew its top. I don't know, I'm no geologist, but I'm sick of having that thing hanging over our heads. I can't help thinking we need to *go*."

Tex patted him on the shoulder. "I'm with you. I get this creepy feeling all it was doing today was clearing its throat. What a mean, vicious bitch!"

Irvin nodded. "We'll finish repairs, as best we can, sitting right here. No sense in even going ashore. There's nothing left."

"We've got water, but we'll be awful short of food," Tex warned.

"Yeah, but we're not going to find any here. All the more reason to get underway as soon as possible."

"*How* soon?"

"A few days, no more. Who knows if we even have *that* much time?"

Tex exhaled noisily and coughed, hacking roughly. He spat. "What do you want me to do, sir?"

"Your division's priority'll be comm, beyond any new electrical repairs we need after today. What'll it take to let us scream for help?"

"A better antennae aerial, mostly." Tex blew his nose on the inside of his bandanna. "The number two periscope is thrashed. We secured it and packed it, best we could, after that ashcanning in the Java Sea. Maybe we could rig an array on it, extend it, and repack it again?"

"Do it, if you think it'll work."

"What else?"

"Sandy's priority'll be the port diesel. I'd like to run direct drive, and we'll need the charging backup."

"And?"

Irvin shrugged, gazing around at the island in the deepening gloom. The fires were growing. "Inferno," he said absently.

"What?"

Irvin shook his head. "Vent the boat before the smoke gets too thick; then we'll button up for the night. After that, we'll do whatever else it takes to get us the hell out of here."

CHAPTER 20

Respite Island

Matt felt like he was fighting for his life. His opponent's sword tip seemed to be everywhere at once, striking like a snake and slashing at him like lightning from a clear blue sky. He was on the defensive and he knew it—hated it—reduced to parrying the blows and jabs as they came, and he just couldn't keep up much longer. Steel clashed against steel in a veritable blur of blades, and he knew he was giving ground even while his soul screamed attack. Attack! He couldn't. He'd never been much of a swordsman at the Academy. He'd never expected to ever *need* to be, and though his fine sword had seen much more use on this accursed world than he would ever have imagined possible, he'd never faced an actual skilled swordsman—or swordscreature—before. So far, when the necessity arose, he'd just muddled along, hacking at Grik. They had no real "swordsmen" that he'd ever met. Mainly you just had to keep their teeth and claws and short, sickle-shaped swords at arm's length until you saw an opening—or until one of the spearmen at your back did them in. Personally, he'd rather shoot them.

He was gasping for breath and the sandy shore dragged at his feet as he tried to make the half-remembered responses to the attacks. Not that what he'd learned at the Academy was doing him much good . . . The man he faced was doing things with a sword he'd never seen before and he had no choice but to try and do the same. Again, it hardly mattered. He felt the growing, sickening certainty that he would lose. His responses were just too slow, and he'd never developed the muscle memory required for such a contest. He had to *think* about everything. That he'd lasted as long as he had might speak well for his ability to think under stress, but it wouldn't save him. Besides, having *suspected* the battle was lost, he *knew* it already was. There was nothing left but to see it through. He parried a lunge against his flank with a crash of steel—just a little late—and realized the attack was just a feint as his opponent took another long step, past his sword, and planted his own sword tip in the center of Matt's chest. The blade bowed slightly as the blunt point pushed against the padding.

"You've improved," Jenks complimented. Naturally, both men were sweating at that latitude, but maybe Jenks was sincere. At least he was breathing hard this time.

"I'm still dead," Matt objected.

"True, but as both our cultures recognize, Rome wasn't built in a day. Honestly, you are much better. Certainly better than most of the young Imperial hotheads who take the field on the New Scotland dueling ground! You almost got me there, at the beginning, with your . . . unorthodox attack. Nothing to it, really, but experienced aggression, but sometimes that's enough to give you an advantage over more classically trained opponents. It's distracting, and not at all expected. If you can finish it then, why, what difference does it make how good you actually are?"

Matt took a deep breath and managed a wry grin.

"Sounds like a good description of every scrape I've been in since the Japs bombed Pearl Harbor."

Jenks remained silent. He'd learned a good deal about the "other earth" the Americans came from, and the war that raged there, just as Matt and his people knew a lot more about the Empire now. The mention of Pearl Harbor tweaked Jenks a bit, however, as did any reference to Imperial territory that had belonged to the Americans on that other world. Pearl Harbor simply didn't exist, as the Americans remembered it, but the "Hawaiian" Islands did—in a sense. They composed the very heart of the Empire. He knew that as far as a few of the remaining Americans were concerned, Pearl Harbor, or the "Hawaiian" Islands, *still* belonged to them. Most were more philosophical than that, including Matt. They recognized that tiny Tarakan Island, for example, had never been a U.S. possession before they "got here," and Matt used an interesting phrase to describe the situation: "Possession is nine-tenths of the law." That didn't mean that knowing parts of their "homeland" was under "foreign" occupation was easy on them. Jenks could sympathize. None of his people had any idea who, if anyone, occupied their own almost mythical ancestral Britain. In that sense, both the human destroyermen and Jenks's Imperials had a lot in common with the Lemurians, whose homeland had been under Grik occupation for untold ages.

Jenks realized that the Imperial possessions in North America might someday become a source of contention as well. For the time being, however, territorial ownership was the least of their concerns. They were united—the Americans, and at least that portion of the Empire that Jenks and Governor Radcliff represented—in a task that might prove difficult enough even if they all worked in perfect harmony.

"Let's get something to drink," Matt suggested. "All this Errol Flynn stuff is hard on you in this heat!"

"Indeed," said Jenks, unstrapping his own padded vest and then helping Matt with his. He'd noticed before that Captain Reddy sometimes had a little trouble removing things from his left shoulder. An old wound, he assumed.

"Particularly if by that you mean 'capering in the sand with swords.'"

"That's exactly what he means," supplied the Bosun in a gruff tone. "The Skipper's a regular Captain Blood. You might be a little better at all that fancy ballroom dancin', but in a real scrap with no rules and real killin' to do, the Skipper's a regular artist!"

"Of that I have no doubt," Jenks replied seriously as he and Matt stepped through the sand to a small thatch pavilion erected at the edge of the trees. Chief Gray was reclined on a wickerlike lounge alongside O'Casey. Neither man stood as their superiors approached, but Gray leaned forward and tilted an ornate pitcher of chilled nectar into a pair of mugs for the two men.

"Thanks, Boats," Matt said sincerely, and after he removed the iron face guard he'd been wearing, he greedily gulped the sweet fluid. Jenks nodded his thanks as well and took a long, slow sip. Matt set his mug on the table and stared at the two reclining forms as he poured it full again.

Today, Gray and O'Casey were the only "security" personnel accompanying Matt and Jenks. As always, Gray carried his 1911 and a Thompson submachine gun. With only his right arm, O'Casey made do with a cutlass and four long-barreled flintlock pistols stuffed in his belt. Matt knew he was a cool and formidable opponent. That neither commander would allow, or felt the need for, a larger security force reflected the fact that Matt and Jenks really had come to like and trust one another. That their combined "squadron" and Governor Radcliff had firm, uncontested control of Respite left no one with any real concern for their safety.

Matt had grown to appreciate that "Respite" was the perfect name for the island where they took their enforced ease while waiting for the Allied supply ships to arrive. Despite the oppressive heat of the latitude they'd all more or less grown accustomed to, and the daily rains that kept the humidity high, the place was a virtual paradise in many ways. From the perspective of the human destroyermen, there was liberty, of course, and a kind of liberty none had enjoyed since they'd been forced to flee Surabaya in the "old" war. Commerce at Respite's suddenly booming brothels was carefully regulated because the ladies there were still "obligated," but Courtney's mission to "buy" indentured women was beginning to bear fruit. Matt hated that his men were visiting brothels full of what were essentially slaves, but he'd literally had no choice but to allow it . . . at least for a while. He couldn't, in good conscience, explain to his long-deprived men that the smorgasbord of smooth, nubile, female flesh displayed for all to see was not—could not be—for them. He would probably have faced a real, albeit temporary, mutiny. His old maxim to "never give an order you know won't be obeyed" still rang true.

He'd assembled the men and told them that Respite had . . . facilities . . . for seafaring visitors, and there'd be liberty on the standard rotation—as long as the men behaved. He then went on to explain a little of the "way things worked around here," and he'd been stunned by the response. He had to immediately quash a rising, incredulous, spontaneous crusade among his crew—human *and* Lemurian—to "Free the Wimmen!" He'd been stunned . . . and proud. As miserable as the scarcity of women had made the men of USS *Walker*, their daily association with " 'Cat gals" in labor or combat had made the revelation that Imperial women lived in almost universal servitude even more horrifying to them than it might otherwise have been. Once, some might have even wistfully dreamed of a place where women could be their virtual slaves. No more. They wanted women, and no mistake, but their perhaps unique experience with the prolonged "dame famine" made the very idea that "some Joe" might practically *own* a whole passel of them utterly hateful.

He went on to explain the use to which they intended to put some of the gold on board, news that was met with universal acclaim. That lowered the steaming, evangelical kettle aboard *Walker* to a simmer. Now, though the men still visited the brothels fairly regularly, he'd noticed some had begun to "make friends" with other island women, both indentured and "free." He encouraged that. Not only did friendships with un-obligated women gain them female "recruits," on whose behalf Bradford was negotiating with Governor Radcliff to allow unrestricted emigration, but honestly, it gave Courtney an idea of which indentured women to focus on for "purchase" with their limited gold. Matt had already ordered the men not to ever come to him with any "special requests." If a girl one of the guys was sweet on just "happened" to be chosen, that was one thing. If the men thought he was letting them go on a "shopping spree," that would be something else, probably bad in any number of ways.

Respite had other interesting aspects as well. For example, the dreaded flasher fish so prolific within the Malay Barrier apparently hadn't ever crossed the vast, deep ocean to this place. There were strange creatures, to be sure, and most of the more unusual probably guarded dangers as yet unsuspected. There were even vast numbers of perfectly ordinary-looking sharks clustered around the barrier reef that protected the fine, clear anchorage within the broad lagoon. But amazingly, for the first time since that terrible Squall brought them to this world, they'd found a place where they could actually take a refreshing dip.

Much to the incredulity of their Lemurian shipmates, human destroyermen thoughtlessly leaped over the side and capered in the water like children whenever their duties allowed. Armed watchers stood guard, of course, ready to warn of the approach of anything dangerous-looking beneath the crystal water, but simple, innocent pleasures such as that worked wonders on the men's morale. The upbeat mood was infectious, and it benefited the 'Cats as well. Within a couple of days, a few of them were even goaded into the utterly unnatural element. They were watched like infants, and their reactions were almost always hilarious—and predictable. Spanky likened the spectacle to throwing housecats in the bathtub, and he wasn't far off. Some of the hardier 'Cats eventually got sort of used to it. A couple even at least pretended to enjoy swimming as much as their human shipmates did.

Some days Spanky brought Tabby on deck where she could breathe fresh air into her damaged lungs. She still wore bandages over the worst of her burns, but many had healed enough that they could endure the open air, at least with some polta paste applied. To those who watched, Spanky was gruff but attentive, and Tabby, despite her pain, seemed happy. All were relieved that she would mend.

With that image in mind, standing there now with Jenks at his side, Matt was struck by the irony that ultimately, his people had more in common with the Lemurians than they did with the only human civilization they really knew on this world—one derived from the very same culture his own nation had sprung from. He shook his head. If there was one thing he'd learned since they'd wound up here, it was that his crew, his men, had a distinct talent for disrupting the status quo. That was perhaps the supreme irony of all: before the war, any change in the status quo in China or the Philippines was met with stiff resistance.

He smiled.

"I might better get back to the ship, Skipper," Gray said. "Stites'll be along directly to spell me at protectin' you." He grinned, but waved out at the lagoon where *Walker* lay at anchor amid the Imperial ships. "I swear, Bashear's a good hand, but he don't know how to be a proper bosun yet. Can't get any work outta the men. Look at all them hoodlums jumpin' in the water and splashin' around! And our poor ship ridin' there with new rust streaks down her sides!"

Stites arrived only moments later, '03 slung on his shoulder. Instead of the usual banter with Gray, however, he stepped up to Matt, saluting. "Skipper," he said anxiously, "I got a message here from the tanker squadron. Some's from them and some's been relayed on, tacked on, sorta. I, ah, read it, Skipper."

"Thanks, Stites," Matt replied. Grinning, he returned the

salute. "That's okay. I trust your *discretion*." Everyone had been keeping close tabs on the aftermath of the Rangoon campaign and the buildup for the push against Ceylon. They were also hooked on the drama surrounding the expedition to salvage *Santa Catalina*. Of course, any news about Allison Verdia Letts was quickly passed around her shipful of "uncles" and "aunts." Matt saw no reason to censor the transmissions they received. He took the message, written on Imperial paper Jenks had given them.

FROM COMMODORE SOR-LOMAAK COMMANDING FDFS (FIL-PIN DEFENSE FORCE SHIP) SALAAMA-NA AND ELEMENTS USN TASK FORCE OIL CAN X

Matt looked up. "I really don't know this Sor-Lomaak," he admitted. "I assume Saan-Kakja does, and trusts him. *Salaama-na*'s a Fil-pin-built Home. . . ." He looked back at the next part, then read it aloud for Jenks's benefit.

EYES ONLY MP REDDY CINCAF X DISTRIBUTE FOLLOWING AS YOU SEE FIT X ENCOUNTERED—RENDERED AID—TOOK IN TOW—DISABLED IMPERIAL SHIP ULYSSES X VESSEL HAS SUSTAINED SERIOUS STORM DAMAGE BUT IS SEAWORTHY X LARGE PERCENTAGE SURVIVORS X BETTER CHARTS AIDED DECISION DISPATCH AHEAD THREE (3) LIGHT OILERS IN COMPANY NEW FIL-PIN-BUILT USN STEAM FRIGATE USS SIMMS THAT JOINED US THIS DAY X ETA 100 NM ENE YOUR POSITION FOUR (4) DAYS X PLEASE PROVIDE PILOT AND ESCORT X REMAINDER OF SQUADRON APPROX NINETEEN (19) DAYS OUT X SAAN-KAKJA SENDS COMPLIMENTS AND DEVOTION X MOST RESPECTFULLY SOR-LOMAAK SALAAMA-NA X END MESSAGE XXX

"That *is* good news!" Jenks exclaimed. "How very excellent! I had despaired of *Ulysses*! I should be glad to send *Icarus* to pilot your other ships in!" He paused, wearing an anxious smile. "I must say, I'm fairly bursting to view this 'new' *Simms*! She was named for Captain Lelaa's ship, was she not? The first steam frigate out of the Fil-pin yards! I'll warrant she's a beauty!"

"Thanks," Matt said, reading further. "I'm sure she is." His expression had changed. "*Icarus* will be much appreciated," he murmured, then he began to read aloud again. The next part seemed to have been composed in a hurry.

ADDENDUMM X A MAJOR REPEAT MAJR VOLCAANIC EVENT OBSRVED SSE SOUTHERNMOST FIL-PIN SETLEMENT MIN-DAAN-AO VICINITY TALAUD X ALL COMUNICATIONS USS TOOLBOX LAUMER EXPEDISION LOST X HEVY SEA SURGE SOUTH ISLANDS X MUCH DAMAGE X FEAR WIRST NOT YET HAPPEN X SAD CONDOLINCES ALL OUR PEEPLE X WILL UPDATE X MESSGE END XXX

"Good God!" Jenks exclaimed, stunned.

"Yes, sir," Gray agreed somberly. "God help 'em."

"Commodore Jenks, please arrange a meeting with Governor Radcliff," Matt said woodenly. "We have a few things left to sort out before we take off, and the date for that's finally near. If our replenishment vessels arrive in four days, I want to be underway in six." He shook the note in his hand and looked at the men around him. "We're running out of time, gentlemen, I feel it. We may not be trying to refloat a submarine on top of a volcano, but events might still overwhelm us while we sit here goofing off. Before much longer, Billingsley'll be arriving in Imperial waters. It stands to reason that with the princess captive, whatever scheme the Company's cooking up will likely hatch shortly after that." He looked at Jenks. "I'm sorry, Commodore, I wish you could be with us, but we're going to have to sprint for it. Fine a ship as *Achilles* is, she just can't keep up when *Walker* stretches her legs."

Jenks nodded slowly, thoughtfully. "Very well, Captain Reddy," he said and sighed, looking out at his ship in the harbor. "I will arrange the meeting, but if you mean to move that swiftly—something I cannot debate, since I too feel a growing sense of urgency—I must leave my ship in the hands of Lieutenant Grimsley and accompany you. *Walker* might be able to sink half the Imperial Fleet, but she can't sink New Britain. You simply can't stand offshore and demand all Company officials be marched down and hanged at the execution dock." He chuckled grimly. "Again, it is amply demonstrated that neither of us can succeed alone. I can't get there in time without you, and once there, you can't accomplish anything without me." He paused. "No offense meant, and I don't mean to boast, but I do think I can secure the aid of the one other person who might be in a position to help us." In response to Matt's blank stare, he shrugged and elaborated. "The Governor-Emperor, of course. You see, despite everything, the Governor-Emperor and I are . . . well acquainted. He *will* see me if we make our presence known, and he *will* believe me about his child."

The "Governor's Palace" was an impressive edifice. It wasn't the biggest independent dwelling on Respite—that title belonged to the Company Director's Mansion—but completely enclosed within the formidable harbor defenses they'd seen from sea, it was the most secure and commanded the preeminent view. The structure itself was the most "familiar" Matt had yet seen on this world, in terms of architecture. It looked much like the homes dedicated to the commanding officers of any number of American military facilities back in the States and abroad. It was large, airy, comfortable, and tastefully decorated. The elevation and an unopposed breeze from almost any direction provided Matt with a tantalizing, nostalgic hint of an early fall day on the coast. Except for the plastered limestone columns supporting the seaward-facing porch roof on the ground floor, there was little ostentation. The porch also overlooked a rather radically sloping "parade ground" surrounding a flagpole resembling a topmast and ending with a line of officers' barracks just short of the defensive wall. The grade was such that one could sit on the porch and see the harbor and the vast sea beyond with a view unobstructed by anything but the Imperial flag. It was breathtaking.

Matt and his companions stepped down from the donkey-drawn "land barge" with spoked, wooden wheels that had carried them up the impressive slope like a San Francisco streetcar. The conveyance had pleasantly surprised Matt the first time he rode it to the palace. It was a simple affair, built with a single back and two outward-facing benches. Even with six admirably teamed and amazingly dedicated donkeys pulling it, it moved at a ponderous pace, but though unsprung, it was surprisingly comfortable. On that first visit, he'd expected to have to hoof it all the way to the Governor's Palace dressed in his deteriorating best or, worse perhaps, *ride* one of the ridiculous donkeys. Either eventuality might have caused an international incident. Juan Marcos had performed miracles maintaining Matt's original "Mess Dress," and the sweaty damage of such a trek might have driven him to fire on the palace with one of *Walker*'s guns. Since then, he'd enjoyed riding the land barge several times during its winding, scenic, relaxing ascent. Sitting on it, calm and still, was a little more difficult when it came *down* the hill, though.

Matt, Gray, Bradford, Spanky, and Chack were received at the fortress gate by an Imperial Marine, who saluted and politely escorted them across the stubbly parade ground and the palace lawn to the porch. Commodore Jenks, O'Casey, and *Achilles* Marine Lieutenant Blair were already seated upon colorfully cushioned wooden chairs, attending Governor Radcliff, his adjutant, the Respite militia colonel, and several diaphanously dressed ladies. Drawing closer, Matt recognized the governor's wife and three daughters. The wife, Emelia, was a short, round, but surprisingly attractive woman who habitually wore the amused expression of one who observed but wouldn't stoop to dabble in the affairs of men. The daughters shared the attractiveness of their mother in younger, slimmer forms, visible in the breeze despite the shapeless clothing. They shared a trace of her "look" as well. In Imperial society, Emelia's was probably an extremely liberated life, and Matt suspected that Radcliff appreciated her opinions, in private at least. They seemed comfortable together, and the governor, as in the past, didn't immediately shoo his women away.

The Imperial men stood as the destroyermen approached.

"Captain Reddy of the United States warship *Walker*,

come to call with companions, Your Excellency," barked the Marine escort. Matt saluted, as did the others except for Bradford, who swept his ridiculous hat from his head and bowed, pointing his ruddy, balding pate at their hosts.

The Imperial officers returned the salute in their slightly different fashion, but Radcliff was beckoning them forward. "Please do come aboard," he boomed. "These militant ceremonials waste time we may later regret! Nothing against ceremonials, militant and otherwise, but everything has a season and we face a stormy one indeed."

The ladies didn't rise or move in any way, but all seemed intensely focused on Chack, as before. His "American" English was near perfect now, as the first Lemurian who'd ever begun to learn it, and he was the very personification of military professionalism and bearing. He'd clearly impressed the governor, but he was just as clearly aware—and mortified—that the Imperial ladies considered him exotically cute. Matt saw it too and was amused by their fascination and Chack's discomfiture, but doubted the governor's ladies would consider Chack so cute and cuddly if they'd ever seen him in battle.

"Please, gentle . . . ah . . . gentlemen," Radcliff continued, suddenly a little discomfited himself, "do join us. Watch your footing on the steps there—the spacing's all wrong. I've been meaning to have it fixed. . . . Well done! True seamen never even notice! Please be seated, everyone. We have much to discuss!"

Matt sat on one of the empty chairs and removed his hat while the others did the same. Raking his fingers through his hair to slick it back, he noticed one of the daughters had shifted her attention to him. He tried to ignore her gaze.

"Your Excellency," Matt began, "I'm sure Commodore Jenks told you the news we received yesterday?"

"Indeed." Radcliff's expression turned grim. "You have my most sincere condolences. We have considerable experience with volcano-ism and the sea surges such activity can produce. I do hope the ultimate toll won't be as high as you fear."

"Thank you, sir. Another message today added little new information."

Radcliff paused briefly, then shook his head. "Pardon me, Captain Reddy. Please know I sympathize with your concern, but I cannot restrain my wonder regarding your devices for communicating over such vast distances! The message Jenks conveyed to me was saddening . . . and disturbing in other ways that we must discuss, but the means of its delivery . . . I cannot comprehend it."

Courtney Bradford leaned forward in his chair. "My dear Governor Radcliff! It's really quite simple, once you understand some very fundamental principles—"

"Courtney," Matt interjected, hoping the Imperials hadn't been too offended by Bradford's exuberant and completely unconscious condescension. O'Casey, at least, understood a few of those principles. "Later." He looked at Radcliff. "Right now, let's focus on the message itself. What else about it is 'disturbing'?"

Radcliff glanced at his adjutant, his face reddening a little. "A single moment more, if you'll indulge me. First, to complete an understanding reached between Mr. Bradford and myself, let me say that I understand that there are . . . certain aspects of our civilization you may not be comfortable with." He sighed, and his eyes flicked toward his wife. "I might even make so bold as to propose that I . . . increasingly share a measure of discomfort regarding one issue in particular." He spread his hands helplessly. "Sadly, momentous change often requires considerable time. In our negotiations, Mr. Bradford has proposed ways those changes might be accelerated, if not instantly achieved." He looked at Bradford. "I believe you summed it up nicely by referring to a 'balance of supply and demand'?"

"Indeed," Courtney said, somewhat pleased with himself. "An end to this hideous 'Company' and its abhorrent trafficking in human flesh must necessarily precede any real progress, but the Alliance does offer an immediate, if modest, 'safety valve' to alleviate the 'oversupply' problem here on Respite, at least. Over time, a decreased supply of a certain . . . commodity . . . within the Empire must necessarily appreciate its value and, eventually, status."

Radcliff nodded seriously. "Ingenious and succinct," he said. "In that respect, on that subject, I have made my decision. With your guarantees of decent treatment and these somewhat unprecedented 'rights' you speak of, any Respitan woman who has completed her indenture or is otherwise free of any legal or commercial indebtedness is also free to choose for herself if she wishes to emigrate to the lands or 'Homes' collectively constituting these 'Allied Powers' of yours." He glanced again at his wife and grimaced at her apparently . . . more satisfied amusement.

"I regret, however," he continued, "that with the exception of a few dubious Company contracts I'm inclined to throw out, you must continue to purchase the obligations of other . . . persons so . . . encumbered. Should you choose . . ." Radcliff's grimace grew more pronounced as he spoke. It was apparent that he'd never contemplated this aspect of his culture's "institution" so deeply before. He cleared his throat and marched determinedly on. "Should you choose to retire a . . . debt with anyone who holds it," he finally managed, "and they refuse to sell said . . . debt, for any reason, they shall be liable to a charge of usury." He glanced at his wife again. "Owning debt is one thing," he said defensively, "but owning people, quite another!"

"Thank you, Your Excellency," Matt said simply. It was a major concession, he knew—one he'd held out for. Despite Courtney's arguments about "commodities" and "supply and demand," he would pay the actual value of the obligations of the women Courtney chose—but no more. There must be no "price gouging." He'd argued that that would imply the owners of the debt truly did consider the women who "owed" it to be their property. The Respitan economy might even take a hit, particularly if a lot of "free" women actually chose to emigrate. By the look of things, they did a lot of the hard work on the island. The signs were that many would, but how would they decide when the time actually came to step aboard a ship crewed almost exclusively by another species and leave behind everything they'd ever known? For that matter, how would his own destroyermen respond if they went from famine to feast virtually overnight? He had no concern that the women would be well treated by the Lemurians, and there'd be plenty for them to do. In that respect, their lives might not even change that much. But they would be free and equal—and they would know what respect felt like.

Radcliff had extended an olive branch, but Matt could see there was a catch. He waited for the other shoe to drop and when it didn't, he spoke. "That has nothing to do with the message we received yesterday," he prodded. "What exactly 'disturbs' you about it?"

"Well . . . I mean no offense, please understand. It's just that this apparent armada of yours, advancing toward Respite, leaves me uneasy."

"Uneasy," stressed the militia colonel.

"I understood you had an . . . oil collier, a 'tanker' squadron coming to supply your needs," Radcliff continued, "but the message hints at a considerably larger force. Large enough to take one of our biggest ships in tow." He held out a hand. "Don't mis-take me, we are all very grateful for the rescue of *Ulysses*, but let me explain. As you know, there are elements on this island that have flirted with secession from the Empire. I am one of those 'elements' myself." He became agitated and abrupt. "But, well, let it be said: we pray the Empire might be repaired, and Commodore Jenks assures me that you could be of tremendous help in that regard. I do hope and believe you are the friends you seem to be. If the effort should fail, however, if the Empire should continue its suicidal slide, we will secede. We have no choice. Even as we flirt with secession, our beloved Empire, through the Company, flirts with even darker things. We will not," he added, suddenly forceful, "throw off one corrupted master only to be enslaved by another!"

Matt was taken aback. He looked at Jenks and knew the

man must have explained, but still the governor wanted more guarantees. Upon reflection, he supposed that was reasonable, given Respite's position. He saw Emelia staring hard at him and realized she was probably the ultimate source of the governor's sudden apprehension. Oddly, he was pleased. If someone as powerful as Governor Radcliff would listen to a woman's concerns in this society, even when privately expressed, there might be hope for the Empire yet. He felt another stab of anxious fear and loss. He knew that without Sandra backing him up, he never would have accomplished half of what he had.

He cleared his throat. "Governor Radcliff, you have my personal guarantee, upon my honor as an Officer and a Gentleman commissioned into the United States Navy, that my country . . . the Alliance we represent . . . has no territorial ambitions here. We're engaged in a terrible war with an unimaginably brutal foe thousands of miles from here, and that's where I'd be if the criminal Billingsley and the 'Honorable' New Britain Company hadn't abducted . . . some of our people as well as your Imperial Princess, and perpetrated an unprovoked attack on Allied persons and property. We now know that not only Billingsley but the Company he serves was responsible for that, so we're at least as much at war with the Company as you are. We're natural allies in that respect, but we expect no further assistance from you than that war will require. To that end, Mr. Bradford will hopefully conclude negotiations for basing and quartering treaties to support the logistical requirements necessary for that operation."

"As I said," Jenks explained, "their 'Task Force Oil Can' will arrive, and most of its elements will move on to New Britain, escorted by *Icarus* and assorted Allied warships. *Achilles* and USS *Simms* will follow almost immediately in our wake with a couple of fast, 'razeed' oilers. All that will ultimately remain here is a communications facility—to transmit and receive the amazing messages you admired—and some support personnel to ensure a steady flow of supplies to support the campaign Captain Reddy described. It really is that simple, and that's all there is to it. I have seen their real war and their real enemy, gentlemen, and claiming Respite for themselves is not even on their horizon. They don't *want* to be here."

"But what constitutes the 'end' of that 'campaign'?" Emelia suddenly blurted. The men looked at her, stunned, and in the governor's case, clearly somewhat angry. Emelia defiantly held her ground.

"The destruction of the New Britain Company, ma'am," Matt said simply. "And frankly," he added after an introspective pause, "getting even. Saving your country after that is up to you."

CHAPTER 21

North of Tjilatjap (Chill-chaap)

Santa Catalina's engine room telegraph rang up "Astern Slow," and Dean Laney stood up from the rough box he was sitting on. (Strangely, though a few chairs had survived the "lighten ship" purge, every single chair, stool, or anything even vaguely comfortable to sit on in engineering had vanished.) Thinking dark thoughts, he winced at the resurgent piles that had begun tormenting him again. As quickly as he could, he moved to shift his own lever in response. "Astern slow!" he shouted at the 'Cat throttlemen.

The 'Cats'll love the thing, Laney thought. *If it works.* He crossed his fingers. The best 'Cat snipes understood turbines now, but they knew those were beyond their capability to build from scratch—at least in the near term. The compound engines they'd been making worked well, and so did the huge, crude, bulky, triple-expansion monsters being built for the "flattop Homes," but this was the first "American" reciprocating engine they'd ever seen. They were familiar with the principle, but this machine represented the virtual "state of the art" of its type.

With mutual encouraging blinks, two Lemurians turned

the grimy wheel on the main valve. High-pressure steam *hooshed* into the first massive cylinder of the triple-expansion engine dominating the compartment. The three big piston rods twitched. Then, with a mighty, joint-sore shudder, accompanied by hoots of glee, the crankpins slowly moved the webs that in turn spun the shaft. They were all one huge casting, but at that moment they seemed separate entities, working together like long-lost friends. With the first piston approaching the bottom of its stroke, the valve chest vented the now lower-pressure steam into the next, even larger cylinder, pushing that piston down. Just before the first one finished its stroke, the third and largest piston tasted low-pressure steam once again and helped heave the first one back up—to start the process again.

The hoots became a cheer, and even Laney's face creased into a grin. Over the noise, they heard cheering all over the ship. Steam hissed here and there, but not from any major leaks Laney could see. Certainly not in the lines, which had been his biggest concern. The shaft was turning, and 'Cats scampered to spew oil on anything anywhere that they hadn't been able to get at before. The bottom shaft webs and rod caps had been in the water, and they got liberally doused when they came up. There was a diminishing rumble aft as the stuffing box and shaft bearing returned to their duty and oil was sloshed on them as well. *It'll be an oily, slimy mess down here*, Laney thought happily, *until we can secure and wipe some of this shit up*.

A steady, thrashing, *whumping* sound came from aft, and he knew the screw was beating at the water. The bow was still stuck lightly in the silt and the hull began to groan as the engine strained to pull it free. The telegraph rang up "Astern Full."

Laney blinked. "Damn. I thought the Skipper was going to try to ease us off, not horse her." He didn't reflect on the fact that Lieutenant Commander Chapelle had suddenly become the "Skipper" as soon as the engine came to life. He answered the ring, then turned to the throttlemen. "Open her up, boys!"

* * *

Dark smoke piled into the still, humid air. Russ Chapelle couldn't hear much over the cheering, but he could feel the life returning to the old ship beneath his feet. Her bow was still stuck, however, and the deck shuddered with restrained energy. Sammy was his talker, stationed near the speaking tubes, ready to shout if anyone reported a casualty. So far, the old girl was holding together. Russ remained anxious, but wasn't surprised. Most of the Navy 'Cats on this expedition had been involved in refloating *Walker*, and the little guys had really learned their stuff.

"Full astern," he ordered. Ben Mallory looked at him nervously. "Don't worry," Russ said. "I know what's behind us. I won't crack us up." *Santa Catalina* was about four hundred feet long. With her stern swung out from the beach, there was a shallow sandbar studded with ancient drowned tree trunks little more than a thousand feet aft. The vibration began to build and the cheers started to ebb as murky water churned around the laboring screw. Then, suddenly, something gave. Maybe it was suction, or the ship was still too heavy forward, but without warning, the old freighter just seemed to *ooze* away from the beach. There was a slight dipping sensation as the bow abruptly discovered that nothing supported it but water, and Chapelle instantly rang "Stop Engine" on the big, dingy brass telegraph.

"Lookouts!" he shouted at the bridgewings. "Range estimates every fifty . . . uh, tails!" A "standard tail" was close enough to a yard that he wouldn't need to convert it. He moved the wheel experimentally. They *had* tested the steering engine. . . .

"One hundred yards!" called the port lookout, estimating the range to shore and using the accepted Navy measurement.

"Around nine hundred!" came the range from starboard, looking aft. He couldn't see for himself, but he was relaying the estimate of another lookout on the aft deckhouse, above the fantail.

Russ began turning the wheel. "I'm giving her 'right

standard rudder,'" he explained to Ben. "I hope that even with the engine stopped we gained enough steerageway to bring her stern around." He grinned. "Slow and easy, that's me! Hell, I've been conning a ship with no engines at all lately! That makes you start thinking ahead!" That was also why *Tolson* hadn't come any farther upriver. Without engines, if she got into trouble in the confined space, she was stuck.

"You're doing fine," Ben assured him. "Just remember, this rusty old tub of yours isn't what's important."

"She's more important than you think," Russ retorted. "But don't worry, I won't break any of your toys."

"Two hundred yards!" called the lookout. "Stern started to turn, but the current stopped it."

Russ rang up "Astern Slow" and the vibration beneath their feet resumed. "I don't think I can turn her into the current," he said aloud, maybe to Ben, maybe to himself. "But maybe I can hold her by the tail while the bow swings out." He looked at the starboard lookout. "Range?"

"About seven hundred. The . . . ah . . . closing rate? It is less."

"Good," Russ replied. He rang "Stop Engine" again, and spun the wheel before ringing "Ahead Slow." The vibration ceased momentarily, then resumed with an entirely different resonance. He glanced at Ben with a self-deprecating grin. "Should've brought a couple of bridge officers along! Frankly, though, I don't think anybody ever thought we'd really be steaming this bucket out of here." He shrugged. "I didn't."

Ever so slowly, *Santa Catalina* coasted to a stop, her screw partially exposed, ponderously slapping the murky water. Just as slowly, she began to move forward—leaving only the slightest wake to wash over fascinated, watching eyes.

"Lookouts and leadsmen to the fo'c'sle!" Chapelle ordered. Sammy loudly repeated the command through a rusty speaking trumpet on the starboard bridgewing.

Sammy was shaping up to be a pretty good bosun's mate, Chapelle thought. Too bad he couldn't blow a pipe.

"You want me to take the wheel, boss?" "Mikey" Monk asked. He'd suddenly become Chapelle's exec.

"Not just yet," Russ replied. "If anybody's gonna crack this egg, it better be me." He cast a look at Ben. "I don't think the good major will shoot me if I do it. He might if I let somebody else, and I'd probably have it coming." He called out to Sammy. "What's our depth?"

"Five fathoms, Skipper," came the reply. "Get deeper now," Sammy added hopefully. He was watching a 'Cat stationed just aft of the forward crates, holding up the number of fathoms with his fingers as they were relayed to him. Ahead of the ship, several hundred yards, the steam barge putted along, testing the waters with its own lead, prepared to wave a red flag if the bottom came up.

Russ grunted, estimating just about zero margin for error. With her present load, *Santa Catalina* drew nearly twenty-four feet. Five fathoms was thirty. The ship wasn't particularly heavily loaded, and she'd made it into the lake half full of water, so it seemed reasonable she could get out again, especially riding higher. But Russ didn't know what the channel had done in the year and a half she'd been on the beach, or what the tide had been like when she came in. New snags or sandbars might have formed; even the channel might have shifted. That didn't matter, since he didn't know the channel anyway, and they'd just have to grope along, but a sandbar could be bad.

Slowly, slowly, they steamed to the south end of the lake, creeping along just fast enough to keep steerageway. The jungle closed in as they neared the river channel, clutching at them as they passed, it seemed. Clouds built up and they proceeded even more cautiously through an afternoon downpour. At one point, through the nearly opaque rain, Moe used his keen eyes to spot the red flag on the barge waving frantically, and Chapelle called down to reduce speed even more. They couldn't stop because the current would move them unpredictably, so they began preparations to moor. Then word came that the depth at the river mouth was four fathoms—*Santa Catalina*'s exact depth.

"Okay," Russ said, licking his lips. He'd spent a lot of time poring over a yellowed Solunar chart on the wheelhouse bulkhead. The next time the tide would run higher than it now did would be at 0126 on the morning of November 12. He didn't want to wait that long. "Dump the guns," he ordered regretfully. The old freighter had been armed with a dual-purpose five-inch gun forward, and a three-incher aft. Both were badly corroded, their bores pitted beyond serious use, but he'd hoped to save them. Still, they'd been dismounted and rigged to go over the side in a hurry, prepared for this very eventuality. The ship needed only a few inches, and hopefully the guns would provide them. Massive splashes preceded a slight lurch aboard the ship, and tentatively, *Santa Catalina* eased forward.

Except for the drumming rain, the lethargic throb of the engine, and muted reports from Sammy, standing soaked on the bridgewing, there was complete silence on the bridge. They felt the slightest, prolonged, quivering shudder through their shoes as the keel kissed the bottom and slid through the silt. He hoped the rusty hull and ancient rivets would stand the strain—and they wouldn't discover a random rock or boulder.

"Ahead one-third," Russ ordered, hoping increased inertia would carry them across. They were committed now. They'd make it or get stuck, probably for a couple of weeks. There was little more they could do to lighten the ship, not without dipping into their precious cargo itself. He risked a glance at Ben and saw that the flier's knuckles were white as he gripped his hat in his hand, poised as if preparing to wipe sweat from his brow with an imaginary sleeve.

He'd never seen Ben like this before—this . . . intense. He sensed what the man was straining against: the horror that after all they'd been through, fate might still steal their prize. Even now, on the brink of success, after all they'd struggled for and lost, a simple capricious sandbar might rob them of the unexpected—unimagined—treasure stored in those moldy wooden crates. Maybe for the first time, Russ truly understood what the planes meant to Ben; what they might mean for all of them.

To Ben, they were the ultimate expression of technology on this planet. They were also an almost holy connection to everything he'd personally lost. They were *his Walker*. Becoming a pursuit pilot and learning to tame P-40s—the hottest things America had in the air—had defined who Ben Mallory was. Since the "old" war had started and they'd wound up here, Ben had accomplished amazing things. He'd saved them all, most likely, by flying the battered old PBY until it literally disintegrated around him. Since then, he'd been instrumental in providing primitive but apparently reliable airpower to the Allies. He hadn't been in the Philippines, but he'd made no secret of his disgust regarding MacArthur's failure to bomb Formosa with his flock of B-17s during the brief but God-sent space between Pearl Harbor and the air attacks that ultimately slaughtered the big bombers on the ground.

The Air Corps in general and the vaunted P-40s in particular had garnered a poor reputation among the destroyermen as they'd watched them swatted from the sky by the nimble Jap "Zeros." Ben still argued that those same, possibly preventable air attacks, had ultimately pared away the P-40s in the Philippines before their pilots ever really had a chance to learn to use the better, heavier E models. He often pointed to the successes of the AVG B models in China to prove there'd been nothing wrong with the planes that a little practice couldn't cure. He clearly loved the things, and to have them back was the greatest reward he could possibly receive for all his service to date. To lose them now might actually destroy him.

To everyone else, and certainly to Ben as well, the planes represented an insurmountable leap ahead that their enemies couldn't hope to match. Of the twenty-eight planes on board, Ben estimated they could assemble at least eighteen, maybe twenty. Through salvage and spares, they'd have the parts to keep them going for some time, but they would inevitably lose some to training accidents, maintenance foul-ups, and—to Russ—the simple quirky, unexplainable disasters that eventually befell all extraordinarily complicated equipment. Hell, what about those stupid MK-15 torpedoes? They would have to husband the planes that survived, cherish them, and treat them like the temperamental thoroughbred stallions they were—lavish them with attention and keep them in tip-top shape. *Ride them easy*, he thought with growing confidence—and a growing anxiety similar to Ben's—because when the gate pops open, they're liable to win the war.

"S'okay, Mr. Mallory," Russ said gently as the rumble under the hull died away. "Maybe I'm just a jumped-up torpedoman, but I've done this sort of thing before. We'll get your toys out for you, me an' this old rust bucket. Then me and *Tolson*'ll be back in the Navy war. You kick their heads off from the air, will ya?"

"You . . . you think we've made it?" Ben asked cautiously, hushed.

Russ released his own white-knuckle hold on the wheel, stretched his fingers, and clasped it again more loosely. "Yep, I think we have." He actually giggled. "God help me, I think we have." He sighed and turned to Monk. "Send to *Tolson* and the salvage squadron: 'Expect company for dinner, and it better be good.' Then get back here as quick as you can. We'll be in the clear in a few minutes, and I think it's time your 'Air Snipe' ass learned to handle your 'new' ship." He grinned at Monk's expression. "Hey, Mikey, don't look at me like that! I already have a ship, and she's a lot prettier too! You want me to give her to *Laney*?"

"Hell, no!" Monk exclaimed. "I just wasn't expecting it! Imagine, me with my own ship!" He still looked stunned, and Russ and Ben both laughed. "Hard to imagine a lot of things these days," Russ agreed. "Now run along and send that message!" He paused. "Oh, and send to *Tolson* to have an extra set of colors, Stars and Stripes, sent across as soon as we arrive. There's nothing left of the flags aboard here, and *Santa Catalina*'s been without one for far too long."

CHAPTER 22

Yap Island (Shikarrak)

Dennis Silva was snoring loudly in the gray half-light of dawn. Sometime during the night, they'd decided the shiksak activity below had begun to taper off, and he'd produced a bottle of his reserved prize "medicinal" rum to celebrate. He'd shared—a little—and the bizarre phenomenon they experienced later, after he was liberally medicated, had blended into a twisted dream in which their boat was sailing through the air above the roaring rapids of a boundless river. Even now, as consciousness threatened, he remembered that the roar had been pretty loud, and somehow their little boat had become *Walker* from time to time. He was pretty sure Spanky had "blown tubes" at least once, judging by the sooty taste in his mouth. The dream was a hoot, even if the ride was a little bumpy. The circumstances were strange and maybe even ominous, but that wasn't the point. He wasn't sure, but he thought he'd been singing, and he imagincd he'd been particularly witty when he ridiculed Rajendra for his girlish squeaks of alarm.

In any event, for once Silva wasn't already fully awake

before everyone else. The others had endured a long, tense, "unmedicated" night that hadn't been entertaining in any way, and all except Rebecca Anne McDonald were still asleep after their ordeal, snoring under this momentous, utterly changed dawn.

"Mr. Silva," Rebecca whispered, again prodding him disapprovingly with her toe. "Do wake up; something is eating our ropes." She'd barely slept at all, staring down, trying to see what was happening during the seemingly endless, terrifying night. Long after the roar had passed, but before the meager light revealed a dark, diminutive shape near the falls, she'd heard gnawing sounds coming from the aft tackle.

"Mr. Silva!"

Dennis's good eye popped open, and seeing Rebecca in the gloom, he immediately groped for his eye patch. Oddly, despite his bizarre behavior in most respects, he didn't like it when his "little sister" saw the gnarled, sunken socket where his left eye had been. His next priority was True-love's long-barreled pistol tucked in his rope belt.

"Umm?" he demanded groggily.

"The aft tackle. The falls."

"What's wrong with 'em?" he managed thickly.

Rebecca sighed exasperatedly. "Something is there, chewing on them!"

Silva twisted to look. "I'll be . . . derned. You're right!" He squinted. "Silly bastard's gonna drop us on the water—I mean the ground! Hey, there, you little freak!" he growled menacingly, "get away from there, or I'll blow your god-damn head off!" With his left hand, he pitched the empty rum bottle at the thing.

"Goddamn! Goddamn!" shrieked the creature, dodging the bottle and scampering up into the lower branches above.

"It spoke!" Rebecca exclaimed, shocked.

"Yeah," Silva admitted, trying to draw a bead on the ill-defined shape above. "Sounds kinda like a parrot, don't he? You know parrots?"

"Unfortunately, yes," Rebecca admitted. "The Founders carried some and they have quite devastated the indigenous songbird populations of New Britain. Horrid, obnoxious creatures!"

"Well, let's see if they can be ate," Silva murmured.

"Don't you dare!" Rebecca objected. "It may be more than a strange parrot! What if it's like Lawrence?"

"Not like Lawrence," the Tagranesi proclaimed disgustedly, awakening to the voices and quickly grasping the situation. There was little trace of sleep in his voice. "They are annoying 'ests, and they *can* 'e ate. Tasty too."

"Well, then!" Dennis said, aiming at the dark shape more carefully. Over the last few days, they'd supplemented their rations with various arboreal denizens. It often sparked a race between them (usually Lelaa on a rope) and their native "neighbors" to retrieve the fallen creatures, and of course if any shiksaks were nearby, they didn't want to draw their attention by leaving food beneath the boat. There was nothing they could do about their waste, and that was bad enough. Shooting and eating their "neighbors" was a diversion from the monotony of their situation if nothing else, and it kept them from digging too deeply into their increasingly limited supplies.

"No!" Rebecca exclaimed, glancing darkly at Lawrence.

"No! No! Goddamn!" came a shrill, indignant cry from above.

Silva shrugged. "Well, whatever the little bugger is, he talks as good as you, Larry." He looked at Rebecca. "He's gotta leave off chewin' on our rope, though."

The others in the suspended boat began to stir.

"What's happening?" Sandra asked. "Is it over?"

Despite her bedraggled state, Silva couldn't suppress a thrill at the sight of her pretty, morning face. He physically shook himself. *Damn!* He told himself. *Don't even think like that!* It was hard not to after all this time. He'd even occasionally caught himself looking speculatively at Sister Audry. She was a damn fine-looking gal, after all. *Such a waste . . .* He shook himself again.

"*ERRRrrrrr!*"

"What?"

"Oh, nothin'. What do you mean, 'is it over'?" He shook his still groggy head, deciding to answer Sandra's first question before pondering the second. "The squirt wants a new pet. The bloom's wore off poor Larry, I guess."

"That's not true!" Rebecca scolded. "And Lawrence is *not* a pet!"

"What is a pet?" Lelaa asked.

"A dog," Lawrence said, a little wistfully.

"Pets ain't all dogs," Silva retorted, "but dogs can be pets. A pet's just about any critter that likes it when you pet 'em on the head."

"My God, Mr. Silva, you *are* a philosopher!" Sandra exclaimed, still muzzy herself.

"Yep. All I need's a Navy-issue Greek suit."

"Hand me a piece of biscuit, if you please," Rebecca demanded. Half asleep, Rajendra grumpily fished in a canvas bag and produced a mildewed cracker. Snatching it away, Rebecca held it up to the creature, near the falls. "Here you are, little fellow!" she entreated. "Won't you come down and eat? Show yourself! That's a *good* little creature!" Tentatively, perhaps coaxed by her pleasant voice or the smell of food, the little vandal eased back out of the shadows.

"Why, it looks like an archaeopteryx!" gushed Abel Cook. The young midshipman/naturalist-in-training had improved considerably over the last few days. He was still weak, and like them all, literally covered with mosquito bites, but the lightly feathered creature sniffing its way skeptically down the falls had stirred his interest. It wasn't much bigger than a cat, with a long neck and a toothy head just like any other lizard bird they'd seen, but its abbreviated wings and long, feather-vaned tail looked more suited to gliding than flying. Silva chuckled as the light improved because the thing was colored predominantly greenish blue and yellow. The creature retreated at the sound, hissing at Silva with an open mouth full of small, razorlike teeth.

"Sure *looks* like one o' your relations, Larry," Silva prodded.

Lawrence hissed at him too. Rebecca gave them both withering stares.

"Come on, little fellow!" Rebecca cajoled again. "Wouldn't you like something to eat?"

"Eat?"

"Yes!" Rebecca teased it with the cracker. "Eat!"

"Eat!" the creature mimicked doubtfully.

"Yes, eat!"

Quick as a shot, the little thing raced down the falls, snatched the cracker, then disappeared again in the canopy above. Rebecca checked her fingers to make sure they were all there while Silva laughed. A moment later, they heard another querulous cry from above.

"Eat?"

It was immediately echoed by others. "Eat? Eat? Eat!"

"Uh-oh, now look what you've done!" Silva said, turning serious. In a blurry streak, what looked like the first creature bolted down the falls and bounded around the boat shrieking, "Eat! Eat! Eat!"

It bounced off Dennis's leg and dug in its claws—which hurt—but it wasn't even as heavy as it looked. Lawrence took a swipe at it with his sword, but it was just too fast.

"Well . . . give it something to eat!" Rebecca commanded. The entire canopy above was beginning to thrum with the chant "Eat! Eat! Eat!"

"You feed that thing, it'll never leave!" objected Silva. "Them other bastards'll be down in a instant and eat us too!"

"Feed it!" Rebecca ordered, and Rajendra obeyed, tossing another biscuit at the creature.

"No!" Sandra almost shouted. Dennis was right, she thought, but it was too late. Seizing the morsel, the creature stuffed it in its mouth, showering crumbs in all directions. Lawrence was trying to get close enough to take another swipe with his sword when another, similar creature swooped down into the boat and defiantly demanded, "Eat!" To their amazement, the first one launched itself at the second, spewing crumbs and shrieking, "Eat! Goddamn!" It struck the stationary "intruder" like a bullet and, as quickly as that, in a shower of feathers and blood, the intruder was dead. Frizzed out now, its meager plumage standing on end, the first creature scampered back up the falls almost to the limbs above and spread its long arms, feathery, membranous wings taut. With formidable claws bared at the ends of long fingers, and its neck stretched out, teeth exposed, it *gobbled* thunderously like a tom turkey. All protests of "Eat!" ceased in the branches above, and triumphantly, the little creature strutted warningly back down the falls. Finally, hopping the distance to its dead cousin, it clutched the corpse and tore away a feathery gobbet. "Eat!" it chirped contentedly. "Goddamn!"

"Goddamn!" echoed Dennis Silva approvingly. "Little guy's got the basics down!"

"Look," breathed Sister Audry, pointing at the brightening world around them.

Sandra gasped. For nearly the last week, while they swayed between the tree trunks, living a miserable, virtually seagoing existence with all the attendant hardships and inconveniences (particularly on the ladies), Yap Island had worked with shiksaks. It had been almost like watching maggots in meat, except these maggots were nearly as voracious toward one another as they were intent on their primary goal. Mating pairs coupled everywhere, briefly and violently, and the act ended, as often as not, with the death of at least one of the participants. Abel speculated the fighting was the natural outcome of cramming so many highly territorial carnivores together in one place for any reason, but it seemed utterly senseless and unnatural to everyone else. Males died, females died, shiksaks of both sexes died fighting over the carcasses of the slain. When a clutch of eggs was laid, almost as casually as defecating, they were often eaten or crushed by their own mothers. Despite Abel's speculation, he was at a loss to explain this aspect of their behavior, this utter disregard for their offspring.

Apparently, once laid and forgotten, the eggs were safe unless a creature just happened upon them, so maybe they exuded no attractive scent or maybe, as they'd speculated before, shiksaks just didn't have a well-defined sense of smell out of the water. There was no telling. Abel and Brassey had calculated that despite this apparently self-destructive behavior, there would still be a net increase in the ultimate number of shiksaks. Even given the inevitable infant mortality, this annual smorgasbord/orgy might be the only way the creatures had to keep their numbers at a sustainable level. At sea, they had no (known) natural enemies except mountain fish and one another. Sandra was surprised that even Sister Audry allowed that, sickening as it was, God may have allowed shiksaks to sort this hideous arrangement out for themselves, since she was incapable of believing he'd designed it thus. Secretly, Sandra reflected that Courtney Bradford would have felt somewhat vindicated after Audry had so violently attacked his faith in a partnership between creation and natural selection. She was glad he wasn't here to crow about it.

That morning, however, when the day began to break upon the virtually denuded, devastated . . . battlefield . . . that Yap now resembled, all that remained of the great infestation was the destruction left in its wake—and the wake of something else that had happened in the night they still didn't understand. Bloated, festering carcasses lay scattered among fallen trees and sandy, almost rippled soil. The whole place looked like reels Sandra had seen of Poland after the Nazis bombed whole areas into desolation, except that instead of dead livestock, dead shiksaks were littered about. She was fascinated to see green kudzu shoots already bursting forth from some of the dead, and wondered if those that had eaten of them had been infected as well. In all her view, there remained only a single, badly wounded shiksak, and it was determinedly dragging itself toward the sea.

"They're gone," she murmured in wonder.

"Gone," Rajendra agreed. Until last night, he'd still

maintained that Silva's scheme of "riding things out" had been a mistake. Now he seemed as relieved as anyone else.

"Gone and washed away, by the look of things," Silva said. "I would've expected even more bodies . . . and look, there's puddles all over the place, with junk all tangled up like after a flood." Silva looked at Sandra. "Say, what *did* happen last night? I musta been . . . preoccupied."

"You were drunk," Sandra said scornfully. "Not really your fault, I suppose. I should've stopped you, but I had no idea . . ."

"A surge of seawater, like a tidal wave, came in shortly after midnight," Abel said seriously. "Several surges, in fact. All were relatively gentle in a sense—no monstrous, crashing waves—but for a while, seawater surged right beneath the boat at the base of the trees. It gave us some concern," he added as an understatement. They'd been very concerned that their trees might be undermined and fall, as a matter of fact.

"So it wasn't all a dream," Silva muttered. "Did Rajendra really squeak?"

"I wouldn't have heard it over your yodeling!" Sandra said in an accusatory tone. She rubbed her brow. "Chorus after chorus of 'In the Jailhouse Now,' for God's sake!"

Dennis looked at her blankly. "I cain't yodel," he said.

"No," Sandra agreed, "you can't. *Never* do it again. That's an order."

Silva arched his eyebrows and looked at Lawrence. "Ever seen anything like this before? A tide high enough to cover an island like Yap?"

"Yes, 'ut only when the ground shakes. Large tides cross Tagran then. Tagranesi feel earth shake, go to high grounds." He looked worried. "Tide cross here, it cross Tagran too. Ground not shake, late at night, Tagranesi 'ight not go to high grounds . . ."

"The surge came from the southwest. Perhaps it didn't reach as far as Tagran," Brassey said, trying to reassure Lawrence.

"Let's get down and out of here," Rajendra urged angrily. His carpenter agreed.

"Not so fast," Sandra replied. "Captain Lelaa?"

"The surge, or whatever it was, has completely subsided now. We should be able to cross the breakers with the tide around midday," Lelaa replied, glancing at the moon beginning to rise. "We have sufficient time to observe a while longer, to make sure the infestation is indeed over. All I see is that one injured creature, but it is possible more will arrive. We should not wait too long, though, if we want to leave today."

With the full sun, there were no more shiksaks, and the stench of rotting corpses and vegetation became overpowering. Sandra was convinced they needed to leave regardless. Thank God they still had sufficient rum-dosed fresh water. She doubted that any uncontaminated water would be found on the island for some time. Carefully, they lowered the boat to the damp, mushy ground. Abel could help a little this time, and all others were sent down by rope before they made the attempt, both for safety and to decrease the weight.

Silva was annoyed to see how far Rebecca's new pet had chewed through one of the ropes. Another few minutes might have done for them. "Stupid shit," he muttered accusingly at the creature, which seemed perfectly content to remain with them.

"Stupidshit!" the parrot lizard agreed enthusiastically. Uncharacteristically, Silva was at a loss to come up with a clever name for the thing, and that left him a little morose. He'd always thought he had a talent for names. His perpetual fallback, calling it "Spanky," fell on deaf ears as usual. (Nobody knew why he always suggested naming anything ridiculous or inconvenient after *Walker*'s engineering officer, but he apparently had a reason.)

"Stupidshit Eat?" the thing demanded hopefully after the boat touched the ground.

"Hey!" said Dennis, inspired. "Let's call him 'Stupidshit'!"

"Absolutely not!" Rebecca decreed, coaxing the creature out of the boat and onto the ground.

"Stu'idshit sounds good to 'e," Lawrence agreed.

"No."

"Hmm," said Silva, coiling and stowing the falls after Lelaa brought them down. Rajendra and his men were positioning the rollers. All were alert, but in spite of everything, a festive mood prevailed. "Let's see. Eat—Pete! We can call him Pete!"

"I think General Alden might take some offense at that," Sandra observed dryly.

"Well . . . let's call him 'Petey' then! That's a fine, upstandin' American pet name!"

Sandra giggled. "What, make him a member of 'Our Gang'?" Of course, the reference was lost on everyone else.

"Petey!" shrieked the gluttonous tree-leaper. "Petey Eat?"

"I guess that's settled," Silva quipped in the face of Rebecca's glare. "C'mon, let's get a move on. I've seen enough o' this dump. Time to get back in the Navy."

CHAPTER 23

Mid Eastern Sea

USS *Walker* was steaming at twenty knots—her best, most economical speed—almost due east through moderate seas into the rising sun. Commodore Harvey Jenks stood on the starboard bridgewing, enraptured by the seemingly effortless sense of motion. His hat was held tightly under his arm and his hair whipped in the breeze. The pitching, streaming bow tossed occasional packets of spray in his face as it sliced the marching swells, and he laughed like a kid, with closed eyes and a drooping, dripping mustache. O'Casey was beside him, crowding the lookout, and despite having experienced it before, he seemed to be enjoying it just as much as Jenks. Their immediate past had been put far behind them and the two men had apparently resuscitated their old friendship to a degree at least as strong as ever.

Lieutenant Blair of the Imperial Marines was the only other Imperial officer aboard, but he'd brought a small detachment of his men from *Achilles* and was currently drilling them alongside Chack's Marines, aft. He was a bright officer, and he'd learned a hard lesson in warfare at Singapore. He'd also become a fervent convert to Allied infantry tactics—particularly now that he understood and respected them. He even made valuable tactical suggestions, regarding the addition of muskets to the shield wall, that Chack was perfectly willing to test. Later that day, they planned to "shoot at shields" again. Apparently Chack and Blair both thought they'd figured "something" out.

"Skipper on the bridge!" came Fal-(Stumpy)-Pel's high-pitched cry.

"As you were," replied Matt, and Jenks and O'Casey stepped into the pilothouse to see an amused Captain Reddy, towing a beaming Courtney Bradford in his wake. "It looks like you're enjoying yourselves, gentlemen," Matt said, taking in their semi-soaked appearance.

"Captain Reddy," Jenks practically gushed, "before now I could only imagine what it must be like, but now I'm utterly smitten, sir!"

Gray stomped up from below, pushing Bradford forward. He'd heard the exchange. "This is twenty knots," he growled proudly. "If the sea was a little calmer and we had the fuel to throw away, we'd show you thirty!" He leered at Jenks's expression of wonder. "Once upon a time, she'd crowd forty! Might still can, when we get a fourth boiler back in her."

"Lord above, to experience that!" Jenks muttered.

Matt's grin spread. No skipper is immune to compliments about his ship. "I don't know about that, Boats," he demurred, "but if any crew could coax it out of her, this one could." He chuckled. "Spanky's been running around like a mother hen, checking every little thing. Him and Miami. I think now that Tabby's finally back on limited duty, he might take a breath." He shook his head, looking at the Bosun. "I tried to leave her behind, you know. Send her home on one of the supply ships after it shows up and off-loads. She's still got a lot of lung damage. Spanky actually insisted on it. Told her she could rejoin her pals—the 'other' Mice—when she was fit." He looked proudly back at Jenks. "She said she'd quit the Navy if we left her behind!

Wouldn't fight, wouldn't speak, wouldn't teach a soul a thing she knew! I thought Spanky was done for. His face was so red, I started to call Selass!"

Gray laughed.

"You have quite a crew, Captain Reddy," Jenks said, complimenting him.

"Yes, I do." Matt's grin faded. "Now, what you and I have to do, over the next week or so before we reach your home, is figure out how best to accomplish our mission without anybody—particularly this crew and the people we're trying to rescue—getting hurt. Obviously, I want to do that while making sure some other deserving people *do* get hurt." He glanced at Norm Kutas, who still had the conn. "Carry on, Quartermaster." To the talker: "Please pass the word for Captain Chack, Lieutenant Blair, Misters Steele, Campeti, Reynolds, and McFarlane to join us in the wardroom." He looked back at Jenks and O'Casey. "Gentlemen?"

"I don't really know what more I can add," Jenks said, sipping hot tea from a cup. Spread out on the green-topped table between them was a chart showing the four main, or "Home," islands of the Imperial heart. Matt had seen it before, but in the past Jenks had always covered the coordinates to salve his conscience, since it was treason to reveal the location of the islands. For a long time now it was understood that Matt knew precisely where they were, and under the circumstances, such fictions no longer existed between them. Jenks would doubtless be called a traitor by the Company when his story was told, but he considered the Company—and the Dominion—a far graver threat to the Empire than the Grand Alliance was.

Courtney leaned forward for a closer look at the map. Most of those present also knew where the Imperial capital was, by deductive reasoning, but this was their first "look" at it. Matt had been right when he told them it wasn't the "Hawaii" they remembered. The island shapes were tantalizingly familiar, but bigger, and in some cases joined.

Lower global water levels—which Courtney had long suspected—and random volcanism probably explained that.

"We've been gone an awfully long time," Jenks continued, "and I know little more than you what conditions may prevail within the Empire. We might even receive an unfriendly welcome. As I said before, that would be almost certain if I were not with you, but if the Governor-Emperor has been deposed, God forbid, I doubt my welcome will be warmer than yours."

"You, O'Casey, and the princess have all hinted you're a 'big wheel' in the Empire," Matt observed. "I suppose your sympathies are well known."

"Indeed. I'm known as a staunch Loyalist, as are most Imperial officers."

Mat grunted. "Hmm. Well, speculation is almost pointless," he said. "If you don't have any pals left in government at all, we'll have to wing it anyway. Let's assume the situation remains essentially the same as when you left, probably a little tenser, of course, judging by what Governor Radcliff had to say. His was the most recent news. How do we proceed in that 'best-case' scenario?"

"We must assume Billingsley will have beaten us there," Bradford interjected, brooding. "We should know that quickly enough, shouldn't we?"

"I'm certain of it," Jenks replied. "That we would know," he amended. "There is frequent, rapid commerce between the Imperial Home Islands, and almost no clandestine anchorage. *Ajax*'s arrival would be recognized, reported, and known across the islands within days. If her crew is paid off, rumors of the princess would spread immediately. They might keep the crew sequestered, pleading sickness, but that would be widely known as well. If she's there, we'll know. Beyond that, much depends on what Billingsley and his superiors hope to gain, and what their timetable might be. If the princess has become their ultimate weapon against the throne, I think they would act quite quickly. Remember, they had no more certainty that she'd survived than I did, so I have no doubt they've continued their long-term scheme of subversion in our absence. With the princess in hand, I believe they would be overwhelmingly tempted to act precipitously, to 'wing it,' as you said, themselves. The Company and their creatures in the courts are known to take the long view of things, but they are also impetuous and grasping. In the past, the best check we've had against them in government has been their tendency to overreach and bleed support when the people see their true agenda."

"So, if they have indeed won the race, we may find opportunity in the midst of a chaotic upheaval," Courtney mused aloud.

"Possibly, but it could be messy."

"Best case?" Matt asked again.

"Well, obviously, the best thing that could happen is that we get there before Billingsley, tell our story, and wait for him to arrive." Jenks looked serious. "Tempting as it would be, I must caution against trying to stop him at this stage. Better to let him think he's won. If we sight *Ajax*, we should steer clear. If he fears he will be foiled, his only recourse might be to 'eliminate' any evidence against him."

"Agreed," Matt said reluctantly. He paused. "What do you consider the worst-case scenario?" he asked at last.

Jenks shifted on his chair. "Well, certainly, objectively, the worst possible thing that might happen is that Billingsley never shows up at all. Not only would that imply that his ship is lost with all aboard—with the attendant grief for all concerned—but it would substantially undermine our testimony. At least until *Achilles*, *Icarus*, and *Ulysses* arrive. Unfortunately, at that point we will of necessity be ashore and we, as well as the Empire, might not live to see it happen." He looked at Matt. "One of the reasons the Company has survived so long to contend with an entity as powerful as the Imperial throne is that it can be . . . remarkably resourceful and ruthless. Our arrival will threaten its position because *some* will believe us. That alone might precipitate action on their part. One way or another, whether Billingsley has beaten us or not, when *Walker* steams into Imperial waters, the . . . ah, how do you say? Yes. The 'shit will hit the fan.' "

"Pardon me," Chack interrupted. "Viewing this map from a military perspective, I see a number of anchorages, particularly on this New Scot-laand. I see no 'Pearl Harbor,' however. Assuming the names are different, where was it? Where would it be?"

"It ain't there," Spanky said, rubbing his chin through his white-shot brown beard. His expression was as empty as a 'Cat's. He pointed. "Here's where it would be, on the south coast of this 'New Ireland' place, near this 'Waterford' burg. Looks like a lake on a plain." There was a moment of silence while the others in the room absorbed that. "There's that old company flag, without the blue too," he said.

"Yes," Jenks agreed, sensitive to the men's emotions. "New Ireland practically belongs to the Company, for all intents and purposes. There is only one good anchorage, but it's rather exceptional. It's the best-protected harbor on the windward side of any of the islands."

"Best-protected from what?" Chack asked.

"From storms—and attack. Edinburgh is good, on New Scotland, but it's too broad to easily defend against an attacker. New Dublin is well sheltered and fortified, and as you can see, any landing and approach from another part of the island itself would pose a serious problem. Let us fervently hope things do not come to that."

Matt took a breath. "Well, Jenks, we're here for the Company—and our people. Where do we go? Where will the Governor-Emperor be?"

"New Britain or New Scotland. New Britain is the largest island with the largest . . . unindentured population. It is where most people of substance live, and despite their representative duties, most members of both courts live there as well. There are vast plantations and timber holdings. The Imperial capital is at New London on the west coast fronting New Britain Bay alongside Portsmouth. Those are the two largest cities, and they've become practically one."

Jenks thought for a moment. "In normal times, that's where we would find him, but I think Government House on New Scotland at Scapa Flow is where we should steer."

"Because?"

"It's the headquarters of Home Fleet. The Admiralty is there, and nowhere will he find a higher concentration of loyal subjects, indentured or not. Even the 'obligated' are Tories because their debt is to the throne and the Navy, not the Company, for the most part. They're considered 'Naval auxiliaries' and many work in the yard." He shrugged. "Some of our brave sailors are literal gutter-sweepings from the other islands, sent to the Navy instead of to gaol. A few of our officers are men with well-placed relations. Most of our *best* sailors, however, are Scots who spring from obligated mothers living in Scapa Flow or New Glasgow. Most midshipmen come from long-established families, but like your own navy, there are 'mustangs.'" He glanced at Spanky, who reveled in his status. "A fair percentage of them had 'Navy mothers.'"

"Okay, Jenks," Matt said. "First stop, Scapa Flow. We'll come in under both our flags, on opposite foremast halyards to show everybody we're friends. We dock, you throw your weight around and demand to speak to the Governor-Emperor. Simple."

"Hopefully," Jenks hedged.

"Just in case," Chack said, glancing around at the other officers, "I will study this chart, along with Lieuten-aant Blair, of course, and attempt to prepare for a 'worst-case scenario' on any of the islands shown." He bowed his head at Matt. "Captain Reddy has taught me well to always hope for the best, but plan for the worst. I find it difficult to imagine the worst in this situation, but in my 'Maa-reen' capacity, I will endeavor to do so."

Matt managed a smile. "By all means, Captain Sab-At. I rely on it."

Spanky was following a "feel" he couldn't identify. He stopped occasionally, listening, feeling, then moved a few paces farther on. It seemed like it must be coming from the forward fireroom, but he just couldn't be sure. Ever since he'd joined *Walker* on the China Station (he and the Bosun were the longest-serving hands), he'd made a practice of learning her every sigh, screech, rattle, and groan. After so much work had been done to her, her various refits and the recent rebuilding, he'd found himself relearning her sounds and "feels" all over again. He certainly wouldn't complain; with number three almost restored, *Walker* was as healthy as he ever remembered her being. But there was one frustrating new "feel" he hadn't "pigeonholed." He couldn't decide whether it was just part of the new "normal" or something to worry about. To make things worse, no matter what he did, he couldn't find what was causing it, and it was driving him nuts.

He paused his inspection under the amidships deckhouse/gun platform and swiped a sandwich off a tray just as soon as Earl Lanier set it down on the stainless steel counter.

"Hey, you m'lingerin' bastard," came an indignant growl from within the galley. "Them sammitches is for them Marines playin' sojer, aft! . . . Oh," Lanier said, recognizing Spanky. He stuck his droop-jowled face through the little window. "I guess m'lingerin' *officers* can swipe sammitches outta the hardworkin' bellies o' anybody they want."

Spanky took an ostentatious bite. "I could work a hundred sandwiches out of *your* belly and nobody'd even notice, Lanier," he mumbled around his mouthful.

Lanier grunted, satisfied with the response. He abused everyone on the ship—except the captain and his "lemon-limey" guests—by rote. He considered it as much a part of his job as cooking. The fellas, even the 'Cats, needed an outlet to relieve their stress, and the sometimes bitter banter between them and their cook was one of the least destructive, and backed by ancient tradition. Besides, Lanier could take anything—and nearly anybody. His bloated form required real, substantial muscle to heave it around, and he'd proven many times he had plenty of guts . . . beneath his expansive gut.

"Pepper," he roared at someone behind him. "No, goddamn it, Pepper ain't here! Bastard's back in Baalkpan, runnin' the Busted Screw! Prob'ly got it took over by now!" The Busted Screw, or Castaway Cook, was a saloon/café Lanier had opened near the shipyard, and Pepper had remained behind to keep it going in his absence. It was considered "necessary to the war effort" by now. "You, swabbie, what's your name again?"

"Taarba-Kaar," came an indignant response.

"Yeah, Tabasco! Hell, I don't care what your name is. Get a mop and run out there an' clean up *Mr.* Spanky's crumbs!"

Spanky left the argument behind, shaking his head. Aft, in the cramped space around the searchlight tower and the secured Nancy floatplane, Chack and Lieutenant Blair were drilling their troops. Together. *Interesting*, he thought. He stopped and listened. *Damn, it's* got *to be in the aft fireroom!* Number three was almost "back up"; maybe that was it, *something goofy going on in the new tubes*. He dropped down the access trunk. Sitting there, between the hatches, he could definitely feel "it" again, and more distinctly. He opened the bottom hatch and slid down to the catwalk above the number three boiler. Closing the hatch behind him, he carefully felt the rail, a pipe, but whatever "it" was, "it" was gone again.

"God*damn* it!" he roared.

"What the matter, Spanky?" one of the 'Cat firemen asked from below.

"Oh . . . never mind." He slid the rest of the way down the ladder to the deck plates. "Where's Tabby?" he demanded. "She ain't in her rack like she's supposed to be this watch."

"She hide when you yell," ratted one of the other 'Cats. Tabby's division had sworn not to cover for her when it came to her health.

"I ain't hidin', you fink," Tabby exclaimed in her new, gravelly voice. She stepped from behind the boiler, wiping her hands on a rag. She still looked awful—fur blotched, gray skin, no longer pink and angry but scarred now on her arms and neck. "I was checkin' stuff," she said, a little petulantly. Spanky motioned her forward and together they sought a little privacy, from ears, anyway.

"If you want to stay down here, you have to follow the rules," Spanky scolded.

"Why? What'll you do if I don't? Get rid of me?" She held out her arms, exposing the scars. "Make me freak deck ape? I say 'hell no,' I stay down here." Her drawl had begun to slip again. Never a good sign. "I already lose everything I want. I lose my Mice, I lose my Spanky—I *ugly* now! I lose my boilers too? You take that from me?"

"Tabby, I . . ."

"No! You no 'Tabby' me! I *chief*. You say so. I feel swell! You make me lay sick, no work, I lose chief. You make some dumb-ass chief!" She shook her head. "I chief, I work. I no work, I no chief. Boiler chief all I am now, all I ever be. You take that, I die." Tears started down Tabby's face again, just like before in this very spot, and Spanky felt like a heel.

"You just don't get it, do you?" he said slowly, huskily. "I'll always be 'your' Spanky; you haven't 'lost' me and never will. I *do* love you . . . but more like a . . . a *daughter*, like—than maybe like you think you wish I did." He shook his head and sighed. "Don't get me wrong, you're a swell dish, a knockout. I wouldn't give a damn about all them little scratches if I loved you a different way . . . but I just *can't*, see? Even if I could, it wouldn't be right. Over time, I figured that out, but I also figured out I *do* love you—like my own sweet daughter that makes me proud of what she does. Can you see that?"

"You love me?" Tabby asked, sniffling.

"Sure."

"But like a daughter, not . . . not like wo-maan? Would it be different if I not . . . wasn't a 'Cat?"

Spanky shrugged. "Honest to God, I don't know. Maybe. You do make me sneeze. . . . But that doesn't matter, and we'll never know. I love you the way I love you. I can't change that . . . and if you weren't a 'Cat, you never would've been down here in the first place."

Tabby seemed to consider that for a while and her eyes dried up. "I love you the way I love you too," she said. "I not change that either. But I be Spanky's daughter for better than nothing." She managed a slight grin, then it faded. "Just don't take chief away!"

"Whatever gave you the notion I would?"

"You tried to send me away!"

"Sure I did, because I care about you! I want you well again, damn it! If you keep fooling around down here in all this steam and crap before you're healed completely, you're liable to get pneumonia and die! Then I'll have to make some other dumb-ass chief."

Tabby hugged him and he patted her gently on the back. His eyes were starting to water. Damn fur! "There, now," he said. "Go see Selass and get her to listen to your gills. After that, light along aft and get in your rack! Me and Miami can keep things going 'til you're fit. Nothin' but smooth sailin' from here."

Weird, Spanky thought later when he reemerged into the light and started trying to locate the "feel" again. He couldn't find it at all. "Great," he muttered. "It's off and on. I'll never figure the damn thing out."

CHAPTER 24

Mid Eastern Sea

Alone upon the wide, vast, empty blue, *Walker* churned onward, her abused but faithful sonar scouring her path of lurking denizens. Jenks said mountain fish, or "leviathans," were rarely encountered in the empty spaces between the India Isles (what should be the Marshalls) and the Home Islands. Apparently, there was insufficient sustenance for the gigantic creatures there. Only occasionally, truly monstrous specimens were seen pursuing an apparently oblivious eastward course. He had no explanation for that behavior, but some Dominion officers he'd met in less tense times had hinted it might have something to do with a strange name they had for a long, shallow gulf on the northwest coast of their realm: El Mar de Huesos. "The Sea of Bones." He'd never been there. Matt and the rest of *Walker*'s senior officers kept that disconcerting name to themselves—not that they planned to go anywhere near the place. Many 'Cats aboard had just recently come to grips with the fact that they *weren't* about to steam off the edge of the world into the void. They didn't need exotic, menacing place-names stirring any lingering superstition.

The sea remained relatively placid and the omnipresent heat grew less oppressive. *Walker*'s speed and the prevailing winds kept the ship wetter than her Lemurian crew preferred, because the swells were sometimes higher than her deck, but it was often actually pleasantly cool. They began to see lizard birds unlike any they'd seen before. They had long necks and tails and incredibly broad wingspans of five or six yards, perfect for cruising endless miles on the firm sea breeze with hardly any effort at all. Courtney amused the crew by chasing from one side of the ship to the other with a pair of binoculars in his hands. The creatures—he insisted they were almost true pterodactyls when Bashear called them "dragons"—seemed aware that he was intent on studying them, and constantly avoided his steady observation. Other flying creatures, wildly colorful, began to visit. There was the usual animated excitement aboard that prevailed whenever they neared a new landfall, but there was a large measure of tension as well.

The Lemurians were mindful that they were about to see where the "ancient tail-less ones" had ultimately gone, but along with the fear that they would fall off the world, they'd largely shed the reverence they once felt for those ancient visitors. The bloom was off the rose. After all, they'd met them, fought them, and knew they were capable of treachery. The question that animated most discussions was whether they would have to fight them again. *Walker*'s mostly new crew had become nearly as fatalistic, and in some ways jaded, as her original crew of Asiatic Fleet destroyermen had ever been. But in contrast, they also felt a confidence that they could deal with unknown threats, a confidence that their human predecessors had never enjoyed, and the outnumbered "old hands" tried their best to ensure that that optimism remained realistic, but Jenks, Blair's Marines, and Respite aside, the crew was generally angry at the Empire.

In the way of most Lemurians, they wanted to get along with the strangers, but they were equally ready for a fight. *Walker* had stood toe to toe with *Amagi*, after all, and despite the mutual destruction they'd wrought on one another, *Walker* still swam, wearing *Amagi* steel. To some—who hadn't been there—it was as simple as that. They'd come to expect misery, deprivation, and daily toil in the way all destroyermen did, but they'd missed the sense of being a tiny, wounded, hunted animal, which the humans still remembered. They believed they were steaming toward a final, straight-up confrontation with whatever power had attacked them and stolen their people, and it was difficult for some to grasp that it might not be as simple as that, and even if it was, *Walker* couldn't smash the whole Imperial Navy by herself. They expected miracles from their special ship, and the "old hands," Matt included, increasingly wondered and worried if that was a good thing or not.

On November 25—Thanksgiving Day—1943, USS *Walker* steamed into the New Scotland port of Scapa Flow, and the budding hubris that had begun infecting *Walker*'s crew vanished as quickly as an ice cube in the fireroom. Earl Lanier tried to lighten the mood in the spirit of the holiday by unveiling an immense roasted skuggik he'd smuggled along on the trip, deep in the ship's laboring freezer. He'd spent the entire night before preparing the thing, complete with what notionally struck him as "traditional" trimmings. His well-meaning efforts were met with obscenities (which he duly bellowed in return) and genuine, universal horror. Skuggiks were, after all, giant earthbound buzzards, for all intents and purposes. Lanier failed to see the distinction between a cooked skuggik and a catfish, and went into a profound pout.

What had been a virtually empty sea, except for a blue-brown mound at dawn, practically filled with sails of all sizes and shapes as they neared New Scotland's leeward coast. Most of the ships, fishermen, coastal luggers, and inter-island packets fled at the sight of the strange iron steamer racing out of the southwest. A few deep-draft "freighters" flying the Company flag ponderously turned away or hove to as the old destroyer approached the achingly beautiful mountainous isle, rising monolithically from the dazzling sea.

"Ain't that something?" the Bosun said, gaping at the exotically familiar, but eerily . . . wrong . . . land. New Scotland retained a semblance of the distinctive crests of the islands now joined to form it, but it was higher, more imposing, more sharply defined. Gray's question seemed sufficient for everyone.

"A beautiful land," Matt said wistfully, and Jenks nodded in appreciation of more than the words.

"Thank you, sir."

Juan Marcos, his arm still in a sling, had joined them with a carafe of coffee. He knew how the captain and the other human Americans felt. He'd been similarly overwhelmed when he first saw what his beloved Philippines looked like on this world. Of course, Matt and the others had had much longer to get used to the idea than he had at the time, and their reactions were more subdued. Still, he could sympathize. The driven-home *fact* of the thing was harder to bear than the sight of it.

Walker was finally challenged by a swift paddle-wheel sloop with an Imperial jack, just a few miles short of the harbor mouth. Jenks appeared slightly scandalized by the tardy challenge, but it served their purposes. By then, *Walker* was flying the U.S. and Imperial flags, as well as an extensive colorful signal proclaiming her to be a friendly vessel transporting Commodore Harvey Jenks and urgent "dispatches" for the Governor-Emperor. The signal was authenticated by *Achilles*' number and Jenks's code group. Probably considering *Walker* to be a remarkably fast but lightly armed vessel, the sloop was content not to attempt to stop her but to escort her in—after a flurry of signals appealing for her to slow down.

"Jumpin' Jesus," Spanky declared when they cleared the western harbor mouth and saw the fortifications guarding it. The "west fort" was in the shape of a vast leaning wedding cake, three tiers high, bristling with forty heavy guns that Jenks assured them could reach two-thirds of the distance across to the opposite, similarly impressive works. The construction was an aggregate of coral and volcanic rock that was "spongy" and thick enough to absorb the shot of any known gun almost indefinitely without communicating any structural damage. Currently peacefully smooth, the walls of both forts glistened white.

"Ahead one-third," Matt ordered. "Mr. Campeti will fire the salute."

The Japanese alarm bell "salvo buzzer" rattled on the chart house bulkhead immediately before four guns barked in perfect synchronicity. Smoke streamed aft and Jenks nodded respectful appreciation. The Empire had no designated numbers for gun salutes, and though long-absent naval vessels sometimes fired them, they were required only of foreign powers. In such cases, protocol demanded that visiting ships fire all their "great guns" either in broadside or succession to signify that they were thus no longer loaded and incapable of causing harm. Since the Empire knew only one foreign power, and official (overt) Dominion visits to Scapa Flow were rare, few salutes ever sounded in the harbor. In this instance, *Walker*'s meager "broadside" would be noted and—hopefully—appreciated, but the utter perfection of the timing, possible only with her magical gyro and electronic fire control, would be noted with amazement as well. Everyone, Jenks included, considered that mixed message of respect and an apparently unprecedentedly high degree of professionalism a good one to send.

Matt watched with satisfaction as the crew of the number one gun on the fo'c'sle below commenced a rapid, well-choreographed gun-cleaning drill, much like that used on any Imperial ship. He knew the guns would look wildly bizarre enough to observers, but hoped they could keep their breech-loading nature a secret as long as possible. The crews had been instructed to cover the breeches with canvas shrouds as soon as their evolution was complete.

"It won't fool everyone," Jenks warned, watching. "We have experimented with breechloaders before. It is your self-contained 'cartridges' that make them practical. Perhaps you can keep that back for now."

Within the harbor's embrace, Scapa Flow grew even more impressive. Jenks had described it and drawn a few pictures for Chack, but even Matt was amazed by what the Empire had wrought on this isolated speck of land. He'd been proud of what the Allies had accomplished at Baalkpan, impressed by the exponentially greater capacity of the facilities building at Maa-ni-la, but combined, the two Allied industrial powerhouses weren't a match for Scapa Flow in terms of infrastructure and scope. Here was a true well-established industrial city in every sense. White buildings, both stone and wood, with shakelike shingles predominated. There was color as well, if not the riot of it that one usually saw in Lemurian ports. Cranes and warehouses stood on every hand, and jetties extended outward from long piers, accommodating the forests of masts. A large shipyard lay directly ahead on the western end of the harbor and sleek hulls with *Achilles*' lines stood on blocks surrounded by scaffolding. Great mounds of stacked timbers dried under sheds. Jenks had told him the New Scotland and New Ireland "oaks" made excellent ships, but they imported most of their timber, like everything else, from their continental colonies. Smoke rose everywhere, carried off to the west, from smokestacks, foundries, apparent machine shops, and great steam-jetting engines situated here and there that powered the various enterprises.

And there were people. *Human* people in an abundance Matt hadn't seen since they fled Surabaya on that other world in another war. He glassed the shore. Women here didn't run around mostly nude, he noticed with some relief, but they were doing the lion's share of the labor. Dark-haired, dusky-skinned women in practical working attire crawled around the building ships, swinging mallets and plying saws. He refocused on a party of women led by a gray-haired matron, caulking the seams of a new hull with every bit the same professionalism he'd seen Jenks's crew employ. Other women casually drove wagons and carts pulled by honest-to-God horses! Horses, donkeys, and cattle had all been aboard the original ships, according to Jenks, but the horses had never done well until they traded for more from the Dominion. Matt was glad to see the familiar creatures. He wished there'd been dogs, but Jenks said no. There were cats, in their teeming throngs, as well as flocks of parrots that swarmed everywhere like pigeons. Matt was curious how 'Cats would take to meeting "cats."

He shook his head. On second thought, the Fil-pin shipyards were probably more expansive, and certainly had more space to grow. They could also handle larger ships with their bigger, purpose-built, Home-constructing cranes. Baalkpan could too. With some smugness, he saw no evidence of a dry dock either. But in terms of a dedicated populace with the proper, well-honed skills, and long-established support industries and facilities—complete with offices and barracks—Scapa Flow rivaled Pearl Harbor. And if the city beyond the waterfront didn't match Honolulu, it was the biggest he'd seen on this world from a perspective of the numbers of dwellings. He doubted as many people lived here as lived in Maa-ni-la, but there, many families—often whole "clans" like their seagoing cousins—occupied a single large dwelling. There were a lot more houses here.

"I think our escort wants us to dock over there, Skipper," Kutas said, nodding at a long, isolated dock under the guns of an inner harbor fort.

"Yes," Jenks confirmed, studying signals through his telescope. "The escort and the fort are both signaling the 'approach of strangers.'" We will be met by an armed party at the dock," he warned.

"Well, until we know the deal here, we'll have to respond in kind," Matt said. "Sound general quarters," he ordered. "Gun crews will stand away from their weapons, but small arms will be issued and Chack will prepare to repel boarders." He looked at the Bosun. "Side party to the gangway, prepared to receive a reasonable delegation. If they don't want to be 'reasonable,' stand ready to help Chack."

"Aye, aye, Skipper," Gray said, and thundered down the metal stairs aft.

"Captain Reddy!" Jenks protested. "After all, you must not start a fight here!"

"I don't intend to, but I won't let them just run loose all over my ship as soon as we tie up."

"They won't do that."

"By your own admission, we don't know *what* they'll do. I'm playing it safe until we do. Mister Steele? You have the conn. Lay her alongside the dock—gently, if you please. I'm going to go change clothes."

Ultimately, a hostile-faced Marine lieutenant did seem ready to try to sweep aboard with a substantial "escort," but Jenks, now standing in his best Imperial Navy uniform beside Matt at the gangway, ordered the lieutenant to leave all but two men behind.

"Commodore Jenks!" the lieutenant exclaimed when he came aboard. "It *is* you, sir! We couldn't imagine . . . no one could. We expected some sort of trick!" The man looked almost wildly about, at the destroyermen, the steel deck beneath his feet, the strangely shaped guns. He actually did a triple take when he noticed Chack, and visibly paled at the sight of so many . . . non-human crew. "What the devil . . . ?"

"These are friends, Lieutenant," Jenks said forcefully. "I understand your confusion. There is much to be confused about, but my signal was clear and true. I must see the Governor-Emperor at once. Is he on New Scotland?"

"Ah . . . aye, sir. In Government House these last five months. The courts haven't met, and we don't know much about what's happening on the other isles, beyond what we hear from sailors. The Prime Proprietor, Sir Reed, is here as well, and him and His Majesty's been goin' at it hammer an' tongs, tryin' to govern the Empire from here, without—an' in spite of—one another."

"I feared as much," Jenks murmured. "Things are truly that bad?"

"I'm not sure it's all *bad*, sir," confided the lieutenant. "His Majesty is safe here at least, and since Sir Reed doesn't dare let him out of his sight, he's had to come here as well. You might say they've got each other bottled up. In the meantime, the Proprietors can't meet without Mr. Reed, and His Majesty has to call the Directors to court—" The man's eyes fell on Chack again and he was distracted.

"So in the meantime," Bradford interrupted, "bureaucracy reigns! Splendid. 'He who governs least governs best,'" he quoted.

Jenks gave him an odd look. "That . . . might be so, in ordinary times. But decisions must be made." He turned back to the lieutenant. "And we have news of great urgency for His Majesty. Please do escort my friends and myself to Government House without delay."

The lieutenant looked uncomfortable. "Aye, aye, sir," he said, "but I fear I must collect the harbor fees from this ship before anyone may disembark from her."

"What is this nonsense?"

"Yes, sir. Mr. Reed's orders. As exchequer, he has established many new fees to cover the costs of what he calls his 'government in exile.' All non-military vessels tying up at military docks—all docks in this harbor—must pay a use fee." The man cleared his throat. "It's a rather large fee, sir."

"I'm sorry, Lieutenant, there will be no fee for this vessel. As you can clearly see, she is a ship of war and flies the Imperial flag."

"But . . ."

"No 'but.' Sir Reed may bring his fiscal concerns to me." Jenks looked at Matt, Courtney, and Gray. "Shall we, gentlemen?"

Matt wanted to bring Chack along so the Governor-Emperor could meet a representative of his people, but that would have to wait. For now, leaving him aboard ship with his Marines was the better course. Courtney was the de facto ambassador for the Alliance, and Gray . . . well, Gray would go regardless.

Flanked by a squad of Imperial Marines, their lieutenant leading, the small party marched through the curious throngs of brown-eyed female yard workers. As on Respite, most were strikingly attractive, at least until reaching a certain age, apparently. Their exotic beauty left them then, but they retained a sturdy handsomeness that Matt, at least, had rarely seen, and that he suspected lingered for the rest of their days. Bradford removed his hat and beamed all around at young and old alike. They continued beyond the waterfront and into what looked like the business district of the city.

"This way, gentlemen, if you please," the lieutenant said.

"I know where Government House is," Jenks retorted.

"Of course, sir."

They strode on in silence for a considerable distance, through crowded streets full of staring people. There were more men now, most in uniform, but a few women drifted along behind them in their brightly colored, shapeless gowns.

"Jeez, Skipper," Gray whispered at his side. "You go from feastin' your eyes to famine around here. What's with the dead balloon suits?"

"I guess they're practical, sort of," Matt replied. "Now pipe down. What is it with *you*? Every time we meet new folks, you're always saying something that'll make me crack up and get us killed." Gray looked at him curiously.

Ahead was a broad square with an impressive columned building. Matt was struck again by the strange attempt at a classical style of architecture. The Governor's Palace on Respite had reflected it as well. This building was much larger, though, and four stories high, with a shining metal observatory dome perched on top. Matt was fascinated to see the large telescope protruding through a pair of open shutters, pointed at the harbor, not the sky.

More red-coated Marines with yellow facings and heavy gold lace received them at the massive door of the structure and took charge of them from the Marine lieutenant.

"Your arms, sirs," one of them said, "if you please." It wasn't a request.

Jenks looked at Matt uncomfortably. "I'd forgotten," he admitted. "One gets as accustomed to wearing weapons as to clothing. Forgive me—it is required."

Matt nodded. "Of course," he said, unbuckling his belt, which supported his Academy sword and holstered 1911 Colt.

Gray grumbled, but handed over his own belt and the Thompson he'd been carrying on his shoulder. "Don't monkey with them things, fellas. You'll shoot both your feet off."

"Your arms will not be tampered with, sirs."

The Marines escorted them into a large, ornate reception hall furnished in an understated Queen Anne style. A bulky man in an elaborate black-laced green frock met them.

"Commodore Jenks!" he exclaimed. "How nice ye have returned! I must say, we despaired of ye some time ago!"

"Andrew," Jenks acknowledged, smiling. "I assume His Majesty spied our approach?"

"Aye! He was quite animated. More than he's been fer . . . Well, he'll be anxious ta see ye!" He paused, looking at Matt and the others. "Bringin' visitors, though . . . Most irregular."

"Unprecedented," Jenks conceded.

"Ye vouch fer 'em, I assume? There's restrictions, as ye know," the man stated.

"I know. I will bear any consequences."

Andrew shooed the Marines back to their posts. "Carry on," he told them, then gestured at the visitors. "This way. His Majesty awaits ye in the library."

"Yeah," Gray said to the Marines. "As you were. Nice, ah, muskets, fellas."

Matt glared at him.

Matt assumed Andrew was a butler, or something of the sort, but when they reached a tall hardwood door at the end of the hallway, he opened it and preceded them inside, moving slightly to the left to stand before a massive overburdened bookcase. Jenks had told him that every book aboard the "Passage Squadron" of ancient East Indiamen was in Imperial custody. The printing press existed here, and other books—copies and new works—were available to anyone who could afford them, but the originals received the same protection as the Governor-Emperor did.

The library was big but cozy, even cluttered in an absentminded, professorial fashion. Books (reprints, by the look of them) were scattered about, lying open. Strange machines stood on shelves, and on virtually every surface. The wood decor was dark, but the vast windows at the far end of the room permitted ample light to see and even work by, reflected by the almost universally white architecture outside. In the center of everything was a big, graying man, probably as powerful as the Bosun. He was in shirt-sleeves and weskit, and a pair of spectacles rested on his nose. His silver-streaked hair was gathered in a queue with a black ribbon near the nape of his neck, and he regarded them with a magnifying glass in his left hand. Matt hadn't really known what to expect. Jenks had described the man, but at first glance he seemed a decade older than Jenks had led him to believe. Apparently, by Jenks's quickly concealed expression, he was surprised as well.

"Commodore Jenks!" the man exclaimed, rising to stand nearly as tall as Matt. "Harvey!" He strode across the decorative rug and embraced Jenks long and hard. "I feared you were lost as well!"

"Not lost, Your Majesty," Jenks replied, "but considerably inconvenienced for a time. May I present my friends?"

"Of course. You must, in any case."

"Indeed. Your Majesty, Governor-Emperor Gerald McDonald, sole sovereign, by the grace of God, of the Empire of New Britain Isles and all her possessions . . ."

"Yes, yes, Harvey, do get on with it," the Governor-Emperor said with a slight grin. "And no more 'Majesty's,' if you please. It has always been 'Gerald' between us."

"Very well. May I present Captain Matthew P. Reddy of the United States warship USS *Walker*. His preferred rank of 'Captain' does not reflect his full authority. He is, in fact, the Supreme Commander of all military forces united beneath the Banner of the Trees. I will explain all that implies in due course, but suffice for now, in this company, he has become my particular friend."

"An extraordinary achievement, surely," the Governor-Emperor commented wryly, but without sarcasm. "There must be quite a tale behind that."

"Yes, sire," Jenks agreed, dispensing with "Majesty," but refusing to go further. "I must also present His Excellency Courtney Bradford, Esquire; scientist, naturalist, and plenipotentiary at large for the aforementioned Alliance. Accompanying them is Chief Bosun's Mate Fitzhugh Gray. He's more than he appears as well, despite his best efforts to conceal it."

The Governor-Emperor forced a chuckle. Matt could tell there was one question he wanted answered before any other. Still, he faced Matt and offered his hand. "A pleasure, sir," he said. "And please accept my profound admiration for your unusual, splendid ship. I've never seen her like!"

Matt bowed slightly. "Thank you, sir, and the pleasure's mine. Your city here is beautiful, and most impressive." He paused, glancing at the commodore. "And before saying more, I'm compelled to note that it's my understanding that Commodore Jenks might face some . . . difficulty for having supposedly brought us here."

"It's not ordinarily done," the Governor-Emperor confirmed.

"Well, then, let me put that issue to rest. It should be obvious to anyone that he didn't bring *us*, we brought him. You see, we pretty much knew where you were without a word from him. Like your ancestors, we come from another world, and we've got it mapped out reasonably well. Through historical accounts, conversations with another of your subjects, and a process of elimination, we knew . . . these islands were the only place your civilization could be."

Governor-Emperor McDonald gazed intently at Matt. "What subject?" he practically whispered.

"A brave, beautiful, and intelligent young lady named Rebecca Anne McDonald, sir."

The Governor-Emperor visibly tensed. "How . . . extraordinary," he managed. "And where is this . . . young lady, Captain? Where is my daughter?"

"It's a long story, sir, and you're not going to like it any more than I do," Matt said softly.

Over the next two hours, Matt, Jenks, Courtney, and Gray told how Rebecca had survived the shipwreck, been rescued, endured the Battle of Baalkpan, and ultimately been abducted by the Company warden, Commander Billingsley. Throughout the story, the Governor-Emperor asked sufficient questions to ensure that they were telling the truth and, as Jenks foresaw, became completely convinced. He called for refreshment, chewed a quill, jumped to his feet and ranted around the room, and even shed miserable tears. He couldn't hear enough about his daughter's adventures, but he was in agony all the while. He blamed himself completely, since it was he who'd sent her away in the first place—to protect her from just such an attempt by the Company to gain her custody and use her welfare against him.

"I love her quite desperately, you see," he tearfully explained. "She is my only child." He glanced at the ceiling and by inference, the living quarters above. "*Our* only child. My wife has not been the same since . . . Oh, God damn those evil creatures! I will have all of them hanged!"

"Of course, sire," Jenks agreed, "but first, we need more proof than our own mere words. Ideally, we've beaten Billingsley here. I take it there's been no news of *Ajax*?"

"None. Nor has New Dublin declared a quarantine—the only way to prevent news of her arrival there," answered the Governor-Emperor. He paused for a moment, a troubled expression clouding his face. "Of course, there has been precious little out of New Dublin of late." He shook his head. "But surely, they could not hide *Ajax*."

"Then we must wait a bit longer," said Jenks. "Either until *Ajax* arrives . . . or *Achilles* brings *Icarus* and *Ulysses* in. Either will provide sufficient proof to destroy the Company and hang half the Court of Proprietors. If you act before then, it might well fracture the Empire and cause a civil war."

"It might regardless, but you're right, of course." The Governor-Emperor sighed. "What to do in the meantime? As your battle would testify, the Company certainly knows you found my daughter; they sent more ships to seize her. They cannot know of *Ajax* yet, so they must assume she's either with you or left behind. Safe from them, at any rate. What will they do? We cannot pretend we know nothing of their scheme."

"With respect, sir," Courtney interjected, "I believe we can. They have no way of knowing we ever met their, ah, criminal squadron—not yet. I propose that Mr. Gray immediately return to *Walker* and make sure everyone aboard understands they must make no reference to the hostilities, or to any meeting with other Imperials besides Jenks and his people. As far as any of us are concerned, the princess is safe with the rest of Jenks's squadron and coming on directly."

"Oh, if only it were true!" the Governor-Emperor practically moaned, then shook his head. "Of course. An excellent stroke, Your Excellency. Playing that role might be more than my wife can bear, but I shall try to manage. Andrew?" He gestured to the man still standing just inside the door, where he'd remained since they entered. "Please escort Mr. Gray back to Captain Reddy's ship—with your permission, Captain."

Matt whispered something in Gray's ear, and the older man nodded. "Absolutely, sir."

When Andrew and the Bosun left, Jenks looked questioningly at Matt. "Is there a concern you'd like to share?"

"Not really. I hope not. It just occurred to me, though, that this 'Andrew' guy has heard everything we've said. I told Boats to keep an eye on him."

The Governor-Emperor looked shocked. "Preposterous! I've known Andrew my entire life."

"As you knew Sean Bates?" Matt asked.

"How the devil do you know that name?"

"Through Commodore Jenks," Matt replied. "I knew the *man* by another name—'Sean O'Casey.' I still call him that."

"Good God!" The Governor-Emperor looked at Jenks in amazement.

"Yes, sire," Jenks admitted. "He never abandoned us, though we abandoned him. It was he who first saved your daughter, and lost an arm doing it."

"Good God!" he repeated. "Bates! Where?"

"Aboard my ship," Matt said.

Governor-Emperor McDonald's face worked. "He was right all along," he said. "We knew it too. We just didn't know *how* right." He straightened. "You were wise to leave him aboard ship. Even missing an arm, he would be recognized. Please convey to him my deepest appreciation, affection . . . and apology, until I can do it in person."

"Yes, sire."

There came a knock at the door, and a sentry opened it slightly. Without waiting to be announced, a small, plain, unremarkable-looking man strode through the gap, an annoyed expression on his baggy face. "We are invaded by strangers, and I only learn of it from my barber!" he complained. Despite his bold entrance, the man's voice was wispy, almost whiny.

The Governor-Emperor regarded the man coldly and Matt feared that Courtney's new plan would disintegrate immediately. Instead, Jenks spoke. "They're not strangers to me, Sir Reed, and they have certainly not invaded. They brought me here at my request aboard their remarkably swift vessel so I might acquaint His Majesty with the results of our expedition."

"Jenks!" the man exclaimed, taking a step back as if he'd met a ghost.

In the meantime, the Governor-Emperor had regained his composure. "Yes, it is Jenks," he said. "Not lost after all. You'll have to withdraw your self-serving appropriation to erect a monument to 'the noble explorer.'" In an aside to Matt, he said, "This is the 'Honorable' Harrison Reed, supposedly *former* Director of Company Operations. He is currently my chief antagonist in the Court of Proprietors, among whom he holds the Prime Seat."

So this—unimposing person—was the instigator of all the hardships and loss they'd endured, first through Billingsley, then through his subsequent responses to news of the princess's rescue. Keeping his features carefully neutral, Matt stood. "Mr. Reed," he said in greeting, "I'm Captain Reddy." Was there the slightest hint of recognition?

"*Sir* Reed," the man said, almost absently. "But where is *Ajax* . . . and *Achilles*?" Reed plowed on, clearly dismissing him. "And the other two—I can't remember their names."

"*Achilles* will be along shortly," Jenks said. "I regret to report that the others were variously lost, one to a leviathan, and *Ajax* is missing and presumed lost. There were storms. . . . In any event, I dispatched *Agamemnon* home some time ago with news of our situation and the happy rescue of the Princess Rebecca. Did *Agamemnon* not arrive?"

"She did not," Reed lied smoothly with just the right tone of regret. If anyone had harbored the slightest doubt that this ridiculous man was involved in the conspiracy, it was swept away. *Agamemnon* had returned with the others as part of the "criminal" squadron and engaged them in battle alongside the other Imperial and Company ships. *Agamemnon* had been destroyed by *Walker*.

"Most tragic," commented the Governor-Emperor. "Unless *Ajax* turns up, *Achilles* will be the only survivor."

"A stiff price to pay for the life of a single girl," Reed stated. "As I initially argued."

"But well worth the price," Jenks jabbed, "since the princess was indeed rescued. Even now, she returns aboard *Achilles* in the company of a protective Allied force that carries enough fuel for Captain Reddy's ship to return home."

"What size force?" Reed demanded, suddenly less

haughty. "How do we know their intentions? If all Captain Reddy needs is fuel enough to go home, we can provide that."

"*Walker* doesn't burn wood or coal, sir," Matt said simply.

"Ridiculous! She's a steamer—I saw her myself on the way over."

"She's a steamer, all right," Matt agreed, "but she burns oil—refined petroleum. You have none here."

"Preposterous," mumbled Reed. He looked at Jenks. "Where's Commander Billingsley? Company wardens are sent aboard Imperial ships to ensure there are no grievous lapses in judgment—such as bringing strangers to our sacred home. I'd like to hear what he has to say about all this."

Jenks shook his head. "Regrettably, Commander Billingsley desired transfer to *Ajax* some months ago, and as a Company warden"—he almost sneered the words—"it was not my place to discourage his whim."

"Then send me his deputy!" Reed demanded, his voice rising.

Governor-Emperor McDonald stood. "You *do not* shout demands in *this* house, Prime Proprietor!"

"Of course not, Your Majesty," Reed replied, practically simpering. "I beg your forgiveness. I am overwrought with grief. Mr. Billingsley had entered an engagement to my niece. Regardless, I do beg an interview with his deputy."

"None are present," Jenks said. "Those who remain"—he hoped there weren't any, but it was nearly impossible to be sure—"are aboard *Achilles*. Captain Reddy's ship has little extra space. Only Lieutenant Blair and a dozen of his Marines accompanied me. There was no room for more."

"Well, then," Reed replied stiffly, "I suppose we have no choice but to accept your version of events until *Achilles* arrives."

"I suppose not, Prime Proprietor."

Reed turned to face the Governor-Emperor. "But what of these . . . animals . . . infesting that . . . wrongly appointed ship in question? Surely the thing must be quarantined? There has to be disease aboard. Filthy, furry creatures! Keeping an ape for a pet is one thing. My son has a parrot. But allowing them to romp all over one's ship is quite another!"

Matt took a step forward, but Courtney placed a hand on his arm. "Those 'apes' constitute a large percentage of my crew," Matt said, seething. "They're *not* apes, but people, just like us. They don't look like us, but they're highly intelligent, loyal, and honorable friends. The weakest among them could also unscrew your head without effort." Matt looked at the Governor-Emperor. "*Not* apes," he emphasized again. "We call them Lemurians and that seems to suit them. They're our friends and allies. Those aboard my ship have sworn the same oath as my men and are our countrymen. You might want to pass that word."

"Dear me," Reed proclaimed with mock regret, "I seem to be striking raw nerves with every word! Perhaps I should go before I inadvertently instigate hostilities!" He bowed to the Governor-Emperor. "Joy to you, sire, for the imminent return of your daughter. Now that I have some notion what the fuss at the waterfront was about, I'll let you treat with these strangers in peace. Please excuse me."

"Good-bye, Mr. Reed," Matt said in a neutral tone. "I'm sure we'll speak again."

Reed paused in the doorway, looking back. For the first time, it seemed his full attention was focused on Matt. "Indeed," he said, then was gone.

After Reed departed, they talked a while longer about their plan, then shifted topics to the Lemurians and the Grik, the war raging far to the west, and the stakes involved. The Governor-Emperor seemed oddly sympathetic.

"You have told Captain Reddy of the Dominion, have you not?" he asked.

"Of course," Jenks said.

"Well," continued the Governor-Emperor, looking at Matt, "with the . . . displacement . . . of our government here to New Scotland, the Dominion ambassador, a particularly unpleasant Blood cardinal with the perversely ironic name of Don Hernan DeDivino Dicha, has followed us here. I shouldn't wonder if he contacts you, quite soon in fact, requesting a meeting."

Matt was taken aback at first, but supposed he should have expected it. "He'll be just as curious about us as your people are," he surmised, then snorted. "Divino Dicha! Shit! . . . Ah, excuse me, sir."

"Precisely."

"What do you recommend I do?"Matt asked.

Governor-Emperor McDonald looked at Jenks.

"As I said, sire. He is my friend. I trust him completely."

McDonald looked back at Matt and shrugged. "Meet with him," he said. "As these Grik of yours might someday threaten us here, his nation could eventually threaten yours. I suggest you get to know him."

It was almost dusk before Matt, Jenks, and Bradford left Government House on their way back to the ship. The Governor-Emperor had halfheartedly asked them to stay and dine with him, but everyone was tired, and Matt suspected the man needed some time alone with his wife. Now they spoke quietly as they walked, so the squad of Imperial Marines escorting them wouldn't overhear.

"Lord," Matt said, "what a screwed-up mess." He felt the reassuring weight of his belted weapons. "Good thing I didn't have either of these with me. I might've killed that slimy bastard Reed."

Jenks shook his head. "You wouldn't have. I've seen you angry—very angry—but never enough to lose your senses. We've constructed a delicate web of deceit for Reed and his creatures to entangle themselves in. No doubt they have planned a similar trap for us, with much more time to prepare. Hopefully ours will startle them into revealing theirs, or launching their plot before it is complete." He shook his head and slowed. "With your permission, Captain, I won't return to the ship tonight."

"Why, what's the matter?"

"Well, I've been away from home a long time, and certainly by now my wife has learned of my return. . . ."

"Oh . . ." Matt said, his face reddening. He'd been around bachelors for so long it had completely slipped his mind that Jenks was married. "Harvey, I'm sorry," he said. "Of course you need to see her. Ah, give her my best."

Jenks chuckled. "She has an unwed sister, you know."

Matt shook his head. "Thanks, but no thanks." His voice was hard.

Jenks was seared with regret. "Of course. How ridiculous of me."

"Skip it. You run along, though. I'll see you in the morning."

Almost as soon as Jenks veered away, walking briskly, a man in an elegant frock coat and a large, wide hat appeared in the gloom ahead, forcing the escort to pause. One of the Marines, a corporal, spoke to him and then turned to Matt.

"This villain of a Spaniard asks if you'd join his master for dinner," the Marine said.

"Who is his 'master'?"

"Which it's that slicky-fish Dom ambassador, Hernan the Happy. His residence is in the Dom embassy."

Matt turned to Courtney, frowning thoughtfully. "Well, Governor-Emperor McDonald *did* say we ought to get to know him, but I wasn't expecting the . . . opportunity so soon. Are you up to it?"

Courtney grinned gamely.

"What about you, Marine?" Matt asked.

"Which I'm at yer disposal 'til yer back on yer skinny ship, Your Honor."

Matt considered. "Very well. We won't dine, not tonight, but we'll meet him briefly. It's been a long day. I'm sure you wouldn't mind a rest either."

"No, Your Honor."

"Please send a man to my ship, if you please, and tell them where we're going and who we'll see." He made sure to speak loudly enough for the messenger to hear. "We should be along shortly."

The corporal—who didn't look much different from the "villainous Spaniard"—and his squad led them through a seedier part of the city. "Professional" ladies lewdly entreated them to join them in a guttural English-Spanish mix that Matt would once have considered a type of "Tex-Mex," but this he could barely understand. Courtney beamed at them and tipped his hat as they passed. They pressed on into the gathering gloom.

"Which here it is," the corporal said.

The building looked like a smaller version of Government House, but it didn't stand independently. Other, somewhat dingy white structures butted right up to it. The Dominion embassy, or whatever it was, had fresher paint, and flew an odd red flag. Embroidered upon it was a large golden cross with some kind of weird bird perched on top.

"Fascinating symbolism," Courtney muttered. Matt was an historian of sorts, having received his degree in history at the Academy, but it didn't mean anything to him. The "messenger" with the big hat who'd led them there told the Marines to wait, then stepped forward and knocked sharply on the large, iron-reinforced doors. A small window slid aside, revealing a peephole, and muted words were exchanged.

"The Imperial heretics will await you here," the man said, speaking to Matt for the first time. "Since you will not dine, your visit will be brief. Follow me, please." The door creaked inward.

Matt looked at Courtney and, somewhat ostentatiously, waved him forward. "After you, Mr. Ambassador."

Inside, the reception area was gloomy, all red and gold, with baroque iron lamps adorning the walls. Busy tapestries hung between them with far too much detail to absorb as the visitors were led past. The "messenger" preceded them up a winding staircase to an upper floor that opened into a broad, uninterrupted audience chamber. At the far end of the room, suffused in an orangish light, rested a dark-skinned, silver-haired man dressed entirely in red, except for the frilly gold shirt peeking from beneath his crimson robe. Beyond him on the red wall was a huge gilded cross with crude golden spikes jutting from the areas where Jesus had traditionally been nailed to his. The man stood to meet them as Matt and Courtney were presented to him—by name. Obviously, the ambassador had spies—and didn't care if they knew. They'd have to be careful.

Thank God the Bosun isn't here, Matt thought. Gray was Catholic, but he just couldn't have stopped himself from making cracks about "popes and witch doctors." It was his way. The man before them clearly took his position very seriously, and if Matt had burst out laughing this time, they probably would have wound up impaled or burnt at the stake—assuming everything he'd heard about the Dominion was true.

"My friends." The man greeted them in a strangely silky-gentle, cordial voice, "I am Father Don Hernan DeDivino Dicha, Blood Cardinal to His Supreme Holiness, Messiah of Mexico, and by the Grace of God, Emperor of the World."

"The entire world! How impressive," Courtney blurted out. Matt could have kicked him. Apparently he didn't need Gray to get him killed—and at least Gray could fight.

"Oh, how charming!" said Don Hernan, with evident pleasure. "You truly *are* from an unknown land! Your manner of speech is most refreshingly odd. Perhaps the rumors that you come to us from the Old World are true as well!"

"Rumors spread fast," Matt commented. To his surprise, their host chuckled and touched a golden goblet. Wordlessly, a beautiful, unadorned, and entirely naked girl—who might have been fourteen, Matt realized in horror—raced in and filled three goblets, then virtually sprang from the room. Somehow, she hadn't spilled a drop—Matt watched their host actually check to see if she had. He shuddered, wondering what the penalty would have been.

"Indeed," the man continued in that disconcertingly soft voice. "Quite 'fast' indeed. Almost as quickly as your extraordinary ship!" He paused. "And never doubt that all of this world will one day beg for the benevolent rule of His

Holiness! It was given unto him and his order by the very breath of God!" He shook his head, still smiling. "Of course, spreading the Word and Intent of God is a tedious process. The world is filled with unbelievers and heretics who must be forced to come to His understanding." The ambassador performed a slight, modest bow. "I merely state the fact of the matter. Time and perseverance alone will make that fact clear to all." He paused and smiled more broadly. "Call me Don Hernan. Wine?"

Courtney began to accept, but Matt held him back. "Thank you, no. Spirits aren't allowed on United States ships, and while I may not be aboard right now, I am on duty. As is Ambassador Bradford. Perhaps another time."

"Perhaps," Don Hernan answered pleasantly. "Tell me, how stands the Faith on the Old World?"

Matt shrugged. "Pretty well, I guess. Lots of people believe in God. I do."

Don Hernan's lip twitched. "I mean the Roman Faith. Is it universal?"

Matt looked at Courtney. "Ah, no. It's spread all over the place, but it's not universal."

Don Hernan's smile faded slightly. "As I feared," he said. "Too weak. Force is the key. They must have forgotten that. All will be heretics now, to one degree or another." He looked at Matt. "Tell me of your faith."

"Why don't you tell me about yours first?" Matt replied, hedging. "We're new here, and everything we've heard comes from the Brits—I mean Imperials."

"Yes," agreed Courtney enthusiastically. "We know almost nothing about your . . . crossover experience. We've heard tell of an Acapulco galleon, but that's about the size of it."

"Ah, so you know some small part, even if it has been . . . corrupted." He sipped his wine. "*Nuestra Senora de La Quezon* was indeed a Galeon de Manila y Acapulco." Don Hernan warmed to his subject. "She was a noble ark, gentlemen, made of teak, mahogany, and lanang wood, almost as if her builders were divinely inspired to prepare her for the Holy Pilgrimage she would make. She departed Manila to serve God on this world in July of 1681. Her logs still exist, and are as revered as the Book of Exodus!"

"Oh, how marvelous!" Courtney gushed. "Such a tale they must tell!"

"Well," Don Hernan said, his smile growing again, "I am always pleased to tell how God took messengers from one imperfect world and placed them here to make a better one. Perhaps a longer . . . interview might be arranged." He focused on Courtney. "With you, at least." He closed his eyes in sadness. "In sum, mistakes had already been made, you see, terrible mistakes. The conquerors of New Espana conquered too well, destroying the fiercer, purer words of God already known by the native peoples. Things may still have been salvaged, but the Church was weak and did not press its victory. Here, we rediscovered those crucial instructions God had left for us, and added them to the ones we knew. After that, we . . . resolutely advanced the true, complete Word and never looked back. This will be our world, in His name."

"So your Founders encountered natives who'd crossed as well—earlier!" Bradford said eagerly. "What were they? Inca? Maya? Tol . . ."

"What they *were* is unimportant," Don Hernan interrupted, with a first trace of annoyance. "What we are now, all of my people, are children of God, and subjects of the Holy Dominion!"

"But . . . Well, what was gleaned from them? What 'Word' was rediscovered?"

Don Hernan smiled, pleased by Courtney's interest. "Simply that as Jesus Christ suffered for us, we must suffer for Him. Pain alone is the purifier of sin, and the blood, the Precious Water, He *sacrificed* on our behalf must be returned manyfold. That is the Word that awaited those who came to this world! That to be truly holy in the eyes of God, one must emulate his Son in all things, but most particularly, one must ultimately die in pain at the hands of another!"

Bradford could only gape, stunned by such profound perversity.

"Dear God," Matt murmured aside to him, "Jenks was right. These guys are crazier than bilge rats!"

Don Hernan was pleased as he watched the visitors leave. He thought the interview had gone quite well. Captain Reddy was doubtless an unrepentant heretic. The man had disrespectfully called directly upon God several times—such impudence!—but at least he did believe. Bradford displayed genuine fascination, perhaps even an attraction to the True Faith. At least he'd been eager to learn more about it. Don Hernan cared little exactly where the strangers were from, or what their situation was; he already knew much, and his spies would discover the rest. He'd wanted to learn about the *men* themselves and thought he had. Their animalistic "allies" never entered his thoughts. He'd determined, despite their advanced ship, that they couldn't pose much of a threat. They were clearly somewhat tentative—understandable in this new setting. They would move slowly, feel their way, try to be "friends" with everyone. They shouldn't be a factor, particularly after they were conveniently dead. A waste, it was true; he would have liked to explore further possibilities with the curious one, but that would only have edified him, and such deep curiosity was a mortal sin in any case. He sighed.

"Tea?" he asked aloud after a long moment.

Prime Proprietor Reed entered the room, huffy. "Your Holiness, you simply must not summon me here like a wayward child," he insisted. His wispy voice was adamant but querulous. "It grows more difficult to move about unobserved, and at this late date I cannot be thought to be closely associated with you! Not just yet."

Don Hernan understood Reed's concern and realized, with a bit of surprise, that his admonishment had required a measure of real courage. Despite Reed's nervous tone, Don Hernan knew the man wasn't a complete coward; he couldn't be to have facilitated such a lengthy and risky scheme, but his voice and demeanor were incapable of conveying forceful resolve. He was perceived as timid, which was possibly appealing to his ever-fearful constituents, but not very inspiring to others. It was just as well. That very demeanor allowed him to be profoundly underestimated by his opponents.

"I apologize, my son," Don Hernan said smoothly, calmingly. "So tedious. Our 'association' will be apparent soon enough, and we no longer need pretend. In any event, I thought you should like to hear my interview with the heretics. The sea captain, particularly."

"Well . . . yes, of course."

"You spent some time with him today. What do you think?"

Reed sighed and sat, uninvited, then poured a cup of tea from the pot just brought by the naked girl. "Dangerous, unpredictable. A complication we did not need."

Don Hernan was surprised. He considered himself a good judge of character, but he knew Reed was better. The man was a "politician," after all. "Well, then, if you're sure . . ."

"I am."

". . . perhaps I shall order them killed as they return to their ship. I can easily arrange an attack on the Marine escort by the 'disaffected mob.'" He chuckled. "Regrettably, the strangers would die in the scuffle."

Reed shook his head, horrified. "No, Holiness! That won't do at all! My spies have been badgering the crew of the iron steamer all day, and have learned little except that their Captain Reddy is a most formidable man. Simple street thugs would likely not succeed, and he might suspect the true motive for the attack and become remarkably vengeful! Apparently, he has a towering temper." Reed paused. "Perhaps worse, Jenks and His Majesty would surely suspect, and they might well take precipitous steps."

Don Hernan tugged at his sculpted chin whiskers. "Interesting. Very well. There will be no . . . covert assassins. You say Captain Reddy has a temper?"

"That is what I understand. I have begun to learn a few things that provoke it. . . ."

"Excellent." Don Hernan sipped the wine still before him on the table, then looked at Reed and smiled. "As you know, my first inclination has always been to destroy the enemies of God, but I can be patient when I sense opportunity. Perhaps the arrival of Jenks and these 'Americans' is heaven-sent."

"How so?"

"It could provide just the right distraction. We are not quite ready—another month would have been ideal—but the 'complication,' as you put it, of their arrival and the approach of *Achilles* makes that month uncertain. You agree there is more to their story than we know?"

Reed nodded. "There's been nothing out of Respite in weeks. That is the course they would have taken. I fear, if nothing else, they know that *Agamemnon* did return and the Company sent ships to intercept the princess."

"But they said nothing of it . . . to you. I would warrant they shared considerably more with His Majesty. *Achilles* must bear proof, and they are awaiting her before the Empire goes on the rampage, leveling accusations against the Company. *Achilles* has an escort?"

"American ships of unknown power, but if their iron steamer is any indication . . ."

"Certainly *faster* than anything we might confront them with. If we attempted another interception, even if we succeeded, they wouldn't have to fight—they could just outrun our ships . . . and arrive here with even further proof." Don Hernan tapped the goblet with his fingers. "As I said, we are not quite ready, but with a distraction . . . we are surely ready enough." He stood, decisive. "We cannot wait until the planned 'Founders' Day' date for the operation. I will have to send dispatches, speed things along, but the gift of the moment must not be ignored. You say this Captain Reddy has a temper? What makes it burn most bright?"

"I do not know, but I provoked him several times . . . as I do . . . and in our brief exchange, I learned he takes especial offense to slanders against his ape-like crew! He protects them vigorously and they are one weak spot, at least."

"Would he rise to a challenge over them?"

Reed smiled. "I should think so. I didn't even press him. He seems quite fond of the creatures. I suspect that if any were present when offense was given, he would be even more likely to rise."

Don Hernan chuckled. "The Pre-Passage Ball is in three days. I think we should arrange an . . . entertainment that should quite consume Imperial attention while we implement our plan. Commodore Jenks will be there, of course. Ensure that Captain Reddy is invited—make it impossible for him to refuse—and do invite at least one of his . . . animals."

"You are most wise, Holiness," Reed said, bending to kiss the offered ring.

The music was Vivaldi and Courtney Bradford was entranced by the unexpectedly familiar melody of the "Spring (La primavera)" concerto from *The Four Seasons*, played by an excellent violin quartet. "Unbelievable," he muttered over and over when not distracted by the apparently endless stream of people trying to meet him. Matt was at least as overwhelmed by guests and dignitaries, many in Imperial Navy uniforms. Jenks and his wife stood near Matt, and Jenks did most of the talking, while Matt tried to be engagingly distant to the horde of young ladies fluttering around him in their colorful, cloudlike gowns. The Bosun stood off a little, virtually alone, toying with a glass of something and generally grimacing all around.

The fish-flesh clouds were bright pink overhead as the sun vanished in the gap between the high, distant mountains. The Governor-Emperor spoke to the attendees with his wife, a frail-looking thing, smiling bravely, beside him. He said something about Jenks's miraculous return, and welcomed their distinguished guests from another land. Courtney didn't catch it all. Lanterns and torches sprang to life, dancers orbited one another on the close-cropped

Government House lawn, and the music became increasingly difficult to hear as the Pre-Passage Ball commenced in full force. Jenks had told them that the festivities commemorated a ball (or it might have been a small dinner party) that occurred a week or so before the three ancient Indiamen departed some East Indian Island (Bradford couldn't remember which, and it hardly mattered now) bound for India. The Founders' Day celebration, barely a month away, took note of the survivors' arrival here, thirteen months later. It was a kind of "before and after" observance. Over the years, the Founders' Day event had become more a time of remembrance and thanksgiving, while the Pre-Passage Ball evolved into a party.

Bradford didn't much care just then, as he was nearly half drunk. It was time to taper off, he decided. He'd promised Captain Reddy that he'd keep his wits about him. He noticed Chack was still under siege and began moving toward him. Besides himself, Matt, Gray, and Chack were the only people from *Walker* at the ball. The entire crew was anxious for liberty, but they understood things were tense ashore, and they needed to remain ready for anything. People came every day to gawk at the ship and the Lemurians aboard her as they went about their duties. There'd apparently even been an attempt to abduct a 'Cat who'd jumped down to the dock to help a screaming child. At the 'Cat's cry of alarm, Spanky and another pair of 'Cats leaped to his aid, sending four rough-looking men running back into the crowd. The distressed child was nowhere to be found, and even some of the onlookers suspected a plot and urged them back to the ship.

The people of New Scotland were fascinated by the Lemurians, however, and what little they'd learned about them was the talk of Scapa Flow, and even posted on broadsheets. Therefore, while all of the visitors were celebrities and near the center of attention since arriving at the ball dressed in their best, the very center space had been unwillingly taken by Chack—and he was in hell. Despite his immaculate and very martial Marine dress, every diaphanously dressed female in attendance stopped to fawn over him like a helpless, squirming youngling. Some even stroked his fur! He was mortified, and Captain Reddy glanced his way almost constantly, clearly tense on his behalf.

Bradford plowed onward, dispensing apologies. His vision was a little blurred and he stopped for a moment to clear his head. There was a commotion to his right, and he noticed a man with slick black hair doing much the same as he, working his way toward Chack with a purposeful look on his face. Courtney felt a gust of alarm and tried to pick up his pace. He tripped. So many people tried to help him up, laughing, happy, swirling people, that it seemed forever before he reached his feet. With another string of apologies, he tried to swim through the bodies.

He heard shouts. People pressed back against him, crying out in surprise. A commotion erupted where Chack had been, but he couldn't see the Lemurian anymore. A woman screamed. Courtney began to panic. What was happening? He couldn't see! What was he doing? He didn't even have a weapon. Already he feared the worst. There were more shouts—indignant, offended, enraged. He thrashed his way through a ring of people, practically panting with terror—and was completely taken aback by what he saw.

In the light of the torches, Chack stood safe and sound, but he was holding Captain Reddy by one arm while Harvey Jenks held the other. The captain stood, knuckles bloody, staring at the slick-haired man with that . . . frightening . . . look he so rarely got. The Bosun burst into the ring, eyes casting back and forth, searching for a target for the "dress" cutlass (he'd painted the scabbard) at his side. The slick-haired man stood, a little shaky, daubing his mouth with a handkerchief. Daubing wouldn't do the trick. Both lips were split wide open, and dark blood practically covered the silky cravat and white shirt down to his weskit.

"I velieve I 'ust de'and satisvaction!" said the slick-haired man.

"You got it, you cowardly bastard," Matt hissed. "Anytime, anywhere! I *ordered* Captain Chack not to respond to rats like you. I can, by God!"

"Excellent." The man seemed to be trying very hard not to show any pain. "The Impherial dueling grounds, then. Just after se'vices. Swords." With that, the man turned and paced calmly through the crowd.

"What the hell?" Matt asked, stunned. He seemed to be getting his rage under control and his expression showed uncertainty. He'd been prepared for a fight right then. "When's that? What's going on?"

"Next Sunday, a week from today—after church services," Jenks said severely. "Sunday's the customary day." He shook his head and took a breath. "We've been done, my friend." He released Matt's arm and strode out into the circle, looking at the faces there. He lifted his gaze until he seemed to see who he was looking for, some distance away. "I want there to be no doubt among any man here that this despicable episode was premeditated and engaged upon by none other than Prime Proprietor Harrison Reed!" He pointed in the direction the slick-haired man had gone. "That creature, you know! How many times has he taken the field for the '*Honorable*' New Britain Company? He's an assassin! A hired killer! He does nothing on his own account! He is but a tool, a coward's weapon in the hand of Harrison Reed!"

There was a gasp and the crowd began to shift, as if unconsciously realizing that it formed a barrier between two adversaries. Eventually, a gulf widened between the circle and the Prime Proprietor himself, standing on the steps of Government House. Just a short distance away, unnoticed by most, stood the Dominion Ambassador, Don Hernan DeDivino Dicha. Reed glared back at Jenks, then flicked his kerchief as if to say, "As you will," and turned away.

Courtney swayed just a bit and wondered if he alone noticed the odd, benevolent smile on Don Hernan's face. "A bloody duel!?" he roared. "Seriously, we've come all this way for a bloody *duel*? Buggery!"

*   *   *

After the bizarre confrontation most everyone, aside from a few well-wishers, seemed willing to leave the "celebrities" alone, and they managed to secure a well-lit table away from the dancers. The ball slowly gathered speed again, but there was a new, electric excitement as people began to contemplate the "Duel of the Decade." Jenks recognized the mood and sighed. He'd seen it before. He looked at Chack. It wasn't the Lemurian's fault, but Chack couldn't help but blame himself, and it showed in his body language.

"They suckered us," Matt growled, rubbing his torn knuckles.

"They suckered *you* if by that you mean they lured us into their trap instead of the other way around," Jenks said. He smiled slightly. "I must admit, it was a glorious thing to see, however. You knocked at least two teeth out of that vile man's head, and he's never even been touched on the field, with sword or pistol." He smirked. "Dueling to the death is a common occurrence in the Empire. A serious, honest punch in the mouth is rare."

"Who was that guy?" Matt asked.

"An assassin, as I said," Jenks replied. "A damn good one, actually. If you'll pardon the irony, you should feel flattered."

"I feel like an idiot."

"You don't understand. One way or another, there was going to be a duel provoked this night. I should have expected it, but I never dreamed Reed would be so bold . . . or is it boldness? Desperation? What if *time* is the issue?" He shook his head. "Put that aside for a moment. That man—that assassin—knew exactly what he was doing, and which keys to stroke. I doubt he expected quite as vigorous a response to his taunts"—he grinned again—"but he knew you would react the way you did. Who else has insulted our Lemurian friends lately?"

"Reed."

"Precisely. The thing is, it didn't matter if you responded or not. Say Chack had responded. There'd be a duel. If neither you nor he responded, I'll wager Mr. Gray would have, and there'd be a duel."

"Not without orders," the Bosun stated piously.

"Oh, don't be absurd, you ancient beast!" Courtney burst out. "Of course you would have—but that's not the commodore's point, is it?"

"No, it's not," Jenks said. "There would have been a duel if that man had had to bite your feet to provoke one. That's what he *does*. All you lost by striking him was the dubious advantage of choosing weapons."

"I'm good with a pistol," Matt said.

"A licensed, inspected, flintlock dueling pistol? Mmm. I thought not. That may have made you almost even, at best. No, it will have to be swords now, and you simply can't beat him . . . in the kind of fight he expects. I doubt I could."

Matt sat up straighter, but didn't speak.

"Well . . . then how come you jumped in too?" Gray demanded, a little loudly. He glowered at a man at a nearby table who'd glanced up when he spoke. Gray's question was mirrored in the eyes of Jenks's attractive young wife, seated beside him. She had dark hair and was dressed just as ridiculously as all the other women, but somehow she pulled it off. She didn't voice the question as Gray had, though; it wasn't her "place."

"Why not? The incident was obviously contrived. No doubt there was another hireling in the crowd waiting to challenge me, or vice versa. I simply beat them to it by publicly blaming Reed to see his reaction—and the reaction of others. Most interesting."

"At least you get to kill Reed," Matt said, almost jealously.

"What? Oh, of course not! He'll hire a substitute. It's his right as the offended party. Can't have people running around picking duels with others simply because they dislike them or they're weak," he scoffed sarcastically.

"Then . . . why do it?"

"*Because* it was contrived. 'They'—Reed, the Company . . . perhaps even Don Hernan, by the look on his face—have an agenda, that's plain. What isn't at all clear is what it is . . . and what next Sunday has to do with it." He became silent, thoughtful. Matt looked at the others. Clearly he was missing something. Finally, Jenks shook his head. "I did what I did to surprise them, to see their unprotected reactions."

"You're gonna fight a duel 'cause you wanted to see the look on their faces?" Gray demanded.

"Quietly!" Jenks cautioned. "We don't want *them* to know that! Besides, once more, I presume I would have been compelled to in any case. Consider this: if they only wanted us dead, I assure you they would resort to assassination. What do they have to gain by a public duel?"

"Excuse me, Jenks," Matt said. "You keep forgetting we're new here. Dueling's illegal in the U.S. Navy! What do you mean, *public*?"

Jenks looked around the table. He even had Courtney's attention now. "Oh. I see. I was beginning to wonder why you were being so obtuse! Duels in the Empire are very public affairs. That's probably why there aren't more of them. They're not rare, by any means, but I suspect some are more afraid of the crowd than they would be of an opponent on the field!"

"Crowd? Like this?"

Jenks almost laughed. "Um . . . not exactly."

"Bigger?"

"Exponentially. Even under normal circumstances."

"Normal?" Courtney asked.

Jenks sighed. "I am, deserving or not, a fairly well-known personality. Particularly in certain circles." He grimaced. "I've been 'on the field' twice before, for various reasons." He patted his wife's hand when it suddenly touched his arm. "On both occasions, the event was . . . quite a spectacle."

"That's it!" Courtney said emphatically, and Matt began to nod.

"Indeed. It must be," Jenks said seriously. "Imagine the spectacle at a multiple duel involving not only myself but the primary representative of the first 'new' people the Empire has encountered in over a century. The *spectacle* is the thing!"

"And the timing," Matt reminded.

"The timing," Jenks agreed. "I'm convinced of it! Somehow, our arrival or the impending arrival of *Achilles*—perhaps their belief that the princess is aboard her or that we have some proof of their scheme—has put that scheme, whatever it is, in jeopardy!"

"Ahem," said Courtney. The table grew silent and they all looked up to see Andrew, the Governor-Emperor's man, approaching. Without waiting to be invited, he sat.

"His Majesty has asked me ta ask all of ye, quote: 'What in the name o' God those fish-headed sailors think they're about?' Ah, end quote." He looked around the table severely.

Jenks looked at the man with a calculating expression. "How long have we known each other, Andrew?"

The man blinked, but stared right back. "I'm forty," he said. "Ye and His Majesty is both thirty-nine. As the eldest, I was in charge when we all first went a'fishin' at the docks when we was tots. The Empress Mother, bless her lovely, sweet soul, bade me take ye both, as well as young Sean, sport shootin' in the Highlands for the first time when I was ten, so ye an' His Majesty woulda' been nine. Ye got excited reloadin' fer a second shot at a dragon foul, an' fired yer rammer away. Ye cried." Andrew sighed. "I stayed on when ye an' Sean went off ta sea, ta fight Dom pirates an' have yer fun. It was I, stood by His Majesty when his mother died, an' the . . . Rebellion came. Aye, even then! An' it's me that's stayed ta brother him when his sweet daughter was lost. You tell me, Harvey Jenks, how long have we known one another?"

Jenks nodded and looked at Captain Reddy. "Andrew *Bates*," he explained, ironically, and Matt's eyes widened. Jenks looked back at Andrew. "I'm sorry, old friend, but we can leave nothing to chance, and I wanted Captain Reddy to trust you as I do. Tell His Majesty that by leaping into the enemy's web, we may have snared him in ours. We're convinced that something will happen next Sunday, either at or during the duel."

"What do ye think it'll be?"

Jenks held out his hands. "We've no idea, not yet, but whatever it is, it will be for 'all the marbles,' as my friends here would say. We have a week to uncover the plot."

"I believe I already know," Chack said suddenly. "Not what they hope to gain, but I suspect I understand the reason for the provocation tonight." He looked at Jenks, blinking intensity. "I will tell you . . . if you tell me how to save Captain Reddy from that . . . aas-saassin."

"Chack!" Matt reprimanded.

Jenks chuckled. "Oh, no, that's quite all right." He looked at Chack. "Do you believe me when I say I have a plan—in that respect at least?"

Chack blinked skeptically, then nodded. "Yes." His tail twitched and he looked around the table. "You may be right about the reasons for this 'duel' thing, but regardless how it started, I believe *you* were the ultimate target, Commodore Jenks, not Captain Reddy. You say a lot of people will come to witness this duel, this fight. More than are here?"

"That's right."

"Many will come just to watch?"

"Yes."

"Who will come to support you? To be on your side? To be your friend?"

"Why, I expect . . ." Jenks's face paled in the torchlight. "Oh my God! Captain Reddy, I apologize. It *wasn't* you who was 'suckered,' it was me! I won't be fighting him, but my duel is, in essence, against Reed! The vast majority of those who will come to directly support me against him are Marine and Naval officers . . . and we don't dare tell them to stay away!"

CHAPTER 25

Off Tagran Island

"There it is!" Lawrence practically squealed. "Home!" *Ajax*'s battered longboat was cruising north, northeast through a sickening, quartering swell, under her dingy triangle of canvas. The sky was clear and blue, but the sea was running fairly high. All the occupants of the boat were "old salts" by now, however, and no one noticed any discomfort, except perhaps from sunburn.

"You're sure this time?" Silva grunted skeptically.

"Sure, I sure! That *is* Tagran!"

"That's what he said *last* time," Silva reminded everyone darkly. Lawrence shot him a savage look and hissed. "Petey" hissed too, and possibly sensing a brightened mood, chirped, "Eat?"

"No eat, dear," Rebecca called. "Later perhaps." They weren't exactly on short rations—yet—but nobody wanted to waste food on Petey except Rebecca and Dennis, and Silva only claimed to want him fed to keep him fat enough to eat themselves.

Petey hop-glided from the bow of the boat, past the

mast, and landed lightly in Rebecca's lap. He wasn't much bigger than a house cat and weighed considerably less. His claws and teeth would have made him a handful for many larger predators, though. He looked up at the girl with big eyes, surrounded by scaly skin, that gradually turned to downy feathers. "Eat?" he pleaded pitifully.

"I'm sorry," Rebecca replied soothingly. "Not now!"

"Little creep," Silva grunted. He looked at Lawrence and patted his arm companionably. "I know how it feels, little buddy, bein' a ex-pet. There used to be this gal in Olongapo . . ." He shook his head and nodded forward. "That little bump over there's Tagran? It don't look any bigger than Yap."

"It is, just . . . not as high, less . . . hilly," Lawrence said. "See that . . . grayness there?" He pointed. "That is the island I lived on as a hatchling!" Lawrence was genuinely excited. Everyone was. Their escape from Billingsley, their existence on the island, and their ultimate departure had been harrowing enough, but then they were faced with a rough voyage in a leaky boat with only a vague idea of their true position in relation to Lawrence's home. The map they had wasn't much good. Silva had been mightily tempted just to say the hell with it and make for the Philippines. Only the current and an insufficient water supply put that notion to rest. He had no doubt they'd make it, they *couldn't* miss the Philippines, but it would be a hard trip. Besides, many islands in the Fil-pin Lands were practically unexplored, with lots of nasty beasties. Now, after all they'd all been through, Lawrence's assurance that they would be met as friends and given aid was a huge relief.

Dennis had a weird thought. "Say, you keep carryin' on about how happy ever'body'll be to see you. After gettin' fooled by the princess, how do I know you ain't some sort o' lizard king, or somethin? Why get worked up over you comin' home?"

Lawrence made a happy sneezing sound, a belly laugh for him. "I not king! I just Lawrence. Tagranesi nice 'olks, though. They love stories, adventure. I have 'oth. Lots to tell! No one has ever returned to Tagran after so long, and I have gone far!"

"Hell, they'll prob'ly just think you're a ghost and ignore you." Silva stopped, glancing aft again, far to the southwest. "Whoa. What the hell?" Others in the boat looked where he was facing. The distant horizon was smudged dark, brooding, where it had been clear just a short time before.

"Is it a storm?" Sandra asked anxiously.

"No," said Lelaa. "I don't think so. I don't know what it is . . . unless . . ."

"Unless it's that damn Talaud." Silva finished for her. "You said it was gettin' antsy. Couple o' times now, I seen som'thin' like that—when we was further south, on Yap. Might be a big ash cloud, spreadin' out from it."

"You said nothing before," Rajendra said accusingly. "Why not?"

"Why should I? It's a goddamn volcano! Nothin' we can *do* about it. Why worry?"

"But . . . it is hundreds of miles away!" Rebecca objected. "Surely it cannot threaten us here?"

"When Krakatoa erupted in 1883, the explosion was heard thousands of miles away, and the shock wave is said to have circled the earth numerous times," Sister Audry said nervously. "Tens of thousands died in the resultant waves."

"Lieutenant Laumer's men spoke of a 'Kraa-katoa,'" Lelaa said thoughtfully. "I think some of them feared Talaud was 'gearing up' to 'pull one,' if I do not mistake the terms."

"No mistake, Cap'n Lelaa," Silva said grimly. "Dumbasses prob'ly jinxed themselves, talking about it."

"You don't believe that!" Audry said severely.

Silva didn't answer. Instead, he looked up at the sail and then turned to Rajendra at the tiller. "See if she'll come another point or two into the wind. Cinch up them sheets, boys," he added to Brassey and Abel Cook. "Time to quit goofin' off."

"Goofin' off!" Petey seemed to scold.

As the day wore on, the lonely longboat drew closer to Tagran, close enough to make out details of the island, but at some point Lawrence's enthusiasm seemed to wane and he grew nervous again.

"What's the matter, Lawrence?" Rebecca asked, increasingly concerned.

"That *is* Tagran," he insisted. "It . . . looks di'rent, though."

"It's been a long time, my dear," Rebecca consoled him. "Perhaps you are mistaken?"

"Di'rent," Lawrence said. "I don't know how."

"Different, like maybe a big wave splashed over the joint?" Silva said suddenly. "I didn't see the one that washed over Yap, but it had to be twenty, thirty feet tall just to rinse all our 'droppin's' out from under us. If it was that big when it hit here, or maybe bigger . . . Looky there! There's a buncha crap up in them trees yonder." He pointed.

"No," Lawrence moaned.

"What sort of houses do your folks live in?" Silva asked, uncharacteristically gentle.

"Tree timbers, like you call ca'ins . . . cav-bins."

"Cabins. Are they built up high, like the 'Cats do?"

"No."

Silva looked at Sandra and Rebecca. Sister Audry shifted to the front of the boat and put a hand on Lawrence's back.

"Well . . . a wave couldn't have washed over the entire place!" Cook said. "There's a small peak upon it. Two, in fact!"

"That is true," Lawrence said, his voice miserable. "Tagranesi go there when ground shakes. None live there 'ut our 'Noble Queen' and her attendants, though. There is little to eat that is not carried there. Tagranesi catch 'ish, raise creatures to eat, grow things . . ."

"There's a sail!" Brassey exclaimed. "There, do you see? It's coming around the headland! Two sails!"

Silva squinted with his good eye. "There's more than

two! Look kinda like proas! A whole swarm of 'em." He glanced around. "You know, like big double-ended canoes, with outriggers and a bipod mast!"

"They *do* look quite like proas," Sister Audry exclaimed, shading her eyes. "Proas were quite common around Java . . . once."

"Who are they?" Rajendra demanded, checking the prime in his pistol. "Are they your people, Lawrence?"

Lawrence shook his head. "I *think* so. Others, not just Tagranesi, use those *kichi-acki*, ah, 'roas."

"But they might be enemies of yours, here to plunder the remains of your home?" Rajendra insisted.

"I think not," Lawrence replied as the vessels began converging toward the longboat. "They *are* Tagranesi! Thank the God!"

"Well, don't just sit there gapin', you nitwitted lizard!" Silva exclaimed. "Shout out to 'em before they think *we're* here a'plunderin'!"

There on the open water beneath a clear, sunny sky, Lawrence was reunited with his amazed people. They weren't the only ones amazed. Silva, Sandra, and Rebecca in particular had come to know the Grik better than they cared to, and the Tagranesi looked an awful lot like their hated enemy. They'd grown used to Lawrence, but to see so many of his people acting like . . . people . . . instead of raving killing machines was so far beyond their experience, it took a while for them to loosen their grips on their weapons. At first Lawrence jabbered excitedly across to one of the larger proas, apparently summarizing their tale and explaining his miraculous return. The Tagranesi listening to him appeared as tense as Silva and the others felt at first, but after a while they too laid their weapons aside and listened as Lawrence spoke. Occasionally, one of the apparent "leaders" made a comment or loudly repeated something Lawrence said.

"What the hell?" Dennis demanded during a brief pause.

"That's Chinakru!" Lawrence replied, referring to what

seemed the "main" leader. The creature looked like an older version of Lawrence, covered with fine orangish "fur" and dark brown stripes. The crest on its head was much longer and flatter than Lawrence's, and fell down around its neck almost like a horse's mane. Even when the crest stood up, as it had when the first words were exchanged, it still covered the top of the creature's head like a horsetail plume. The most amazing thing about Chinakru, however, was that despite his apparent fitness, he looked *old*. His feathery fur was shot with white, and so was the thick crest. Some of his teeth were gone and the others looked none too sharp. There were even dark, wet circles around almost rheumy eyes. None of the humans had ever seen an old Grik.

"Who's he?"

"Chinakru is—used to—ah, he teacher, head'aster, leader on island that I grew to . . ." Lawrence shrugged. "Island I grew to 'Lawrence' on. He knows I! He knows 'Lawrence' now too! I told him the title 'Ecky gave! It is a strange title, true, yet it is I now! It is real! *I* real!"

"That's wonderful, Lawrence!" Rebecca gushed. "Are you sure you don't mind the name? It was all I could come up with at the time. Perhaps one less 'strange' to your people would be best?"

"No! I Lawrence now!" the Tagranesi declared proudly. "I achieved all that is I as 'Lawrence.' Lawrence I stay!"

"That's swell, Larry," Silva gibed, "but what's goin' on? Why's everybody out here bobbin' around on the water to meetcha?" More than twenty proas of all shapes and sizes were in view now, and several had gathered around them, hove to. "Why don't we take this touchin' reunion party ashore?"

Lawrence spoke to Chinakru and then listened as the old Tagranesi told his own people's tale. His voice was grim as he passed the translation. Essentially, though Lawrence was now a "person" in the eyes of his people, his people no longer had a home. They weren't even "Tagranesi" anymore. The great wave had come in the night, as Lawrence had feared, and many had been drowned. Worse, all the survivors' livelihoods, their crops, livestock, everything, had been destroyed as well. All that remained were these boats nestled in a cove on the lee side of the island to carry almost three hundred refugees. Perhaps ten times that number had died, or had been left behind to starve.

Chinakru and his best pupils had left the "proving ground," the "forming" island to help those he now led on a mass migration "somewhere else." It had happened before, centuries in the past, and now they must endure the greatest trial of all.

"But it's right there!" Silva protested. "How come they have to leave? What about us? Can't we at least rest up for a while? Shit!"

The ground had not shaken before the wave, but now it shook all the time. More waves would come, perhaps even bigger. The only "safe" place would be the highest hill on Tagran, and only the "Noble Queen" of Tagran could remain there with a select few to rebuild their people, since there was not nearly enough food for all. The only chance for the refugees was to get as far out to sea as possible before the next waves came, and ride them out. They might not even notice them on the water. After that, they must find a new place or die.

"Jeez," Dennis muttered, looking longingly at the island so close. "I guess it's the Philippines, then, after all. Talk about wasted time!" He looked around the boat. "That's six, maybe seven hundred miles, and the currents won't be any help at all."

"But the current carried Lawrence, Mr. O'Casey, and myself in the right direction," Rebecca protested.

"You were south of here, and lucky too," Dennis said. "Besides, it carried you nearly straight at Talaud. If that's what's causin' most o' this ruckus, that's the last place we want to make for. Cap'n Lelaa?"

Lelaa nodded slowly. "Agreed. Talaud must be the culprit. I hope Mr. Laumer's expedition has already left that place!"

"What should we do?" Sandra asked the Lemurian sailor, seeking her professional opinion.

"Mr. Silva is right—we must make for the Fil-pin Lands."

Rajendra growled something under his breath.

"What's that?" Sandra demanded, but Rajendra didn't answer.

"It's our only real option," Lelaa persisted. "The map from *Ajax* shows other, closer islands, but they will be as vulnerable as Yap and Tagran, and we don't know who, if anyone, might meet us there." She stared significantly at the gathered proas. "We can't stay here. There's no food, and I suspect going ashore to take any that remains would result in violence. Personally, I'd rather die than return to Yap, even without the shiksaks. It *must* be the Fil-pin Lands! Now, if Talaud 'blows,' there will be massive waves, much like Sister Audry described. The southern Fil-pin Lands, Min-daanao particularly, will be swamped. We should steer west, northwest, and sail as fast as we can. With the compass, the Heavens, and Captain Rajendra's quadrant, we will not get lost." She sighed. "Silva is also right about the currents, if not the distance. I have never been this far east, obviously, but I've been off the east coast of the Fil-pin Lands. The currents will be against us. We're now actually about nine hundred of your miles from our destination, a voyage of . . . months. How much food and water do we have?"

"Not *that* much!" Rajendra blurted.

"Have you a better suggestion?" Sandra asked. Rajendra just shook his head.

"We have about a month and a half, usin' just enough to keep body and soul together," Silva said. Lelaa nodded agreement. She'd estimated as much.

Sandra sighed, rubbing her forehead. "Lawrence," she said at last, "your people have no knowledge of the Philippines, correct?"

"None, except I."

"I imagine those . . . proas are a lot faster than this boat, with as little sail as it can carry."

"True," Lawrence agreed.

"Twice as fast?"

Lawrence didn't know. The only one he'd ever sailed, he'd built himself, and it was very small.

Lelaa had been looking at the lines of the boats in question. "At least that," she said, "which would shorten the trip, but those boats do not look as well suited to heavy weather."

"And ours is? How much food and water do they have?"

Lawrence asked, and discovered that the refugees had less than they did, for all intents and purposes.

"Saan-Kakja may kill me," Sandra muttered, "but ask them if they want to go someplace way bigger than they've ever seen; where no wave can ever wash their lives away." She looked at Lelaa. "I don't think Saan-Kakja even has a colony on Samar, does she?"

CHAPTER 26

Talaud Island

"Jeez, Mr. Laumer," said Shipfitter Danny Porter nervously, watching the distant mountain through binoculars, "I don't think I can take this much longer! I'm starting to think poor Sid got off easy."

Irvin Laumer stood beside him on S-19's conn tower, beneath the brown-gray sky. He turned and gave Porter a blistering stare. "Stow that crap right now, sailor! Sid didn't give up, and neither will you." Laumer paused, taking in the hellish scene of desolation surrounding the boat. The island was a dusty, skeletal corpse, and the strange winds and twisting thermal eddies kicked up random vortices that danced among the wooden bones. The air was full of an ash so fine that it resembled a smoky haze, and everyone who came up from below wore bandannas. They didn't help much. The whole crew had hacking coughs, and some were coughing blood. The dust was everywhere, and even below, red, puffy eyes streamed constantly.

"Look," Irvin continued, less harshly, "I know you're scared. Everybody is. This is the screwiest situation imaginable. But think about it like this: you were at Baalkpan, under Chapelle, right?" Danny nodded. "I wasn't even there," Irvin said with a touch of bitterness. "I was at Sembaakpan with the 'women and kids.' Tell me this—which was scarier, this or a couple hundred thousand Grik coming to eat you?"

"Well . . . that was," Danny confessed, "but there was fighting, see? We were *doing* something! There wasn't all this time . . . just sitting and waiting."

Irvin nodded. "Yeah, we've been waiting a few days, but we've been busy too. We've been working on the boat and waiting for the lagoon to clear enough for us to get out of here. That was a chance Captain Reddy, you, and all the 'Cats never had at Baalkpan—a chance to get away from what was coming. By all accounts, you didn't lose it then, and you're not going to now. Got it?"

"Aye, aye, sir."

The steel beneath their feet reverberated with a gasping, metallic groan, and black soot mixed with rusty red dust exploded from the port exhaust, aft. For almost a full minute, they listened to the labored, clattering rumble of the port diesel, before it belched and died.

"Looks like Sandy might finally have a handle on that thing," Irvin observed. "Seems the biggest problem with it was that a leaky exhaust vent let water in, rainwater mostly, thank God, and it rusted everything up in the cylinders and seeped into the crankcase." He raised his own binoculars and scanned the lagoon. There was still a lot of debris, and the water around the anchored submarine was dark and gray with mud. But most of the detritus had washed ashore by now, or gathered into tangled islands close to the beach. "Which is good," Irvin continued, "because we're through waiting. As soon as the tide clears as much of that junk out of the mouth of the lagoon as it's going to today, we're getting the hell out of here!"

"Torpedo room reports that the submerged anchor's secure," Tex Sheider announced over the rumble of the starboard diesel and the distant, fitful cracks booming from the mountain.

Irvin nodded, glaring at the volcano. "Bitch acts like she doesn't want us to leave," he murmured. "Very well," he said louder. "Lookouts to the bow, and as far aft as they dare. Stand by to fend off debris. Make all preparations for getting underway."

Midshipman Hardee tooted a call on a bosun's pipe—the kid had a real talent for the thing—and Lemurians scurried from below, positioning themselves for the prearranged detail, closing the hatches behind them. Just moving around on the boat was a real chore now. With her strakes burnt away, her furry crew had to climb over and under the exposed deck supports and they looked like kids charging through a set of playground monkey bars armed with long poles and lashed-together broom handles.

"The maneuvering watch is set," Tex said, repeating a call from below. "Such as it is." He changed his tone to that of an ominous lecture. "All hands are informed that the submarine service expects every man aboard, from the captain on down, to know his boat from the topmast to the keel," he quoted, then shrugged. "All stations manned and ready."

"Very well," said Irvin again. He took a breath. He'd been in command of the operation from the start, but now, at last, he was about to command S-19 while underway. It was different. "Port motor, ahead slow. Steer zero, six zero, but stand by for prompt course corrections."

"Port ahead slow, zero six zero, and stand by for corrections, aye."

Slowly, almost unnoticeably at first, S-19 began to move under her own power once again. The merest wake ruffled back from her straight up and down bow, parting the mud-thickened sea. Almost immediately, the port screw bit something under the water. They felt it in the fibers of the sub and Laumer's carefully neutral expression ticked just a bit. There was no change in the bass tone created by the turning port shaft, however, so whatever it was, it must have been insubstantial. It might have been the submerged carcass of an animal. The boat crept onward. Several times, the lookouts called out and pointed at something floating in the water and Irvin ordered slight course corrections to avoid the obstacles. Once, the forward starboard lookouts had to heave at something with their poles as they passed. After nearly an hour, S-19 finally eased out of the mouth of the lagoon and into the bigger waves beyond.

They literally weren't out of the woods yet, though. Debris and shattered trees might extend for miles beyond the island, but as the boat began to pitch, Irvin called the majority of the lookouts away from their posts. A few would have to stay, but now, in clearer seas, they should spot any hazards soon enough to avoid them. Tex called some of his electricians to the bridge to resume work on the antennae aerial they'd begun rigging to the bent but now permanently extended number two periscope. Slowly, the dust that had hung around them like a shroud began to clear as a gentle northeasterly breeze carried it away, and a few 'Cats even removed their bandannas experimentally. On impulse, Irvin suddenly turned and looked back at the island, looming there, still dominating the horizon like a malignant blotch.

"Where to now, Mr. Laumer?" Tex asked.

"Hmm? Oh. Well, we'll maintain this course for the time being, maybe add some speed after a while if the lookouts don't see too much junk. Right now, I want to get as far away from that island as we can." He snorted. "And I *don't* want to get between it and Mindanao! We'll steer northeast for the rest of the day and tonight, maybe tomorrow too, depending on how things look, then we'll turn north across the Philippine Sea. We might try the San Bernardino Strait, but as long as we have the fuel and nothing breaks, we'll go all the way around Luzon to Manila if we have to. We got this old gal off, Tex!" he said adamantly. "I'm damned if I'll let that island snatch her back from us!"

"You think Danny's right? You think Talaud's gonna blow its top?"

Irvin shook his head. "How should I know? But if it does, it's not going to get S-19! Too many have died to save her." Suddenly, Irvin snapped a sharp salute toward the island and held it. Tex started to protest, then he understood. Grumbling at himself, he saluted as well. Soon, everyonc topside on S-19 was standing straight, saluting not the island but *Toolbox*, Sid Franks, and all the others they'd left behind. Finally, Irvin lowered his hand and the others followed suit. "So long," he whispered hoarsely and turned to face forward. "Get that aerial up, Tex. I'd sure love to be able to whistle up a tow, if it comes to that. A lot of folks probably think we're dead already."

S-19 gradually increased speed to six knots, a reasonably gentle demand on her single shaft, abused batteries, and the generating capacity of her starboard diesel. The sea remained a little choppy, but not bad enough to button up the boat. She desperately needed airing out after the long confinement of so many filthy and admittedly nauseated 'Cats in her claustrophobic, smoky, ash-filled pressure hull. Add the fact that only the officers' head was working (the sea valve was jammed on the other one, probably from all the time the boat spent wallowing in the sand), and the slop buckets they'd resorted to made matters even worse. S-19 was a "pig boat" again, in most essential respects.

Sandy Whitcomb worked on the port diesel all night, with the eager assistance of his new "division's" strikers. He knew the engine would run now; he just had to refurbish it sufficiently that it wouldn't destroy itself if asked to run too long. Tex Sheider's strikers had rigged what he hoped was a suitable antenna, and he thought he had the voltage requirements for his little transmitter about right. The crystal receiver had already been rigged, but even at its maximum extension, the warped number two periscope wasn't as high as *Toolbox*'s shortest mast had been. So far they weren't getting much but hash. Nothing was coming out of Paga-Daan on Mindanao, and anyone else with a transmitter was probably just too far away. They'd almost never been able to hear Manila directly.

Irvin was on the conn tower, leaning on the rail facing

aft. It was cramped there, like everywhere on the old boat, and two people wouldn't have fit. The painfully bright sun hovered almost directly overhead, and beneath him, a 'Cat emerged, bearing a slop bucket and chittering disgustedly. She dumped it over the side of the outer hull superstructure, then waited for water to surge over the pressure hull so she could rinse the bucket out. She was still chittering when she disappeared, never looking up.

"You okay, Skipper?" Tex asked behind him.

Irvin nodded. "Just tired." He yawned and smiled. "Glad to be underway, though." He gestured to the southwest, where all that remained visible of Talaud was a pinkish-gray pall, almost fifty miles distant now, then turned to face his exec. "Put on a hell of a light show last night," he said, chuckling a little self-consciously. "Almost like it was throwing a fit because we got away."

Tex nodded. "I guess we did, though." He chuckled too. "I have to admit—now—sometimes I wondered! That damn Danny was starting to give me the creeps!"

Irvin began to reply, but stopped when he saw Tex's mouth drop open in stunned disbelief. He looked aft again and was too shocked by what he saw to speak himself. The distant, glowing smudge had become a black, sun-blazed mushroom of titanic proportions, roiling upward and outward with impossible speed and power.

It was almost a minute before Irvin managed to say "Jesus!" and in that time, the hideous stain on the morning sky just continued to grow.

"It looks like God just dropped a bomb!" Tex said, hushed.

"Yeah," Irvin agreed. "A God-size bomb." For a moment he said nothing more, then: "What happens when a bomb hits the water?"

"Well . . . you get a really big splash."

"Yeah . . ."

After a while, the sea began to roar, loud enough to drown out the sound of the diesel.

"Oh, no," Irvin said.

"What is it?" Tex shouted. Cries of alarm came from the hatch behind them.

"It's the sound of the blast! Sound moves four or five times faster through the water!"

Tex's face went pale. "I've heard tidal waves can move almost as fast as a sound through air!"

Irvin snatched his binoculars from his chest and focused them at the base of the distant, towering plume. In the gathering light of the sun, not yet engulfed by the expanding blackness, Irvin saw a distinct white line rising, far away, between the cloud and the deep blue sea. The horizon gave the impression of being almost slightly humped. The binoculars in his hands began to shake. Wrenching his eyes away from them, he turned and looked at Tex. "Rig for dive!" he shouted.

"*Dive?* We *can't* dive! We'll never come up!" Irvin thrust the binoculars at him and Tex took a look. "God almighty. That was one *hell* of a splash!" he said. He spared Irvin a look that could have said, "God help us," "It's been nice knowing you," or "Why'd you let me volunteer for this?" but immediately stepped to the hatch.

"Rig for *dive*!" he bellowed down below. "Secure all hatches this goddamn instant!"

"Clear the bridge!" Irvin yelled, and reached for the dive alarm before remembering they'd never fixed the switch on the conn tower. The suddenly terrified Lemurian lookouts plunged down the ladder, followed closely by Tex. Irvin didn't even take another look before he dropped down after them. In the control room, he twisted the round-knobbed switch three times.

Arrgha! Arrgha! Arrgha!

"Dive! Dive! Dive!" he said into the microphone. Almost immediately, the various station phone lights lit up. Expecting panicked demands for an explanation, he continued: "Trust me on this, people, it's dive or die! Porter and Hardee, report to the fore and aft berthing spaces to pass instructions! Stay off the phones unless there's an emergency." He looked at Tex, who shrugged. "Mr. Sheider and

I have the dive," he said. He hoped they did. "Secure the starboard engine, close main induction. Answer bells on batteries!"

Tex took a breath. "Open all main vents! Vent negative!"

"Flood safety, flood negative!" Irvin continued. He heard Tex bark a laugh.

"Ah, pressure in the boat, Skipper," Tex apologized. "The board's green!"

Feverishly, desperately, Irvin, Tex, Porter, Hardee, and Whitcomb shouted, cajoled, explained, and pleaded with their otherwise Lemurian crew to learn and execute procedures most had never remotely expected to perform. Hardee had been just a frightened child the first time he submerged with the boat, but he'd been interested and picked up a lot then—and since. There were a few "Crazy Cats" who thought it would be fun, and had actually wanted to dive the boat all along, but not many. S-19 was designed as a submarine, but no one had ever expected her to *be* one *again*. Not on this world. With aching slowness, the scratch submariners feverishly struggled to force S-19 beneath the waves they'd tried so hard, so long, to put her back upon.

The sub's bow planes and damaged stern planes clawed at the sea, and her port screw drove with all its might. Sluggishly, the boat started down. The starboard shaft packing sprayed water at twenty feet, and more water gushed down from the number two periscope packing at thirty-five. Water seeped and dripped from her riveted, tortured seams in every compartment. At fifty feet, water exploded inward from the crew's head, and the high-pressure pumps were already being overwhelmed. Irvin risked a look above with the number one periscope, and though it should still have been three feet above the sea, sea was all he saw—like he was looking down at it. As he'd feared, it wasn't an ordinary tidal wave, but a bore—a "splash" wave, as Tex had described it. It wasn't curling over them like surf breaking on the beach, but he couldn't see the top, since S-19 wasn't equipped with a lens adjustment to search the sky for aircraft. Irvin couldn't even estimate how far away it was. He sounded the collision alarm.

Somehow, the old submarine had made it fifty feet beneath the sea. She was critically overstressed, but she could have even surfaced again on her own. The wave didn't give her a chance to try. *It* brought the boat up. Suddenly, after all her desperate effort to escape Talaud's death wave, the depth gauge in S-19's control room swept *backward*, and in mere moments, the rusty old hull lay exposed in the depth of an immense trough, naked beneath the mountain rising against her. It pounced. In seconds, S-19 went swirling from the surface like a twig caught in an underwater vortex. Down she went, almost tumbling, shedding dive planes, superstructure, anchors—and life, as the mountain surged by above.

The vortex released her at last, drifting helpless, twitching like a storm-battered fish, bleeding air and oil at four hundred feet—twice as deep as she was ever meant to go.

CHAPTER 27

New Scotland, Sunday, December 4, 1943

The meeting in *Walker*'s wardroom consumed a lot of Juan's coffee hoard, but didn't produce much in the way of new insights. They'd learned precious little over the past week, not nearly enough to be sure of anything, except a possible "short list" of enemy objectives. What the conspiracy actually hoped to achieve, or how, was still a gnawing mystery. All they could do was try and prepare for as many contingencies as they could imagine. Jenks had come aboard once a day to "train" with Matt in swordsmanship, and he did improve, but mostly they brainstormed and discussed what Jenks had learned. It wasn't much: a swift Dominion dispatch sloop had cleared Scapa Flow, and another later departed New Glasgow to the west the very night *Walker* arrived at New Scotland, but nothing flying the red flag had come or gone since. That seemed to confirm their suspicions that whatever was up, the Dominion was involved and major preparations had been underway for quite some time. Matt was impressed by how quickly the conspirators reacted, and how closely they kept their intentions. It hinted that whatever was coming, *Walker*'s arrival might have advanced the schedule, lit a shorter fuse, but only minor adjustments were required to a plot that had long been in place.

"So all we know—still—is that 'something big' is liable to drop in the pot tomorrow, but we don't know what it is," Gray observed.

"Yeah," Matt said, rubbing his eyes. It was almost 0100 and he had a big day ahead of him. Probably they all did. "Jenks still thinks it's an attack of some kind, probably with Dominion aid for some reason, but he still doesn't know where it'll come from or what it might be composed of." He sighed and swirled the lukewarm coffee in his "Captain's" cup. "The objective might be Government House and the harbor facilities. It could be the dueling ground itself—there'll be a lot of brass hanging around. Jenks has tried to make sure *all* the brass won't be there, but he has to be careful who he talks to. No telling who's involved." Matt gestured at the porthole. "The objective might even be Home Fleet, God knows how. There's six 'ships of the line' and ten frigates in port." He looked at Frankie. "Mr. Steele, so far all you know you can count on, according to Jenks, are the frigates *Euripides* and *Tacitus*."

Frankie nodded glumly. "What about our guys?" he asked Palmer.

The comm officer looked troubled. "Still no news. *Salaama-Na* and her escorts were on their way, last we heard, but there was another big storm out there, and we haven't heard anything since. The 'new' Fil-pin-built *Simms* and Jenks's *Achilles* sailed right after we did, but there's been nothing from them either. Aerials or wind generators probably got carried away, and *Simms* might've cracked her batteries, or shorted everything out. *Achilles*' set was a piece of . . . junk to start with." O'Casey nodded and Palmer lowered his voice. "Then there's that damn Talaud. I hear Respite okay at night, but it's fuzzy. Everything's fine there, but they're worried about a surge from the west. It seems the volcano's been going nuts, and I only get snippets from Maa-ni-la. Respite Station passes stuff along, though, and it's getting scary back home, Skipper."

"So . . . nada," Steele said. Palmer shrugged.

Matt took a deep breath. "And I guess if anybody'd seen or heard from *Ajax*, they would've said something." Only silence answered, and he slowly exhaled.

"Okay," he said, "here's the plan. In the morning"—he rubbed his face—"later *this* morning, at 0400, Mr. Reynolds will take off. . . . Everything still good with the Nancy, Lieutenant?"

"Swell, Skipper. It'll be a little creepy taking off in the dark, but no sweat."

"Good." Matt looked at Frankie. "We'll raise hell on the ship, blow tubes, vent steam, and generally carry on in a variety of loud, mechanical ways, to cover the sound of the Nancy's motor. It'll draw attention, but hopefully nobody'll notice an airplane taking off in the dark." He shrugged. "We goofed up telling them what the damn thing was, but most people here don't believe it anyway. 'It's a proven fact that powered flight is impossible,'" he quoted wryly, and everyone chuckled. He looked at Reynolds. "It'll probably be like looking for a needle in a haystack—and we don't even know if the needle's there—but if anything's coming by sea, we need to know it. Keep a sharp eye off Scapa Flow, New Glasgow, and Edinburgh. I know that's a big grid, and you're only one plane, but you're probably the only warning we'll have."

Fred Reynolds gulped. "Aye, aye, Skipper."

"After that . . ." He paused. "Maybe it'll look like a big send-off. Spin some platters over the shipwide comm too. Boats, Courtney, Stites, and myself will leave for the 'dueling ground.'" He looked at Chack. "As soon as you hear the church bells sound the end to services, form your short company of the 2nd Marines on the dock. O'Casey? You'll command the Imperial Marines. Lieutenant Blair's been feeling out Marine officers, much like Jenks has been doing, to see who he can count on. He'll meet you here with whatever he can scrounge up."

"We should go with you," Chack insisted.

"No, we have to assume they'll be expecting that. It might even be what all this is about. You have to be ready to respond to anything. If we need you at the dueling ground, Stites'll send up a flare. It's about two miles, but you'll see it well enough." He arched an eyebrow. "It's supposed to be a pretty day." He laid his hands on the table, palms up. "Anything else? I think we've covered every base we can. . . . I just wish we knew we're in the right ballpark!" He waited a moment while his crew glanced at one another. "Okay, that's it. I'm going to try to sleep. Wake me if anybody hears *anything*!"

At long last the gathering broke up. Matt started for his quarters, but Spanky blocked his way, hands on hips. Throughout the meeting, he'd done little but chew yellow tobacco and spit in a sediment-filled Coke bottle. "I oughta be with you," he said.

"No. I want Frankie to have three boilers all day if he needs them. You're the only guy in the whole world who can do that . . . and maybe *not* empty the bunkers!"

"Well . . ." Spanky stuck out his hand. "Good luck, Skipper."

Matt took the hand. "You too. I expect we're both going to need it."

The atmosphere at the dueling ground was like a big, garish fair, and as Jenks predicted, attendance was huge, even compared to the Pre-Passage Ball. The event had been the talk of the Empire for an entire week, and people came from almost every island to view the spectacle. Not many came from New Ireland, but it was a virtual Company possession and only a few executives there had the means to hire passage. Even so, oddly, not a single ferry or Company official arrived from New Dublin. That struck many as strange, since New Dublin constituted Harrison Reed's prime constituency. Nevertheless, the New Scotland churches bulged with pious attendees, praying for the souls of the soon to be departed, and bookmakers hawked odds through the teeming crowd.

"Jenks is runnin' about even," Gray announced, reappearing with Courtney, pewter mugs in their hands streaming suds. "Thanks for the loan, Commodore," he added.

Jenks nodded. He was dressed simply in a white shirt with a red cravat, his white Navy knee britches, and a pair of knee-high boots. Around his waist was only a tight red sash, into which was thrust his naked sword. His long hair was clubbed at the nape of his neck, and his mustache was freshly braided. He looked very businesslike, and it was clear he'd done this before. Matt had followed his lead, wearing khaki shirt and trousers, both of Lemurian "cotton." His loose trouser legs were bound by a pair of U.S. Navy leggings. His own naked Academy sword—carefully sharpened—was held against his side by a web belt. He took off his hat and handed it to Juan, who'd sneaked off the ship to join them as they made their way to the grounds. Juan had even shed his sling, gamely moving his arm around when confronted and claiming he didn't think it was ever really broken at all.

"What about me?" Matt asked, tying a bandanna around his neck. He needed something to sop at sweat.

Gray winced. "Lots of sympathy, Skipper, but you're runnin' about twenty to one, give or take. Against."

"Ridiculous," Juan scoffed, tying another bandanna around Captain Reddy's head to keep sweat from running into his eyes. Juan's attitude reflected that of virtually *Walker*'s entire crew. The "distracting" send-off they'd given him had been real, and it warmed Matt's heart, but he'd been a little taken aback by how little concern they'd shown that he might lose his contest. Most just couldn't understand how far out of his element he would be.

"That bad?" asked Matt. "What makes folks so pessimistic?"

Gray cleared his throat. "Well, ah, as we suspected, there's been scouts down watchin' you and the commodore prancin' around on the ship, practicin'. Lots of folks think you'd do well . . . with a lot more practice. But the word is you're too, ah, 'predictable.' Too worried about form . . ." He shrugged. "Sorry, sir. Like I always say, too much calf slobber'll spoil the pie."

Matt frowned. "That's okay, Boats. I'll give 'em a show, whatever they think."

"That's the spirit, sir! You've been in worse scrapes before."

Matt nodded thoughtfully. He had. "Who'd you bet on?"

"You, of course." He glared at Jenks. "Penny-pinchin' devil didn't give me enough money to do it up right, and he demanded fifty percent of my winnings too!"

"It *was* a risky wager," Jenks reminded him. He paused. "The good thing is, your opponent will likely 'stretch it out.' He's a 'professional,' and makes his living at this. He'll want to make it look good; provide a 'spectacle.' That should give you plenty of time to practice your new, 'predictable' style against him." He stopped. "Please excuse me," he said, stepping away to meet his wife, waiting behind the rope line. They saw him cradle her chin with his hand.

"Weird duck," Stites pronounced, fiddling with a tarp-covered crate they'd sent up the day before. "All of 'em. Weird ducks. Treat wimmen like pets, or worse, but Jenks does love that gal. I wonder if he 'bought' her."

"I sorta loved a dog once," Gray grumbled. "Damn fine bitch. Even so, my mother woulda cased me out if I treated a woman like I did that dog." He paused. "Skipper, are we even sure this is our fight? We got women now—though I ain't personally—and a hell of a fight all our own, a long way from here. I know we wanna save *our* girls, and even Silva, but . . . well, you know as well as I do that's . . . probably out of our hands." It was the closest anyone had come to actually saying the hostages were probably lost with *Ajax*. "We still need to kill the Company and that's a fact, but . . . this is a lot bigger than that now."

Matt looked at the Bosun, but for an instant he was seeing the face of Don Hernan, and remembering that . . . twisted interview. He was personally convinced that the "Blood Cardinal" was up to his neck in whatever was going on, though he still didn't know how.

"You're right," he said. "This is way bigger than that. But it *is* our fight because we're here." He snorted. "Hell, Boats, that's what we've been doing for the last two years, since Pearl Harbor: fighting the war we're *at*. I'm not saying we need another war, or even that I like this Imperial setup much, but I have started to like the people. Some of 'em. Right now I think they need us . . . and damn it, we need them. That Don Hernan gives me the creeps worse than the first Griks I ever saw. In a way, he and his Dominion strike me as even worse than the Grik because they're *people* that act the way they do. And this Reed and the Company . . ." He shook his head in exasperation. "Hell, I don't even try to calculate 'shades of gray' anymore. There's just too many. All we can do is try to look underneath them all to see if we can find the basic black or white, good or bad. Maybe I'm a sucker, but I can't help feeling that if we quit trying to find good folks on this world, even if we run into more bad ones while we're at it, we might as well steam back to Baalkpan and wait for the Grik to return and finish us off."

Gray nodded slowly, staring out at the dueling ground. "Aye, sir. Maybe so. I sure would like to get me one of them gals and spend a year or two retired before I croak, though."

Stites rolled his eyes. "S.B., if you ever 'retired,' we'd be buryin' you from boredom in a week."

Horns sounded, and the combatants moved to face one another across the field. It had been decided that the contests would be simultaneous. Despite the gladiatorial atmosphere, the layout of the dueling ground itself reminded Matt of a football stadium in a forest. The architecture was surprisingly familiar, and the thick woods of Imperial Park surrounding the grounds were unlike anything Matt had ever seen on the "old" islands. They looked more like pines. The spectators on one side occupied an expansive set of wooden bleachers, built around the Imperial viewing box. The Governor-Emperor stood in his box with Andrew and a number of military officers. All were dressed in their Sunday best and wore impassive expressions, but it was clear whose side they were on. The bleachers around them thundered with noise, the accumulated effect of perhaps four thousand voices talking at once.

There was a stark contrast between that and the "opposing" bleachers. Don Hernan occupied that box, surrounded by a phalanx of priests and a few local clergy. Matt was surprised to learn that the Empire allowed Blood Priests of the Holy Dominion to preach on its soil, but it did. Only those of the English Church enjoyed full citizenship, but vestiges of Hinduism and Mohammadism still lingered as well.

"Oh, that's *done* it," Jenks said aside to him as they strode forward. He sounded stunned.

"What?"

"Look there." Jenks pointed. Joining Don Hernan in the opposing box was Harrison Reed himself, followed by a large entourage. Many of the spectators on that side hissed and grumbled and began to get up and leave, apparently outraged, making their way to the opposite bleachers. "Good God, we were right! Reed's declared himself!"

"Why wouldn't he be on that side?" Matt asked. "You represent the Governor-Emperor and your argument's with Reed."

"That may be how it *seems*, my friend, but that's not exactly how it *is*. Technically, 'on the field,' I represent only myself. That's why, close as we admittedly are, His Majesty has taken no official notice. Reed should be—normally would be—watching from the same box as the Governor-Emperor, pretending to be his very best friend. By standing with Don Hernan, he has made this a political fight. Worse, he's declared himself against the Governor-Emperor and *with* Don Hernan! See? Even much of the Company baggage is clearing from the opposing stands! For the most part, nobody hates the Doms worse than the Company! Even Billingsley despised them! Called them 'Roman Witches and Freaks.'"

"Then . . . I'm more confused than ever. Why work together? Why would Reed stand with them?"

"They work together for 'the Trade,' the commerce in people that you hate so much. It's the Dominion's cheapest, most plentiful resource and the Company's most lucrative commodity. Otherwise, the Company and the Dominion couldn't be further apart—I see you don't understand, but we don't have time to go into economics. Suffice to say for now that they hate one another. Up 'til now, they needed one another more."

"What's changed? Why would Reed show his hand?"

"*Everything's* changed. We were right, it *will* be today. Reed has chosen his side and thinks he's safe to do so. Stop here."

"Well . . . that's nuts. Won't he be arrested, for treason or something?"

"Just as soon as our little 'entertainment' is over," Jenks swore.

They'd reached the center of the field and the now much larger "home" crowd cheered lustily. An announcer was introducing them with a speaking trumpet, but Matt couldn't hear the words.

"And in *this* corner," Matt muttered to himself as their opponents strode to meet them. The slick-haired man was dressed much as he'd been that night a week before. His lips still bore heavy scabs and his crooked grin was missing a couple of teeth. He moved like the professional he was, but his eyes glinted with hatred and anticipation—as though he expected to enjoy this chore.

"What?" Jenks asked.

"Skip it. Who's your guy?"

"I've no idea. It doesn't matter."

"I don't even know 'my' guy's name. Will we say 'hello,' or just 'come out swinging'?"

"We won't say 'hello.' "

"We'll just start hacking away at each other, perfect strangers?"

Jenks sighed. "As soon as the Imperial Marshal inspects our weapons, reads the complaint, and gives the signal, yes. Now please stop distracting me and concentrate on what you must do!"

Matt smirked. He supposed he should be nervous, but his mind was already far beyond the moment, worrying about everything else going on. Somehow, he couldn't escape the suspicion he was missing something. He knew he had to focus, or all that other stuff very shortly wouldn't matter to him anymore. Like the others, he submitted his sword for inspection and half listened to the various complaints and the Rules of Combat. Jenks had gone over the rules with him pretty carefully. Finally, the marshal stepped back and held a kerchief high, fluttering in the morning breeze. There was a hush in the stands.

"What's your name?" Matt blurted at the slick-haired man. He didn't know why he did it. Maybe it was a final, subconscious attempt to think of him *as* a man. His opponent seemed taken aback, but sneered as best he could around his broken lips.

"Does it 'atter? You'll soon be dead."

Matt shrugged. "I guess it doesn't after all."

The kerchief dropped.

Lieutenant Fred Reynolds knew he was on an important mission, and he was suitably serious about it, but he couldn't help but appreciate the stunning view presented by the early-morning spectacle of the New Britain Isles. He'd never flown above the Hawaiian Islands before. He'd never flown *at all* before he entered Ben Mallory's Air Corps, but he knew he'd made the right decision. Ever since they came to this world, he'd just been a seaman, the last of *Walker*'s original crew who hadn't advanced, or even struck for anything. He'd gained a lot of experience as a talker, but that was all he'd ever really been. Now he was an aviator, a pilot, an *officer*; and all he'd really done was finally pick something to do that didn't scare him or bore him. Sure, sometimes he was scared of flying, particularly when somebody was shooting at him, but he wasn't afraid of the *idea* of flying, and even with the improved ships, it was never boring.

Comm was boring. Constantly listening for messages that never came. He'd had a taste of that, and couldn't stand it. That was Kari-Faask's job on the plane—along with all her other jobs—and he didn't envy her that one at all. She seemed to like it, though, and probably would have liked it better on the ship or ashore. She was no coward—cowardice didn't run in her family—but her courage was of a more sensible nature than the great Haakar-Faask's. Probably more sensible than Fred's—and she hadn't ever shot any holes in their own airplane either. Their pairing made better sense all the time, to Reynolds's mind. He was the increasingly "hotshot" pilot who took their little ship where it needed to go, and had a real feel for takeoffs and landings on the water. She was the workmanlike side of the team, diligently doing her duty, monitoring the receiver, and constantly scanning for the things they'd been sent to look for.

It was no surprise to Reynolds, then, when her tinny voice reached him from the speaking tube, interrupting his enjoyment of the sense of being the very first person ever to view these new islands from the air, as well as simply appreciating the sharp, almost chilly air. They were on the second leg of their pattern, flying northwest along the coast between Scapa Flow and New Glasgow. Ever efficient, Kari had made an observation and monitored a transmission at the same time.

"Surface target, bearing two three zero," she said, and Fred looked to his left. Sure enough, there were shapes to the southwest, sails, lots of sails, coming from a direction Jenks had said no large Imperial force was operating. Either that was *Walker*'s Allied resupply or it was bad guys. It was that simple.

"Transmit the position of the target," Fred said, a rush of heat at the back of his neck, despite the altitude. Uh-oh. He'd seen enough sails from the air now to begin to recognize whose they were, just by their shape. These were even easier to identify. They were red. The Grik used red paint on their hulls, but nobody he knew had red sails except that Dominion dispatch boat. Jenks had said the Dominion sometimes used red sails for official vessels—and warships. It had to do with their screwy, bloodsucking version of Catholicism, or something. The heat at the back of his neck turned to ice. "Ah, send that we're going to investigate the target," he added, banking left.

"Fred," came Kari's voice, "I also got a weak signal from Respite, maybe bounced off sky. They pass along message out of Maa-ni-la, passed from somebody . . . anyway, it is general alarm." She paused. Her voice sounded more concerned than it had over possible enemy action.

"Well, what is it?" Reynolds demanded.

"Talaud blow up. Everybody saying it 'pull Kraak-aa-toaa,' but worse. What that mean? Signal say Min-daanao—Paga-Daan—*gone*. Tarakaan, maybe even Baalkpan, Sembaakpaan, Sular, Respite, Saamir—all land places—maybe get big gaararro, ah, 'tidal wash.' "

"Holy smoke!" Fred remembered that Kari was land folk from Aryaal. Big waves meant a lot more to them than they did to sea folk. Like everyone in the Navy, though, he'd heard tales of Krakatoa and what followed its eruption—ships carried miles inshore and left high and dry with no survivors. It was the boogeyman of natural disasters. Where Talaud was, Mindanao probably did get hammered. Still, he couldn't imagine anything making a wave big enough to threaten Tarakan, much less Baalkpan or Respite. "Settle down, it'll be fine. Just transmit the warning and let's pay attention to what we've got here." He'd steadied up on a heading toward the strangers and was beginning to descend. "I'd say they're definitely Dominion ships," he added grimly. "Get the word to Mr. Steele; the Skipper was right."

Commander Frankie Steele was standing on *Walker*'s bridge, hands behind his back, trying to look like he knew what he was doing. The church bells of Scapa Flow were pealing in the morning air, echoing cacophonously through the streets and alleys. Chack and O'Casey were forming the Marines on the dock as if for inspection, and the few port marshals and Company wardens left watching the ship were growing uneasy over this unexpected and unannounced activity. Blair was double-timing a company of

Marines through the harbor district, and their "shore shoes" thundered in time with the ringing bells. The marshals and wardens didn't know what was happening; it looked at first like the Marines were coming to force the "ape folk" back aboard the strange steamer—but there were a few Imperial Marines mixed with the "apes"! When Blair's Marines arrived fully on the scene, and the lieutenant advanced and saluted Chack, all the civilian guards fled in confusion.

Ed Palmer dashed onto *Walker*'s bridge with a sheet of yellow Imperial paper in his hand. "It's here," he said, pale.

Frankie snatched the message away and quickly scanned it. He worried about the report concerning Talaud—the ship's receiver hadn't caught it—but that wasn't pertinent to them here, now. "They *are* going for it," he said, almost amazed. Somehow he just hadn't imagined he would really have to step into the Skipper's shoes and fight the Skipper's ship. "The whole damn enchilada!" he continued, looking up at Spanky. "Reynolds reports a 'large' enemy force making for Scapa Flow! He got close enough to identify ten Dominion battlewagons, or 'liners,' ten more ships like we call frigates, and what looks like a couple o' dozen transports." His brow furrowed. "He says only the transports are steamers, though, an' they're hangin' back. That's weird." He shrugged. "Prob'ly mean to poke a hole with the liners and punch the transports through, fast like."

"I'll bet you're right," Spanky said.

Frankie looked at him with a strange smile. "Sure you don't wanna switch jobs?" he asked, a strange edge to his outwardly joking question.

Spanky looked at him a moment, actually tempted. Frankie was usually steady as a rock, but he'd been through a lot, right from the start, aboard *Mahan*.

"Naw, Frankie," he said in a joking tone as well. "I got a job. Bashear's already hangin' around the auxiliary conn." He paused. "Why don't you sound GQ and get this show on the road? We can't let 'em catch us in port like the Japs did at Pearl!"

"Yah," said Frankie, straightening. "Sound 'general

quarters'! Make all preparations for getting underway! Signal flags to the yards!" He looked at Palmer. "Send back to Mr. Reynolds that he can play dive bomber if he likes, but take care of that plane!" Reynolds's Nancy had a dozen of Chack's mortar bombs aboard, the same bombs other Nancys had dropped by hand in combat over Rangoon. Reynolds hadn't been carrying any in the battle with the Company ships because they hadn't expected a fight. Now he always carried a crate of bombs whenever he flew.

The prearranged signal, "enemy in sight," along with "southwest" as reported by the Nancy, rattled up *Walker*'s halyards, along with an attention-getting shriek from her whistle. *Euripides* and *Tacitus*, both commanded by close personal friends of Jenks, already had steam up, and they acknowledged the signal. Immediately, both ships also fired signal guns and ran up additions to their own "enemy in sight" flags, announcing confirmation of a "hostile fleet" southwest of Scapa Flow. Maybe a few other Imperial ships would take the hint. *Walker*, now free of the dock, belched smoke and churned forward, squatting down aft as her twin screws bit deep and threw up a churning white wake as she commenced a rapid starboard turn.

Finny was on the starboard bridgewing. "The fort is flying signal!" he said. "It spell English, say 'Amer-i-caan Ship Heave To or Be Fired On'!"

"The hell you say?" Kutas grunted at the wheel.

"Signals!" Frankie shouted aft of the chart house. "Hoist: 'Dom Invasion Fleet Headed Scapa Flow. No Shit!'" He paused. "Tell 'em if they shoot at us, we'll let the bastards in," he snarled. They waited in silence, the blower roaring behind the pilothouse, but the minutes ticked by and there was no change in the Imperial signal.

"Even if they shoot, they'll never hit us," Kutas said. "We're too fast." He couldn't keep all the concern out of his voice, however; the fort had a *lot* of guns.

"*Euripides* and *Taas-itus* are underway," Finny shouted. "They still firing signal guns, flying flags. They flying battle flags now!"

Walker was still gaining speed, and her crew cringed involuntarily as their ship raced under the fort's gaping guns at twenty knots. There were no shots.

"Lookout sees smokes on horizon," called Min-Sakir, or "Minnie" the talker, so named for her size and voice. "Much smokes!" she stressed. "Nancy is pounding craap out of traan-sports!" she chortled.

"Belay sportscaster comments on the bridge!" Frankie scolded, a little more harshly than he'd intended.

"Aye, aye, sir," replied a chastened Minnie.

Far outstripping her Imperial "allies," USS *Walker* sent her own battle flag racing up her foremast and steamed into battle with a new, unknown foe.

The slick-haired man immediately went on the attack. Matt found himself fighting for his life once again with swishing, crashing blades and a blinding-fast sword point that dissolved into a blur before his eyes. The difference was, this time he really was fighting for his life and there was no padding or blunted tips. He was giving ground—he had no choice—and still he suspected his opponent was merely toying with him, showing off. The guy was incredibly quick, even faster than Jenks, and Matt knew with complete certainty that he stood no chance in this kind of fight. He'd improved tremendously—his daily exercises had seen to that—but he still felt stiff, fighting in this formal, almost ritualized style. He stuck with it, though, even after his unnamed adversary pinked him on the left shoulder, cut the back of his left hand when it inadvertently strayed from behind his back, and opened a shallow gash on the inside of his right forearm.

He had no idea how Jenks was doing; he didn't dare take his eyes off that cobralike blade before him. He heard grunting and stomping and the incessant rattle of blades, so he knew his friend was still alive at least. Beyond that, he didn't have a clue. His own fight had backed him up and around, until Jenks's battle continued at his back. The crowd, almost completely on the Imperial side now, occasionally groaned or cheered, and he suspected the groans were mostly for him. He fought on, gasping, sweat soaking his bandanna and blood streaming down to his wrist. Soon his hand would get slippery and he'd be dead. Seeing this, his opponent disengaged and took a few steps back.

"Wipe your arm," he said harshly. At least he was breathing hard as well. "I'm enjoying this, and I want it to last!" He turned his back and walked in a circle, slashing at the air while Matt pulled the bandanna from his neck and wiped the blood away. He held the cloth against his face, soaking up the sweat, then wrapped it around his bleeding left hand, clasping the ends in his palm. There was polite applause from the stands. He looked over and saw that Jenks and his adversary were still going at it.

"Thanks," Matt said. "Sorry, I don't know your name, so I hope 'shithead' is okay?"

The slick-haired man snarled and came at him. As quick as that, the battle was rejoined with the same intensity as before, maybe even more. Matt kept at it, still a little awkward in the stiff form he'd practiced. The other man had a number of advantages besides his vastly greater experience. He was smaller, faster, in much better condition, and his blade wasn't as heavy. On Matt's side was his reach, his thus far almost entirely defensive strategy—and his mindset. Unknown to his opponent, Matt wasn't fighting a duel, he was battling a rabid animal, a Grik, a creature bent on killing him so he couldn't perform his greater duty of protecting the people he'd brought here. The man had been right about one thing—his name meant nothing to Matt.

There was a thunderous cheer, a cheer Matt had been waiting for, praying for, as his arm began to tire. He'd been counting on it, but it drew his opponent's attention just the slightest bit. With a roar, Matt dropped all pretense of form and style and lunged forward, plowing his opponent's sword aside with his own, then grasping the blade with his "bandaged" left hand. Bringing his guard up, he smashed the man in the face again, drew back, and drove his Academy sword into the slick-haired man's chest, all the way to the hilt.

The crowd went almost silent, then erupted once again. Chances were, a few might scoff at his tactics, but they weren't against the rules. Besides, most likely, hardly anyone saw what he did. Attention had probably been focused on Jenks. Matt took the slick-haired man's sword from his loosening fingers and let his body slide off his own blade onto the ground. The crowd was ecstatic. He looked at Jenks and grinned, gasping for every breath. A squad of marshals, muskets on their shoulders, were trotting toward the opposing box where Reed leaned on the rail beside Don Hernan, his face set in stone. Matt watched, perplexed again as to why Reed would so publicly associate himself with the weird foreign priest—or whatever he was. Obviously, the Governor-Emperor also considered it tantamount to treason. Everyone would think so, even the Company. Reed just stood there, waiting for the marshals to come. It didn't make sense.

Something stirred near the bottom of the stands and Matt looked down. About four feet off the ground, the blue bunting parted and exposed five, six, eight! dark, ominous muzzles. Matt spun and sprinted toward Jenks. Just as he performed a classic open-field tackle on his friend, eight medium-weight cannons erupted with breath-snatching force and spewed their double loads of canister into the "Imperial" bleachers.

"My God, it *is* here!" Jenks coughed as the white smoke billowed over them. The cheers in the stands had turned to screams. "No wonder Reed went to that side!"

"Not so much a political statement as self-preservation," Matt agreed, coughing too. He heaved Jenks to his feet. "Cannons! How the hell did they get *those* here without anybody seeing? Didn't anybody think to check?"

"For *cannons* on the ground level under the viewing stands? Be serious. They may have been sneaking them in for months, in carts or wagons. . . ." Jenks seemed disoriented. "The Governor-Emperor!"

"C'mon!" Matt said. "We gotta get out of here before they reload!"

"I must go to Gerald!"

"Jenks, he's either dead, well protected by now, or too busy to notice you!" Matt said sharply. "Let's go!" He sprinted back in the direction they'd previously walked, dragging Jenks by the arm. Stites, Juan, and a puffing Gray met them in the smoke. Stites had a BAR and Gray carried his Thompson. Juan had two 1903 Springfields and he handed one to Matt, along with his other belt with his scabbard and Colt.

"Did you shoot the flare?" Matt demanded. The air was still thick with the white haze of gunsmoke. Muskets began to pop, stabbing orange flame in all directions, but most was aimed at the Imperial stands.

"Aye, sir, as if I needed to," Stites replied. "Goddamn cannons! If Chack didn't hear that, he's . . . well, been around cannons too long!"

Men in yellow and red uniforms were becoming visible at the base of the "visitors'" stands, loading the heavy guns.

"Hose 'em!" Matt ordered. Juan fired the first shot and a man with a rammer staff crumpled to the ground. Gray stitched the blue bunting around each gun, while Stites unleashed several clips horizontally along the base of the stands. Matt held his fire, looking for Reed, Don Hernan, or any of the bigwigs, but the viewing box was suddenly empty. Musket balls *vrooped* through the air around them, and they were driven to cover. All the while, the screaming in the stands to Matt's right continued unabated. They scrambled over a hasty barricade that Courtney had erected around the reinforced crate. He'd added some heavy benches and other odds and ends he'd managed to gather before he drew the enemy's attention.

"Bloody good show, Captain Reddy!" he exclaimed, when they dropped behind the meager protection. A stack of helmets awaited them, and everyone discarded their hats and put one on, pulling the straps under their chins. "If I didn't know better, I'd have bet against you myself. I almost believed you were outclassed there for a moment. Bravo!"

Stites heaved one of the ship's .30-caliber Brownings up

onto the crate. Juan banged open a box of belted ammunition.

"Yeah," said Matt. "Me too." He peeked over the crate. "Damn!" he said. "Where are they all *coming* from? There must be a company of infantry out there, maybe more. Hurry up, Stites!"

"I suppose if the marshals had been attentive enough to discover cannons, they might have found that as well," Jenks said wryly, referring to the Browning. He seemed to have gathered his wits. "Bringing weapons to a duel . . . It just isn't done!" He crouched beside Matt, fiddling with the chin strap of the unfamiliar helmet. "They must have staged the infantry in the woods before dawn, perhaps keeping people out with men posing as marshals."

"Or they had real ones helping," Matt said. Three cannons fired into the opposite stands again, raising another chorus of screams.

"Filthy murderers!" Jenks cried. "They're deliberately killing unarmed civilians!" he exclaimed to Matt. "Give me a weapon, I beg you!"

"Welcome to the kind of war we're used to, Jenks," Matt said grimly. He handed over the Springfield Juan had given him and picked up the BAR, checking the magazine. "You remember how to use that?" he asked.

Jenks looked doubtfully at the '03. "You showed me once."

"You're going to love it," Matt assured him, opening fire with the BAR. Stites joined him with the .30-cal.

Against Kari's adamant warnings, Reynolds took the Nancy into a final dive. The strangers on the ships below were starting to shoot back now, and being mainly infantry, they had a lot to shoot back with. The speed of the plane made individual accuracy from smoothbore muskets poor at best, but with so many firing, even accidental hits were likely. The last dive had resulted in seven or eight brand-new holes in the little ship, one of which was causing a little trouble with the starboard aileron.

Fred Reynolds and Kari-Faask had left three ships burning already, though, and they still had one bomb left.

"Hold on to your hat!" Fred cried. "Just one more run, and we beat feet back to Scapa Flow! We're almost out of fuel anyway." He pushed the stick forward and Kari reluctantly finished cranking the wing floats back down. She was panting from raising and lowering the contraptions and cursed herself for the idea. She'd popped off that they needed to "slow down" in their dives so she could get a better feel for her release point. Fred said they needed more drag and she suggested the floats. Since then, they'd discovered the things made pretty good dive brakes, but improved mechanical advantage over the prototype or not, it was a hell of a lot of work.

Kari finished cranking just as the Nancy lined up on an undamaged transport, and she reached into the nearly empty crate of bombs. Fred was staring at the ship, imagining a set of sights was mounted on the nose of the plane—across the large "NO" painted there. The target was a weird-looking thing, as were all the "enemy" ships. It was a steam-sail hybrid like the Imperial frigates, but the lines remained more classical. There really wasn't much difference between the American and Imperial steamers except that the Americans used screw propellers and the "Brits" used paddle wheels. The Dominion steamers might almost have been galleons, or Grik Indiamen, and their paddle wheels were exposed. As far as Fred could tell, the Dominion warships—and a couple were real monsters—still relied on sail power alone. He knew that could be an advantage as well as a disadvantage, depending on the wind, and their sides seemed to be pierced for an awful lot of guns. "Get ready!" he shouted.

The transport below was trying to maneuver, something the others hadn't done, and he kicked the rudder back and forth, trying to keep the target in his imaginary sights. Human shapes grew visible below, hundreds of them, all seemingly armed with muskets pointed at his nose. Some started flashing amid white puffs of smoke. He bored in, almost until it looked like the Nancy would clip the enemy masthead, and he yanked back on the stick just as the plane shuddered from a number of hits and the air around him thrummed with a hundred more balls as he roared down, almost to the sea, and leveled off into a gentle, distance-gaining climb.

Risking a quick look back to see where the bomb fell, he didn't see a detonation or even a splash. "What the—!" he started to shout into the voice tube, but then saw Kari lolling back and forth with the motion of the plane. "Kari!" he yelled. "Kari, answer me! Are you hit?"

The 'Cat managed to straighten slightly, and shifted her face toward the voice tube. "I hit," she confirmed, barely audible. "Motor hit too." Fred saw she was quickly being covered by atomized oil spraying through the prop. "I tell you we ask for it that time!" Kari mumbled.

"No, Kari!" Fred shouted, "*I* asked for it! I'm *so* sorry! Where are you hit? Put pressure on it, stop the bleeding!"

Kari didn't answer. Instead, she flopped to one side of her cockpit and slumped down in her seat.

"No!" Fred screamed. "You hang on, do you hear? Damn it, don't you . . . Just hang on!" Frantically he looked around. The oil pressure gauge was dropping fast, and the various temperature gauges were beginning to rise. Ahead, toward the mouth of Scapa Flow, he just made out a gray shape, a bone in her teeth and hot gasses shimmering above her stacks. A couple of other ships were underway as well, far behind. "Just hang on," he repeated, aiming his battered plane for the old destroyer, and pushing the throttle to its stop.

With an audible *thwack!* followed by a diminishing, low-pitched *wha-wha-wha* sound, Juan's leg jerked from under him and he fell against the crate and slid down, flat on his face. He'd been kneeling on his right knee and his left leg had strayed from behind cover. Gray quickly dragged him back and inspected the wreckage of his lower leg.

"Shit. Smack in the middle of the shin," he said, tearing

his T-shirt and tying the strips tightly just under the knee. Juan hadn't made a peep. He didn't seem sure what had happened. Gray caught Matt's eye and jerked his head significantly from side to side, mouthing, "It's gone." Juan tried to get back up, but Gray held him down. "No, goddamn it, you stay put! You wanna bleed out?" With that, the Bosun replaced the magazine in his Thompson and fired a long, smoky burst over the top of the crate.

They were nearly out of ammunition for the .30-cal. The tiny cart they'd hired the day before simply hadn't been able to carry much beyond the weight of the large, inconspicuously armored crate—not to mention the heavy weapons inside. Of course, they hadn't expected to fight a pitched battle all alone, and that's basically what they had on their hands. The crate was riddled with holes, but few balls had passed all the way through, courtesy of the two Marine shields inside. Stites had been grazed along the ribs, but otherwise, besides a few splinters, they were unhurt. Until Juan was hit.

They'd drawn most of the enemy fire on themselves, giving the bleachers a chance to empty, and Matt concentrated on the cannons when he could, keeping them from firing at them now. The guns were effectively silenced, but enemy troops continued to pour forward to take the place of the countless slain. They'd been preparing to pull back straightaway behind the crate, and then sprint for the protection of the wall that funneled spectators into the bleachers. With Juan hurt, that was out. They couldn't leave him, and any man who tried to carry him was doomed. All they could do now was hold their ground and hope Chack got there in time.

The machine gun had done the most damage, and Matt was constantly revising upward the number of enemies they faced. He'd never seen human troops take such punishment and just keep pushing, especially into the mouth of something like the Browning, which they'd never encountered before. It was nuts. Twice, the "Doms" tried to cross the open ground on their left flank and come at them from that direction, but Stites literally butchered the attempts. Since then, it was pretty straight up: five men (including Courtney's occasional shot) with modern weapons against an army. Jenks finally figured out how stripper clips worked, and fired away with his '03, with telling effect. Still, they wouldn't last long when the .30-cal ran dry.

"What *is* it with those people?" Matt demanded. "Why don't they break?"

"They are 'Blood Drinkers,'" Jenks snarled. "Elite troops. See their red neckcloths? They are the very 'Swords of the Pope.'" He looked at Gray, almost apologetically. "I'm sorry—that's what they call the fiend. That, or 'His Supreme Holiness.'"

"No sweat," Gray replied. "I ain't much of a Catholic these days." He nodded at Juan, who'd managed to rise, regardless. His left leg was relatively straight now, except for where it bent a little at the shattered bone. He'd grasped his Springfield again and took careful aim with gritted teeth. "He is, though, and he's pissed."

Juan nailed another yellow-and-red-clad man. "Pissed," he agreed harshly, almost moaning with the agony that had finally come.

"Their pope ain't our pope, so don't worry about it. We've even had a few doozies of our own, but this beats me. Do they really drink blood?"

"I've heard so. They believe death in battle, for 'God,' brings them instant paradise. Retreat brings eternal damnation."

"Empty," Stites announced, crouching down. The balls whizzing by the crate or slapping into it became a blizzard. "Whoa, boy!" he yelped, clenching his eyes shut when a ball snatched at his hair. "Sumbitches is gonna drink my blood!"

"Shut up, you nitwit!" Gray said, also taking cover. "Maybe they will, and it'll poison the lot of 'em!"

Finally even Juan fell back down when a cascade of splinters left his face bloody. Remaining exposed now was suicide. The Filipino's bloody fingers groped inside his shirt for a small golden cross and he closed his eyes. "You must leave me, Cap-tan," he said hoarsely.

"Not a chance," Matt said severely. "Who'll cut my hair?"

After an intense fusillade that left them all cringing together behind the disintegrating crate, the firing abruptly ceased, and Matt risked a quick glance. Yellow-and-red-uniformed men had begun to form up on the dueling ground. More and more troops streamed from the woods and spilled out from under the bleachers, adding to the ranks. "Jesus," he said, "I bet there's still three or four hundred of 'em. Maybe five."

"Now will come the charge," Jenks said quietly. "They'll sweep right over us and into the city."

They were startled by a sudden loud drumroll and the initial hesitant skirl of a bagpipe, of all things. Matt turned and looked behind them.

"It's Chack!" he said excitedly.

"About damn time!" the Bosun grumbled.

"Close up, close up!" Chack roared at the "pickup" infantry they'd assembled at the dock. Blair had managed to scrape up about two hundred and thirty Marines, including those from the ships they thought they could count on. With Chack's fifty and Blair's initial dozen, they'd double-timed to the sound of the guns, their shoes and Lemurian sandals echoing off the buildings and stone streets leading through the city from the waterfront. Crowds of panicked civilians cleared a lane in the face of the bizarre collection of troops. Other units were expected, but none had been prepared. It would still be some time before they arrived. One of Blair's volunteers found his note on the bagpipe and launched into a martial tune that was simultaneously stirring and nerve-racking to Chack. "What in the name of the Heavens *is* that thing?" he demanded.

The drums continued to roll as the Imperial Marines jockeyed into the unfamiliar formation Chack and Blair had imposed, and once it looked something like they'd envisioned, Chack raised his voice.

"Battalion!" he roared. "Forward, *march*! Shields, *up*!" The entire first rank was composed of Chack's Lemurian and Blair's human Marines. They'd been marching with their muskets slung and shields trailing to their left. Now they brought the shields around, facing the enemy. A compact block of troops sixty wide and five ranks deep split and surged past the beleaguered men behind the crate, reforming on the other side, just under seventy yards short of the growing Dominion line.

"Corpsman!" Matt shouted, standing and looking around. Selass, complete with Marine armor, scrambled forward from the rear rank with a pair of assistants.

"Cap-i-taan Reddy!" she chattered. "Thank the Heavens you are safe!'

"I'm fine. Juan's hurt."

"Cap-i-taan!" greeted Chack, bringing up the rear with Imperial file closers. Blair was with him. "Thank the Heavens!" he repeated. "I'm sorry we did not arrive sooner. All is chaos in the harbor. Reynolds reports a large Dominion fleet approaching from the south, and a signal calling all Imperial subjects to arms flies above Government House. *Walker*, *Euripides*, and *Tacitus* have sailed, and at first it seemed as though other ships and the forts might actually *fire* on them! Word is spreading quickly, though, and other ships may now join them. It is like your 'Pearl Harbor' all over again!"

"Let's pray not," Matt said grimly. "Goddamn it!" he swore, uncharacteristically strongly. "My ship's steaming into battle, and here I am!"

"You planned for as much," Jenks reminded him. "Trust your first officer and let us finish the fight 'we're at,' yes?" He looked around. "Where's Bates—'O'Casey?' "

"In the front rank, holding a shield. He insisted," Chack replied.

"Fool!"

"Chack," Matt said, "listen. This is your battle now. Fight it your way. You've got to hold them here, but if you get a chance, stick it in!" He paused. Lemurians were only now beginning to grasp the concept of quarter, since the Grik never asked or gave it. "Take prisoners at your discretion," he said at last. "We need to scram. Jenks has to find the Governor-Emperor and report the big picture. If something's happened to him, Jenks needs to be ready to sort stuff out. No telling for sure who's on whose side right now." Matt looked at Jenks. "Find that pretty wife of yours too, make sure she's safe!"

"What are you going to do?"

"I'm going to borrow half a dozen Marines and get that bastard Reed. Where do you think he'll be?"

"The Dominion embassy, I shouldn't wonder," Jenks hissed. "He'll be awaiting the outcome with Don Hernan. I expect he'll seek his protection if they lose!"

"What protection, after this?" Matt challenged.

Jenks blinked, then nodded. "Indeed."

Chack detailed an even dozen Imperial Marines (amazing how readily they followed his orders. Kipling was right about "keeping your head") and Matt, Gray, Stites—and for some reason Courtney—disappeared in the direction of the embassy.

Chack turned to face forward. This would be his first test against an equally armed foe. True, his Lemurian Marines had percussion muskets with tighter tolerances, sights, and therefore better accuracy, but they were holding the shields and their weapons might not load as fast as flintlocks anyway. The "Doms" seemed to be waiting for him, as if battles of this nature, like this one had suddenly become, should have "rules" of sportsmanship. What were they waiting for? he wondered. A pre-battle chat? He looked at the Imperial bleachers, and the bloody corpses heaped and scattered there. His lips curled, exposing sharp canines. Captain Reddy *had* given him "discretion," after all.

"Prepare to fix bayonets!" he cried. The troops shifted slightly, anticipating, and the drumroll became a staccato rumble.

"Fix!"

As his Marines had trained, and the Imperials had been

instructed, three hundred bayonets were jerked from their scabbards with a bloodthirsty roar and brandished menacingly at the enemy.

"Bayonets!"

With a metallic clatter, the weapons were attached to muzzles.

"Front rank, present!"

The Lemurians' muskets were already loaded, and they would be too busy to shoot in a moment at any rate.

"Aim!"

Hammers clicked back and polished barrels steadied at the surprised foe.

"Fire!"

Even before the smoke cleared, exposing the carnage of that first volley, Chack was already shouting: "Front rank, guard against muskets! Shields at an angle! Get them up! Lean them back! Second rank, present!"

"The Nancy in trouble!" shouted Minnie, the talker, relaying the message from the crow's nest. Frankie had been staring at the Dominion battle line through his binoculars, amazed at the size of some of the ships. They weren't nearly as big as a Lemurian Home, but they were easily half again bigger than the largest Grik ship they'd seen—and they appeared to carry a *lot* of metal. He redirected his binoculars skyward. The little blue plane was coming right at them, purple-white smoke trailing its engine. "They no call 'May-Day,'" the talker finished.

So, Frankie thought, *either the transmitter's out or Kari's been hit*. Reynolds seemed to be having increased difficulty keeping the plane in the air. "Range to target?" he called.

"Seven zero, double zero, closing at thirty knots" came the reply, relayed from Campeti above on the fire control platform. *Walker* was making twenty knots, so the enemy must be making ten. Damn. Big *and* fast. Of course, they had the wind off their port quarter, and that was probably their very best point.

"Very well. Slow to one-third. Stand by to recover aircraft and hoist the 'return to ship' flag!"

Even as *Walker* slowed and the whaleboat was readied to launch, the plane began belching black smoke, and with the reduced roar from the blower, they could hear the death rattle of its engine. Fred seemed intent on a spot just ahead, off what would soon be *Walker*'s starboard beam.

"Ahead slow! Stand by to come to course three double oh. We'll try to put her in our lee. Launch the whaleboat as soon as practical and have the gun's crews stand by for 'surface action, port.' "

The Nancy wheezed and clattered past the pilothouse, gouging roughly into the sea with a wrenching splash. Even before the propeller stuttered to a stop, Fred Reynolds dove out of his cockpit into the water.

"All stop!" Frankie cried, a chill going down his spine. There were no flashies in these seas, but there were smaller fish that acted like them. There were also a hell of a lot of sharks. Big ones, little ones, a few truly humongous ones . . . and there was a type of gri-kakka—as well as other things. "Get that whaleboat in the water!" Frankie yelled, even as the boat slid down the falls and smacked into the sea. Fred had swum around to the observer's seat and was trying to claw his way up the oil-streaked fuselage. Kari wasn't moving. Somehow, Fred managed to climb high enough to get the Lemurian by the long hair on her head and drag her from the plane just as the overheated engine burst into flames. Almost immediately, the fuel tank directly above it ignited with a searing *whoosh* and a mushroom of orange flame and black smoke. The right wing folded and the fuselage rolled on its side, and in what seemed a matter of seconds, the entire plane was consumed by fire, its charred skeleton drawn beneath the waves by the weight of the engine.

There in the water, Fred Reynolds was stroking mightily toward the oncoming boat, one arm clawing at the water, the other trying to hold Kari's head above it. "C'mon!" urged someone on the bridge. A dull moan reached their ears and a huge splash erupted a few dozen yards off the port bow. Another splash arose a quarter of a mile short.

"Bow guns—'chasers,' from the Doms," announced Minnie. "Big ones, say the lookout. The first one prob'ly lucky close."

"Range?"

"Four t'ousand."

Frankie glanced back at the sea to port and saw with relief that the whaleboat had reached the aviators. "The main battery will commence firing," he said grimly. "And pass the word: 'lucky close' ain't an option today. We have to keep the range on those bastids an' tear 'em up from a distance." He gestured back toward Scapa Flow. "Our job is to hold 'em back until the cavalry gets here. Like Reynolds, we'll concentrate on the transports if we can, and stay away from the heavies. As many guns as those things have, they don't have to be good to shred us, just 'lucky close,' see?"

The new salvo bell clattered on the bulkhead behind him.

Matt and the others were running, breathing hard. They'd managed to stay together, however, and even Bradford was keeping up. The streets were eerily quiet and vacant. Matt wondered if the inhabitants were sitting things out, or if they'd already responded to the Governor-Emperor's call to arms. For some reason, he didn't think that was the case in this district. He worried about snipers. They turned onto the street dominated by the embassy of the Holy Dominion and were met by a scattered volley that felled one of their Marines and shattered masonry at the corner behind them. Gray emptied a twenty-round stick into the group, sending all but one of the six men sprawling. The other man stood there, stunned, until Matt shot him with his Springfield as they trotted past. Stites had the BAR again, but he was low on magazines for it too. They reached the iron-bound door, and Matt immediately inverted his rifle and drove the butt hard against it. The door didn't budge.

"God*damn* it!" he raged.

"Stay cool, Skipper," Gray said. "I got a treatment for

this." He reached in a satchel and pulled out a grenade, a "real" one, made in the USA.

"I didn't know you had those," Matt said accusingly. "We could have used them!"

"I was savin' 'em for if things got serious," Gray explained innocently. "Bash in the peephole!"

Matt redirected the butt of his rifle and Gray pulled the pin on the grenade and dropped it inside the door. There was a muffled *ba-rump* inside, followed by screams.

"What good did that do?" Stites demanded. "We still can't get in!"

"After the day I've had, it was pretty fun," Gray said. "Otherwise . . ." He fished in his pocket. ". . . Spanky gave me this really swell rubber band! Just look at this thing!" he said, displaying the gift. "Don't know where he got it, but it's a peach. I was gonna make me a slingshot for . . . Anyway, everybody get back!"

He took another grenade, and looping the rubber band around it, hung the little bomb from the top left hinge on the big door. Making sure everyone was clear, he yanked the pin and ran. The spoon flew and the grenade bounced up and down a couple of times.

Blam!

Grenades make poor breaching charges, but the high-explosive inside made short work of the brittle iron hinge. The door trembled, then fell diagonally outward onto the street.

"C'mon!" Matt yelled.

In the grand scheme of such things, compared to other fights Chack had participated in, the Battle of the Imperial Dueling Grounds was a relatively small affair. It was big by Imperial standards, at least as far as land battles were concerned, but it wasn't even close to something like Aryaal, Singapore, and certainly not Baalkpan in terms of scope. The Dominion had landed and secreted away perhaps a thousand troops in warehouses and an abandoned barracks outside of Leith, and the conspirators had considered that number more than sufficient to overwhelm New Scotland's small, dispersed, Marine garrison from behind Scapa Flow's defenses, especially when coupled with the overwhelming surprise that Reed and Don Hernan had achieved. It didn't work that way.

The Lemurian shields made a big difference. For a while. The Dominion front ranks were decimated by those first volleys, but they had greater numbers to start with. Chack and Blair's experiments with the shields paid off, teaching them that the dense hardwood-backed bronze implements would turn a musket ball if held at an angle, and the shields were battered and streaked with smears of lead, while the rear ranks delivered a withering fire. The front ranks suffered terribly from the beating they were taking, painfully flayed by spattered fragments of balls, stunned by incessant impacts, and even struck by balls that skated in or found a gap. The shields could take only so much, however, and they began to be pierced or fall apart under the hammering.

"Second rank! Take shields where you can," Lieutenant Blair ordered, knowing Chack would never do it. "First rank, fall back to the rear!"

Chack spared him a thankful glance. Less than thirty Lemurian Marines were able to obey.

O'Casey appeared, unfired pistols still dangling around his neck. He was covered with blood, caused by dozens of splinter wounds. "This is the damnedest thing there ever was," he gasped.

"It is quite like a duel itself, is it not?" Blair asked. His hat was gone now, replaced by a bloody rag. "A most appropriate setting, I suppose."

"It is *stupid*," Chack growled. "General Alden would *not* approve." He shrugged. "But I don't know what else to do. We cannot maneuver here, and there is no cover other than the stands—and we can't reach them without exposing ourselves. Stupid! All we can do is stand here, trading blows like fools."

"Where's Captain Reddy, an' Jenks?" O'Casey asked.

A ball caromed off Chack's steel American helmet, almost knocking him down. He shook his head and resumed his erect pose. "Stupid," he repeated, looking almost desperately around for some inspiration. "If only we had a single gun!"

"Just be glad theirs are silent," Blair said. He looked at O'Casey. "Captain Reddy has gone for Mr. Reed. Jenks seeks the Governor-Emperor!"

"Then I must assist one or the other," O'Casey said. "I'm of no further use here."

"Nooo, Mr. O'Casey," Chack said. "Untrue. Your collection of pistols might soon be of great use. I weary of this mutual mauling! I ask myself what I would do if those . . . people were Grik, and I see only one course that will decide this before both sides are annihilated! Lieutenant Blair? I see the enemy has not fixed bayonets. Why is that?"

"Why . . ." Blair paused. "Well, they can't."

"They *do* have them?"

"Yes, but they're a different style. A type of plug bayonet. They insert them into their muzzles and they are quite effective, but their shooting is over then. They usually have to drive them out. If they'd affixed them before now, they'd have had to charge, or stand and be shot to pieces."

"Like we are doing?" Chack practically roared. "Why didn't you tell me this before?"

"I—" Blair was confused.

"Listen to me, Lieutenant Blair. You must trust me. We are about to lose a lot of troops, your men mostly, but then we will shortly end this fight. Do you believe me?"

"I . . . uh . . ." Blair suddenly remembered the last time he'd disregarded the advice of a Lemurian commander. Safir Maraan had tried to warn him at Singapore that his tactics simply didn't apply. His command had been virtually eradicated that day, and he'd miserably blamed himself ever since. He'd also come to realize that these . . . creatures, these Lemurians, knew a lot more about pitched battles on land than he did. "Yes, I do, Captain Sab-At," he said finally, formally. "What are your orders?"

"The discipline and execution must be flawless," Chack warned.

Another grenade preceded Matt, Gray, Stites, and the ten surviving Marines through the shattered door of the Dominion embassy. A second Imperial had been killed by a sniper from a second-floor window. The grenade burst amid another chorus of screams, and the group charged in, Gray's Thompson spitting at a trio of men in uniforms crawling on the floor.

The entry hall looked different this time. The lanterns were askew and fresh blood pooled beneath bodies on the tile. The red walls didn't seem any different, but they glistened where fresh color had splashed. The golden tapestries and accents ran with glittering purple-red. There must have been at least twenty men near the door when Gray's first grenade dropped among them, and many had been killed outright. The rest, probably still stunned, had fallen to the second. A few more shots finished the survivors.

"Upstairs!" Courtney Bradford shouted. "Check upstairs! The buggers will likely be there!"

Matt pointed around at darkened alcoves. "You men," he said to the Marines, "check those spaces! Make sure there's not another way out of this joint!"

"Where'll they be?" Gray asked, puffing.

"Upstairs, like Courtney said. I hope."

They thundered up the spiral staircase. A pair of musket shots, fired wildly from above, shattered the banister just a few feet from Bradford, and his enthusiasm ebbed just a little. Stites hosed his BAR upward, stitching back and forth, and they were rewarded by a scream and a thud. As a group, with Bradford lagging slightly, they arrived at the top of the stairs. A man in the uniform of a Blood Drinker, probably one of those who'd fired, lunged at Matt with a bayonet inserted into the muzzle of his musket. Matt knocked it aside with the Springfield and drove his own bayonet into the man's chest with a shout, pushing him back until he'd virtually pinned him to the wall. The dim, orangish light in the room reflected off the glazing eyes that stared back into his.

"Bravo!" came a voice from the far side of the chamber, standing before the garish golden cross on the wall. "You have me, it seems."

Matt turned, yanking the bayonet clear, and saw Harrison Reed dimly illuminated, sinister shadows around his eyes and mouth. He stood with his arms crossed before him, a pistol loosely in his hand. The naked servant girl lay sprawled on the hardwood floor in the center of a spreading pool of blood.

"You will face the very fires of hell for storming this place," he said conversationally. "This is not just an embassy—bad enough, I assure you—but a blessed house of God."

"Where you just murdered a little girl!" Matt said, bringing the Springfield up. "I ought to kill you where you stand!"

Reed pointed the pistol at Matt in a classic style that showed he was proficient. "I did not kill the child. I presume Don Hernan sent her to paradise himself, before he left. He was quite taken with her." He shrugged slightly. "I found her like this, and before you ask, I don't know where Don Hernan is. Directing the completion of our plan, I shouldn't wonder."

"Sumbitch has skipped!" Stites snarled disgustedly.

Reed ignored him, but wiggled the pistol slightly. "Perhaps, Captain Reddy, you would care to exchange my life for yours? You are here, so I assume the fighting went poorly at the dueling grounds?"

"Things were looking up when we left," Gray said harshly. "We got reinforcements."

Reed smirked. "Pity. Regardless, I remain optimistic."

"You wouldn't be if you'd stayed for more of the show," Matt promised. "Is that why you hid here? I wouldn't be 'optimistic' about anything right now, if I were you. Listen." Even through the solid, windowless walls, a crescendo of distant musketry rattled incessantly. "Besides, you're basically the reason we're here."

Reed looked genuinely surprised. "Whatever do you mean?"

"Your Commander Billingsley attacked our Alliance, abducted Princess Rebecca, and . . . took some other people who mean a lot to us," Matt ground out. "That's all on you. We came here looking for Billingsley—and whoever it was who put him up to it."

Reed slapped his forehead. "Oh, dear!" he said. "It seems I was most dreadfully mistaken! You had me quite convinced the princess is safe and you had abundant proof of the conspiracy arriving with *Achilles*!"

"We do have proof. Plenty. We know you sent *Agamemnon* back to kill the girl, along with three other ships. We destroyed *Agamemnon* and captured the others, but Billingsley already had Rebecca and our people on *Ajax*. We came looking for him . . . and you."

Reed shook his head. "I underestimated poor Billingsley! He may have been an apostate with no idea what the true stakes were, but it seems he served *me* quite well, at any rate. The irony is, he would have been utterly horrified to learn who *I* serve!"

"The Dominion," Gray spat.

"Don Hernan," Reed corrected, "and the True Church." He twitched the pistol. "Don't mistake me; I love my country—this land—but no power on earth can hope to oppose the Dominion for long, nor should it." He smiled. "You see, oddly enough, I've become a Believer. In any event, I decided it was better to join the Dominion Church and serve from within, than to be conquered and suffer the devastating consequences. I'm a patriot, working to secure New Britain's proper place *within* the Dominion, as a partner—not a possession!"

"You're a traitorous son of a bitch, serving a sick, perverted, cartoon church full of freaks!" the Bosun stated simply.

Reed's eyes flared. "You may sing a different tune when this day is done!"

"Perhaps you refer to the Dominion fleet coming from the south?" Courtney asked. "Of course you do. In that case, I propose it is *you* who will be dreadfully disappointed. We discovered its advance quite early this morning and . . . um . . . sufficient fleet elements have sortied to intercept it. All of Home Fleet and the harbor defenses have been alerted as well. No fleet can pass those forts, sir! We once nearly stopped a much larger fleet with much less!"

For the first time Reed's expression showed uncertainty. "That's a lie!" he snarled.

"What?" Matt asked. "That we know about the fleet? Or that it'll be stopped? Obviously we know about it, and that's enough to stop it. Courtney's right about those forts. Besides, where *is* Don Hernan? You don't really believe he's off leading a charge. My God, you stupid bastard. Why'd he *kill that poor girl*? The bastard bolted, leaving you with the bag!"

Harrison Reed seemed to sag. "Very well," he said. "Perhaps you're right." He straightened and his aim steadied. Gray tensed, ready to spray him down. "I won't hang," he said simply. "You surprised me today, Captain Reddy. You killed one of my very best." He snorted. "Not exactly sporting, your ploy at the end, but you did hold your own and manage to get the job done." He took a breath and slowly lowered his pistol to the chair beside him. "I'm no Lemuel Truelove," he confessed, "but I challenge you to kill me man to man. You will have your revenge, and I will have paradise."

Matt hesitated only a moment, then inverted the Springfield and drove the bayonet hard into the wooden floor.

"Skipper!" objected Gray, but Matt ignored him while Reed smiled and drew the ornate rapier at his side. Before anyone could say another word, Matt's hand went to his belt and came away with his 1911 Colt .45. Flipping the safety off with his thumb, he shot Harrison Reed four times in the center of his chest.

"The hell with you, you murdering bastard," Matt said as Reed gasped and dropped to his knees. "I hope that didn't hurt much. I'd hate for you to even *think* you were going to paradise!"

Stites giggled. "*Damn*, Skipper!"

Matt looked at him, then glared at Gray. "C'mon," he said, "we've still got work to do."

Commander Frankie Steele was actually secretly a little surprised at how well his first independent action was going. *Walker* was battling virtual behemoths, but all their massive power was no match for the old destroyer's speed and maneuverability. The enemy battle line had broken, immediately sensing Frankie's main objective and trying to put their ships between *Walker* and the remaining transports. The troop-filled transports were the key. Without them, the whole Dominion operation was pointless. Massive red-sailed ships of the line, or "liners," veered to defend the steamers and bring their guns to bear. In so doing, they lost cohesion, massed firepower, their advantageous wind—and all semblance of organized control.

Ponderously, the mighty ships turned, thrashing the sea with their heavy guns, as many as fifty to a side, mostly in *Walker*'s churning wake. They'd scored a few hits with what had to be twenty-four-pounders or better, but the damage had been minimal. Smoke streamed from new holes in a couple of *Walker*'s stacks, and she had a new hole the size of a porthole in the guinea pullman. Other than that, things had all gone the old destroyer's way.

The new exploding shells she employed for only the second time came as a rude surprise to the Dominion Navy. They weren't much, still just hollow copper bolts filled with a gunpowder bursting charge, detonated with a contact fuse. They didn't penetrate worth a damn. They had the math to put them right where they wanted them now, however, even propelled by black powder, and *any* bursting charge going off on a crowded gun deck covered with guns being loaded with fabric powder bags could be cataclysmic.

One Dominion ship of the line had simply blown up, and another was burning fiercely. For penetration of hulls and destruction of masts, *Walker* still had an ample supply of solid bolts. *Euripides* and *Tacitus* were close to joining the action now as well. They didn't carry as many guns as the liners, but theirs were newer—bigger even than *Achilles*'—throwing thirty-pound balls. Frankie estimated that the enemy had wasted more metal shooting at *Walker* than the old ship weighed.

Ahead, in a gap cleared by the explosion of one of the liners, four of the transports lay helpless before *Walker*, seeming almost to cringe like rabbits as the greyhound saw them and turned to give chase. She'd have to steam directly between two liners to get at them, but one had lost its foremast and the other actually seemed to be turning away. Defying his own strategy to remain at a distance, Frankie sensed an opportunity to end the fight with a swift, bold stroke.

Answering bells for "ahead flank," the blower roared, and *Walker* made her lunge for the sheep.

"Concentrate all fire port and starboard with explosive shells at the enemy warships until we pass between them, then hammer those transports!" Frankie ordered. Smoke belched from the transport's stacks as they poured on the coal and tried to turn away even as *Walker* swept down upon them, streaming gunsmoke. She pounded the disabled ship to port with the number two and number four guns, and the one apparently trying to flee to starboard with numbers one and three. The heavy "antiaircraft" guns, mounted in tubs where the aft torpedo tubes had been, raked both ships as well, and their pounding roar was joined by the staccato bursts of the .50s on the amidships deckhouse. Exploding shells penetrated deeply into the relatively unprotected bows of the liner to port and detonated within, spewing shards of copper aft that savaged gun carriages and hewed bodies. One round finally passed nearly the length of the deck before exploding and gouts of white smoke whooshed sporadically out her gunports as exposed powder bags lit. The ship shuddered from almost continuous secondary detonations, and smoldering gunners actually crawled out the gunports and flung themselves into the sea. A greasy black ball of smoke roiled into the sky amidships as something flammable, lamp oil perhaps, ignited and spread burning liquid on the deck. The red main course caught fire and the flames spread quickly upward, devouring the sails above. The ship didn't explode, but she was fully engulfed in flames as *Walker* sped past her.

The ship to starboard had received a severe beating as well, and her ornate, garishly decorated stern galleries were a shattered shambles, gaping wide like an open mouth with broken teeth. Many of the aft guns on the two main gun decks were probably dismounted or crewless, but the ship had turned almost directly into the wind and for a few moments *Walker* was steaming parallel to her, less than five hundred yards off her port beam—and the remaining thirty-odd guns of that broadside. Almost too late, Frankie realized the mistake he'd made. The ship hadn't been fleeing; it had been turning to do exactly this: voluntarily taking the punishment *Walker* meted out, just to bring its own guns around.

"All guns! Surface action starboard!" he shouted, just as the side of the enemy ship vanished behind a dense, white cloud of smoke, lit by dozens of flashes of yellow lightning.

Spanky McFarlane was half deafened by the thunderous blows that hammered his ship. Something had gone insanely wrong. A moment before, he'd been standing there, near the throttle station with Miami Tindal and a centrally located damage-control party. He'd been drinking coffee from his favorite remaining mug—the one with the Chevy emblem, the hula girl, and, ironically, the aerial view of Oahu. In the next instant, he got the blurred impression of roundshot punching a hole in the hull beside him, bowling through the party of Lemurians gathered there, along with a spray of splintered steel and rivets. The shot rebounded off the bulkhead, the hull, and finally came to rest somewhere in the bilge. Miami had been talking and now he was just . . . gone. Spanky blinked and wiped his face with his sleeve. For some reason, he couldn't see very well. That was better. He noticed then that his sleeve was soaked with blood, and all that remained of his sacred cup was the porcelain handle in his hand.

He blinked again and saw the 'Cats at the throttle staring at him, blinking horror. He did a quick inventory of himself and as far as he could tell, he wasn't injured. Looking down, he realized the same wasn't the case for three of the four members of the damage-control party. At least two were dead. One might be, and the fourth was sitting on the deck plates, stunned. Miami . . . Well, he was dead. Spanky shook his head, clearing the fuzz, and realized the turbines were winding down.

"Shit!" He lurched to the speaking tube. They didn't rely much on electronics in battle anymore. "This is McFarlane in the forward engine room. What's going on up there?"

"Commaander McFaarlane!" came a relieved cry. It was Minnie. "You come to bridge quick! You needed on the bridge!"

Spanky paused, looking at the air lock to the aft fireroom. "Uh, what's the story on the boilers? Why're we losing steam back here?"

"I don't know!" came the panicked but strangely distant reply.

"Well, put somebody on that does!" he bellowed.

"I can't!" the girl—he always thought of them as girls now—practically screeched back at him.

"Well . . . who's got the conn?"

"I *DO!*"

"*Jeez!*" That's why the voice sounded so distant. "Okay, okay, pull yourself together! I'll pass the conn off to auxiliary from here, then I'm on my way! Get, uh, Finny! You got Finny on the horn?"

"I got Finny and Tabby in the forward fireroom! Everything fine in there!"

Thank God. "Tell Tabby to bypass the aft fireroom and route steam back to the turbines! Finny needs to take his party topside and get their asses in through the deck access to check on numbers three and four! Warn him to vent the space before they go in. I'm on my way!"

He opened the cover of the tube to the auxiliary conn on the aft deckhouse and was further deafened by the heavy bark of the Japanese 4.7-inch gun. "Bashear!"

"This is Bashear."

"Listen, you got the conn until further notice. We got the talker steerin' the ship! What the hell's goin' on up there?"

"I don't know, Spanky. We just got clobbered, and there's steam and smoke gushin' everywhere. I can't see forward of the searchlight tower! It looks to me like one o' those big bastards suckered Frankie in close and then shotgunned us!" Bashear sounded harried.

"Okay, stay loose. You should have number two back on line directly. Try to get us the hell away from whatever's poundin' on us. You still got Campeti on the horn?"

"Yeah."

"Tell him to pour everything he's got at the closest target. Use the HE in the Jap gun. *Blow* the bastards off us if you have to! I'm gonna try an' get to the pilothouse!"

"Aye, Spanky!"

Spanky glanced at the blood and gore around him, then looked at the throttlemen. Other 'Cats were beginning to arrive from aft. "Listen," he said to Bashear once more. "We got wounded down here. Call around. See if you can round up a corpsman."

"I'll try, but most are ashore with Chack and there's a lot of wounded up here too."

"Right." Spanky directed one of the newcomers to the apparent corpses. "Check them fellas and do what you can for the hurt." He paused and caught the eye of the steadiest-looking throttleman. "I gotta scram, so you're in charge for now. Keep these guys cool down here," he admonished, then launched himself up the ladder to the main deck above. If the aft fireroom was full of steam, he didn't dare open the air lock and let it in.

On deck, he was greeted by a hellish scene, grown all too familiar. Steam and smoke swirled up from the starboard side, filling the deck. 'Cats ran back and forth, some hauling hoses, others just running, screaming, their fur scorched black. The Japanese antiaircraft guns hammered his ears and the number three gun added its smoke to the mix even though its crew couldn't see and had to be suffering in the choking air. That was Pack Rat's gun now, and he knew the Lemurian gunner's mate would never leave it. The Dominion liner lay to starboard, a little aft now, and even through the heavy haze caused by burning wooden ships, he saw it had been riddled with holes. Another comparatively feeble broadside blossomed from its side, punishing *Walker* further with a few more hits. Spanky felt the shot strikes pound through his shoes like trip-hammer blows, but he also noted several small splashes in the sea alongside. Not all the enemy shot was penetrating, he realized. Maybe not even most. Thank God. If it was, after the blows he'd felt, they'd already be sinking. The ship *had* slowed almost to a stop, however, and was beginning to wallow in the swells.

He ran into Jeek, directing his division in throwing a curtain of water on the smoke, trying to get it to lie. Reynolds was probably still in the wardroom with Kari. Jeek yelled that he had no idea whether there was fire under all that smoke, but he wasn't letting it anywhere near the aft deckhouse where the last plane and all the aviation fuel was stored. Spanky repeated what he'd said to Bashear about corpsmen, but Jeek just looked around and shrugged. Spanky raced on, under the amidships gun platform on the port side of the galley, headed for the bridge, but was brought up short by Earl Lanier, calmly sitting on his precious Coke machine and eating a sandwich.

"What the hell are you doing?"

"Guardin' my machine!" the fat cook snarled. "What's it look like? All my mess attendants is on report! Bastards didn't stow my baby below before this fracas, they just hauled ass to their battle stations! I had to drag it around here from the other side by myself!"

"Why aren't you at your battle station?" Spanky demanded.

"I am! Why ain't you at yours?"

Shaking his head, Spanky resumed his sprint. At least Earl *was* doing something. His usual battle station was in the head.

It was awful on the bridge. The new battle shutters covered the windows, so there wasn't much broken glass, but at least one shot had come through the thin side plating of the starboard bridgewing and plowed up the wooden strakes in its passage. The chart table was shattered and twisted askew, and the handle had been sheared clean off the engine room telegraph. The damage to the bridge wasn't what caught his eyes at first, however.

Four bodies lay on the shattered strakes. Norm Kutas was alive, but had splinters running up the backs of his legs, all the way to his buttocks. A pair of 'Cat pharmacist's mates had already arrived and were trying to get him on a stretcher. Ed Palmer, hair scorched and face blackened, seemed okay otherwise, though winded. Two 'Cats were obviously dead, their blood dripping through the strakes from terrible wounds, and the brave Lemurian talker was still at the wheel, holding it in an iron grip even though she no longer controlled the ship. Others began to arrive, grabbing bodies and carrying them away, but none touched Frankie Steele.

Frankie had somehow dragged himself up against the forward bulkhead. He wore a curious expression on his pale face, staring down at the stumps of both his legs, gone above the knees. To Spanky's amazement, he spoke.

"Hey, Spanky," he said, almost whispering. "Skipper gives me the keys, and what's the first thing I do? I wrap her around a tree."

"Oh, Frankie," Spanky said hoarsely, kneeling beside him. "Even the Skipper's banged her up a time or two. You know that."

"Yeah. But not like this. Not stupid." Slowly, he looked into Spanky's eyes. "An' we just got her fixed up from the last time!" He paused. "Mr. Ellis! Where's Mr. Ellis?"

"Jim's fine," Spanky said softly. "Just busy is all." Jim Ellis was on the other side of the world.

Frankie smiled. "Good man. He'll be a swell skipper for *Mahan*, once he settles in." His chin slumped slowly to his chest and he was gone.

"Goddamn," Spanky said, and stood. He looked at Minnie. "Are you fit for duty?" he demanded. Shakily, she nodded. "Then get back to your station! Mr. Palmer, I presume by your presence that you have no more pressing duties, so you have the conn. I have the deck. Talker? Replacements to the bridge, and inform Mr. Bashear to relinquish the conn. I expect he's got other things to do. What's the status on the boilers?" He patted his chest. "And somebody get me some binoculars!"

For the last several moments, there'd been no incoming fire. Taking the offered binoculars, Spanky strode onto the bridgewing and scanned around to determine why. He saw with satisfaction that their primary tormentor was low in the water and beginning to abandon. A few good hits with the Jap 4.7 at the waterline had probably settled her hash. The transports still lay ahead, obscured by a growing fogbank of smoke, but they'd gained some distance, bright sparks in black smoke soaring high from their stacks. They hadn't turned away, however—not yet. They seemed intent on finding protection behind another pair of liners approaching *Walker* from the west. The number one gun barked and bucked, and a round shrieked away to explode in the fo'c'sle of one of them, but Spanky couldn't tell if it did much good. A 'Cat pounced on the smoking brass shell as it fell to the deck from the opened breech. He tossed it in a nearby basket almost full of other dingy, blackened cartridges.

Spanky picked his way across the shattered strakes to the port bridgewing. More liners were approaching from the port quarter. Damn. He needed steam! For a moment, he wondered where the enemy frigates were. They had to be faster, and should have been all over him by now. He shrugged. Gift horses were rare critters. "Steam?" he demanded again.

"Finny report now, daamitt!" the talker replied, frustrated. Spanky couldn't stop a small smile. "He say boilers okay, but main steam line and feed-water pipe is shot. Smoke uptakes too. An' there's oil an' water in the bilge from leak somewhere. . . ."

"Tell Finny I don't give a damn what's wrong, only how long it'll take to fix—and what he needs to do it! Does he need people?"

"Almost all firemen in forward fireroom okay, they cram in air locks on both sides. He got them. Actually, Tabby got them. . . ." The talker paused. "Tabby on the horn."

"Spanky Skipper now?" came the tinny question. No drawl was present.

"Aye," the talker replied.

"Then tell Spanky to fight ship! I fight mess down here! Finny bypassed three an' four. Spanky lucky to have number two back, soon as pressure builds again! I fix the others as fast as I can, they fixed when they fixed! Spanky don't get no more holes in my poor ship! He hear?"

Spanky rolled his eyes and nodded.

"He hear," confirmed the talker.

"What's the pressure on number two?" Spanky asked.

"Ah, eighty and rising," Palmer replied, "but . . . there's still nothing getting to the engine room!"

"Crap. Finny must've shut everything off. Get Tabby on it ASAP. We gotta move." He stepped outside and glassed around again. "Okay, tell Campeti to have the number one gun concentrate on the transports with fire control assistance. All others will stay on the advancing warships in local control. Aim for their bows, tear 'em up!"

"Comm-aander," said the talker, "lookout reports *Taasitus* and *Euripides* have fought through enemy frigates, trying to join us here!"

"Is that so? Well, that explains the frigates. Tell Campeti

to keep firing, but watch his targets! We might have friendlies out there shortly."

The battle off Scapa Flow became a race for position. By all rights and reasonable expectations, it should have been over; the Dominion plan had been thwarted in the sense that there was now no way they could still land troops with surprise, and surprise had been the key to success. Unreadable signals flying from a large, distant liner confirmed that the enemy understood this as well, because even as the Dominion warships jockeyed to reconsolidate and reform, the surviving transports—minus one more that *Walker* had disabled—finally drew away to the west. *Walker*'s lookout confirmed that Imperial ships of the line, "battle waagons," were finally out of the harbor and forming up as well. Fully two-thirds of the Dominion ships were heading for them, trying to cut them off.

At first Spanky didn't understand. Why continue the fight? Intellectually, he expected an interesting match. Several Dominion liners were disabled or destroyed, so the numbers would be nearly equal. The contest between the two fleets would pit ships with many guns, propelled by sail alone, against ships with fewer, bigger guns, powered by sail and steam. There were advantages and disadvantages inherent to the philosophies behind each fleet, and Spanky knew Matt would be fascinated. But then Spanky *did* understand. The remaining third of the Dominion fleet, a little hard-used and frigate-heavy now, was gathering to approach *Walker*. Apparently the old destroyer had made an impression on the enemy commander, because the major battle shaping northeast of her position seemed designed solely to ensure that nothing beyond the now battered *Tacitus* and *Euripides* could come to *Walker*'s aid.

"Oh, shit," he muttered. "Tell Tabby the boilers might be 'fixed when they're fixed,' but we need at least one of 'em fixed *right damn now*."

"She trying!" cried the talker. "She not know why there no steam to engines!"

Spanky looked around, frustrated. He *needed* to be

helping out with engineering, but right now he *had* to be on the bridge. He thought furiously for a moment, battling the various necessities in his mind. The simple fact was, even if the Skipper and the others hadn't been ashore, *Walker*'s bench just wasn't deep enough for this anymore. There were plenty of good, professional 'Cats aboard, but dealing with situations like this could be learned only by experience. He could put Bashear back in charge, but the Bosun was knee-deep as it was. Campeti was busy too. He thought Norm could handle it, but he'd already been taken to the wardroom. He finally came to the conclusion that, however unprepared for overall command he considered himself, he was the only remotely qualified person available. He had to stay where he was. With Miami dead, that left only Tabby to do his job. She knew *Walker*'s boilers inside and out, literally. He just hoped she'd picked up enough of the rest of the ship's engineering plant, and how it all worked together. He sighed.

"Tell Tabby she better find out, and quick. This ship and everybody aboard needs her to be a chief engineer right now. If we're not underway in ten minutes, we're all dead."

The talker gulped, tail swishing, and relayed his words. Tabby didn't reply.

"*Euripides* is coming out of the smoke of that burning liner—off the starboard beam now!" Palmer cried. "She looks pretty chewed."

The Imperial frigate had lost her mainmast and its remains had been cut away. Black smoke poured from a dozen holes in her tall, skinny stack, and bright splintered wood glared from her dark-painted hull. Both her paddle wheels still churned vigorously alongside, though, and she was approaching at a respectable clip. A few moments later, *Tacitus* appeared as well, and if anything, she looked worse than her sister. Only her mizzen and bowsprit still stood, and she was kind of crab-walking around a battered starboard paddle box, but somehow she was managing to keep pace with *Euripides*. Shredded Imperial flags still proudly streamed from both ships.

"Have Campeti pass the word! 'Friendies' on the starboard quarter, do not fire on them!" Spanky ordered. The command probably hadn't been necessary, but Spanky didn't want any mistakes in the chaos.

"*Euripides* signaling to make for our starboard side," the talker echoed the lookout. "*Tacitus* angling aft; she come alongside to port."

Shortly afterward, *Euripides* backpedaled, her paddle wheels throwing up a mountain of foam as she arrested her forward motion alongside the wallowing destroyer. *Tacitus* was still coming up, more laboriously, but bundled hammocks, sails, and other items were being slung over her shattered starboard bulwarks, like bumpers on a tug.

"What the hell?" Spanky muttered.

"Ahoy there, *Walker*," came a cry from the catwalk between the paddle boxes on *Euripides*. Spanky grabbed a speaking trumpet and dashed onto the starboard bridgewing, avoiding the jagged metal there. He saw a man he recognized as a friend of Jenks's pointing a trumpet at him. He'd actually given the man a tour of *Walker*'s firerooms, but he couldn't remember his name.

"Ahoy, *Euripides*!" he cried. "It's good to see you after such a . . . busy morning. I hope we're still friends after all the trouble we've gotten you into."

"Nonsense! Wouldn't have missed it!" came the reply. "I did notice that your wondrously complicated internals seem a bit out of sorts."

Spanky grimaced at the gentle jab. "We'll get our 'internals' sorted out," he said. "But I appreciate your concern."

The figure on the catwalk shrugged. "I'm not terribly concerned, actually. Not after the way you tore through those Dom ships of the line—well done, that—but I do bear orders from the Governor-Emperor himself, via Commodore Jenks, to do whatever may be in my power, regardless of cost, to prevent serious damage to your ingenious, but frankly, somewhat . . . ill-favored ship. I do hope 'ill-favored' is not too provocative?"

Spanky laughed. "Beauty's a matter of perception and

opinion. Your ship don't look too pretty herself right now." A mighty splash erupted off *Walker*'s bow, and the number one gun, now trained out to port, replied at one of the closing enemy ships with a loud *crack* and a long tongue of smoky yellow flame.

"Indeed," agreed the man, unperturbed, "but more enemies approach, and judging by your current inconvenience and the lurid dents in your side, it might be said I've failed my mission in one respect, if not all. Together, we've accomplished our primary task—to disrupt the enemy invasion." The man paused. "I'm honored to have assisted you in that. This was not your battle, and yet you've suffered on our behalf. That will not be forgotten, and thankfully I remain in a position to at least attempt the next most pressing instruction of my sovereign."

"So? What's that?" Spanky yelled.

"To prevent the sinking—or worse, capture—of your ship by the enemy. To that end, *Euripides* and *Tacitus* will protect her with their very bodies, and the bodies of their crews—so please forgive me if I entreat you to 'sort out' your engineering problems as quickly as you possibly can!"

CHAPTER 28

West Eastern Sea

The flotilla of formerly Tagranesi proas skimmed along in a westerly direction with a favorable wind at a much faster clip than *Ajax*'s longboat ever could have managed. The moon was high and cast plenty of light upon the dappled sea to spot any looming leviathans, or mountain fish, that might lie in their path. Silva had the tiller of the "command" proa, enjoying the feel of the water sliding past, and his conversation with Chinakru—through Lawrence—in the stern sheets. "Petey" sat carefully, inconspicuously, perched near him, barely moving and without a peep, as he watched Lawrence and the former "Tagranesi" with profound suspicion. Nearly everyone else aboard, and on the other proas nearby, was asleep, except for their helmsman and a pair of keen lookouts.

Captain Lelaa had calculated, by the moon and stars, and longitudinal observations she'd made at Talaud, that they had just enough food and water to complete their voyage in the swifter vessels—weather permitting. The ex-Tagranesi, soon to be "Sa'aarans"—hopefully—had been excited and friendly to their human and Lemurian guests, but, with the exception of Silva, Sandra, and, to a lesser degree, Abel Cook, the rest of the former castaways kept to themselves. Lawrence was happy to be back among his people, and while his "homecoming" hadn't been what he'd expected, he was warmly welcomed. He was sympathetic to the . . . mild discomfort of his friends, however. When he'd been alone among them, they hardly thought about his resemblance to their mortal foes, but now, surrounded by so many, some seemed reserved, pensive. Even his dear 'Ecky was affected.

Sandra and Silva didn't care at all. They'd used Lawrence shamelessly as a portable translator, to talk to anyone who grabbed their attention. Lawrence's "Tagran" was rusty at first, but soon he was fluent again. Silva was most interested in the surprisingly fast, stable, and forgiving sailing qualities of the proas. Almost sixty feet long and nearly ten feet wide, their hulls were shaped from a single massive tree. The outriggers were big too—sharp, hollow, and relatively airtight. (They were raised from the water once a day or so, by counterbalancing, then drained and replugged.) At some time in the past, their designers had even added a long, submerged keel that reduced their leeway amazingly. Silva pronounced them "neat little boats." He also pestered Chinakru incessantly about how his people killed shiksaks, and how they made war if other groups—usually refugees like themselves, it now seemed—came to call.

Sandra wanted to learn everything about their medical practices, but she'd been particularly interested in talking with the females. No human or Lemurian had ever seen a female Grik. Lawrence's people were clearly just a different race of the same species, and she'd hoped to learn some elemental truths. The Tagranesi "Noble Queen" concept seemed strikingly similar to the "Celestial Mother" of the Grik, but among Lawrence's folk, there were no Hij or Uul. There were just people. The only "lower class" was hatchlings. There were few females in the little fleet, and only half a dozen hatchlings. Chinakru had left "those not ready" on the island, probably to die. It seemed incredibly harsh . . . and yet the few hatchlings among them, too young to begin their "training," acted more like vicious, annoying pets than children. None of the females paid them any heed except to catch them and feed them from time to time. It was shocking and bizarre, but without knowing more, Sandra was at a loss as to how the system might be improved. In the meantime, as the days passed, the former castaways had learned to protect their belongings from pillage—and protect themselves from droppings whenever one of the little vermin leaped across to their boat from another and skylarked in the rigging.

Petey actually helped in that respect. He'd evidently sensed from the start that he was among predators that would eat him if they could, and he stayed very close to the humans, Rebecca in particular. Somehow he must have gathered that she was a cherished and protected member of this new "pack" of his, and he screeched, gobbled, and generally raised hell whenever a hatchling ventured near. He stayed away from Lelaa now too. Life was boring on a boat and once, whatever he used for a mind had decided that her twitching tail might taste good, or at least be fun to catch. He'd barely escaped being hacked apart by her sword. After that, he gave both Lawrence and Lelaa a wide berth. His only concession to the lure of adventure now was to occasionally—carefully—hop or coast after Silva when the big man moved about the boat. He usually indiscriminately screeched one of the few words he knew and glided back to Rebecca if the man came close to someone he feared, but Silva paid no apparent heed to Petey whatsoever.

"Chinakru 'ould like to know 'ore a'out the Grik," Lawrence said.

Silva sighed. He could usually understand Lawrence pretty well, but the lizardy guy still talked like his mouth was full of rocks. A lot of what he said was pronounced almost perfectly, but there were some sounds he still just couldn't do. "Well, tell him," Silva said. "You know as much about 'em as I do. Maybe more."

"He grows . . . exercised. He hates the idea o' the Grik; the things I ha' told . . . I think he wants to kill them."

Silva snorted and dug in his shooting pouch for the last dry yellow tobacco leaves he'd been conserving. He up-ended the little pouch over his mouth, forming the loose leaf fragments into a dry wad. "That's fine. Won't hurt his standing with Saan-Kakja," he said. "Have you explained the kind of war we're fightin'? It's gone way beyond spears an' claws."

"That is the issue that concerns . . . me. He cannot understand, not yet. Still, he desires to assist."

"Hmm."

Petey had seen Dennis put something in his mouth and tentatively squeaked, "Eat?" trying not to draw attention to himself. Silva plucked a leaf fragment from his mouth and tossed it at the little creature. Greedily, Petey snatched it and gulped it down. Almost instantly, he was making *kack, kack* sounds, but Silva ignored him. He looked at the lanterns glowing, swaying at the mastheads of the proas around them. "How many of his folks—your folks—will feel the same?" he wondered aloud.

"A lot," Lawrence said, and Silva caught the concern. He understood it. Lawrence's "new" people didn't have a clue about this war. They were kind of like the Americans that wound up on the western front in the Great War, Silva suspected.

"Well, he needs to talk to Sandra, first off. Maybe Saan-Kakja or whoever's in Manila. Maybe Shinya's still there. Thankfully, I'm just a peon, who don't have to sort things like that out." He paused, looking around again. "Say," he said, focusing on the lanterns. "The swells have laid down." Immediately, he glanced to the south. The sky down there had been dark all day, almost like a Strakka, but he knew it wasn't one. It was the spreading ash cloud of Talaud. Right now, he couldn't see anything, except an absence of stars on the horizon. He reached over, and after a brief consideration of sea monsters, stuck his hand in the sea. There was a strange vibration. "What the devil?" he said. "That's weird. Larry, scamper over there and wake Captain Lelaa. She needs to check this out."

"She just go to slee'," Lawrence said reluctantly.

"Blame me. Tell her I made you wake her up. You'll be amazed what you can get away with when you do that. She can't eat *me*, an' I don't care what rank they scrape off. They'll just make me keep doin' the same stuff anyway. I *will* eat you if you don't get her over here chop-chop!"

"Eat!" Petey chirped happily. Lawrence snarled at him and moved off into the gloom where Lelaa slept. Fairly quickly, he returned with the 'Cat in tow. She seemed alert, but still exhausted.

"What is it, Mr. Silva?" She was glancing at the moon and stars to make sure they were still on course.

"Feel the water." Dennis paused. "Hell. You can *hear* somethin' now. Kinda like a freight train a long way off. And the wind's picking up, but the waves ain't."

Lelaa had never seen a freight train, but the reference wasn't lost on her. She knew it was some kind of land steamer, and she cocked her head, ears questing. Her large, bright eyes widened. "Heavens above!" she gasped. "Wake everyone this instant! Rig lifelines—long ones—on everyone! The proas should float; the wood is naturally buoyant, but many may be swept away!"

Lawrence was translating rapidly to Chinakru, and the ex-Tagranesi raised his voice in alarm, spreading the word from boat to boat. Silva was impressed by how quickly the Lemurian sea captain took unquestioned command, mere moments after being awakened.

"Keep the lanterns lit. Some may survive and we'll be widely scattered. Take in all sail! Out paddles! Steer north . . . for that star!" she instructed.

"Is it a wave?" Sandra asked, drawing near with a sleepy Rebecca in tow.

Lelaa blinked rapidly. "I fear so." She looked at Dennis. "Your primary duty is the protection of these females, is it not?"

"Ah . . . yeah."

"Then get them secured! As I said, use a long line. They may become separated from the boat—or it may overturn. They must remain secured, but not lashed, do you understand?"

"Aye, Cap'n."

Lelaa looked around. The flotilla was disintegrating into confusion. Some were steering north already, but others continued on, seemingly unaware. "Mr. Silva, fire that monstrous gun of yours! Get everyone's attention! Lives are at stake!" She faced forward. "Cap-i-taan Rajendra to the tiller!"

Nodding, Silva snatched up his beloved Doom Whomper and discharged it in the air. The growing, rushing rumble didn't exactly mute it, but it did seem less loud than usual. Chinakru was startled by the shot, but quickly resumed his loud harangue. More boats turned. Silva slung the big musket and pouch tightly around his body, then tied lines around Sandra, Rebecca, and a just-arrived, confused Sister Audry. "Abel," Dennis shouted, hoping the boy heard him, "you and Brassey strap in tight, but with a leader, see? Take a turn around the stoutest thing you can find!"

Finishing with Sandra and Rebecca, Silva interrupted Lelaa's pacing and tied her down as well. She didn't seem to notice. She was staring aft now, into the south. A groggy but almost panicky Rajendra lunged past them to the tiller, yelling for his other surviving Imperials to secure themselves as best they could, and Silva tried to make it to him with yet another line. The stern of the proa began to rise noticeably. A bewildered, terrified Petey cried out and launched himself at Rebecca, who caught him and clutched him close. Dennis couldn't really see the wave; it was black as night, and no discernible crest rode atop it, but the angle of the sea was growing more "wrong" by the moment.

"Damn you, Rajendra," Dennis shouted, flinging the line at the man now struggling mightily with the tiller. "Secure yourself!"

"Damn *you*, Mr. Silva!" Rajendra bellowed back. "Save the princess! We will resume our dispute in hell!" The stern continued its inexorable upward rise and Silva fell roughly atop Sandra and Sister Audry, who lay covering Rebecca with their bodies.

Sister Audry gasped under the weight of the impact. "Have you a line, Mr. Silva?" she demanded weakly as the proa passed thirty degrees—and kept going.

"I'll manage!"

"Then . . . you may cling to me—this once—for the sake of the child! She may need you yet!"

The roar was all-consuming now, and the proa flipped onto its back. After that, there were only the terrified screams.

CHAPTER 29

New Scotland Dueling Ground

"Cease independent fire!" Lieutenant Blair bellowed hoarsely at the top of his lungs. "Load and hold!"

All Dominion reserves had to be present now. The battle, since the despicable opening cannon fire against the Imperial bleachers, had raged for more than three hours, and attrition had taken a terrible toll on both sides. The troops were evenly matched in discipline and roughly so in equipment, but largely due to the Lemurian shields, now practically useless, the exchange had so far been in favor of the Imperials. Another mixed company of Marines had marched to join "Chack's" line, delaying his plan but giving it twice the weight. No such reinforcements seemed available to the Dominion troops. Their infantry still had the advantage in numbers, but by only about two hundred men. That advantage was growing, however, because even as the Doms kept firing, the Imperial line had suddenly ceased. All became quiet there, except for the screams and the sounds of balls striking flesh.

"Battalion," Chack yelled, his voice cracking, "prepare

to charge bayonets!" He was answered by a bloodthirsty roar as nearly four hundred bayonet-tipped muskets were leveled at the enemy.

Seeing this, the fire from the Dominion line immediately slacked, and bloodied troops in now stained and dingy uniforms heard commands from their own officers. Some dumped powder charges on the ground.

"Battalion," Chack roared again, "without cheering, without a sound—*listen for the drums*—charge bayonets!"

The block of Imperials and scattered Lemurians surged forward. Some did cheer, caught up in the moment, but not many. Sword in hand, Lieutenant Blair raced forward, pacing his men, slightly ahead. A flurry of Dominion musket shots staggered the front rank, and Blair himself spun to the ground, but somehow rose and continued on. The gap between the enemies narrowed quickly from an initial seventy yards to sixty, to fifty. Chack trotted behind the troops, surrounded by his own surviving Marines. Blas-Mar was there, bleeding from a neck wound, and Koratin was helping support her, his wild face stained with blood and gunpowder. O'Casey was beside him, a pistol in his hand and a gleam in his eye. When the loud Dom command of "Armen la bayoneta!" came, Chack didn't even need it repeated. *Just a little farther now.*

"Drummers!" he shouted, when less than twenty yards separated the opposing forces, and a thunderous roll sounded around him. The block of infantry ground to a halt, spreading out quickly on the flanks. Ahead, he barely saw beyond the taller men that Blair had stopped, swaying, sword raised high.

"Take aim!" someone screamed. It might have been Blair.

"Fire!" Chack shrieked with everything he had. A single, tremendous, rippling volley slashed directly into the helpless Dominion troops, mowing them down like wave tops scattered by a Strakka wind. "Charge bayonets!" he bellowed again, and this time, the cheer was overwhelming. They slammed into the teetering Dominion troops like a spike-bristling sledgehammer. Out of the corner of Chack's eye, he saw one of his Marines advancing the Stars and Stripes, trilling like a defiant demon. The oddly similar Imperial flag went down, but was immediately snatched up by another man who seemed utterly oblivious to anything other than driving forward, flag held high. Ahead, through the slashing, stabbing bayonets, Chack saw the red banner of the enemy go down. It too rose again, but then went down to stay. A renewed roar swept through the Marines, and they drove forward even more fiercely than before.

They were among the enemy now, even Chack. He realized sickly that this fight had devolved into an "open field melee" such as General Alden had always warned him against—but the American Marine had also told him that any sane enemy would break in the face of a charge like the one they'd delivered. Even the Grik would have broken; he'd seen it before. The Doms were being slaughtered, and they'd recoiled, stunned by the surprise volley and the ferocity of the attack, but they *didn't* break—and now the fighting filled the dueling ground with desperate individual combats, like hundreds of duels themselves. Alone on the field, Chack didn't have a muzzle-loading musket. As always, he carried his trusty Model 1898 (dated 1901) Krag, but with the fighting so close, he was afraid to fire it. He'd foolishly drawn a load-out of precious smokeless, high-velocity, jacketed rounds, seeing himself as standing back and knocking off enemy officers. Silva had always told him that velocity didn't necessarily equal penetration, but he just didn't know if the jacketed bullets changed all that. Better safe than accidentally shooting through an enemy and hitting one of the "good" guys. The heavy musket balls were already doing enough of that, he feared. The '03 bayonet on the end of his rifle worked just fine, however, and it was black with drying blood all the way to the guard and dripping with fresh. Melees like this were a last resort—a failure, Pete had inferred—but at least they'd practiced for them, and the Imperial Marines seemed to know their business too.

Corporal Koratin went down, taking Sergeant Blas-Mar

with him. Chack fought his way to them, but O'Casey beat him there, firing pistols as fast as he could grasp them and pull the triggers. His last one misfired and he threw the whole tangled bundle of pistols into the face of a man while he went for his cutlass. Chack saw Blair dragging himself along the ground. He did shoot a man preparing to bayonet the Imperial in the back. Then the fighting carried him along and he saw Blair no more.

A towering man, evidently an officer, with dark skin and flowing black mustaches loomed before Chack. Even as he brought his bayonet up, the man slashed down with a heavy sword, cutting through the top handguard of the Krag and slicing into the steel of the barrel between the rear sight and the barrel band. The hard steel proved too much for the sword, however, and more than half the blade broke off and stuck into the ground. Chack almost dropped the rifle and his hands stung with the force of the blow, but he brought it back up and drove his bayonet into the man's belly.

"Monos Demonaicos!" The man gasped, and Chack thrust again, higher, riding the weapon down as the man fell. "Mi Dios!" screeched the officer as Chack twisted his rifle and pulled the bayonet clear, "Estoy viniendo!" Blood fountained from the man's mouth.

Something struck Chack's left shoulder, driving him to his knees. It had to be another sword, he thought, belatedly rolling away from the blow. He knew he was cut, maybe badly, and only the tough rhino-pig armor had saved him from being hacked in two. He brought his rifle up and there was nothing on the other side but sky, so he shot the man in the face. A hand grabbed him and jerked him up from the bloody slurry the dueling grounds had become, and to his amazement, he recognized the Bosun.

"What's the matter with you?" Gray demanded, blood pouring from a cut above his eye. "Rootin' around on the ground like a private soljer, when you're s'posed to be in charge o' this mess!" Gray was physically dragging him out of the press.

"Wha—what are you doing here?"

"We finished our little chore. Can't get to the ship—Frankie's on his own—so we decided to help you finish this."

"Where's Cap-i-taan Reddy?"

"With Jenks." He nodded toward the far side of the field. "The whole Imperial Guard, two hundred of 'em, is fixin' to hit the Doms in the ass." He paused. "You done good." Without warning, he flung Chack to the ground. "Have a look at him, Selass. If ten percent o' that blood he's wearin' belongs to him, he's a goner." Selass knelt beside him, covered with blood as well, blinking terrified concern.

"But . . . I'm fine," Chack protested. He gestured at the fighting, still close by. "Blas-Mar, Koratin, all the others . . . they're still in there!"

Gray looked at Stites, who'd replaced his BAR with a Springfield and bayonet. "Relax," he said, "we'll fish 'em out. God knows why, but the Skipper wants *live* 'Cat heroes out o' this fight, not dead ones. You stay put!" His gaze swept across the other Lemurian wounded who'd crawled or been dragged from the fighting. "You fellas keep him here, got that?" With only a muttered "Gettin' too old for this," Gray opened his bolt and checked his magazine before he and Stites plunged back into the fighting.

The Imperial Guard finished it. There were barely two hundred living enemies, almost all exhausted and wounded, when the Guard fell on them from behind. Some fought to the very last, and others even slew themselves, but in the end, nearly forty were taken prisoner despite their beliefs. Those that could walk were quickly rounded up and herded to a livestock pen near the harbor where they could be confined under guard. Forty survivors out of nearly a thousand that began the fight. Of the four hundred who'd made the charge with Chack, a hundred were dead and another hundred were badly wounded.

"They fight just like Japs," Matt muttered. He was limping slightly from a superficial bayonet wound he'd taken in the calf, inflicted by a man he'd thought was dead.

"Are your 'Japs' truly so fanatical?" Jenks asked. Through it all, he'd somehow managed to avoid any injuries beyond a few small cuts and splinter wounds.

"They don't surrender very often," Matt confirmed. "At least where we came from." The memory of a Japanese sailor standing on an overturned boat, surrounded by voracious fish, preferring a terrible death to captivity, suddenly sprang to mind.

"Well, we've finished them here. All that remains is the result of the sea battle off the harbor mouth." He grimaced, knowing Matt was keenly concerned about his ship. "Now that surprise is lost, the enemy can't hope to enter the harbor, but they will still fight to damage as many of our ships as they can. They retain an advantage in numbers, if not quality, and that is their only chance to seize any semblance of victory. There will be war between the Empire and the Dominion; there already is. Thanks in large part to you and your people, it will now be a protracted war instead of a one-day affair. Come, let us hurry to Government House. The Governor-Emperor has had himself moved to the observatory so he can view the battle."

"You think he'll make it?" Matt asked quietly.

"God willing. He will almost certainly lose one leg. The other is in doubt. He'd already be dead if Andrew hadn't thrown himself across him."

"Let Selass have a look at him," Matt suggested.

Jenks nodded. "I will recommend it."

"How's Andrew?"

"Failing quickly, I fear. I've sent for Sean to be taken to his brother's side . . . if he himself survived."

Matt limped quietly alongside Jenks, who deliberately kept his pace slower than he obviously would have preferred.

"At least your wife's safe," Matt ventured. He looked at Jenks's face and saw the tears well up in his eyes.

"Aye. There's that."

* * *

There was chaos at Government House. A large number of Marines—that Matt thought might have been better employed elsewhere, earlier—stood guard, facing outward from the residence with bayonets fixed, but Jenks led Matt through them without being stopped. Messengers came and went, and officers, some bloodied by riots or even assassination attempts, milled about on the columned porches. Tired horses, tied to the columns themselves, leaned against one another with foamy sweat running from beneath their saddle blankets. Some of the officers wore naval uniforms, and Matt wondered how many were in the same "boat" he was. When the bulk of the Imperial Fleet at Scapa Flow steamed out to meet their attackers, most of the ships were commanded by junior officers. Even if he could sympathize a little, he felt a growing annoyance to see so much brass not doing anything.

Jenks paused in his flight up the stairs to the porch only long enough to greet an older man in a cocked hat and a soiled but richly decorated coat. "Lord High Admiral McClain," he said, saluting. "I must see the Governor-Emperor."

The man nodded. "He's expecting you," he said gravely, gesturing toward the observatory with his nose. "Aloft." He looked at Matt. "Both of you." He paused, but clearly wasn't finished. "My compliments, Captain Reddy," he continued. "We've not met officially, but His Majesty speaks highly of you. I was impressed by your swordsmanship—as well as your cunning. Particularly the latter. I find myself lending more credence to some of the wild tales I've heard—which forces me to reevaluate a few opinions I'd formed concerning your entire account of the situation in the west." He waved a blood-spattered kerchief he'd been holding against a cut on his cheek. "Dreadful times lie ahead, I fear. The commodore has long been a proponent of aggressive exploration, at least in the seas of this hemisphere." He sighed. "I have opposed that in the interests of security through isolation . . . but we aren't really isolated here at all, are we? Not anymore. We . . . thought the Dominion was our only real threat, and that they might serve as a buffer for what might lie beyond, but even if they're now our most pressing threat, they're not alone, are they?"

"No, sir," Matt said quietly. "And they aren't even the closest. Reed proved that."

"But apparently he *is* their creature. One must now contemplate how much of this Company subversion over the last decade might be laid at his feet, and how much sway over other Company officials he might still exert."

"Reed *was* their 'creature,'" Matt said stonily. "He was ready to hand your Empire to the Dominion on a silver plate . . . but I wouldn't worry about him anymore, if I were you. I *would* strongly recommend you round up as many of his cronies as you can, though. Even if most didn't know what he was really up to, a lot had to know it was treason of some sort or other."

"Indeed. And we shall 'round them up,' as you put it. You and Jenks are to be commended for your perspicacity in uncovering this evil plot." The admiral's expression turned sour. "I only wish I'd been made privy to the particulars in advance."

"There *were* no particulars, sir," said Jenks. "Only suspicions, and we had little enough to base them on." Jenks's voice became harder, more formal. "Not nearly enough to convince even you, beforehand, sir."

Admiral McClain nodded. "I suppose I deserve that," he said sadly. "I hope you'll accept my assurance that you speak to the converted now, Commodore."

"I sincerely hope so, sir. Now, if you'll excuse me?"

"Of course."

"Who was that?" Matt asked as they entered Government House and made their way through the bustle to the stairs.

"Lord High Admiral James Silas McClain the Third," Jenks replied neutrally. "He's the titular governor of New Scotland and commands Home Fleet—a large percentage of which is now fighting the greatest sea battle of the age without him."

"Huh."

They ascended the staircase that ran back and forth through the Imperial living quarters, until they reached a relatively small, oval room atop the residence. It was hot in the confined space, and crowded with officers delivering reports and departing with instructions. Several grim-faced surgeons toiled over the Governor-Emperor's legs, casting furtive glances at the newcomers and one another.

"Prop me up, damn ye all," the Governor-Emperor roared. "I can't bloody see! If I must lie here among you pack of carrion-eaters, at least let me view the battle!"

The man's pale, almost painfully thin wife gently propped him up with a pillow so he could reach the eyepiece of his telescope again. Matt had seen the woman a few times before, but never like this. He remembered that Princess Rebecca often said that Sandra reminded her of her mother, but Matt hadn't caught any real resemblance beyond hair color. Now he saw it: the way she glared at others in the room, the determined way she swept at errant strands of hair that strayed from her more abundant coif. Before, she'd seemed a broken woman, clinging desperately to the faint hope he'd brought her. Now, even as that hope had faded, she'd risen to protect the last thing in the world she appeared to care about: her injured husband. For an instant, a red-hot knife twisted in Matt's guts as he finally allowed himself to contemplate the probability that Sandra was indeed lost to him. His crew had been practically coddling him in that respect for some time now, he knew, but he'd continued to insist to himself that hope remained. He couldn't do that anymore, he realized. He had to let it go. At least for now, he had to put his own grief aside, as this woman had done, and focus on those things he could still save.

Somewhere out there, beyond the general fleet action that the Governor-Emperor watched even now, his ship might be fighting for her life. There was nothing he could do about that either, and his sense of helplessness was profound. There was *something* he could do, though, and if it might do little to help those he cared about here, it might make all the difference for those "back home."

"Ah, listen up," he said loudly. The tumult in the room and on the stairs behind him froze into a kind of shocked silence. Even Jenks was taken aback by the outburst in this setting. "I'm new here, but some things are the same wherever you go, and I know a chicken with its head cut off when I see it."

"Now see here!" the Governor-Emperor roared. "I may be wounded, but I'm no chicken!"

"It's a figure of speech, Your Majesty," Matt said quickly. "I know you're not, but this is the biggest wild-turkey chase I've seen since the Japs bombed Cavite! The events of the day have come as a hell of a shock, even to those of us who suspected *something* was up, but right now the vast majority of your people are still in shock, and still running around like a bunch of headless chickens! There're things that need to be happening, and you've got senior officers milling around on the porch who don't have a clue what to do. I know you're confused. Everyone is. You've never had an attack here, like this, before." Matt took a breath. "My people, on the world we came from, experienced a similar sneak attack not too long ago, and they didn't react much different. We've been surprised a few times in our war here too, against the Grik, but we've learned a few things!"

"What should we be doing now, that we aren't already?" Jenks asked seriously.

Matt took off his helmet and wiped his brow with his sleeve. "You really want to know?"

"Of course!" insisted the Governor-Emperor.

"Okay. You might even be doing some of this already, but if you are, I can't tell." He sighed. "First, you have to signal other ports—Glasgow, Edinburgh, whatever—and warn them to expect attacks as well. Maybe send out some scouts."

"That we have done," Jenks stated. "We have a network

of semaphore towers across the island, and I directed that warnings be sent immediately, as soon as I first arrived here."

"Good. Has everybody replied?" Matt waited in the following silence. "If not, you must assume there have been attacks there already, or the network's been cut. You need to get warnings to the other Home Islands as well. Next, round up all the Company officials and Dominion representatives. I already suggested that to your Admiral McClain."

"I ordered the arrest of Dominion representatives, but detaining Company administrators is . . . problematic," said the Governor-Emperor.

"Why?"

"Many sit on the Courts of Governors and Proprietors. They are part of the government."

"So? Look, Your Majesty, you're at *war*. A lot of people have died. They're still dying! Civilians, sir!" He pointed at the sea. "And out there! Damn it, *my* people on *my* ship, may be dying for *your* country! Too many of my Marines have already died! Don't . . . lie there and tell me you won't . . . inconvenience a few shady politicians! You can sort the good guys from the bad guys later, but right now you have to catch everybody who might have had a part in this before they get a chance to scram." Matt looked around the room and shook his head. "Our plane, our . . . flying machine . . . must have gone down, otherwise it would have returned here to make a direct observation report. We don't know what's going on beyond your 'scope, so you need to get lookouts to all high elevations, here and anywhere you can communicate with, to watch for other landings."

"Do you believe there will be more?"

"I don't know. I would've made 'em everywhere I could at once, if it was me, but from what we're learning about their plan, they may not have thought it necessary. Regardless, all those troops at the dueling ground and all those ships out there came from *somewhere*. It had to be someplace close enough for them to reach with that dispatch ship that left last week."

"Good God, he's right!" the Governor-Emperor said. "They must have been preparing nearby! Commodore, you must divine the location of the enemy base of preparation!"

"I'll do my best, sir."

"Finally," Matt continued, "you need to get all those officers off the porch. Put 'em to work or send them away, but your people don't need to see a bunch of their leaders sitting around, goofing off after an attack like the one today, and with a naval battle still raging just offshore. Act like you've got everything under control and you know what you're doing even if you don't have any idea."

Those remaining in the room were quiet for a moment. Thoughtful.

"Is there anything else, Captain Reddy?" asked the Governor-Emperor's wife. Her tone said that he'd just voiced much of what had been on her own mind.

"Yes, ma'am. With all due respect, I'd get these learned witch doctors and their probes, saws, and nasty hands the hell out of here—and find Lieutenant Selass-Fris-Ar, if you want His Majesty to ever walk again."

"A savage beast in here, tending His Majesty?" gasped one of the "witch doctors" in question.

"Not a savage beast, you fool!" Jenks stated harshly. "The only daughter of a respected figure in their Alliance—an alliance that has done no less than save our very Empire this day! What is presently more pertinent, she is also a practiced surgeon whom you'd do well to observe!" He looked at the woman kneeling beside his leader. "With your permission?"

Ruth McDonald hesitated only an instant before vigorously, tearfully, nodding her head.

"Please," she said.

The Naval Battle of Scapa Flow lasted for the remainder of the afternoon and into the night as it degenerated into a seaborne version of the melee at the dueling ground. With the wind veering around and driving briskly out of the northeast, there was almost no sound other than a general rolling thunder that added to the impression that they were watching an intensely localized storm at sea. Lightning stabbed horizontally between vague, darkened shapes, and once there was a large, searing flash that signified the abrupt death of *somebody's* ship and its entire crew. There was no way to tell whose it was. Several other ships burned like terrible beacons in the night until either they sank or their crews managed to extinguish the fires. It became impossible to discern how the battle fared. Matt never had been able to see *Walker*, and the bulk of the fighting appeared closer than she'd last been reported. Occasionally he saw ripples of gunfire much farther out to sea and hoped that meant she was still in the fight.

Matt and Harvey Jenks were both in a kind of hell, and paced back and forth between taking turns at the telescope to describe the action as best they could while an exhausted and harried Selass labored to save the Governor-Emperor's legs. Gerald McDonald experienced almost miraculous relief when she applied the polta paste to his wounds, but his right leg in particular was badly damaged. She did what she could, but brusquely informed them that she might have to take it off in a few days, regardless. She couldn't hide her resentment at being summoned from caring for the wounded at the dueling ground just to tend one man, no matter how important, and likely only his importance saved the House surgeons from injury several times when they made condescending remarks. Ultimately, exasperated by their unwillingness to credit any technique but their own, the Governor-Emperor himself sent the men away to ponder their futures.

Sean O'Casey (Bates) arrived near midnight and knelt beside the Governor-Emperor's bed. Andrew Bates was gone. It was a tearful moment for many reasons, but the two old friends and playmates were reunited at last, and Matt got the distinct impression that Andrew's position wouldn't be vacant for long. He was glad, and hoped he was right. He'd finally figured out that Andrew was essentially Gerald McDonald's "chief of staff" and the Governor-Emperor would need a good one in the times to come. Sean's unique perspective would be invaluable.

Eventually Sean left, escorting Selass back to her other wounded. She'd done all she could, and now only time would tell. Despite his desire to see the battle end, Gerald drifted off to sleep in the early hours of the morning—an almost incontestable by-product of such a liberal dose of the curative paste—and Matt, Jenks, and an intermittently dozing Ruth McDonald were left alone to answer questions and pass instructions on behalf of the Governor-Emperor. Matt considered it almost surreal that he'd wound up in such a position, and Jenks probably felt the same way, yet it made sense too. The chaos of the previous afternoon was under control, and reports were returning from around the Home Islands. Not all the news was good, but things were being done.

By then, the sea battle had completely broken apart into widely separated duels between individual ships. Jenks was at a loss to explain the lack of any reports or dispatches from the fighting, but hoped it was a sign that the Imperial Fleet had managed to cut off any enemy retreat. It stood to reason, since the battle had lasted so long, so close to the island, with invasion now out of the question. If that was the case, the enemy would have been caught between the fleet and the crushing harbor defenses—but also in the path of any vessel bearing word.

Roughly two hours before dawn, Fitzhugh Gray was quietly escorted into the room by a Marine and a dark-skinned, matronly woman bearing a lamp. The woman gazed sternly at Matt and Jenks and checked on the sleeping Ruth. Clucking, she draped a light shawl across Ruth's shoulders and eased into a chair behind her. Gray slumped exhaustedly into another chair, earning a disapproving glare of his own. He glared back, and then shrugged.

"Hell of a day," he whispered gruffly.

"Yeah. Day and night," Matt replied. "You okay?"

"Sure. A couple scratches. I should'a paid more attention to that jumped-up leatherneck Alden when he was passin' out bayonet lessons."

"Sorry I haven't been down to see the fellas," Matt said.

Gray waved it away. "You been busy, Skipper. Ever'body knows where you are, and what you been doin'." He looked at Jenks. "A full-blown, man-sized war is a hell of a thing, ain't it?"

It was a jab that went back a long way, but Jenks wasn't offended. He'd now seen this kind of war himself before. "Yes, Mr. Gray. Yes, it is. Murdering noncombatants has never been our way, but like yours, it seems my people have now had a dose of a kind of war in which there *are* no noncombatants."

There just weren't any words after that, and they sat in silence for a while, staring out to sea through the opening for the telescope. The firing tapered off until it had all but stopped, but something suddenly flickered in the far distance, in the southwest, and Matt stood. "That looked like a flare!" he said.

"Yes," said Jenks. "Or a rocket. A distress rocket, I fear." He paused. "We both use them, you know."

Another distant flash lit the night. A green one.

"That *was* a rocket!" Matt said excitedly. "One of ours! It's a 'here I am'!"

Two more green rockets soared into the night, even more distant, followed by gun flashes.

"What the . . . ?"

"Skipper! It's *our* guys! *Achilles* and *Simms*!" Gray insisted. "Has to be! I bet they were in communication with *Walker* and saw something. She sent up her 'here I am' and said 'if it ain't me you see, hammer it'!"

The Governor-Emperor's eyes fluttered. "What is it?" he asked, dry-mouthed, smacking his lips. "What did I miss?"

CHAPTER 30

Scapa Flow

Dawn broke on a dreadful scene in the harbor of Scapa Flow. A pair of splintered Imperial "battlewagons" limped in first and tied up at the main Navy dock, barely able to remain afloat. Both were dismasted, and their pumps sent bloody water gushing down their sides from the scuppers. Steam and smoke filled the air, their guns' muzzles were gray with dry fouling, and the wood around their ports was spattered black. Wounded and dead were carried ashore while the crews and mostly female yard workers labored to get ahead of the leaks. There were a few wailing women and some of the "usual" scenes, but many women, like their Lemurian counterparts, merely rolled up their sleeves and set to with a will. They carried moaning bodies and hacked at tattered cordage, cleared lanes through splintered timbers and corpses for canvas hoses and bucket brigades, and helped rescue men trapped beneath wreckage. They worked without being told and took instructions without complaint.

"They act almost like free women," Gray growled. He, Matt, and Jenks had finally received word, signaled by the forts, of the "victory," and they'd rushed to the docks along with High Admiral McClain and his staff to catch the first reports. Admiral McClain looked at Gray strangely, but Jenks nodded.

"Yes, well, as I've said, things are different here on New Scotland. Those are *their* ships, *their* men."

"You could probably get every woman in the Empire to act that way if it was 'their' country," Matt said.

Jenks looked appraisingly at the admiral. "I expect you're right, Captain Reddy. Who knows what changes this war may bring?"

Chack and Sergeant Blas-Mar met them there in their bloodstained armor. Chack still wore his dented steel helmet and Blas-Mar's bronze version had a new, deep, lead-smeared dent of its own. The ball that did it probably knocked her silly, but except for a stained bandage on her neck, she seemed unhurt. Stites emerged from the growing crowd, two rifles slung. He handed one to Chack. "I found your old Krag," he said. "Be sure and get all that blood off the metal. Bring it to me . . ." He paused. "Later, and I'll patch that gash in the hand guard. The nick in the barrel won't hurt nothin'."

"You come from the hospital?" Gray asked. A church near the dueling ground had been turned over to Selass for the Lemurian wounded, but the Governor-Emperor had decreed that she be given access to *any* hospital and that any suggestions she might make were to be considered Imperial edicts.

"Yah," Stites said, shifting a wad of yellowish leaves in his mouth. "We ain't lost nobody else. Corporal Koratin's bad, but 'Doc'selass' says he'll likely make it." He looked at Matt. "She had to take Juan's leg off."

"I know." Matt stared at the harbor mouth. Other ships were beginning to come in. "Doc'selass?" he asked at last. Stites had pronounced it "Doxy-lass."

"Yeah, well, she earned it. And I don't mean it the way you might think. That Bradford said it comes from a Greek word for knowing stuff and teaching—which I guess a regular doxy does too. . . . Anyway, she's been teaching them Brit doctors up a storm."

"Where *is* Bradford?"

Stites shrugged. "Old Silva'd say he's been 'sankoing' around, but that ain't quite true. He was at the hospital most of the night, tryin' to help out. Even talked Spanish to some of the Dom wounded the 'corps 'Cats' was patchin' up—guy speaks more languages than a Chinese tailor—but he jumped up and went to see the Emperor about the time I left. Said he was a 'pleni-potency' or somethin', not a doctor, and he had his own job to do."

"Oh, Lord," Matt said, and contemplated that off and on over the next several hours while they watched the Imperial Fleet—what was left of it—return to port. It was true, though, he finally decided. It was time for Bradford to go to work. Right then, Matt had other concerns. Every Imperial ship was damaged to some degree. It had been a hell of a fight. A lot of the "liners" had serious damage to their paddle wheels despite the heavy wooden boxes that encased them, and Matt felt at least a little vindicated regarding his insistence on screw propellers for the Allied fleet. A couple of Imperial ships with sound propulsion had badly battered Dominion warships in tow, with the Imperial banner streaming above the red ensign of the enemy, but apparently, not many Dom ships had surrendered. Matt still didn't know if that meant they'd escaped or been destroyed. As time went by, however, with no sign of *Walker*, the scene in Scapa Flow; all the drama, horror, relief, and even the dawning jubilation of victory, faded to insignificance as the fiery fist of anxiety for his ship continued to tighten its grip on his heart.

"My God!" Jenks exclaimed, staring through his telescope. He looked at Matt and handed the instrument over without a word.

Just becoming visible beyond the gaggle of limping Imperials, USS *Walker* steamed into view. Matt had never seen his ship return from a desperate battle; he'd always been aboard her. But now he knew how his people—and he unconsciously included the Lemurians in that category—must have felt every time he brought her in. She looked like a floating wreck. Several gaping holes were visible in her starboard side, surrounded by dozens of deep dents that ran her entire visible length, and she had a slight list to port. Water gushed over the side, and even a couple of auxiliary pumps were running, the hoses pulsing with pressure and adding to the torrent returning to the sea. The splinter shield on the number one gun was knocked askew, and the starboard bridgewing rail stood naked where the side plating had been battered in. The searchlight above her fire control platform was completely gone, leaving only the tangled rail and twisted conduits.

Matt absorbed the initial impact of what he saw, then began to observe details. At least two boilers were operational, judging by the smoke curling from her dented and shot-pierced funnels. There were no bodies strewn on her deck and "apes" were hosing blood and other debris from her fo'c'sle. Much of the junk included shattered wood and charred canvas that had to have come from other ships. The battle flag still stood out, straight and proud near the top of her foremast, and all the smoke-stained guns were trained fore and aft. In addition, the old girl's heart was still as strong as ever, because the only reason she seemed to strain at all was because of the two savagely mauled Imperial frigates she was towing in her wake.

Jenks must have mistaken the expression on Matt's face when he lowered the glass and unconsciously handed it to Gray. "I'm so sorry," he said.

Gray looked away from the glass he'd raised and glared at Jenks, eyes red. "What the hell for?" he demanded savagely. "She ain't sinkin'. Sure, she's taken a few dents an' a little smut, but I seen her look worse the mornin' after a hard liberty! She went toe to toe with *Amagi*! You seen *her* sunk-ass carcass at Baalkpan. You really think them pipsqueak battleships the goddamn *Doms* think are so hot are even close to a match for our ol' *Walker*?" He slammed the telescope back in Jenks's hand and stormed off, swearing, toward the dock *Walker* had steamed away from the morning before.

"Quite an excitable fellow," Admiral McClain observed awkwardly.

"Indeed," Jenks replied, "but right, more often than not." He gestured beyond *Walker* and his own voice gained excitement. "And look there, Captain Reddy! I do believe I see the source of the other green rockets we saw!"

Appearing somewhat incongruous among all the war-ravaged ships returning to port, *Achilles* was just passing beneath the guns at the harbor mouth. Beside her steamed what could only be USS *Simms*. Both looked sharp and fresh despite their long voyage, and the contrast between them and the battered prizes trailing behind could not have been more profound. Two relatively unmarked Dominion transports were towing a pair of ravaged liners and the Stars and Stripes and the Imperial banner floated proudly above them all.

"Now that's what I call a stylish entrance," Matt said.

CHAPTER 31

Ceylon

N'galsh, First Hij of Ceylon and Vice Regent of all India, personally awaited the longboat from *Giorsh* at the "Hunter's Ramp" in the still strangely unpronounceable harbor at Colombo. (N'galsh, like Tsalka, was endeavoring to change the name.) N'galsh's presence at the dock, even with his army of attendants, was unprecedented and demeaning, since this "General Halik" wasn't born "of the Hij." Halik was reputed to have "talent," however, and that's what they needed. N'galsh would sacrifice a few prerogatives, at least for now, and bend to the shifting imperatives within the realm of the Grik. His own personal concern regarding the cause behind those imperatives made it easier to choke down. Typically, a regent—or in his absence, a vice regent—was subordinate only to the Celestial Mother herself, but he'd been given clearly to understand that he would follow the directions or commands of the two generals in the longboat without question. The world had been gutted, turned upside down, inside out; its entrails exposed where they should be concealed. Personally meeting the longboat was a minor concession in the grand scheme of things and literally the least he could do under the circumstances. It might also be essential in the sense that, had he not come, it might have been the *last* thing he *didn't* do. The way things were going, he just didn't know, and he didn't care to discover mistakes the hard way.

"In the name of the Mother, I greet you, General Halik . . ." He paused. "General Niwa," he added. N'galsh loathed the "Jaaph" hunters, the "Hunters previously of the Iron Ship." In his view, they were responsible for much of the vile change sweeping the Grik world. He didn't know Niwa's status, however, and suspected it would be easier to later retreat from excessive civility than to repair a slight.

Halik jerked a nod and Niwa saluted. "Vice Regent N'galsh," Halik said. "Regent Tsalka and General Esshk extend greetings and blessings as well." His eyes narrowed. "You will extend the same courtesy to General Niwa that you do to me."

Good. N'galsh sighed. He'd guessed correctly. "Of course. Thank the Mother you both arrived safely. The prey—the 'enemy,' rather—has an ever-tightening grip on the sea approaches. Honestly, I'm shocked you were not intercepted. Nothing gets through."

"We *were* intercepted," Halik said bitterly. "A single of their ships, little different from ours, flying the 'A'ery-can' flag, destroyed our entire escort. Only its sacrifice allowed our arrival here."

"Indeed? Then please accept my most profound congratulations. The enemy demonstrates a fascinatingly effective grasp of the Sea Hunt, at least. Their ships are well found, even those they took from us, and they are artists when it comes to this 'gunnery.'"

"General Esshk says the same. That is one thing we hope to improve before we depart."

N'galsh's jaw fell slack. "Depart?" he asked weakly.

"As we have been commanded," Halik replied.

"But . . . surely you will defeat the enemy first?"

"If we can," Halik conceded. "But General Esshk is not

hopeful. We will do what is possible—test new weapons, learn the ways of the enemy and bleed them with attacks when and where we can support them. We have new programs, new 'trainings' underway to make hunters that contest rather than conquer, but as you point out, even if those 'troops' were ready now, we could not get them here as long as the enemy controls the sea." He took a breath. "We will do what we may, but we must be prepared in the event that the enemy succeeds in his campaign against this place."

"Succeeds?" N'galsh murmured, suddenly distraught. "But the Celestial Mother *cannot* spare this land! It is the most precious of her eggs!"

"She *can* spare it . . . and she will, if necessary. Ceylon is precious, but not nearly as much so as other eggs and the sacred Ancestral Lands that lie closer to the nest. Certainly you understand that?"

"Of course, but . . . how can they be at risk while this one remains?"

"As long as the enemy controls the sea, no 'egg' is safe," Niwa said, and Halik translated. "That will . . . not always be the case. Other programs are underway that will eliminate that control in time, but time is the essential element."

"So . . . you have not come to save this land, but only to trade it for 'time' to save others?" N'galsh questioned, bitterness creeping into his voice.

"Essentially, yes," Halik confirmed. "But fear not, Vice Regent, that same 'time' we hope to win here will ultimately allow our reconquest of this 'egg,' as well as those of the enemy." He looked behind him, confirming that his and Niwa's staff had all arrived ashore. It was composed of other . . . unusual Grik. They had a sizable personal guard of "elite" warriors as well. It would be interesting to see how they performed. "Now, if you please, do show us the tools at our disposal, the tools with which we might shape that time we need."

"Of course," N'galsh said hesitantly. "I have arranged for you to review a gathering of the warriors here."

"Thank you," Halik said, "but there is no need for that. I

know precisely what I will see—a mob of wild hatchlings, for the most part. General Niwa and I require interviews with . . . others such as myself." Halik coughed ironically. "Hunters 'past their prime,' who have faced the enemy, in particular. I also want those who have been defeated, but were not 'made prey.'" He looked ominously at N'galsh. "Unless they have been destroyed?"

"No, no, General Halik! General Esshk left strict instructions regarding that, before he and Regent Tsalka went to meet with the Celestial Mother!" He paused. "Despite the . . . irregularity . . . of that meeting, I obeyed!"

"Good. Additionally, General Niwa and I require transportation to various points on the land. Have those we wish to meet assemble in those places. Our staff will supply a list of locations."

"Of course," N'galsh replied. He hesitated. "Forgive me . . . Generals . . . this is all quite new, and I confess some confusion. I pray you will suffer my presence on your travels? Perhaps I may attend your councils? There is much I have to learn; much I crave to know."

"You are most welcome," Halik said. Suddenly it was his turn to display self-conscious confusion. "Perhaps," he began, paused, then continued. "We are all 'new' to this, with the exception of General Niwa, and this situation is beyond even his experience. Personally, I crave an answer to an extremely profound question, and you may be the only one with an answer of any sort."

"Why . . . surely I will answer, if I can," N'galsh said, surprised.

"Why are we even here?" Halik asked. "More specifically, why is the enemy *not* here already?"

N'galsh sighed with relief. He didn't know the answer, but he did have a guess. "A most interesting question," he temporized. "After the hideous, wrongful defeat at their 'Baalkpan,' we abandoned Aryaal, lost Singapore, and there is every indication that the enemy has conquered Rangoon as well. All that happened in rapid succession—yet they have stopped short of attacking us here. I confess complete mystification. I do not complain," he hastened to add, "but . . . I think perhaps . . . their mouth is full. They must chew before they take their next bite?"

Halik looked at N'galsh with new respect. "I think you are right, Vice Regent." He glanced at Niwa, who was nodding thoughtfully. "They have suffered no reverse—that we know of—yet they pause. As so recently . . . elevated . . . I am sometimes painfully reminded that fatigue and hurts often do not show, but they can shorten the reach of one's sword." He grunted. "And of course, a hunter—a warrior—must eat. It may be that their sword has reached its most extreme reach—for now. Perhaps they gather their strength for the next mighty blow. Possibly they await the arrival of a new, sharper sword. Regardless, their delay has already given us *some* time that may be crucial." He hissed a chuckle. "It has given *us* the crucial time to arrive here, General Niwa, if nothing else!"

"True, General Halik," Niwa replied in the English Halik now more perfectly understood. They'd had a long voyage to get to "know" one another and strangely, something resembling friendship, a form of "warrior bond," had evolved between them. Neither was exactly "of" even his own people anymore, and despite their vast dissimilarities, they had much in common. "But without reconnaissance," he continued, "we can't know what 'new' swords they may have been given. I can *imagine* a few, and we can try to prepare for some of those possibilities, but you must understand that other than the war in the Philippines on our old world, my people had rarely faced American tactics before, and those were strictly defensive. 'General of the Sea' Kurokawa has a low opinion of their discipline and capabilities, but I do not. When we were intercepting their un-encrypted messages, we learned that their 'ground' commander is a Marine named Alden." Niwa shook his head. "I have never faced this 'Alden' before, but he is clearly talented—and a Marine."

"What is a 'Marine'?" N'galsh asked after Halik translated.

"Marines were some of the finest warriors our old enemy possessed. No doubt this Alden has taught their methods to many of our new ones." He looked at Halik. "American Marines are notorious for their ferocity and oddly, considering their high level of discipline, their initiative. Initiative is not encouraged among Japanese troops, and has been virtually unknown among the Grik. I suspect that when the enemy does come, it will be amid a firestorm like we have never seen."

CHAPTER 32

Fil-pin Sea

Dennis Silva was scratching his name on the rough-hewn wood of the boat with a small knife he'd always kept in the shooting pouch he'd managed to save. He'd already carved abbreviations of the names of all the other Allied "survivors" of the monstrous wave: Princess "Becky," "Lt. Tucker," "Lelaa," "Cook," "Brassy," "Sis Audry," "Larry." For some reason, he'd even added "Petey" before adding "D. Silva." He thought it was important, if the boats they'd gathered and lashed together were ever found, that folks would know they'd made it this far. Otherwise, nobody would ever know what happened to them. He considered carving Rajendra's name, but didn't know how to spell it, and didn't have the energy. He couldn't remember the carpenter's or engineer's names. *Dumb-ass*, he thought of Rajendra. *Silly, useless dunce finally rears up on his hind legs like a man—when it didn't make a difference anymore. Hanging on to the tiller might've seemed like a brave stunt at the time, but the boat was going over no matter what.* Silva shook his head. *The rest of the Imperials probably never even woke up—*

never knew what hit them. Whether they did or not, they didn't tie themselves in. Buncha dopes. Or were they? A quick drownin' might've been better than this slow, desiccatin' to death.

No. Scratchin' names on a boat is one thing—never hurts to cover all the bases—but just givin' up and dyin' is for pansies. One way or another, somethin's going to have to kill *Dennis Silva!* He finished his wood work and put the knife back in his pouch. They'd collected and lashed together eleven proas that would float, but all had lost their masts and there wasn't an intact sail left among them. There'd been no sign of the rest of their little "fleet" and all the food, and virtually all the water had been lost or spoiled. Over a hundred of Lawrence's people survived the wave, but they'd begun dying almost immediately. The creatures could handle the sun and heat extremely well, but only if they had plenty of water. Now, most of the survivors were bundled beneath scraps of the rough Tagranesi sailcloth, seeking protection from the sun. Looking around at the mounds of gray "canvas," Dennis saw little sign of life, and he began to imagine he was the last one alive. The proas themselves looked more like a logjam than anything else he could imagine, bobbing and undulating with the swells beneath the merciless sun, inexorably coasting northward with the current. They might wash up on Japan someday, he thought, but they'd be long dead before then.

He caught sight of a blurry figure on the far side of the "logjam." That was about as far as he could see with any clarity anymore. Squinting, he recognized Chinakru. The lizard leader had posted himself there as a lookout, much as Silva had done on this side. Silva was strangely encouraged that the old guy still had the juice to do it, even if there was little point. Maybe, like Silva, he just didn't have it in him to give up while there was any life left in him at all. He felt light-headed, and his tongue was swollen so tightly in his mouth that he doubted he could speak, but he nodded solemnly, respectfully, at the old lizard. Chinakru nodded back.

The boat shuddered slightly and Sandra moved slowly, painfully, out from under the modest shelter they'd rigged. Seeing Dennis, she crawled in his direction, clumsily seating herself beside him.

"Three days," she managed to say thickly. Her lips were cracked and her eyes looked dull.

"Yeph," Silva replied, surprised that he could talk—and by how bad his voice sounded. He wished Sandra hadn't come out. She looked terrible, and seeing her only reminded him how badly he'd failed to protect her and the others.

"S'vivors won't 'ast much 'onger now," Sandra gasped.

"I know."

The canvas moved again, and Lelaa crawled out to join them, panting. She didn't look as bad as Sandra, but only because of her fur. If anything, she'd probably suffered worse. 'Cats generally needed even more water than humans did.

"Wat's dat sound?" Lelaa asked, after several tries.

"What sound?" Dennis croaked. All he could hear was a constant, ringing "*reeeee*" in his ears.

"Dat . . . rumble, bubble sound." Lelaa put her ear to the damp hull of the boat and listened again. "Der it is," she almost crooned. "Louder now. I hear it asleep, and it waked . . . woke me up. It's real."

"So? It's prob'ly a mountain fish down there, fartin'. I bet somethin' that big could fart for an hour."

Sandra shushed him. "No, I hear it too." She looked around them at the sea and saw a large, low, fuzzy shape, creeping toward them from the south. "My God!" she practically shouted, and fell down in the boat. Chinakru was yelling something and the mounds of canvas began to stir.

"It *is* a mountain fish!" Silva hissed, groping for the Doom Whomper. "A baby one!" He tried to raise his massive weapon, but it was just too heavy. "Hel . . . Help me with this thing, Cap'n Lelaa!" he almost roared.

"No!" she said, wonder creeping into her voice. "That's no mountain fish!" she declared, surprisingly clear.

"Well, whatever the hell it is, gimme a—" Silva stopped, staring at the closing apparition. "Uh . . . Is that . . . ?"

"Ess nineteen!" Lelaa confirmed with utter certainty, helping Sandra back up. She worked her mouth and tried to lick her dry lips. "Though maybe only your God knows what she's doing here . . . and how she managed it!" The excitement in her voice aroused others in the proa and the canvas fell away, revealing blinking eyes and haggard faces. "Former" Tagranesi on the other boats began to stir as well, and Chinakru was moving around his boat, alerting others.

The battered submarine didn't look much like her old self anymore; most of the superstructure atop her pressure hull was twisted or gone. She resembled a wallowing, listing, waterlogged tree trunk that had been chewed on by a super lizard, but enough of her distinctive characteristics remained to identify her. The four-inch-fifty gun still stood, supported by the naked, reinforced structure beneath it that had once been concealed by the foredeck. The straight up and down bow was unmistakable, and though both were now fully extended, the aft periscope was decidedly bent near the top. Of course, the filthy, bloodstained men and 'Cats clinging to the remains of the shattered conn tower removed any possible doubt.

"Ess nineteen!" shrieked Captain Lelaa, trying to make her cracking voice heard over the two rumbling diesels as the sub slowed to a stop nearby.

"Ahoy there!" came an answering, almost unbelieving cry through a speaking trumpet. "Captain Lelaa? Is that really you? Who the devil are all those . . . creatures?"

Princess Rebecca stood unsteadily, supported by Lawrence—who was in turn supported by Abel.

"They are Lawrence's people," Rebecca managed to cry. "Would you happen to have any water to spare?"

Sandra looked at Dennis, a grin further splitting her dry lips. "Your gun is empty anyway, Mr. Silva, and your gunpowder is all wet!"

"A good thing too," Silva replied, strength seeming to surge back into his limbs as he stared at the battered wreck before him. Clearly, the old submarine had been through hell. He couldn't wait to hear her story. "I bet one shot would've finished her."

Petey squirmed out from under the heaped canvas and sluggishly hopped to the bulwark beside Rebecca, where he goggled at the submarine. "Eat?" he moaned plaintively.

EPILOGUE

Baalkpan

Alan Letts, chief of staff to Adar—the High Chief and Sky Priest of Baalkpan and chairman of the Grand Alliance—bounced the burbling infant in his arms. Across from him on a similar, decidedly human-style chair, Adar himself lounged awkwardly, but as comfortably as he could. They were in the "living room" of Alan's new "house," provided by the "grateful people of Baalkpan." Alan and his wife, Karen, had both refused the gift as originally presented, but Adar assured them that homes such as theirs would eventually be available to all "mated" officers. There was already a bachelor officers' quarters and numerous barracks for the single enlisted soldiers, sailors, and Marines. The small female bachelor officers' quarters, or "fem-box" as it was called, had been around ever since the human females spent their first night ashore. Now there'd be quarters for married officers, according to Adar. Something like "base housing."

Alan wasn't sure that was the original plan, and frankly doubted it would be the case if he and Karen hadn't raised a stink. He was pretty sure the initial idea arose because Adar wanted his chief of staff and his family—particularly young Allison Verdia—to have a suitable roof over their heads. The home was relatively modest—by an admiral's standards—and would have been "suitable" for a very extended Lemurian family, but Adar had hinted more than once that Alan and Karen should quickly add to their brood. Alan wondered how Adar would cope with the anticipated flood of mated officers once the "liberated" women of Respite began to arrive—and, of course, there were already plenty of mated Lemurian officers, though most had homes of their own.

A lot would depend on how the fragile new "financial system" they'd created held up. The Alliance was now officially on the "gold standard," and the transition from the age-old barter system was moving in fits and starts. Gold was recognized as "pretty" by the aesthetic Lemurians, but with the possible exception of the Maa-ni-los, few 'Cats recognized the metal as possessing any intrinsic value, particularly when compared to iron. Gold was easy to form and didn't corrode, but it made poor tools and weapons. Alan explained that besides its value as a "pretty," decorative, metal, gold could be used as a symbol to represent the relative value of goods and services that Lemurians had always kept up with by means of a complex system of tabulated obligations. Gold would eliminate the need for that—once they calculated a baseline for what a given quantity of gold should be worth. Adar complained that "anybody" could just go out and "find" gold, but Alan countered that simply finding the stuff required labor too, and maybe that time and effort might be used to establish a "baseline" of sorts.

It was all very complicated, and Letts was no economist. His experience as a Navy supply officer actually had more in common with the old Lemurian system. He'd always relied on sometimes complex and overlapping commitments and favors to get what he needed for the ship before their "old" war with the Japanese began, but that experience had also reinforced his firm commitment to the capitalist system. He'd been lazy then, because he was good at his job and hadn't had to work very hard. Besides, there'd been an all-pervading "what's the point?" attitude in the Asiatic Fleet. Still, with his family's farming roots, he knew that the harder you worked, the more you should make, and the more you made, the more people you could hire to help you make more. He devoutly despised the socialist systems in Nazi Germany and the Soviet Union, and like most of his human destroyermen comrades, didn't see much distinction between the two. Both were brutal totalitarian regimes, and he blamed the socialist-leaning American "progressives" for his own country's utter unpreparedness for war. He knew something had to be done, and gold was the simplest, most obvious answer.

The likely inclusion of the Empire of the New Britain Isles in the Grand Alliance reinforced that conclusion, since gold and silver were their only currency. There'd be "growing pains" and a lot of confusion at first, but at least those with property and goods wouldn't "lose" anything, and services would have immediate value. The value was yet to be determined, but Alan had faith that the free market would quickly establish that on its own. A lot of "debt" would have to be forgiven at first, since the war effort had required much of everyone without anyone being paid, but at least the "government" would start with a surplus. It would retain ownership of all community industry created for, and essential to, the war effort. That meant Adar would still control those industries over which he'd placed the various ministers, at least until they were sold to budding "industrialists." Needless to say, all military assets already complete, the ships, ordnance, fortifications, dry dock, etc., as well as *Amagi*'s steel, would remain the property of the Allied powers and the US Navy.

"I never tire of looking at your delightful youngling!" Adar practically gushed, leaning forward to stare at the squirming, cooing creature. They'd already kicked around a few more of Adar's concerns about the economic revolution, and they'd settled into a simple, friendly visit. Adar stopped by several times a week now, mostly for that very purpose, and Alan suspected the chairman needed the break. Adar's own residence was within the Great Hall itself, so he was never truly off duty even at home.

"Neither do I," Letts confessed, "but the . . . smell gets old. Ah . . . Karen?" he said, raising his voice.

Karen Theimer Letts swept into the room and snatched the child away. "There's no law that says you can't change a diaper now and then," she scolded.

"I do!" Alan replied in his defense, "but I can't do it here, in front of the Chairman!"

Karen harrumphed, but Adar saw a smile on her face as she retreated from the room.

Letts sighed, his eyes following the pair. "You know," he said softly, "in spite of everything, these last few months have been the happiest of my whole life."

"All the more reason why I do not understand this request of yours," Adar said, just as quietly. They were resuming a conversation that wasn't for Karen to hear . . . yet. "I do not know how I would ever manage without you. If you join First Fleet now, all we have accomplished, all we have set in motion, might be undone."

"We've already been over this," Letts insisted. "I'm *not* 'essential' here anymore. Brister, Riggs, or even Sandison has a better handle on this economic stuff than I do, and with their greater combat experience, they'll be better advisors on defense. My staff can easily take up the logistical slack around here." He paused. "Besides, you read General Alden's report. Logistics on the sharp end is a mess. They *do* need me in the fleet, and . . . damn it, I've been on the sidelines almost from the start! It isn't right and it's not fair!"

"Fair? To whom?" Adar almost snapped. "Fair to you?"

"No! It's not *fair* to all the guys who've been putting their lives on the line while I sit here, nice and comfortable, with a wife I love and a kid I adore! It's eating me alive! I've done some good work here," Alan admitted. "I'm not complaining about my job. It's just . . . It's time for me to 'pitch in,' to 'do my part.'" He rubbed his eyes. "We don't know what's going on in the east yet. Captain Reddy's helped the Imperials win a battle, but that's all we really know. What's next? There's a real mess out there, and we may have a whole other war on our hands! In the meantime, General Alden and Admiral Keje are building for their push against Ceylon!"

"All the more reason you should remain here!" Adar argued. "Coordinating logistics for two possible fronts should be at least twice as difficult!"

Letts shook his head. "There's nothing we can do for Captain Reddy; any help he gets will have to come directly from Saan-Kakja, not through here—and Saan-Kakja's got problems of her own, after that damn volcano went off. That's going to make it even harder on First Fleet, because who knows when we'll get the promised reinforcements?" He shrugged. "That might sort itself out over time, as the Fil-pin Lands get over their current emergency. If we get sucked into a full-blown war in the east, it's liable to be a Navy show for the most part, at least for a while. Saan-Kakja is better situated to support that. The war in the west is about to become increasingly land-oriented, though, and that's where I need to be! We can't afford another logistical fiasco like the one at Rangoon. We can't afford the lives it might cost."

Alan let that sink in for a moment before he continued. "Ceylon will be the biggest stunt we've ever pulled, maybe bigger than Baalkpan. Surely our biggest *offensive* to date. If, God forbid, it all falls in the pot and I'm not there, how will I live with myself?" He gestured in the direction Karen had taken Allison. "How will I look *them* in the eye, when I might have made a difference?"

Adar shifted in his chair, but said nothing. After a while,

he steepled his hands, elbows on his knees, and stared long and hard at Alan with his large, penetrating eyes. "I will consider it," he whispered at last. "In the meantime, please do concentrate on helping get *Aracca* out of the dry dock." He chuckled, in his Lemurian way. "Major Mallory pesters me constantly about putting *Saanta Caat-alinaa* in there to retrieve the rest of his toys from her hold. He fears she will sink beside the dock! Moving his great, heavy boxes to the still incomplete 'airstrip' is proving quite a chore as well!"

USS *WALKER*—Scapa Flow

"It's official, Skipper," Ed Palmer said, handing over a sheet of the yellowish Imperial paper. It was a report via Government House forwarded straight to Matt. "Two Imperial frigates tried to enter the harbor at New Dublin and take possession of the Dom ships that escaped the battle and wound up there. The frigates were fired on by the forts! There was no damage, and they lit out, but New Ireland's either been occupied by the Doms—or they've thrown their hat in the ring with 'em."

Matt had been leaning on the rail by the signal lockers behind the pilothouse, surrounded by Bradford, Spanky, Chack, and the Bosun. All were staring aft at the repairs underway. Sparks jetted from torches, and lines and hoses littered the deck. Almost all the hull damage was on the starboard side, and scaffolds had been rigged to straighten plates and rerivet seams near the waterline. When that work was finished, they'd turn the ship and continue upward from the safety of the dock. (Even if the local variety of flashies weren't as big, or apparently as insatiable, as those within the Malay Barrier, they were still damned dangerous, and there'd been a lot more in the neighborhood since the battle.)

They had all the help they needed. *Walker* had actually been given priority over the Imperial ships in the yard, but she had plenty of hands with the arrival of *Simms*, and local technicians and specialists were better employed fixing Imperial damage. Some of the female yard workers still tried to do anything they could. They *wanted* to help. Chief Bashear finally told them to get scrapers, chippers, and brushes and turned them loose with paint cans. The portside had barely been touched, since *Tacitus* had absorbed most of the shot fired from that direction. They could paint there until the starboard side was ready.

Spanky was a hero—again. He'd fought *Walker* brilliantly after power was restored, and through speed and maneuver he'd savaged most of the Dom ships that *Tacitus* and *Euripides* had protected *Walker* from—then worked tirelessly to save them in turn. Matt finally forced him to accept that he was *Walker*'s de facto exec. Either Tabby could handle engineering or she couldn't. Which would it be? Reluctantly, Spanky admitted she was "better than most" engineering officers he'd known, and if he "helped her out" now and then, she could probably "manage."

The new Nancy had been assembled and lowered over the side to keep it safe and out of the way, but Reynolds was in no shape to fly it. He was banged up and needed a rest, but his worst injury was mental. He blamed himself for Kari-Faask's critical condition, and even if she lived, Matt wasn't sure the young flier would bounce back. Maybe he should talk to him. He knew all too well how it felt when someone died because he'd made a mistake. Ultimately, he would order the kid to fly if he had to—they needed recon now more than ever—but it was important for Reynolds to snap out of it on his own . . . if he could.

Matt took the sheet from Palmer and looked it over before passing it to Spanky. "Stupid," he said.

"Yes, sir," Palmer agreed. Everyone was mentally and physically exhausted from the labor of repairing the ship. The services for Frankie, Miami, and nearly thirty 'Cat sailors and Marines had left them emotionally drained as well. Sensing the dark mood that prevailed, Palmer quietly left the bridge.

"So what's the deal, Courtney?" Matt asked. Almost a week had passed since the battle, and Bradford had spent most of the time sequestered with the Governor-Emperor and Sean "O'Casey" Bates. Gerald McDonald was much improved, almost magically so, and Selass had decided not to remove his leg. He would limp forever, but he would walk—and live. Even as the man's health improved, his rage toward the Dominion became more acute. "Has anybody found Don Hernan yet?"

"Regrettably, no. It's assumed he's still hiding on New Scotland, and no leaf shall be left unturned. . . . Realistically, it's suspected that he already made his escape aboard one of several small craft seen departing Leith, even while the outcome of the battle here was still in question. Unfortunately, no word of the attack reached the town until the following day."

"Damn." Matt looked at Spanky. "No, he bolted at just the right time. As soon as *Walker* steamed into battle, the outcome wasn't in doubt."

"Thanks, Skipper, and damn straight! But all we had to do was make a stir while everyone else woke up."

"And he knew that," agreed Matt, "so my bet is he's gone. Damn!" he repeated. "Having that sick bastard on the loose is like walking barefoot and blindfolded through a pen full of rattlesnakes."

"Silly devil in a red dress—he don't scare me," said the Bosun.

"He should, Boats," Matt told him, "because I'll also bet that most of this crackpot, shoestring scheme—that almost *worked*—was his. Had to be. Reed was a true 'convert,' and he might've even had some pull, but I don't think the Dominion was taking any orders from him."

"I doubt our Imperial friends would call a major fleet action a 'shoestring' affair either!" Courtney said.

"But it wasn't *supposed* to be a fleet action," said Spanky, "and it wouldn't have been if us and Jenks hadn't sniffed a rat." He shook his head.

"So, Courtney," continued Matt, a little hesitantly, "you thought you'd wrap up your other 'negotiations' today?"

"Um, yes. The Empire of the New Britain Isles formally

requests full membership in the Grand Alliance—pending ratification by the other members, of course."

"That's what I figured," Matt replied flatly.

Courtney's face reddened. "Captain Reddy, you've done your job and now I've done mine! One reason we came here in the first place was to secure an alliance with these people."

"Yeah, and maybe we've 'done that job,' " Matt ground out, "but we haven't accomplished our mission."

"The Company is dead, at least as it was," Chack offered lamely, blinking uncertainty.

"Yeah, but we didn't . . . find the girls . . . and damn it, we didn't get . . . *even*!"

"You killed Reed," Gray pointed out.

"Not good enough! Not anymore." Matt gestured around at the ravaged fleet in the harbor and the damage to his own ship. The destruction and loss suffered ashore weren't visible, but it was present in all their thoughts. The civilian casualties from the indiscriminate Dom artillery had been appalling. "And the list has gotten a whole lot longer. To 'get even' now, we've got a full-blown, two-ocean war on our hands! You think Adar will thank us for that?"

"Adar will understand, Cap-i-taan Reddy," Chack said. "Never forget the person he is. He knows the evil of the Grik. Do not doubt he will recognize the evil of the Dominion, and he is not alone. Most of our people have come to understand that evil, in whatever form, cannot simply be ignored. We have as much reason to help these people against their evil enemy as they have to help us."

"I guess we've just got to fight the 'war we're at,' Skipper, like you said," growled the Bosun softly. "Wherever we are."

Ed Palmer rushed back onto the bridge, flourishing another sheet. "Skipper!" he almost shouted.

"What now?" Spanky growled. "Every time you show up like this, somethin' has just come off the rails. Makes it easier to understand why folks used to kill messengers!"

"We got another transmission from the resupply squadron out of Respite! They finally heard from Manila—good news for a change, sir!" Ed said, glancing at Spanky. "Well, not all good . . . but the good part's *great*, I swear!"

Almost reluctantly, Matt took the sheet and began to read, skipping the preface.

TALAUD ISLAND OBLITERATED BY UNPRECEDENTED VOLCANIC EVENT X MASSIVE WAVE UNKNOWN SIZE HAS STRUCK SOUTH FIL-PIN LAND MINDANAO X NO SURVIVORS FOUND VICINITY OF PAGA—DAAN X SEARCH CONTINUES X SLIGHT DAMAGE MANILA BUT MANY OTHER SETTLEMENTS SEVERELY AFFECTED X RESCUE EFFORT COORDINATED BY COLONEL SHINYA AND ARMY—NAVY ELEMENTS X MAY DISRUPT LOGISTICS TRAIN CEYLON OPERATION X ADMIRAL KEJE-FRIS-AR AND GENERAL ALDEN ADVISED TO COMMENCE OPS AT DISCRETION XXX

US SUBMARINE S-19 DISCOVERED BADLY DAMAGED BUT UNDERWAY WEST OF SAMAR X EXPEDITION HAS SUFFERED SEVERE CASUALTIES BUT HAS RESCUED SEVENTY ONE (71) SURVIVORS TAGRANESI PEOPLE X LT IRVIN LAUMER ALSO BEGS TO REPORT RESCUE XXX

IMPERIAL PERSONNEL X PRINCESS REBECCA ANNE MCDONALD X MIDSHIPMAN STUART BRASSEY XXX

ALLIED PERSONNEL X MIDSHIPMAN ABEL COOK X TAGRANESI LAWRENCE X SISTER AUDRY X CHIEF GUNNER'S MATE DENNIS SILVA X CAPTAIN LELAA-TAL-CLERAAN X MINISTER OF MEDICINE SANDRA TUCKER X GOD THE MAKER BLESS THEM X MESSAGE ENDS XXX

The page began to shake in Matt's hand and a bright sheen covered his eyes. "My Lord," he said hoarsely and wiped his face with his sleeve. He cleared his throat. "Uh, please send this to Government House, with my congratulations, to the Governor-Emperor and his wife."

"What is it, Captain?" Spanky asked.

Matt's lips formed a genuine, delighted smile, and he handed over the message. "Read it aloud, Spanky, then post a copy. Everybody aboard deserves to see it." His eyes started to fill again. "Now, if you gentlemen will excuse me,

I think I'll . . . take a short nap on my cot in the chart house. I'll be along shortly with a reply, Mr. Palmer," he said, and turned away before the tears spilled down his face. "Carry on," he added, closing the chart house hatch behind him.

Spanky read the message, but then he, Gray, Courtney, Chack, and Palmer remained by the rail in silence. They were exuberant, but also a little uncomfortable. Unspoken, all their thoughts were on Captain Reddy and how this latest news would hit him. He'd always been a rock—but a hot rock will crack when you pour cold water on it. Less than a minute later, to their surprise, Matt banged open the hatch and strode back to face them, a huge grin splitting his lips. His eyes were still red, but no trace of moisture remained.

"Belay that, Palmer," he commanded. "Let's go send a reply right now; then I'll take the message ashore to the Governor-Emperor myself! I've got some ideas about this 'new' war I'd like to kick around with him anyway."

"Well, sure, Skipper . . ." Palmer said.

"What about that . . . nap, Captain?" Gray asked, a little concerned. "You been pushin' yourself awful hard. . . ."

Matt laughed, and the sound was . . . right. "So have you, Boats. So has everybody. The hell with that. All of a sudden, I'm not really tired anymore!"